The
Mother House

a novel

Katherine Doyle

This book was created with the assistance of CanamBooks self-publishing services

www.canambooks.com

ISBN 978-1-7775900-0-0
ISBN (EPUB) 978-1-7775900-1-7
ISBN (MOBI) 978-1-7775900-2-4

Cover art: Linda Bell/www.lindabell.ca

Author photo: Ian Cameron

Editor Jess Shulman/www.jessshulmaneditorial.com

Design & layout: Ted Sancton/Studio Melrose

This book was set in Scala Pro 11/16

In memory of my mother

MARY EILEEN DOYLE

1913 – 2000

PART 1

1

THE MOTHER HOUSE 1930

THE LAST THING Frances remembered was kneeling, before she slumped onto the girl beside her.

She came to when the girl fumbled and grasped her under her arms but Frances did not open her eyes. She had made a scene.

I'm in trouble now, she thought.

A hoarse whisper: "Girls, girls, come away. Give her some air. Back to your pews."

Frances recognized Sister Alfonse's voice, their dormitory Sister. Her job was to watch over the new postulants at night and herd them to the chapel by six every morning. This ruckus was unexpected, and Sister did not like disruptions to the routine.

Routine was everything here: the hours they kept, how they dressed, how they did their chores, who spoke to whom, where they sat, how often and how long they prayed. There was some comfort in it, but all in all, Frances found it monotonous.

Somebody dragged Frances onto the floor and placed her on her back. Soft rustlings of fabric, squeaks of new shoes close to her head, and the continuous prayers and chants of the congregation drifted around her... *Patris, Filii, et Spiritus Sancti*...

The coolness of the chapel's marble floor seeped into Frances's back and a small shiver rippled on the nape of her neck. She kept her eyes shut. Her thoughts were racing, crashing into each other, but she stilled herself and listened. She must have fainted.

The Sister shook her shoulder.

"You, you, wake up," Sister whispered.

Frances opened her eyes and grasped the nun's hand. Sister Alfonse tried to pull it back, but Frances held on and drew her closer.

"Please help me. I need the toilet."

Sister pointed to a hefty girl with a pimply chin at the end of the pew beside them. "Help me."

They hoisted Frances under her arms and shoved her into the girl's seat. Sister pushed her head down aiming it toward her lap but instead banged it on the back of the pew in front of Frances.

"In, out, in, out." Sister said. She demonstrated by gasping and blowing out through flapping lips.

"Please, Sister, the toilet," Frances mumbled into the pew.

Frances knew Sister was flustered. She could hear the Directress of the Novitiate, leading the morning prayers from the front of the chapel, hesitating and missing her cues.

Sister Alfonse pointed to the big girl. "Take her to *la toilette* in reception."

As the girl's arms encircled her, Frances took comfort in the girl's strength. She leaned her tall thin frame against her unknown helper. They took long strides to the back of the chapel under the sidelong scrutiny from each pew. As the chapel door closed behind them the girl released Frances. They stepped away from each other and looked left and right down the long, empty corridor. Everything was still, and the morning light dappled the black and white marble floor.

"Wait here", Frances said. "I'll be all right alone." Giving the girl no time to respond she walked away staying close to the wall. She was weak and dizzy and could have used some help, an arm to lean on, but her embarrassment was too great. She wanted to be alone.

Frances glanced out the windows as she passed them. The trees in the garden between the Mother House and Sherbrooke Street were limp and dusty. It had not rained in the two weeks since she and her friend Patsy had come up on the train. It was their "grand adventure", leaving home for the Montreal convent, using their proper names, trying to shrug off their girlish selves. Frances and Patricia acting grown-up.

Who was she kidding? Frances entered the empty circular entrance hall and saw the dark wood door with the small sign: La Toilette. But the lure of the front door was too much to resist.

The only sounds were muffled kitchen noises coming from downstairs. She went to the elegant double doors with frosted, etched glass panels, put her eye to a clear part, and looked at the long path that led out of the Mother House. What a thought – to walk out the door and stroll down Sherbrooke Street. Frances had been in the convent with a hundred other girls and several Sisters for two weeks and the notion of walking free and alone outside filled her with giddiness. The feeling evaporated.

But where would she go?

Frances turned away from the door. As she did so the smell of breakfast – coffee, bacon, toast – wafted up the staircase. The soft underside of her tongue quivered and filled with spit, her stomach heaved up, and she ran to the toilet, her hand clapped over her mouth.

Afterward, she was leaning against the wall of the tiny closet-like room with her hand still clutching the chain suspended from the water tank above the toilet. Her mouth was sour from vomit. The door opened a few inches and the pimply-chinned girl poked her head in. She squeezed in, pushing Frances behind the door then turned and shut it. She sniffed.

"My word, there isn't room to swing a cat in here," she said. "And look at the state of you. Sit down, my girl." She took a glowing white handkerchief from her pocket, wet it in the small basin and held it to Frances's forehead.

After a few moments she said, "You'd feel better if you took off your cap. May I?" She reached over to take the pins from the black close-fitting cap that went from Frances's widow's peak, down over her ears and around the nape of her neck. She slipped it off. She dampened the handkerchief again and put it around Frances's neck. "Better?"

"Yes." Frances hesitated. They were breaking the Rule of Silence. "You're very kind. I don't want to get you in trouble though. You should go back to the chapel."

"Old Alfonse won't miss us. There's so many of us and we all look the same in this get-up. We have five or ten more minutes. I'm Rosemary Egan. What's your name?"

"Frances Dalton. I'm from New Brunswick. You?"

"Right here in Montreal, from a place you've never heard of, Griffintown."

Frances thought of Thomas and her heart squeezed. Before she could censor herself she said, "Yes, I know someone from there. I'm sure he said Griffintown."

"What's his name? I bet I know him or some of his cousins. It's a small place." She let out a hearty laugh.

Frances hesitated and then looked up as though searching for Thomas's name. "John, I think. I only met him once. Please pass me my cap. We'd better go back."

"Right. We can't avoid it any longer. Turn your head and I'll pin up your hair. It's come undone at the back." She combed her thick fingers through Frances's fine, mousy brown hair, twisted and pinned it, and put on her black hairnet. She handed Frances her cap.

"Thank you, Rosemary."

"I've had lots of practice. I'm the oldest of six girls and four boys." She paused, "Fixing hair isn't the only thing I know, Frances Dalton." Rosemary put two fingers under her new friend's chin and raised her head until they were eye to eye. She held her gaze for a long moment.

What's she getting at?

"Squeeze behind the door so I can get out of here. And rinse out your mouth." They both giggled as they manoeuvred themselves out of the narrow room, but when they stepped into the hall they put on their solemn postulant faces and posture. They walked to the chapel in silence. The Mass was over and everyone was filing out, two-by-two.

Sister Alfonse was standing outside the chapel, near the door, her wooden clapper at the ready, as the novices and postulants came out of the chapel, eyes downcast, hands clasped at their waists. Sister gestured for Frances and Rosemary to stand beside her and put her finger to her lips. When the last couple passed, Sister struck her clapper once and the line of postulants stopped. Sister pushed Rosemary into the line and then took Frances by the arm and got in line too. She clapped twice and the line moved forward.

"*Tu vas bien, ma petite?*" You're okay, Sister asked in a hushed voice.

"*Oui*, Sister, I mean *ma Soeur*." Frances was shy speaking French. "I was very hot, *ma Soeur*, that's all. I'm okay now."

"What is your name, *ma petite Soeur?*"

"*Je m'appelle Frances Dalton, ma Soeur.*"

Sister looked her up and down, raised one eyebrow and said, "*Dalton?*" She scrutinized her again. "*Bien, Francoise, vas manger.*" Go eat. Sister stepped out of the line and walked in the opposite direction.

Oh God, she knows my aunt, Frances thought.

Frances caught up with Rosemary who faced forward with eyes down but managed to whisper, "What did she say?"

"Just asked my name."

They were going through the refectory door. "Hush now," Frances said glancing at the head table where the Sister Superiors sat.

They took their places near the back with the novices and postulants and bowed their heads to say grace with the community.

⚜

That night small sounds filled the dormitory as the girls settled for another night – the scrape of shoes on the bare wood floors, stifled coughs, quiet sniffles. Silent prayers – for strength, for comfort, for salvation – also rose to the heavy ceiling beams and out the dormer windows. Frances didn't know what others prayed for but for her, it was being someone other than a nun.

There were fifty postulants, the beginners, twenty-five on each side of the room, each in her white-curtained cubicle. The cubicles reinforced the Vow of Poverty with only a narrow bed, a small cabinet with a drawer for a rosary and missal and a cubby for wash things and underwear. Each girl had two hooks on the wall for her habit and cape. The girls' possessions had been inspected when they arrived and anything contrary to The Rule was sent home.

The number of girls in the community hall had astounded Frances and Patricia when they had arrived from down home. The Rule of Silence had not begun yet and they heard muffled conversations in every corner.

Patricia had craned her neck around. "Golly, there's probably more than a hundred of us. Where will they put all of us, eh, Francie; I mean Frances?"

That was early August, less than a month ago but it seemed longer to Frances. They were not in the same dormitory and rarely had a chance to steal a few words.

❧

During the previous four years in the boarding school in Newcastle Frances and Patricia had talked about everything. After the dormitory lights were out they would get out of bed and rest their bare feet on the cold linoleum floor. Patsy would haul the rough wool blanket from her bed and they'd wrap it around their shoulders as they huddled on a bench in front of one of the tall paned windows that looked over the Miramichi River. On moonlit nights they could see the river current as it flowed out to sea. The river had taken their thoughts out to an unimaginable future.

With Patsy, Frances had felt like a different person. She wasn't just the baby, the third daughter anymore. She wasn't the sickly one. She was herself.

She talked about role models, a term she had learned recently "I never knew we could choose a way to be. We didn't have to just follow along. There's got to be more."

"You're right, Francie. Doing what you want to do is better than doing what someone tells you to do."

One moonlit night Patsy had told Frances she thought she had a religious vocation. Vocation was the favourite topic of the nuns who taught them. According to them, to be called to the religious life was the best thing to hope for. It was in first place; marriage and motherhood second; and far after that, spinsterhood, the word alone having a pinched, mean sound.

Patsy's oldest brother Tim had entered the seminary in Montreal recently to become a priest. Her parents were very proud and talked about him all the time. Patsy saw her parents from time to time because they lived in Chatham, across the river from the school.

"I think they'd be happy if I took the veil," Patsy said.

"But what about you? Would you be happy?" Frances was surprised by her own question. She'd never thought about her own happiness or the fact that it might be connected to decisions she'd make. It was a distant, unformed idea.

"Yeah, I think so. I could become a teacher like Sister St. Maureen."

Frances said, "What would you like about being a nun?"

"Well, I could become a really good teacher. I would have a place where I belonged." Frances nodded.

After a few moments Patsy continued. "Maybe I could become a Sister Superior like your aunt!"

Patsy gave her friend a little poke in the ribs and started to laugh. She was the only one who could tease Frances about the Provincial Superior aunt. She got enough pressure from the nuns who seemed to think she also was destined for a religious life.

"What do you mean about a place where you belong?"

"I'm not sure." Patsy was quiet for a few minutes. "The convent seems to be the Sisters' own place. If I went home, I'd be in my parents' home. If I got married, I'd be in my husband's home. But if I was in the convent it would be my home."

Patricia looked at Frances. She was red in the face and peering at Frances with a furrowed brow. "Do you understand?" she asked.

"Yeah, I think I do. I never thought about my future until I came to St. Bridget's. I thought I'd see what my sisters did and then follow along. Sister St. Jerome always talks to me about my aunt so I think out of spite I never even considered being a nun. But I see what you mean. It's kind of a secret life." She paused. "But I wonder if it's the only way to have your own place, a place where you belong?"

Her question had hung in the air.

⚜

Sister Alfonse opened the door at the end of the dormitory. Every sound halted as though the room held its breath. "*Bonne nuit, mes petites Soeurs. Dormez bien.*" Good night, sleep well.

Although the postulants were separated according to language for their lessons, the dormitories were mixed. "*Bonne nuit ....* Good night ... *Soeur Alfonse ...* Sister ...". Frances joined the French chorus thinking of Cecile, Mamma's helper.

Frances wasn't homesick – four years boarding at St. Bridget's had seen to that – but she yearned for Cecile. In the summers they often did the chores together. Cecile didn't think Frances was weak or sickly. She talked to her about her own family in ways that showed Frances she thought she was trustworthy.

Frances knelt beside her bed with her arms held out straight to her sides emulating Jesus on the cross and trying to remember all the required prayers but her attention – maybe her devotion – wandered.

This brief time in her cubicle each night, unseen, unobserved was a reprieve. Frances knew, however, that at any moment, Sister Alfonse could draw the curtains aside and oversee what they called the Practice of Humility, the recitation of a litany of self-abasement.

Her brother Jimmy's voice came back to her. "See how holy they think you are now." Frances knew she was far from holy after what had happened.

Sister Alfonse's wooden clapper and the sounds of the other girls getting into bed jolted her back to the dormitory. She didn't know if she had prayed at all, but she got under the cool sheet and drifted into sleep.

But deep, relaxing sleep was not hers. Frances reached for the chamber pot under the bed but when she pulled it out it was full of tiny mice. She got up and peed on top of them. A relief.

She awoke with a start still in her narrow bed. A dream, it was only a dream. She felt herself, relieved she hadn't peed the bed. But she couldn't hold it another minute, even though getting up after the evening bell was against The Rules. She put on her shawl and went on cat feet between the rows of cubicles, pleased to hear heavy snoring coming from Sister's private alcove. The bathroom was off a small corridor. She crept along until she came to the toilet stalls, used one and made her way back to the dormitory.

She paused to look out the window. The high, crystal-clear moon threw sharp shadows across the room. She thought of home and how in the early evening the rim of the full moon peeked, soft and yellow, over the roof of the barn. This bright, fierce moonlight was foreign.

She was four beds away from her own. A movement of air and the bed curtains beside her parted. Rosemary reached out and pulled Frances into her cubicle.

"What are you doing?" Frances was astounded by the girl's boldness. They were in the period of Profound Silence and this was a serious breach.

Rosemary pulled her down onto her bed, put her finger to her lips and pursed them in a hush sign.

"I heard you tippy toeing to the bathroom. Wanted to follow you but was chicken. Heaving your guts out in the morning and up peeing all night. When are you due?"

Frances stared at her.

"Well?"

"I ... what do you ... due?" Frances wrapped her arms around her stomach and leaned over her knees, rocking up and down.

"You don't even know, do ya darlin'?"

"What are you talking about?"

"You're expecting a baby, aren't you?"

"For the love of God. How would you know such a thing if I don't even know it?"

"I was standing behind you the day we got fitted for our habits. Remember, two weeks ago when we arrived? I heard the old crone in the sewing room say whoever sent her your measurements didn't know one end of a tape measure from the other. I didn't think much of it at the time but your sick stomach this morning and now not able to hold it till morning ..."

"But —"

"I could be wrong, but I've seen it lots of times – my Mama, my Aunties and a few of my cousins." Rosemary put her arm around her shoulder. "What about your breasts? Are they sore?"

Frances pulled away and shook her head. "Stop it, will you?"

"Mama said she always knew because of that. Go on, give them a squeeze."

Frances turned away from her and raised her hands to her chest, winced then dropped her hands in her lap. "It can't be, Rosemary."

"What? You never had ... never ... with a boy?"

Frances bowed her head and picked at her cuticles.

"Never?" Rosemary waited. "Not once?"

More than once, thought Frances. How could it have happened? It was over so fast. Making a baby should take more time. And ... and ... She couldn't speak.

She didn't look at Rosemary, didn't want to see the disgust on her face. She said, "Yes." Then choking, said, "What am I going to do? What can I do?"

Rosemary put her arm around her new friend's shoulder. Frances glanced at her. No disgust there, only a puzzled look. "I don't know. We can't do anything tonight though so let's try to get some sleep. But we have to do something soon before one of them catches on."

She jerked her head sideways toward the snores from Sister Alfonse's spot. "They're as sharp as crows' beaks."

She stood up and gave Frances her hand and pulled her to her feet. "Go back to bed. We'll think of something." She gave Frances a gentle shove.

Frances took a deep breath and started to speak. Rosemary nudged her again. "Hush now, go on." She closed her curtains.

Frances mulled over what Rosemary said. We'll think of something. She said that. We'll think of something. Us.

Frances lay awake a long time. She was relieved it was out, not in the open, but at least she wasn't alone. She'd been holding her breath for weeks. She couldn't stop herself from pretending when Rosemary said it, but she had suspected.

When she had been packing to leave home, Mamma had put a box of sanitary napkins in her suitcase.

"What will I do when they're finished?"

"I don't know. They'll take care of it."

The box sat unopened in her bedside locker. She tried to remember when she had had her last monthly, but she drew a blank. Then she remembered the whispering in the orchard at St Bridget's about the monthly curse and babies.

*

There had been twelve of them in the boarding school class at St Bridget's, the class of 1930. A lot of the talk had been about the future, the same old choices – nun, wife and mother (those two went together), or spinster – teacher, secretary, or nurse – but definitely spinster.

One brilliant autumn Saturday in their last year they'd been in the orchard. A few, like Frances and Patsy, were picking apples but the rest were sitting in twos and threes chatting. Frances heard a few gasps and squeals of laughter. She looked over. Now all the girls were clustered around Avelda, leaning in to catch every word.

Frances tilted her chin toward them. "What's that about?"

"Avelda's probably talking about how 'mad' she is about Rudi Valentino."

"Meow, meow," Frances said, shaking her finger at Patsy. "C'mon, let's join in."

They set their basket against a tree and worked their way into the circle.

"That's what she told me." Avelda looked around at them. "I told her I want to marry Bobby when I finish school. She thought it was time I knew about it."

Frances leaned over to Annie. "What's she talking about?"

Annie cupped her hands around Francie's ear. "S-e-x."

Frances leaned over to Patsy and relayed the three-letter word.

That night the three of them sat at the window. Annie filled them in. "Our monthly visitor means we aren't going to have a baby but if we have s-e-x with a boy – she called it intercourse – our monthly will stop and then we'll have a baby."

Frances frowned. Annie crossed her finger over her heart. "Honest, that's what her mother told her."

Patsy spoke up. "My sister told me the same thing this summer. She's having a baby in December."

They fell into an uneasy silence. They were thinking about the same thing, the same girl: Isabelle. She had been in the class behind them and had left the school in March with no explanation. It wasn't long before the story had come out. Patsy's mother told her. Isabelle was pregnant and had gone to her aunt's in St. John's. The aunt had a handicapped son and Isabelle would care for him. She wouldn't be coming back. She wouldn't finish her schooling. And what about the baby? Nobody knew.

Frances had been having her monthlies for two years by then. She'd started when she was fifteen just like her sisters. The conversation in the orchard had upset her for a few reasons. The worst was Isabelle, her disappearance and the seeming erasure of her from the life at St. Bridget's. The second reason was Avelda, getting married at seventeen. No other ambition. But the third reason had angered her the most: having not connected her monthly with having a baby.

She'd seen cats and dogs in heat on the farm. She knew Papa paid attention to when the cows were ready to be bred. But there was a lot of secrecy around it for girls. They were never to mention it at school. If a girl didn't come to class because of it the nuns rolled their eyes and pursed their lips.

Her sister Jo called it "Eve's curse."

It was a secret, a shameful secret.

❖

A week dragged by in the convent. Panic and worry ate into Frances. She moved the buttons on her skirt, so it wouldn't cut her in two, and she bound her breasts with her extra slip and some safety pins.

She and Rosemary talked another night after she had been to the toilet. Rosemary said, "Mama is coming on Sunday for her first visit. She'll know what to do."

Frances gaped at her. "Don't tell your mother! She'll think I'm horrible and she'll tell Sister St. Boniface. They'll kick me out. I'll have to go home. And they won't want me there. Nobody will want me. What if they kick me out of here?" The pitch of her voice was rising with each word. She picked at her bottom lip and crushed Rosemary's hand.

Rosemary laughed in a soft, low tone. "Getting out of here is what you want, Frances. Where you're going to go is the problem. This isn't much consolation now but you're not the first girl who has gotten into trouble. Mama has helped other girls."

Frances remembered Isabelle, the girl sent to Newfoundland, and the rumours, the mean things some of the girls had said about her. And her fate, being a servant, maybe forever.

Rosemary's certainty – "getting out of here is what you want" – brought Frances up short. Until that moment she had not admitted the seriousness, the finality of the situation to herself.

"How old are you, Rosemary? You know so much."

"I'm twenty-four. You?"

"I'll be eighteen this month."

"Being the oldest in a family with lots of aunts and cousins meant I heard many conversations that weren't meant for me. Mama used to say to my aunts, 'Little pitchers have big ears', but after a while she just gave me a hard stare and put her finger to her lips."

"What do you think your mother will say?"

"I don't know. I never heard that part of the conversation. Now you get to bed. We're lucky for old Alfonse's sleep of the dead."

"Rosemary!"

Rosemary rolled her eyes. "It's just an expression. Off you go."

When Rosemary mentioned her mother Frances thought of Mamma. She remembered how awkward Mamma had been when she talked about Frances going to the Mother House.

What would Mamma think now?

Barely a month had passed since that conversation with Mamma, but it felt like a year. Frances had finished her last year at boarding school and had had no notion of what she would do with herself while she waited for the teachers' college to be rebuilt after a fire. She had been doing the dishes with her sisters when Mamma yelled for her to come out to the porch.

"What's going on?" Josephine had asked, her voice low and urgent. Frances knew Jo hated not being included in every conversation.

"Who knows? Back to the dishes, girls!" Frances snapped her damp tea towel at Bernadette's bottom and ran out to the porch.

Papa was sitting in his old rocker. They used to tease him that he'd stolen it from a dollhouse because his lanky frame was too much for the chair. His knees stuck out high in front of him and sloped down toward the seat of the chair. Two thick, cream-coloured pages rested on his left knee. Frances knew she'd seen that deluxe stationery before but couldn't recall whose it was.

Mamma patted the seat beside her. "Francie, sit down here. We've had a letter from your Aunt Sister St. Benedict.

Oh no, her again. She recalled the other letter from her aunt.

Papa went on. "Beatrice's letter is about you, Francie." That was her aunt's name before she became a nun.

Frances's insides shrivelled, and her heart pounded in the cavernous space left behind.

Thomas ... they know!

"Aren't you curious, dear?" Mamma's voice was gentle and coaxing. It didn't make sense.

Why isn't she cross?

"What would Sister St. Benedict have to say about me?" Her voice was a whisper. "She hardly knows me."

"I better just spit it out." Papa took a deep breath. "Your aunt has offered you a place ... in Montreal ... in the Mother House."

Silence.

Mamma reached out and shook her daughter's knee. "Francie, you're as white as a ghost. What is it?"

"I ... I wasn't expecting it, that's all. What would make her think of me? I'm not holy or even a very good student. I'm just ordinary."

But she'd known in an instant. She remembered her aunt's stinking letter from three years ago. It had been addressed to her parents but she had read it in secret. This had been her aunt's plan all along. One of them had to become a nun and Frances was the one. Sacrificed.

"Frances, it's an opportunity," said Papa. "There's nothing for you here with the teachers' college closed. You and Mamma talk it over. But we've got to let them know soon." Papa handed the letter to Mamma, put on his cap and unfolded himself from the rocker. "I'm going to the barn."

"Papa's right," said Mamma. "I don't like the idea of you wasting your time here. You'll be able to get more schooling in the Mother House and that can lead to other opportunities."

"But I don't want to be a nun. It's not right to pretend."

"Think of it as trying it out. Not every girl who starts there takes vows, you know. It won't be much different from being at St. Bridget's."

"It sounds like you want me to leave, like you don't want me here. Have I done something wrong?"

"No, no, no. My dear, no." Mamma went silent and stared at her hands in her lap. Finally, she said, "There are men and boys around here who would be happy to know a nice girl like you." Mamma studied her hands again, glanced at her, looked down again, and then looked up at her. Frances knew what was coming.

"You're seventeen, too young to think of marriage, but not too young for boys to start showing an interest in you. And long courtships are a problem. A man can put pressure on a girl that leads to no happy end." Mamma's face was flushed.

"The crux of it is I don't want you getting mixed up with a young man and ending up with all your chances ruined. Do you understand? It's not that I want to get rid of you, Francie but better to be using your time well."

Frances felt the pulse of the ugly blotches on her neck and chest.

She knew about men's desires, and her own.

Mamma reached over and took her daughter's hand in hers. "If you stay here, even for a year, until the teachers college reopens, you'll be stuck in the house with Cecile and me, baking bread, separating milk, churning butter, darning socks. I want more for you."

"I guess I know what you mean, Mamma. I'll think about it tonight. We'll write to Sister in the morning."

Frances stayed awake a long time thinking about entering the Mother House. She was one hundred percent sure she didn't want to be a nun. The very thought of it, made her feel like something was pressing down on her, pushing her into a corner.

But she didn't want to take the expected route and be a teacher like her sisters either. That would be as though they'd plowed the way to make it easier for her because she couldn't do something else on her own, without their help.

But going to the Mother House doesn't have to be final.

What if it could be a stopgap measure, a time to figure things out? She didn't like the pretense, but it wasn't her big idea in the first place. Why not take advantage of the time? Maybe she and Patsy would have some fun.

In the morning, after she told Mamma she would go, Mamma told everyone else. She said it at Sunday supper as casual as could be as if Frances was just going to Borden's store to get some sugar.

"Francie is going up to Montreal this month. She's going to enter the convent so she can continue her education."

Stunned silence. Then everyone had their say.

"What the dickens!" Josephine said. "You never said a word, Francie."

"*Sister* Francie, now," said Bernadette.

Her brother Jimmy banged his fork on his plate and glared at all of them in turn. "Jesus, Mary and Joseph! What about me? I never do nothin'. Why's Francie get to do everything, the little snot?"

Bernadette muttered into her pie, "She's going to a *convent* for crying out loud."

Papa stared at his plate and spoke in a low monotone. "Watch your mouth, son. If you'd stayed in school maybe you'd have some opportunities too. You made your bed already, now lie in it."

Jimmy jumped up, knocked over his chair and stormed out, slamming the door behind him. Mamma started to get up but Papa put his hand on her shoulder. "Leave him be, Agatha."

Josephine got in the last word. "He's not thinking straight, as usual."

After supper Frances had gone out to find Jimmy. But Jimmy was gone. She'd seen him out on the road with two of his pals, smoking and kicking mindlessly at the road gravel.

She'd wanted to tell him that it was no privilege to be entering the Mother House but rather, a family debt owed to Papa's sister. He was resentful, getting all the hard chores and farm work because he was the only boy, but she'd be paying too, maybe for her lifetime.

⚜

In August a month later, after Mamma had told the family, Frances was in the convent in Montreal. Pregnant and desperate she now wondered if the conversation she and Jimmy never had would have made a difference to what happened.

On the first Friday of the month of September, a Monsignor and a priest came to the Mother House chapel to say a special Mass. Frances went through the motions without needing to think about them. All her thoughts were on what was happening to her. Like many girls in trouble she asked herself how it could have happened. But she knew. She was lost in thoughts of the summer.

After Mass they had a special breakfast, larger than usual, because they would fast the rest of the day. When the meal was over, all the nuns at the front table rose to their feet in unison. Like a wave, the next table rose, then the next, then the novices and finally the postulants. Sister St. Boniface had entered the refectory by the side door.

She beamed out at them. "Sisters, Novices, Postulants, please sit down." She waited until there was no more chair scraping, rustling or throat clearing. The room was still. "As you know, Monday is the Feast of the Nativity of our dear Blessed Virgin." A few quiet murmurs around the room.

"Sisters, remember Silence, please. We have received an invitation from the Archbishop for a group to attend Holy Mass on Monday at Notre Dame de Bon Secours Chapel. Your respective Mistresses will inform you on Sunday which of you have been chosen to go. Now let us give thanks and pray for the good health of Archbishop Bruchesi and also for fine weather on Monday."

⚜

That evening a group of them sat on stools in a circle in the recreation room with their needlework on their laps. They were allowed thirty minutes of restrained conversation but only with the girls on either side of them.

"I hope we're chosen," Patricia said. "It would be an honour and a great treat to get out of here for a few hours. I wonder how far away it is. Maybe Rosemary knows. She's from Montreal, isn't she? If we go, I'll write to Sister St. Maureen about it."

Frances was tired and couldn't match Patricia's enthusiasm. She bowed her head to her work, but her eyelids drooped.

"Frances, don't fall asleep. Sister St. Louise will be here in a minute." Patricia nudged her. "Maybe Sister will give us a hint." She paused. "What's the matter, Frances? Don't you care if you go?"

"Yes, it would be nice. I'm just worn out." Frances heaved a sigh. She had had kitchen duty for the last five days. Each week ten postulants were assigned to help the kitchen Sisters to prepare the meals for the entire community. It was tedious work. "I've never peeled so many carrots and turnips in my life."

Now the Mistress of the Postulants came into the recreation room. Everyone stood, clutching her sewing. "Good evening, Sister St. Louise."

"Good evening, Postulants." Sister sat on her armchair in the circle. "This Monday, September eighth, will be a special day for all of us and an extra special day for some of you. I will spend an hour with you on Sunday evening, so you know what is expected of you.

"Let us now spend some time studying and contemplating. Why is the Bon Secours Chapel so important to us? Doreen, you may answer."

Doreen's face erupted in red blotches and her upper lip sprouted beads of sweat. "Th ...th ... thank you, Si ... Sister. I ... I ..." She gave up and hung her head.

"Well, Doreen, we can't wait all evening for you to get it out. How are you ever going to be a teacher if you can't even speak to us, your Sisters? You must pray to our Blessed Mother to cure you of this affliction. Now, who can tell us? Mildred?"

"Our founder, Venerable Marguerite Bourgeoys, built the first pilgrimage chapel there in the sixteen hundreds." Frances heart went out to Doreen; she wanted to slap the smug look off Mildred's face.

"Yes, exactly. Well, not exactly." Sister gave a cool smile. "She influenced others to build it. She was too busy teaching and converting the Indians to build a chapel. Now we will meditate on the meaning of the Nativity of the Blessed Virgin Mary."

Sister spoke, almost chanted, about Mary, the mother of Jesus, being their role model of purity, obedience and humility. She was chaste, whole, untainted. She was the state of perfection they were expected to emulate.

Frances dared to peer around her. All the girls' heads were bowed, eyes closed, lips moving in silent prayer. Frances was ashamed, most impure, spoiled. She was unworthy to be with them.

✣

Sunday dragged on. Duties were kept to a minimum – cold meals, no laundry or cleaning, just busywork and prayers. The postulants who had visitors waited for them in the formal reception hall at the front of the convent while the rest were in the recreation room with their needlework and prayer books.

Frances and Patricia were mending a large tablecloth. It was too big to keep in their laps, so they were allowed to sit at a table. It was a relief for Frances because her legs and back were aching. She was wretched. She wanted to tell Patricia. She wanted to fall into her arms and bawl her eyes out. But her shame hardened her into silence.

Patricia was excited; they'd both been chosen for the outing to Bon Secours chapel. She could hardly keep her voice to a whisper. "Francie, Francie, we're both going! I wonder what Sister will tell us this evening? Probably more about 'custody of our senses' and all that rigmarole. Isn't it great?"

"It will be nice to be in the sunshine and see something other than this place." Frances looked around and avoided looking at Patricia.

"You don't sound very keen."

Frances raised her voice as much as she dared. "No, I'm not keen, to be honest. Just leave me alone, Patricia."

Frances took a spool of white thread from the mending box and turned away from her friend. A hard lump formed in her throat and her eyes stung with tears.

"Francie?" Patricia tugged the piece they were working on, but Frances didn't look up from her work.

One by one the girls who had had visitors came into the recreation room. Rosemary was among them. She looked at Frances and Patricia and winked.

"So that big galoot is your pal now, is she?" Patricia kept her head down and her needle in the tablecloth. Frances knew she had hurt her best friend.

"No, Patsy, no. I just can't talk to you right now. Please understand."

Patsy yanked the tablecloth away from Frances. "That's just it. I don't understand anything. And don't call me Patsy."

2

ESCAPE

Frances was lightheaded and nauseated but kept pace with her fellow postulants. They'd had nothing to eat since eight last night, a special small meal before they went to bed. They were on Sherbrooke Street now and she moved her eyes from side to side, thinking of Thomas's fond descriptions of the grand mansions. Thomas was never far from her thoughts. The thrill of the last weeks at St. Bridget's made her heart thump. She remembered his lemon scent and could feel his hand on the small of her back. Less than three months ago; could it have been as recent? It seemed like years ago in another country.

The sun was low in the sky now and cast long shadows behind them as the column of young women wended its way down gentle slopes to the right, then left, then right and on and on.

Rosemary had told her the chapel was on the river's edge in the old part of the city. As they went further east and south the life of the city rose up to greet them – cars, streetcars, horse- drawn carriages, men unloading boxes in front of shops, men in suits and hats going into buildings, boys on street corners holding up newspapers and yelling in French. They passed several churches, the bells pealing out the hour. Seven o'clock.

Frances understood why Sister had warned them against gawking. The buildings soared above them, inviting with their wide staircases, arches and pillars in warm yellow and beige stone. Here and there the brass fittings, engraved plates and doorknobs gleamed in the morning sun.

A sharp contrast to the grandeur of the stone buildings were the scenes in some of the alleys they passed. Men in tweed caps and worn-out clothes stood in silent lines, hands shoved deep in pockets and shoulders slumped. Midway up the alley the line stopped in front of a door that was propped open with a rock. A pair of hands holding a bowl reached out to the first man in line. The man took the bowl, crossed the alley to the red brick wall and spooned the contents into his mouth as the next man shuffled up to the door.

Because Rosemary was from Montreal, she had been selected to marshal the column of postulants. She tilted her head toward the alley and whispered to Frances, "Soup line."

Mamma and Papa had talked about men begging for food from complete strangers, but she'd never seen it. She was embarrassed for them. To swallow their pride like that for a bowl of soup.

Don't they have family to turn to?

A burning shame rose within her. She was no better than them. Ashamed to turn to her family, she was going begging for food and shelter... and more.

The smells and sounds of the market reached them before they saw it. The stench of rotting vegetables, horse manure and sewage hung in the air. Men and boys were unloading carts, setting up tables and baskets brimming with corn, tomatoes, beans and more. They greeted and cajoled each other, rough but companionable. Frances held her handkerchief over her mouth and nose. She tried taking small gasps through her mouth to quell her nausea.

One man looked up from his work as they approached. He stuck his thumb and index finger into the corners of his mouth and emitted a shrill whistle then barked a command at the other workers. Many of the men turned away from their work and stood with their heads bowed and caps in their hands. The whistler led the Sisters' procession onto a narrow walkway free of straw and horse manure.

Frances didn't like the market smells, but they did remind her of home. A wave of nostalgia for the barn and the henhouse washed over her.

Their procession turned into a grey building that fronted on the street. Frances was surprised at the chapel's modesty. Despite its name, she'd expected something very grand with a big garden. It really did look like a simple chapel.

They filed in one by one. Progress was slow. Some of the postulants came to a full stop when confronted with the spectacle of the interior. The painted dome soared above in turquoise and pink and gold where an image of the Blessed Virgin Mary floated amidst cherubs, her holy garments swirling around her. The morning sun sparkled through the stained-glass windows and broke into jewels that scattered across the white marble floor and the upturned faces of the devotees.

An insistent throat clearing and the sound of the wooden clapper brought them to their senses and they filed into the pews. Frances was on the dimmer west side of the chapel where the stained glass merely glowed, waiting for the afternoon sun to bring it to life. The postulants stood like statues until the clapper sounded, then sat in unison. It was a relief to sit after the long walk.

Frances took a few deep breaths. She was uncomfortable, wearing all the extra underclothes she could. She had pinned the envelopes Rosemary had given her last night to the inside of her vest.

She looked for Rosemary but couldn't find her. The rows of young women in front of her were indistinguishable from one another in their black caps and habits. Nausea and panic vied for her attention.

The windows offered a distraction. Starting on the sunny side of the chapel they depicted the life of Mary, first with the Annunciation by the Angel Gabriel of Mary's virgin motherhood. Frances sat under the Flight into Egypt where Mary, holding her newborn, sat on a donkey being led by the sainted Joseph.

Mary had to flee from her enemies too.

Anguish flooded through Frances. She closed her eyes to capture her tears.

The Mass began. Frances went through the motions – standing, sitting, kneeling. She responded to the Latin prayers, sang the hymns but was distracted. She kept rehearsing her role.

"Keep your wits about you and you'll know when the time comes," Rosemary had said.

"What if someone stops me?"

"The market will be heaving. No one will pay you the least bit of attention."

The altar bells tinkled. They were on their knees; holy, holy, holy, the bread, the wine and then the communion procession. Frances's row filed out on the side aisle, moved to the back of the chapel and then around and up the centre aisle.

"Urrgh, urrgh." Thud, clatter. "Urrgh." All heads turned toward the commotion in the centre aisle.

Frances was on her tiptoes like everyone. Her heart squeezed and turned to stone. Rosemary was on the floor thrashing to and fro. The procession had halted. Frances was beside the church door.

Oh, Rosemary. This is it, isn't it?

She pushed the door and stepped into the outside world, a world of sunshine, horses and carts, vegetable sellers, and streets leading away from Notre Dame de Bon Secours Chapel.

Move with purpose, like you're on a mission, Rosemary had said.

Frances stepped into the busy street, lifted her skirts to step over a steaming pile of manure and headed up the hill that led away from the chapel. She kept her head down and strode, stretching the umbilical cord that held her to the congregation until it snapped.

3

BECOMING GEMELLE

MINUTES UPHILL FROM the chapel, was the grey building Rosemary had described. It took up the whole city block. The main part was set back and three wings jutted out toward the street.

The entrance was halfway down the block. Church bells rang nine o'clock just as Frances lifted the big iron knocker. She was wrung out but knew she had hours of uncertainty ahead of her.

The nun who opened the door was tiny and ancient. She raised her knob of a chin and peered out at Frances from behind sparkling rimless glasses, scanning her from the top of her black cap to the hem of her postulant habit.

"Oui, qu'est ce que vous voulez?" What do you want? The nun leaned to her side looking around Frances.

Frances spun her head around to look.

They've come for me. They found me, she thought

But no, they hadn't. She was just such an oddity to the old nun that she was looking for the person in authority who had brought the young postulant here.

"Ma Soeur. Help me, please. *J'ai un bébé."* Frances didn't know how to say pregnant in French.

"Où est le bébé?" Sister asked with a small furrow between her sparse eyebrows. Again, she moved from side to side, now looking for a small bundle.

Frances reached out, took the nun's hand and placed it on her belly. *"Ici, ma Soeur."*

The nun yanked back her hand as if it was on a red-hot stovetop. *"Mon Dieu Doux, non."* Then she reached out and grabbed Frances by the forearm. *"Entre, vite, vite."*

Frances found herself in a similar but much older building than the convent she had left at dawn that morning. The same hushed, stale stillness, the faint smell of beeswax and incense. The old nun took her by the hand and led her to a small parlour. *"Attends ici."* Wait here.

"Ma Sœur, ôu est la toilette, s'il vous plait?"

"Par là." She tilted her chin toward a door across the corridor.

The Sister was gone when Frances returned to the parlour. She listened to the ticking of the clock and the churning of her stomach. She took out the envelopes Rosemary had given her. One had her name on it and the other said "Director of the Miséricorde Hospital". Fatigue and hunger blunted her curiosity. She returned her letter to her undershirt and put the other in her pocket. She rested her eyes and tried not to think but soon saw images of her sisters, Patsy, and her classmates from St. Bridget's. Everyone else was moving forward – education, careers, marriage, even becoming a nun – but not her. She was lost and floundering, not knowing even what the very day would bring.

The wall clock chimed eleven and a young nun came in. She thrust a bundle of clothing at Frances and turned her back to her.

"Put this on. Leave your tings here." Her accent was French but Frances was happy to hear someone speak English.

The first thing Frances removed was her tight-fitting cap and the black hairnet underneath. She tidied her hair as best she could.

"Depeche-toi. Je t'attends." Hurry up, I'm waiting.

Frances hurried out of her black habit and pulled the shapeless grey dress over her head. She kept on the triple underpants and vests. She had little enough. At the last minute, before the nun turned, she remembered the letter in her habit pocket. The well-worn grey dress she now wore had a pocket, so she tucked it in there.

Frances folded the black habit. She wasn't sorry to leave it.

She followed the young nun out of the parlour. They turned right in the corridor, walked to the end and went down a worn granite staircase. At the bottom they turned left then right down another narrow corridor. It was hot and humid. Loud clanking and grinding of machinery added to the oppression.

The young nun hustled. Frances felt light and uncorseted in her used, baggy dress. They entered a long narrow room with high windows at ground level along one side. Dozens of young women sat side by side doing needlework at tables facing the windows. They all wore the same shapeless uniform and no head coverings.

One woman stood up and stretched, her hands on her lower back. She waddled over to the laundry baskets, her enormous belly leading the way. Frances looked at the women again, and realized they were here for the same reason she was. All of them – *all of us* – she corrected herself, pregnant.

⚜

When the noonday meal was over, and the rows and rows of young women were finishing the last of their tea someone tapped Frances on the shoulder. "Come." Another walk, through long corridors, up the stairs and around corners led to the office marked *La Directrisse*. The silent escort sat with Frances until the inner door opened and a nun, tall and burly, came out, looked Frances over, and said, unsmiling, "*Bienvenue a la Miséricorde. Entre.*"

Frances looked at the nun as she went around her desk and settled herself. These Sisters wore a different habit but the essentials were the same – a long heavy black dress and a crisp white wimple encasing her face. The sides of the wimple formed a curve above the nun's face and a white band covered her forehead to a half-inch above her eyebrows. Not a wisp of hair.

"I am *Soeur Philomène*, the director of this hospital. You have caused quite a stir here today. We have not, in our long, long history, had the honour of registering a postulant."

Frances heard the sarcasm.

Sister Philomène sat watching her, a cat waiting for a mouse.

"Sister, my name is Frances —"

"*Silence.* You will not say that name again."

"Sister, I have a letter for you. May I show you?"

"*Oui.*" She reached out and took the envelope.

The letter was one page, but the nun took a long time to read it. She glanced at Frances. "It is in English. I must be careful to understand the meaning. *Assieds.*" Sit.

Some moments passed.

"So, you have run away from a convent. And you have had help. This *Madame ...*". She broke off and looked at the letter. "Ellen Egan, your cousin, she is worried about the shame and disgrace you will bring on your family, especially your aunt." She spoke in affirmatives, no questions.

Frances kept her head bowed and said nothing.

"Your silence and composure are commendable. I will ask questions and you will answer. Were you sent to the convent because of your condition?"

"*Non, ma Soeur.*"

"Your parents know nothing of this?"

"*Non, ma Soeur.*"

"Have you been examined by a doctor?"

"*Non, ma Soeur.*"

"But you are sure you are with child?"

"*Oui, ma Soeur.*"

"Who is the father of the child?"

Frances held her breath as long as she could. Tears filled her eyes and when she took a breath it came as a strangled sob. She kept her head bowed and let the snot and tears cover her face. Sister Philomène sat in silence and Frances continued to sob and gasp for a few minutes before coming to an exhausted stop. Her shoulders sagged, and she snorted to try to stop the mess on her face.

"*Tiens.*" The Sister passed her a white handkerchief that she took from her top drawer. Frances raised her face and met the Sister's gaze. "I cannot tell you that, Sister."

"*Un viol*, perhaps." Rape?

Frances remained silent. She turned the word over in her mind. *Viol.* Violate?

"More than five hundred penitents come here every year to hide their shame and sin. You cannot tell me anything I have not heard before. But sometimes it takes time." She got up and moved to the window and opened it a few inches.

Five hundred every year!

"Do you know the meaning of Miséricorde?"

Frances never thought her Latin classes at St. Bridget's would come in handy. "A merciful heart, Sister?"

"*Précisément.* The Sisters of the Miséricorde serve the Lord by sheltering women who have gone astray, by taking care of them and their children, by being merciful. We will take care of you. But there are rules and you must follow them." She looked at Frances and waited.

"Yes, Sister."

"*Soeur Ignace*, our registrar, will see you today to tell you the expectations. But I must tell you my special expectation, given your unusual circumstances. You must write to your parents today telling them where you are and why. They will hear from your congregation about your disappearance very soon and I do not want them to be worried. I will read your letter before it is posted." She stared at Frances until she nodded.

"*Bien.* What your parents tell your aunt and her congregation is no concern of ours. You can be assured of our discretion. Only two of my Sisters saw you in your habit today. I have instructed them that your previous situation will not be mentioned again." Frances had no doubt that was true. To cross Sister Philomène would be unthinkable.

Sister rang a small bell on her desk. The door opened and the escort was waiting.

Frances rose. "*Merci, Soeur Philomène.*" She backed out toward the door. The escort steered her to a small writing desk where a pen, official hospital stationary paper and a plain stamped envelope were waiting to receive the words she dreaded writing.

⚜

Sister Ignace, the registrar wasted no time. "Your name here is Gemelle. It is the only name you have. We do not have a rule of silence, but we do have a rule of privacy. Do not tell anyone your old name or anything about yourself. And do not ask questions. Do you understand, Gemelle?"

"Yes, Sister."

"*Bon.* You have come with nothing. We will give you what you need." Sister raised her hand to stop Frances from speaking. "We are merciful but also practical. You will work here to pay for what you receive. Do you understand, Gemelle?"

Frances was cowed by the nun's abrupt manner. "*Oui ma Soeur.*"

"Only your cousin, Mrs. Egan may visit you once a week, on Sunday afternoon, for thirty minutes. Sister Thérèse, our Secrétaire des Visites will send her a letter and tell her the rules. It is up to Mrs. Egan whether or not she comes. She is the sole person we will communicate with unless your parents contact us." Sister Ignace looked at Frances with raised eyebrows, waiting.

"*Oui ma Soeur.*"

The remainder of the registration was more of the same – rules, the daily schedule, duties, and the repetition of her new name. Aside from the renaming business, it wasn't that different from St. Bridget's or the Mother House. Learn the hierarchy, follow the rules.

After she left Sister Ignace's office she did as she was told, followed the other penitents, as they were called, and got into bed just as the bell chimed nine o'clock.

Her first day, over.

✤

Frances was in the fusty, old bathroom down the hall from the dormitory she was assigned to. The bathroom was an echoing cavern with four toilet stalls and two tubs around the corner, with only one dim bulb lit during the night. She looked up at the high window and thought of Rosemary in her curtained cubicle a few miles away. She took out Rosemary's letter and squinted.

> *Dear Frances,*
>
> *I am writing this on Sunday night in our dark dormitory. You are brave to do this, and I pray it is a solution to your trouble.*
>
> *We cannot write each other directly, for obvious reasons, but I would like to know how you get on. Please write to my mother. It's 86 Murray Street. I imagine they will read everything you write like they do here. Mama will write to your own mother if you wish. It is hard to know now how things will unfold.*
>
> *May God bless you,*
> *Rosemary*

Tears sprang to Frances's eyes. She brushed them away, memorized Mrs. Egan's address, tore the flimsy sheet of paper into shreds and flushed it away.

Rosemary was right about the difficulty of writing to each other. All letters here, incoming or outgoing, were reviewed and it was the same where Rosemary was. If she wrote to Frances or wrote to her mother about Frances, they would figure out Rosemary's involvement

35

in her disappearance.

She passed two cots before reaching her own, muffled cries coming from one and peaceful, quiet snoring from the other. There were curtains around the cots here too, but the rule was that they were closed only while the penitents were undressing. The rest of the time they were pulled back. Nothing to hide, no privacy, despite their rule of privacy.

Frances lay awake on her iron cot going over the events of the day. She tried to remember everything Sister Philomène and Sister Ignace had said to her, but it was no use. Everything was a jumble. But it didn't matter. The main thing was to be obedient, humble, and penitent.

The blazing thing in her mind was the letter that the Director had made her write to Mamma. Frances calculated that Mamma would receive it on Friday or Monday. Would she write back?

⚜

A loud feral grunting dragged Frances from her sleep. She turned her head from side to side trying to get her bearings. The girls on either side of her slept now, neither crying nor snoring, but the one across the aisle from her was sitting up looking into the lit corridor. She saw Frances and tilted her chin.

"It's Potamie. Her time."

Frances was about to ask, "What time?", and then she realized. "Shouldn't we help her?"

"No. The Sisters are there. They'll take her downstairs."

She came over and sat at the foot of Frances's bed. "You came today?"

Frances hesitated remembering Sister Ignace's warnings.

"Yeah. You came today. Afraid to make a peep. We're all the same after meeting Ignace." She laughed. "My name here is Rogata."

"I'm Gemelle."

"You don't look pregnant. I'm surprised they took you."

Frances couldn't say she had come from the CND convent.

"I had to get out of where I was."

"All of us. We have to be hidden away. What job did you get?"

"Job?" Rogata's direct questions and matter-of-factness surprised Frances. "Oh, my duty? I'm helping in the kitchen. I start tomorrow."

"That's where I am. I'll show you around. Good night, Gemelle."

Rogata's friendliness buoyed her up and shone a tiny beam of light into her misery. Although the Miséricorde was similar to the Mother House, there was an important difference.

She's not going to be a nun. She has to pretend to be Gemelle, but not a nun.

Her optimism was short-lived. She imagined Mamma reading her letter and a cringing sickness overcame her. Frances remembered it word for word. She imagined Mamma turning it over to examine the return address and the stamp, the two vertical lines between her eyebrows deepening.

September 8, 1930
Montreal
Dear Mamma and Papa,

I have some difficult news. Please read this when you are alone.

I left the Mother House today and came to the Miséricorde Hospital on Dorchester Street. I am expecting a baby. The nuns here offer asylum to girls in trouble.

Nobody at the convent knows about my situation, but I expect they will realize soon that I'm gone and will contact you. Please don't worry about me. And please don't tell them where I am.

Our cousin, Ellen Egan, wrote a letter of introduction for me. Her address is 86 Murray Street, Montreal. It would be best if you wrote to me care of her so as not to give Mrs. Beaton in the post office anything to gossip about.

I'm ashamed of myself for bringing disgrace on you and our family. Please forgive me.

With love and regret,

Your daughter Frances

She hoped Mamma would understand the need for secrecy and what she meant by giving her Rosemary's mother's address. She was asking Mamma to take her side, and really, she had no right.

Despite the exhaustion deep in her bones, she lay awake for hours.

⚜

Rogata was true to her word and eased Frances into the routines at the "Mis", as a lot of the girls called the hospital – short for *la misère*, destitution, misery. Rogata spoke English and French sliding from one to the other without thought or hesitation. Every day they washed an enormous pile of breakfast dishes and had a ten-minute break before starting to peel potatoes for lunch.

When Frances got some tea for Rogata at break time a girl called Salome laughed and said, "Hey, *l'anglaise*, don't spoil her too much."

Some of the girls called Frances that, but she didn't mind. It was often said with more affection than Gemelle. Most of the girls hated their imposed names. They were all in the same boat and the enforced limits on their conversations – no past and no future, no name – kept them in a suspended, temporary state.

Almost every day, sometimes twice a day, a girl's labour would begin. The nursing Sisters took them to the delivery ward. Those remaining usually didn't see them again.

On the day Salome didn't come to work in the kitchen Frances asked Rogata, "What happens after the baby comes? Where do we go?"

"You get two weeks off work and then get assigned another job, in a different area. You get moved to a new ward too." Rogata pointed,

"Fetch me the salt."

They were making pastry for pies. Frances got the salt then said, "Another job? I thought they'd ... we'd go home after... after the baby came."

"You have to work to pay off your debt. Didn't you know that? All of this," Rogata waved her arms around, "it's not free."

"Oh .... I guess I didn't understand."

"Everything has a price, room and board, the doctor's fee, the de-livery, the adoption. They add it all up and give you a bill. Then you work it off."

"How long will I have to stay here?"

An older girl called Nymphodore had joined them at the baking counter, "You? You came very early. You'll have to stay a long time."

⚜

Frances worked in the kitchen and saw none of what went on in the rest of the hospital. She knew the girls she ate with and shared the dormitory with were having babies and new girls were arriving at a steady rate, but she felt isolated from the very purpose of the hospital. No one talked about any of the details.

Frances didn't want to know. She tried not to think ahead. The Misericorde and the fact of her pregnancy were temporary, something she would endure. She didn't think of having a child, only of coming to the end of the pregnancy. When it was over she would begin her real life; and even that, she gave scant thought.

Frances and Rogata were rinsing sand from spinach leaves when a Sister Dolorosa sent for Frances. She didn't know why. She turned to Rogata. "Me?"

"It's not easy," Rogata said, "but there's nothing you can do about it. No point in worrying." Frances was no wiser but followed the mess-enger up the wide staircase to the third floor.

Now she was in the Sister's examining room, naked on her back with her knees bent and her feet in cold metal contraptions. Although the room was warm, and she was covered with a crisp white sheet, a coolness in her private area shamed her.

Sister Dolorosa stood beside her holding her hands. "Be calm, my dear. Don't fuss. This will take only a few minutes." She continued to stand there, staring out the window at a maple tree that had the first hints of autumn in its leaves.

Do what you have to do Sister. What are you waiting for?

The door swung open, men's loud voices. Frances tried to close her knees and move her feet forgetting about the straps on her feet. She was splayed open. She couldn't see the men. Sister gripped both her hands in one hand and put the other on her knee.

"Be calm, dear. The doctor is here now. He will examine you. Be still so it won't hurt."

A lanky, grey-haired man loomed into Frances's view over her left shoulder. He glanced at her then turned to Sister. "What have we here, Sister?"

"Eighteen years old, maybe three months, no reliable information, first examination, Doctor."

The doctor made a gesture behind his back. "Over there, gentlemen near her feet, so you can observe the examination." Four young men, little older than Frances, dressed in white coats and carrying notebooks, scuttled behind him settling into place. Frances squeezed her privates tight as though to retract them from the men's gaze. She followed Sister's eyes out to the maple tree.

The doctor reached across and took her cheek in his hand and turned Frances to face him. "When did this happen, *ma fille?*"

My daughter? Frances closed her eyes and turned her head away.

"She just came here this week, September the eighth, and has not revealed anything to us, Doctor. Her early registration has Sister Philomène's approval." Sister Dolorosa said the last bit with a different tone as though Frances was an exception to the rules.

"*Et bien*. Let us proceed and see what we can determine." He turned away from Frances. "Gentlemen, this is an excellent case for you to learn from. Mr. Deserres please proceed with the history and the examination. We will discuss your findings later." He stepped back toward the wall.

A young man with thick glasses and a hawk-like nose stood beside Frances. "*Mademoiselle*, my name is Gregoire Deserres and I am a medical student. I am going to ask you some questions. How old are you?"

Frances kept her head averted and mumbled. "Eighteen."

"When was your last menstrual cycle, Miss?"

Another mumble. "In June or July, I'm not sure."

"Are your cycles regular?"

"Yes."

Gregoire Deserres's voice was calm and neutral. After a few more questions Frances turned her face toward him and saw him waiting for her attention.

"I'm going to do the physical examination now. I will start by looking at your eyes and then work down." He turned to Sister and put his hand out. She passed him a flashlight that he shone in Frances's eyes.

Frances turned away again when he felt her breasts. "When did you notice the tenderness?"

Frances couldn't speak. She was ashamed of being naked in front of Sister and the men. All the rules in boarding school and the convent about modesty, keeping herself covered even when taking a bath, striving for purity and perfection, it was all for nothing. She was an impure sinner. And they knew it.

"Miss? How long have your breasts been tender?" Again, that patient but almost indifferent voice. This wasn't about purity or shame. It was routine for them.

"August. I noticed it then, sometime in August."

Sister stepped close to the examining table and put a small sheet over Frances's chest and then pulled the big sheet low exposing her abdomen. Mr. Deserres roamed his hands over her, prodding and tapping. He stepped back and nodded at the doctor who stepped forward and repeated the motions. Despite her shame Frances noticed the way they did it. She realized that they did it the same way, step-by-step. She watched the two men talking. She couldn't understand them because they were speaking French, but she was intrigued that they had so much to say about her stomach.

"Now I'll exam you down below." Mr. Deserres looked at her and then slid his eyes down below her waist and back to her eyes. Frances nodded and looked away. The leaves on the maple tree were now a blur of orange and green and gold.

Sister held her shoulder for a moment and said, "Breathe, don't grip your muscles." Then she moved down to where everyone was gathered, opened a linen-wrapped tray and passed something metal to Mr. Deserres who was seated between her upraised knees.

The cold contraption moved into her, creating pressure that was not painful but mortifying. And worse was to come. When the man removed the thing he stood up and pushed his fingers inside her and with his other hand, prodded her belly, his face averted, his fingers groping and searching.

After the cold ordeal, Sister pulled the sheet over Frances and opened the door for the men. They left without a word or glance to Frances.

Sister undid the straps on Frances's feet and helped her to sit on the side of the table. "You did very well, my dear Gemelle. That Mr. Deserres is a good one. He will look at the results of your urine and blood tests and then write his report. I'll see you again in a week or so. Please get dressed and go back to work. I'll leave you for a few minutes, so you can tidy yourself." She handed Frances a small cotton pad, glanced below her waist, and left.

When Frances came out of the examining room Sister was at her desk making notes in thick brown cardboard folders that were piled on both sides of the desk. Frances approached her.

"Sister, may I ask you something?"

"Yes?"

"Are you a nurse?"

"Of course I am. All of the Sisters here are nurses." Sister gave her an impatient look. "*Pourquoi?*"

"My aunt is a nurse. She took care of wounded soldiers a long time ago." Frances hesitated. "I didn't know nurses took care of girls ... girls like me."

"Nurses take care of everyone – men, women, boys, girls – from birth to death. Now get back to work before someone comes looking for you."

"Yes, Sister. Thank you."

⚜

Ten days later Frances sat outside Sister Dolorosa's clinic with six other girls. When Perdita, the girl beside her, was called in, Frances and another girl helped heave her to her feet.

"*Merci.*" Perdita walked into the clinic and Sister closed the door.

"I don't think she has long to wait," a girl named Babel said, looking at the closed door. "What about you, *Anglaise?*" she whispered, not looking at Frances but turning a bit toward her.

Frances said nothing at first, just twisted her fingers around each other. "I'm not sure. I'll find out today."

"*Mon Dieu!* You don't look like the kind of girl who couldn't figure it out. You don't forget something like that!"

Frances squeezed her eyes hard to blot out thoughts of the summer. "We're not supposed to talk about it. I'm in enough trouble already."

"We're all in trouble, *Anglaise*. Not talking about it doesn't make it go away." Babel put her hands on her round tummy and rubbed them around in circles. "Me, I'm having dis one at Christmas. *Quel cadeau!*"

Despite her edginess, Frances smiled. A gift indeed. Babel's light heartedness gave her a little lift, but she couldn't think of anything to say.

The clinic door opened. Sister came out with Perdita and led her down the hall to two wide swinging doors. Perdita turned and, unsmiling, gave them a weak wave. They went in.

"She's going to the delivery ward. It'll be very soon." Babel waved back as Perdita went through the doors.

Sister Dolorosa was striding back toward them. "Gemelle, *viens avec moi.*" She held her office door open and ushered Frances in.

While Sister wrote in a file, Frances looked around the boxy office, taking in the small desk and chair, the tall filing cabinet with four drawers, an extra chair and a narrow table with brilliant blooming African violets on it under the window. And the holy paraphernalia, the Madonna and Child, the crucifix, and beside the door, the small font of holy water for blessing yourself coming and going.

It's better than the examining room, anyway.

Sister said, "Sit down. I have the report from Doctor Goudreau." Frances frowned.

"He is the doctor who examined you with the students last week. The best estimate, with so little information from you, is that on – let me see, September tenth – you were ten to twelve weeks pregnant. Very small, perhaps underweight but ..." She looked at the report again and nodded. "Not less than ten weeks."

A numb ringing in her ears, stomach clenched, her breath coming in small gasps, Frances stared at the floor. Ten or twelve?

"*C'est vrai*, Gemelle. It's true but not what you expected to hear?"

A hoarse whisper. "I didn't want this ... I mean ... it's the first time I've heard it. I'm ... please help me, Sister." Then, sobbing and moaning, Frances put her head on folded arms onto Sister's desk.

Sister came around the desk and pulled a chair close to Frances. She held her hands and squeezed them. "Gemelle, it is hard to bear but you must. You have sinned, and this is your punishment. You and the secret of your sin are safe here." She paused trying to look Frances in the eye.

"We will talk again soon. Eat more and walk in the garden every day. I have other girls to see. Go back to work now and pray for the Virgin's mercy."

⚜

Back in the kitchen, Frances didn't pray for mercy. Instead she thought about Thomas and Jimmy and how in the last six months she had gone from exhilaration to desperation.

The first time she had seen Father Thomas Byrne, was last January, when he had come into the St. Bridget's altar to say Mass with old Father Donnelly. The senior girls in the front pew had felt an electric current run through them.

"Who's he?"

"A tall drink of water, that one."

"What a carrot top!"

It was the novelty of it. They had watched Father Donnelly waddle around the altar and drone on for four years, or even more for some of the boarders. He also taught them Latin twice a week. He was as familiar and dull as the furniture.

But Father Byrne! His lean figure gliding across the altar. His liturgical responses to Father Donnelly, pious and musical to their ears.

Then February came and it was Lent. The purple sheen of his vestments set off his luxurious red curls. The girls knelt at the altar rail waiting for communion. When the solemn priests paced toward them, Frances was sure they all prayed that Father Byrne would turn to their side. To have Father Byrne place the blessed body of Christ on their tongue was their girlish longing.

He approached Frances. She looked up. He held the white wafer between them. She looked past the consecrated host to his fine hands, then up into his eyes. She had never, since her First Communion, looked at the priest who gave her the host. And now she did and she saw not the Vicar of Christ, but a man. She lowered her eyes, put out her tongue, and took what he gave her.

Some weeks later Sister Claire asked her to take some altar linens to the church sacristy. Frances was eager to avoid the Saturday study time. "I'd be happy to help, Sister."

The nun had hurried Frances into a heavy cardigan and some boots. "It may be the first week of spring but it's mighty cold and damp. Now, put your arms out straight." She placed the bundle of pristine linen on them. The lace edging hung over each side. Frances curled her fingers over the top of the pile and moved toward the open door.

Sister said, "Please don't mention this to any of the Sisters. I shouldn't be keeping you from your studies."

"Not a word, Sister."

The sacristy, the place where all the sacred altar items and the priests' vestments were kept, was a room beside the altar in the church which was across a field from the school. She trudged through a slushy track balancing her precious load. Though it only took her two or three minutes her cheeks grew rosy from the cold air.

Frances went through the side door of the church. The door to the sacristy was up three steps beside her. Once inside, Frances stood with the closed door at her back and looked around. It wasn't a comfortable room: long and narrow, dim and damp, bare and utilitarian. She was let down. She'd been expecting something mysterious in this holy secret place.

Frances didn't want to get back to the school during the study time so she took her time exploring the room, usually out of bounds to women, except the Sisters. An oak table stood in the centre taking up most of the space. Still bearing the linen, Frances walked around the table toward the back of the room. At the end of the left wall a heavy black curtain about four feet wide ran from floor to ceiling. Beside it a tall mirror, stippled with age. Her reflection caught her off guard – there were no mirrors in the convent. She peered at herself for a moment. Beside the mirror was a small table with a plain white metal basin and a water pitcher.

The oddest thing in the room was a one-armed Victorian sofa. The elegant red brocade upholstery and the carved mahogany frame were worn and scuffed but Frances imagined a grand dame reclining, fanning herself.

As Frances moved back toward the table, the door opened and Father Byrne stepped into the room. He closed the door and squinted at her in the weak light.

She took a quick breath.

He met and held her gaze. Something passed between them, a tingling, a shiver. Some wrongdoing or sin? Arousal she'd never felt before.

She lowered her eyes, keeping her neck and back ramrod stiff and made a graceful curtsy despite the rubber boots. "Good morning, Father. I'm sorry to disturb you."

He didn't respond. He looked to either side and beyond her. She knew he was looking for her companion.

"You're alone." Part question, part statement.

A sudden rush of heat rose in her face.

He went on. "Please, no need to apologize. I believe I'm disturbing you, not the other way around. Let me help you with that." He took a few long strides and slid his arms under the pile of linen. A thrill ran up her arms.

Once unburdened, she stood still, feet together, hands held at her waist one palm resting in the other. He smiled at her.

"I hope you didn't have to iron all that linen." He laughed a little. Frances was peeved to think he was laughing at her, but in an instant she saw he was nervous and was making a little joke to set them at ease.

He stuck out his hand. "I'm Father Byrne, Father Donnelly's new assistant."

"It's a pleasure to meet you, Father Byrne. I'm Frances Dalton." She kept her hands cupped in front of her. She hesitated.

"We met ... at the communion rail, Father." She glanced up at him, looked him in the eye then looked down. The heat was in her belly now, her palms damp.

"I must be going," she said.

Frances stepped around his still-outstretched hand and hurried to the door. The priest followed her. With her hand on the edge of the door, she turned. They were so close that Frances caught a faint scent of lemon. This time she smiled and held his gaze. "I didn't iron the linens, Father. You need to thank Sister Claire for that." Before she stepped out and pulled the door shut she made sure he was still looking at her and zipped her finger across her sealed lips.

Outside in the slush Frances gripped her hands together to stop them trembling. Her heart pounded in her chest. She was torn. It was a sin to feel like this, especially about a priest. Exhilarated.

Father Byrne, apologizing and worrying about whether Frances had ironed the altar linens. She'd never seen the like of it. The few priests she'd ever known set themselves apart, above. But this one saw her and spoke to her. From that first brief exchange, and all that followed it, he had changed her idea of what a priest was.

Months later, in the Mis kitchen she sat on the bench with a pile of potatoes in front of her staring into the past. And Jimmy? No matter how hard she tried to obliterate him he lurked on the edge of her mind. He had changed her idea of what a brother was.

4

The First Letter

Papa's oldest sister – Sister St. Benedict – was the reason Frances and her sisters were sent to St. Bridget's Academy boarding school. It was run by her religious order, the Congregation of Notre Dame or CND. As Papa said, "She's a woman of influence."

Frances remembered seeing the nun-aunt only once at home when she was six. Sister had been strange and distant to the girls. They had peeked around the doorframe to look at her and then giggled about her white chin board and pointy headpiece that were part of the get-up she called a habit. The sides of her face and her chin were framed with a roll of unyielding, white linen that came to a steeple on top of her head. A giant wooden rosary hung from her waist almost to the ground. Her skirts and rosary sounded as she moved among them: swish, rattle; swish, rattle.

Frances and her older sisters Bernadette and Josephine, would get used to nuns after being at the convent school, but that first time, when they were all still at home, their aunt was a great novelty. In their bedroom they folded white paper and put it on their heads with bobby pins and shuffled around tittering and whispering Hail Mary's.

Sister was the only family person Frances ever heard speak French. She had asked her mother how Aunt Sister St. Benedict had learned.

"She learned in the Mother House,"

"Her mother's house?"

"No Frances, in a convent in Montreal where your aunt went to become a nun. Many of the nuns there spoke French so she had to learn too."

"You mean she wasn't always a nun?"

Mamma had laughed. She'd handed her the egg basket. "No. Now run along and collect the eggs."

✤

On the day Frances left for school she was thirteen. Bernadette and Josephine had spent two and three years at St. Bridget's already. Papa took each of their faces in his hands, kissed them on the forehead, and helped them into Mr. McNaughton's wagon. Mamma accompanied them to the train station seeing them to their seats and giving them each an apple.

The conductor on the platform hollered, "All aboard, all aboard!"

Mamma turned to Frances and gave her a kiss and a hug. "I'll write to you every week, Francie. Study hard and listen to the Sisters."

She kissed Josephine and Bernadette and went to the end of the car. Frances looked out the window. The conductor was holding up his hand to help Mamma down the steep, metal steps. The train clanked forward and Frances was weightless. Her mother receded to a smudge on the platform.

Three hours after leaving home the train pulled into the station in Newcastle. A nun stood on the platform with a man in clean but worn work clothes a few feet behind her.

The girls picked up their bags. Josephine nudged Frances ahead of her and cast an exasperated backward glance at Bernadette. "Bernadette! Take that chewing gum out of your mouth before Sister St. Maureen sees it!"

Bernadette stuck the gum underneath her seat, pulled up her ankle socks, straightened the pleats of her dress and followed behind.

Once they were on the platform Frances stopped to pat her hair and let Josephine and Bernadette get ahead of her. They were taller and she tried to hide behind them. After brief introductions to Sister

St. Maureen they all climbed onto a horse-drawn wagon. Sister pulled Frances beside her, wrapped her arm around her shoulder, and gave her a smile and a nudge.

The road from the station to the school ran straight along the river on their right side, the riverbank sloping down to the water. A peaty smell hung in the September air. There was a faint saltiness to it but nothing like the sharpness of the bay at home. The movement was different too, no waves going in and out, just a constant eastward flow, a huge, turbid, brown swath. At the furthest point ahead, the river widened and its brown path dissolved into a greyish haze, indistinguishable from the sky.

Frances knew she'd get an earful from Jo but she asked anyway. "Is that the bay, Josephine?"

"Of course not. That's the Miramichi River. This side is Newcastle and the other side is Chatham, where Mamma grew up."

The driver murmured to the horse who then turned left onto a worn track to a solid red brick building.

Frances thought the building was grand with its wide stone steps leading up to the high double doors. The brass doorknobs and knocker and the arched transom window above gleamed in the afternoon sun. She craned her neck and looked up. High above the doors and the transom window, up near the roof, were four tall, multi-paned windows. Atop it all was a white crucifix. She turned and looked back down the way they had come. Being at the crest of the river slope, Frances had an expansive view of the river.

The door opened before they got to the top step, but there was no one there. Sister St. Maureen ushered them in. "Josephine and Bernadette, please go to the dormitory now. You may unpack your things. Prayers will be at five o'clock in the chapel."

"Thank you, Sister St. Maureen," they intoned in unison and curtsied. Frances watched them leave.

"You will see your sisters later, my dear." Frances turned back at the sound of Sister St. Maureen's soft voice and only then, saw another nun standing behind the still-open door. She moved forward and closed it.

"Thank you, St. Maureen," the other nun said, "That will be all."

Sister St. Maureen smiled at Frances. "I will see you soon in your mathematics class." She turned and walked down the hall on the right, to a door with a small brass sign that said Convent.

The new nun didn't smile. Frances thought maybe she had never smiled in her life. "I am Sister St. Jerome. Welcome to St. Bridget's Academy, Miss Frances. I am the head of the First Year Class. I hope you will follow the example of your sister Josephine and eschew Bernadette's bad habits."

Frances didn't know what shoeing habits meant so she looked at the floor and said nothing.

"Your new classmates are in the First Year Classroom. You will have refreshments and then some instruction. Follow me."

Papa would have said Sister St. Jerome was built like a brick shit house. Frances clamped her lips together to stop herself from smiling. Even with the thick heels of her sturdy shoes Sister St Jerome was shorter than thirteen-year-old Frances.

Frances took tiny steps so she wouldn't overrun the nun. They passed a narrow staircase and went in the first door after it. The classroom was sparse, the only decorations being a crucifix over the chalkboard and a blue and white statue of the Blessed Virgin Mary in the corner. There were three long wooden tables and at each one sat five silent girls, staring at the chalkboard that declared "Welcome First Year Class".

The welcome tea was weak – and there was no warm bread and molasses to go with it – but Frances was thirsty and hungry so she took lots of milk and sugar in it. Sister gave her the first of many disapproving looks. The new girls sat in silence drinking tea and stealing glances at each other. The instruction comprised a litany of rules and routines that would be unaltered for the next four years.

Silence was the biggest rule. Silent in class unless asked to speak. Silent in the dormitories. Silent in the chapel. Silent during meals. Silent during arts recreation, which was what they called sewing and painting.

The exception to the Rule of Silence was the prayers: before meals, after meals, before bed, during daily devotions, before classes in the morning, before classes in the afternoon. The girls took to heart the opportunity to pray aloud and belted out the prayers to a seemingly deaf God.

Cleanliness was another rule but most of that was left to the Sisters with no Saint before their names, the domestic Sisters. They performed a constant cycle of brass polishing, floor waxing, window shining and linen laundering. The girls didn't see a lot of them – they did their duties while the students were in class – but the lingering odours of polish, wax, and soap reminded them they were there. Frances found it a lonely sort of cleanliness. She missed the sharp, cedar scent at home that came into the kitchen every time the shed door opened.

✤

Something Frances didn't know before she went to St Bridget's was that her aunt, Sister St. Benedict, was an *important* nun, the *Provincial Superior*. No one had told her.

When Provincial Superior Sister St. Benedict made an appearance, things changed. The silence was deeper, backs were straighter, prayers were holier.

The first time Frances saw her aunt at St. Bridget's was after Christmas of her first year. She was surprised when she and her sisters were called out of their classes and were instructed with no explanation, to follow Sister St. Matthew who led them to the convent door and told them they were going to the parlour.

Frances had never been in the convent part of the building. She was curious. It was sparkling clean, of course, but there were no cushions or footrests, no cards or checkers, nothing that made it feel homey or lived in. In the corner on a wooden stand that came up to her chin, was a life-size head of Christ wearing his crown of thorns. Blood streaked down his anguished face and his eyes were flung up to the heavens. She stared at Him.

A rattle of beads. Frances turned away from Jesus.

A tall unfamiliar nun was sitting in an armchair flanked by Sister St. John, the principal of the school, and Sister St. Jerome, her thick black shoes dangling a few inches from the floor.

Frances and her sisters bowed their heads, held their hands together palms up at their waists and made a small curtsey. Frances kept her head bowed.

The tall nun leaned forward. "Good afternoon, girls and a special good afternoon to you, Frances. Welcome to St. Bridget's. I hear from Sister St. Jerome that you have settled in well and are applying yourself to your schoolwork." She was smiling and looking at Frances.

They talk about us?

"Come, come, Miss Frances. Say good afternoon to your aunt, Sister Superior St. Benedict," said the principal.

Her aunt pulled her right hand out from her sleeve and made a curt gesture, silencing Sister St. John.

She smiled at Frances and reached out and took her hand. "I can see you are confused, Frances. You haven't seen me since you were sick with typhoid and you probably don't remember. My Sisters and I prayed for you. I am the Sister Superior of our convent schools in the Maritime provinces. I am here occasionally and wanted to take this opportunity to say hello to you and to wish you well in your studies. I visited your parents last month and they asked me to look in on you and your sisters."

Her voice was low-pitched and gentle. Frances remembered laughing at her as she swished and rattled down the hallway at home. Her face reddened. "Good afternoon, Sister Superior Sister St. Benedict," she said with another small curtsy.

Her aunt laughed. "You may call me plain Sister St. Benedict."

She turned to Josephine. "I'm surprised you didn't tell Frances she was apt to meet me here, Josephine. Please be more thoughtful in future. This is your last year here and I expect you to set an example for her and Bernadette, and to help them achieve the excellent grades that you have. Bernadette, Sister St. Maureen tells me she believes you are gifted in mathematics. I hope you will take advantage of the Lord's gifts, my dear."

There was a quiet knock at the door. "Come in," said Sister St Jerome. "Girls, please sit and have tea with our Sister Superior."

Sister Henriette wheeled a two-tiered trolley into the room. On the bottom tier were plates of ginger snap cookies and chocolate brownies!

Sister St. Benedict smiled. "Girls, your eyes are as big as saucers. Please help yourselves. It is good to be able to give you a treat once in a while. This is your home now and you are very welcome here."

Her aunt gulped down her tea and asked Sister St. John to see her out. She said good-bye to her nieces. Frances thought it was a peculiar family visit. No laughter, no friendly gossip, no lingering over endless cups of tea. Not homey, really.

They were left sitting with Sister St. Jerome. "What a saint your aunt is. She has so much to do and still, she made time for you. She is kindness itself and such a role model for you. Now finish up that tea. I'll take you back to your classes."

Later that evening, after prayer, Bernadette and Frances grabbed a few quiet words together.

"I can still taste the walnuts in that brownie." Bernadette smacked her lips and rolled her eyes.

"What does role model mean? Jerome said Sister St. Benedict was a role model."

"She means we could be like her. Because she's a nun, an important one to boot. Ha! Maybe Josephine could be. She's the bossy teacher one. Shh, here comes Jerome."

Frances got into bed thinking of what she could be. She didn't want to be a copy of anyone.

᪥

That brief conversation about being a role model – being like her aunt – came back to Frances when she was home in the summer after her first year at St. Bridget's. It was hot as blazes and they were sitting on the front porch. Jo and Bernadette were teaching Jimmy how to play Auction Forty-Fives. Frances rifled through some papers on a low table beside the old couch. A creamy-coloured envelope fell out of one of Mamma's knitting patterns. She picked it up and saw it was from Nova Scotia.

It was already open. She looked at her sisters and Jimmy. None of them noticed. She tucked it into her waistband and folded her blouse over it.

She got up and said, "Jimmy, watch out for Bernadette. She's a card shark." They all laughed. She went inside and took the stairs two at a time and flopped onto her bed.

May 15, 1927
Dear Edward and Agatha,

I hope this finds you well. The weather in Antigonish is lovely.

As you know, I saw your girls a few months ago. They were very well. One of the cooks expressed some concern about Frances's weight, but I assured the principal that her tall, slender frame was a family trait. Her cheeks are rosy and she has not missed a day of class.

I hope you will encourage them toward a religious vocation. With three of them, and one son, it would be reasonable, and a

*great source of pride, if at least one of them chose to follow in my
footsteps. The Congregation has been very good to me, enabling
me to go to university, something that would have been
impossible otherwise. Armstrongs Brook didn't have much to offer
me in 1882 when I entered the Congregation and I doubt it has
much to offer your girls even now.*

*Sister St. Jerome described Frances as quiet and polite, self-
contained and contemplative. High praise and excellent qualities
in a Sister, I believe.*

*I am pleased to be able to provide a quality Catholic
education to your girls. I hope you appreciate it.*

*I know you will be very happy to have the girls at home for
the summer. Please remember these words of encouragement.*

Your Sister in Christ,

Sister St. Benedict

Frances was dumbfounded. This was the first time she had ever
heard about a vocation for herself and she thought it was ridiculous.
She wasn't like those nuns. She didn't even know how to pray. They
prayed a lot at school but most of the time she recited the words while
entirely different thoughts ran through her head.

Sister St. Jerome's opinion of her was a surprise, too. Frances
thought she went unnoticed which suited her just fine. This nun
business didn't. Jo was the one who should be a nun. She was already
halfway to being a teacher.

Josephine had finished fourth year and was going to teachers'
college soon. Bernadette would leave St. Bridget's in a year. They both
had lots of friends and their lives seemed to be unfolding according
to a clear plan. Frances thought for the first time about being different
from her sisters.

She knew she wasn't like them, wasn't content. When people
thought she was weak, she chafed. Until last year Doctor Shannon had

checked her once a year, so he could listen to her heart – something to do with having had typhoid. A part of being "sickly" was that everyone thought she needed help. That was the worst. Before leaving for St. Bridget's she'd helped her brother Jimmy to carry the milk pails from the barn just to prove she was strong. Jimmy had been nice. He liked sharing his chore and gave her the smallest pail. It had always felt like her arm was going to tear out of her shoulder but she'd been determined.

She tucked her aunt's letter into her waistband again and ran downstairs. The porch was empty. Once the letter was back where she found it she went out to the garden to pick carrots with her sisters.

Her sisters didn't know about the letter or she would have heard otherwise, and Frances hoped the idea of a vocation would be forgotten. Her parents had never raised it. Being a "Bride of Christ", words Sister St. Jerome often used, was nightmarish. She wasn't even sure what it meant, but she knew it wasn't for her. Being thought of as nun material was even worse than being thought of as sickly.

And now, as the Thirties started and Frances and her classmates worked toward graduation, all Frances could think about was the handsome new priest. The girls' talk about their futures – whether it was Avelda getting married or Patsy entering the convent – unsettled her. She tried but she couldn't see any future self. It made her mad. She was mad at the choices in front of her: nun, wife and mother, spinster.

A nun. Patsy's idea about having a place where you belonged, being in a community, was appealing but it was all the rest – the seriousness, the silence, the sameness – she just couldn't get it. And the holiness, the piety. Sometimes she would sneak peeks at the girls and the nuns as they prayed, hands clasped at their chests, eyes closed, lips mumbling. She wished she could feel what she assumed they felt. But there was nothing.

Wife and mother. She thought about the women at home, Mamma's friends and others. They seemed to be backdrops to their husbands' lives. The women kept everything going, repeating the same dull chores alone in the house day in and day out. But they didn't have anything that was just theirs.

Spinster, that mean-sounding word. Frances had looked it up in the dictionary. It just meant unmarried. Mamma had two sisters who were unmarried. One was a teacher in Boston and the other one a nurse, who had even gone to England during the Great War. They had jobs. They had left New Brunswick.

Frances was still mulling over her future. She was seventeen, almost eighteen, and the future was demanding a plan.

But lately something else, someone else, had caught her attention.

Patsy came back from the toilet and pulled down her covers. "Don't go to bed yet," Frances said. "What do you think of the new priest?"

"Well, to be honest, if he wasn't a priest, he'd be out breaking hearts somewhere. But Father Byrne is God's man now."

"Yeah, a crying shame. Nicer to look at than Father Donnelly though."

Frances was bursting to tell Patsy about her encounter with Father in the sacristy but something stopped her. Their meeting was merely a coincidence, but her endless thoughts about him were not.

The afterimage of Father Thomas Byrne was seared in her mind.

5

FATHER THOMAS BYRNE

FATHER THOMAS BYRNE arrived at St. Bridget's Parish on a bitter morning in the first week of January 1930. The sun was barely up when he stepped off the overnight train from Montreal. The east wind howled up the river carrying the cruelty of the North Atlantic onto the platform.

A sturdy bundle of a man grabbed his bag, mumbled through his thick scarf, "Father Byrne?" and walked toward a horse and sleigh. He hurled the bag up and motioned for Father to climb aboard. He thrust a worn wool blanket at him and looked at Father's knees. Grateful, the young priest wrapped it around his legs. The journey was short, and they sat in silence, but the muffled man looked at Father a couple of times. His eyes crinkled and tears from the cold leaked from the corners. Father took it as a welcome sign, a smile perhaps.

⁜

One of Father's first jobs as the new parish priest was to train some altar boys. It hadn't been part of the seminary curriculum, but he knew he had to start somewhere. And it was bound to be more amusing than canon law and ancient Church history. He was eager to make a good impression on Father Gregory Donnelly, the old priest who was his superior.

On his first Saturday morning in Newcastle, Thomas had four scrawny ten-year-old's lined up in front of him in the church sacristy.

"Allan, name the priest's vestments on the table in front of us."

The boy muttered barely above a whisper keeping his eyes on his scuffed shoes. "Father Byrne, this is my first lesson."

"I see." The priest took a deep breath. "Have any of you had lessons?"

They shook their heads.

Thomas blew out a long-held breath and snorted a short laugh. "Well, let's get started. Sit over there on that bench. I'll put on the vestments one by one and explain them to you."

By the time he was putting on the chasuble the boys' attention was gone. "Boys! Let's go out and get a breath of air. We've got a small break in the weather."

Father Byrne pulled his coat and scarf from the hook and lead them out into brilliant sunshine. The boys stumbled after him, pulling on galoshes and coats.

"Ah! This is more like it! Now why don't you boys tell me about what sports you like?"

Not a word. The boys looked at the tall redhead then looked at each other with furrowed brows and hunched shoulders.

"Come on boys! What about hockey? Joe Lamb – he's one of yours, from New Brunswick. I think he's going to prove himself. He's a rough one but a good scorer."

Father Byrne stopped short. The four boys were staring at him.

"What is it, lads?"

Flynn, an angular boy with a shock of dark curly hair, spoke up. "We know about hockey, Father, but we ain't got skates. We just play around a bit."

"And we never hearda Joe Lamb, Father. Or ... or ... heard a priest talk about hockey." Eddy had his head down and was shuffling in a brown puddle with shards of ice crystals piling up on top of his galoshes. "Father Donnelly don't talk about hockey."

Father Byrne threw his head back and whooped with laughter. "No, I don't imagine he does. But I do! I'm from Montreal and up there hockey is the game. Being a priest isn't all praying and teaching boys how to assist at Mass you know.

"Come on. We'd better put away those vestments before I catch it from the Sisters. Then we'll talk about hockey!"

By the time Lent got underway, one of Thomas's four young charges was assisting with Mass every morning. They had their duties down pat so they spent some of the time with Father Byrne playing makeshift hockey in the flat field behind the cemetery. Father Donnelly complimented Father Byrne on the boys' altar performance and didn't mention the hockey.

Thomas was proud of the boys. They were keen to learn and took their duties seriously. He knew part of it was getting away from their regular chores at home but there was also a childlike piety and devotion in them that resonated deep within him.

❧

When he was fourteen Thomas had assisted with Mass whenever he could. It was such a relief to get out, to get away from the sadness and chaos at home. The church was the cleanest place in Griffintown, the shabby Montreal neighbourhood where his family lived. He'd leave their cramped, grimy house, festooned with laundry that never seemed to dry, at six o'clock in the morning and let out sigh of relief. At home, he was always holding his breath and looking over his shoulder for his father.

He especially loved the cold, dark Montreal winter mornings after an overnight snowfall. The silence blessed him, and the sparkling crispness held a mystery that he felt nowhere else.

When he arrived on those wintry mornings, he was always alone in the sacristy for a while. The cleanliness and orderliness soothed him. The silence held him. He went about his duties precisely the same way every time laying out the vestments and polishing the sacred gold vessels with reverence. Sometimes when Father Monahan entered the sacristy to dress for Mass, Thomas was roused as though from a trance.

When he started his religious training at the seminary, he remembered his altar boy days and recognized those times as a sort of meditation. His course of studies in the seminary was rigorous and challenging. When the seminarians had time for meditation and reflection, Thomas turned his mind back to those times and found peace.

Thomas wondered now about his boys. He didn't pry but he liked to think that their altar boy duties provided some sort of anchorage in the swell of their juvenile worries.

⚜

After Frances had left the sacristy that day they met, Thomas leaned against the table, his hands spread on either side of the pile of linen. He patted the edge where she had clutched it, imagining a faint pulse of her warmth. He'd closed his eyes and recalled her. She was almost as tall as he was and thin. Her light brown hair looked soft. Some wisps had come loose from the bun at the nape of her neck and settled on the white collar and necktie of her uniform. Her neck just below her ear was blotchy red, her eyes a soft grey.

His sharp memory of these details startled him. She was playful. A girl had never talked to him like that. Thomas didn't know any girls, except his sisters. They had had some friends but they ignored him. He had attended the boys' school in Griffintown and spent all his spare time playing games in the streets with the other boys. He sometimes swept up Mr. Martin's shop and piled the bottles at the back for two bits. He kept his altar boy routines to himself and then at seventeen, he entered the seminary.

We met at the communion rail, she had said. He remembered that. She had shaken him then. Her knowing look had opened something in him. He had spent that bleak March Saturday afternoon alone in his study. The vicious Northeast wind battered the rectory. The trees around the old house groaned their displeasure. The wind was relentless as were his thoughts of the grey-eyed girl, Frances Dalton.

Thomas knelt in front of the statue of the Sacred Heart of Jesus and lit the votive candle. He held his intertwined fingers at his chest, gazed at the icon, and prayed: *Lord, please help me. I want to be true to my calling, to my vows. But I'm weak. Thoughts of her are tormenting me. Please help me to be strong, to bear my loneliness. I'm afraid I'll let you down. My devotion is shaky. I want to be a good priest. Am I an imposter, Lord?*

6

CONFESSION

AFTER THE SOMBRE rituals of Lent and the jubilation of Easter the students spent April and May preparing for the provincial exams in June. The meagre slip of time the girls had to themselves after class and before afternoon prayers was taken over by Sister St. Maureen for extra math tutoring.

In the second week of the new regime Sister came into their room accompanied by Father Byrne. Annie was the first to notice. "Psst!" They looked up, straightened their backs, pencils down, hands in their laps. They were well-trained in demure posture.

An unfamiliar lightness billowed inside Frances.

"Girls, I have some grand news for you. Say good afternoon to Father Byrne."

They scrambled out of their seats. "Good afternoon Father Byrne." In unison.

"Father Byrne has agreed to lend a hand with the math tutoring. In addition to our group sessions, he and I will do one-to-one tutoring with each of you once a week. Introduce yourselves, girls. You start Annie." Sister St Maureen was giddy with excitement.

One by one each girl said her name and added something.

"How do you do, Father?"

"Thank you for helping us, Father."

"Welcome to our school, Father."

Frances thought Sister St. Louise would have been pleased. Once a month they had a class on Ladies' Comportment with her, where they rehearsed lines like these. The goal was to be restrained without being dull; to be able to put others at their ease without drawing undue attention to oneself.

Frances wondered if he would remember her.

Father Byrne hesitated. "Uh, thank you for your kind words." Turning to Sister St Maureen, "I hope I can help, Sister." He blurted out a short, sharp laugh. His smooth cheeks reddened.

"Sit, girls. Father is going to listen and watch today. He'll want to see your copybooks as he goes around. Before we begin, let us pray." Sister lowered her head and invoked the name of St. Hubert, the patron saint of mathematics, and soon they were bent over their copybooks.

All heads were down but eyes swivelled to and fro. Father Byrne's cassock rustled as he walked around. Then he was behind Frances, a little to her left. He placed his left hand beside her elbow and leaned over her. Frances kept her head down but looked at to his hand resting so close to her. Long fingers with white crescents at the base of each clean smooth nail. A smattering of light brown freckles across the top of his hand faded out toward his fingertips.

"Well done, Miss Dalton. You had no trouble with that equation."

Frances looked up at him and then snapped her head back to her copybook surprised he remembered her name. "No, Father. Some of them are easy."

She glanced up at him again and smiled. She looked at his hand resting next to her elbow and then up at him again.

"Girls! Patricia is having an interesting time with problem number six. Let's all take a look at that one." Sister moved up to the chalkboard and started writing a string of numbers.

Father was still leaning next to Frances and everyone was watching Sister St. Maureen at the chalkboard. Frances took a quiet, deep breath. She reached over and touched the top of his hand with her fingertips. "Thank you."

Her voice was low. She retracted her hand and put it on her lap. Thomas looked at her, frowned, and then moved away.

✠

"Tim's heard things about our Father Byrne." Patricia whispered. It was well after lights out and they were lying in Patsy's bed. Frances held her breath. They'd been in silence since after math tutoring and she was fit to burst. Her fingertips still tingled.

"Well? Do you want to know what Tim said?"

"You know I do. Go on."

"Tim was home at Easter. He told me he's met some priests at the seminary who knew Father Byrne when he was there." She paused. "Our Father Byrne had a brother who was killed in France during the war."

"What a tragedy. He must have been so young."

"Who? Father B.?"

Frances laughed at her friend's familiarity. Then seriously, "Well, both of them! It was a long time ago. Father must have been only a boy."

"I guess so," Patricia muttered. Frances could tell she was falling asleep but she still wanted to talk about Father Byrne, what she'd done.

"Patsy, I touched his hand today," she blurted, unsure about telling her. Patsy sat up, wide-awake.

"His hand was so beautiful resting on the table. I just reached over and gave him a little tap. It was when you got stuck on one of the problems. No one saw."

"Boy oh boy Francie! What did he do?"

"He frowned. Do you think I'll get into trouble?"

"He frowned, did he? Do you think he was angry or maybe just surprised? Maybe puzzled?" She rushed on. "I bet that's it, just puzzled. He couldn't believe a chaste St. Bridget's girl would be so bold."

69

"There's more." Frances was holding her breath.

"Well ...?"

"Remember the day Sister Claire asked me to take the linen over to the church?

"Yeah?"

"I was in the sacristy. What a dreary place. I was just about to put down the linen when he walked in. I froze. Stood there looking at my boots."

"That doesn't sound so bad. What are you worried about?"

"I think I flirted with him. I don't really know, 'cause I'm a chaste St. Bridget's girl!" They covered their mouths in a fit of giggling.

"But I sure felt giddy and bold. I was ... I was ... bold. I didn't want to be chaste. I wanted to be bold."

"You're sweet on him, aren't you? Shh, shh, no. Don't say anything," She gave Frances a gentle poke in the ribs. "A girl who thinks a boy's hand is beautiful must be sweet on him!"

"I think I am sweet on him. I've never felt like this. He's on my mind all the time ... and not just his hands. Oh, Patsy. I get warm and tingly just thinking about him." Frances stroked her bottom lip.

Patsy put her arm around Frances. "I think Avelda would say 'You're m-a-a-a-d about him'!" Another fit of giggling. "I think you're just plain mad. Father is a priest. You can't be sweet on a priest, Frances."

⁂

Father Byrne and mathematics mingled in Frances's mind. She had told Patsy she didn't want to be chaste. She chafed under the daily restraints and was fed up being told who to be. Something new stirred in her.

Sister St. Maureen and Father Byrne split the small group of students in two and each gave individual tutoring to six of them, one by one. Frances was in Father Byrne's group. She imagined that Father finagled that.

They had had four lessons of an hour each so far and the routine was set. They met in the senior classroom, Sister St Maureen at the table facing the tall paned window; Father at the table facing the door.

Four whole hours alone, almost alone, with Father Byrne. Frances was thrilled.

Frances and Mary, her mathematics partner, walked into the class-room carrying their copybooks. They were still in their uniforms. Frances had been wearing the same one for four days and it was grimy and rumpled. Father Byrne looked up as she was straightening her tie and adjusting her collar. He smiled for a moment then quickly checked himself and looked away.

"Miss Dalton, please sit here." He pulled out the hard, straight-backed chair on his right. "Let's see how you did with those isosceles triangles."

Frances sat beside him and placed her copybook on the table in front of him open to the page with her recent problems. Frances had worked hard on the problems until they were perfect. She didn't want to spend her precious time alone with Father doing geometry.

She turned her head toward him and watched his hands as they flipped through her copybook. Frances smiled remembering Patsy's teasing. At that moment Father turned and looked at her.

"You have good reason to smile, Miss Dalton. Your calculations are all correct."

"Oh no. Father. Please. I ..."

"What is it? Please go on, Miss Dalton." He lowered his voice and leaned closer to her.

Frances Put her head down and mumbled into her copybook, "Call me Francie, Father. Everyone does."

Father took his cue from her. He turned his back so it was squarely toward the Sister and lowered his voice even more. "May I call you Frances? Such a lovely name."

"Uh ... uh, sure Father."

"My name is Thomas." He was watching her. He raised his eyebrows in a question, an invitation almost.

"Oh Father. I couldn't call you by your Christian name. If the Sisters knew they'd crucify me."

Father laughed quietly and shielded his mouth with his hand. "Yes, they are a stern lot! I wouldn't want to see you crucified, Frances. It'll be between us. No one here calls me Thomas. You can help me to feel like I belong."

"All right ... Father Thomas." That was as far as she could go. She was flabbergasted.

"We'd better move on to the next set of problems."

He glanced over his shoulder to Sister and Mary who were laughing and chattering like old pals. Mary's sister had entered the Mother House last summer. Since then the nuns were more familiar with her.

"Fa ... um ... Father Thomas. I'll work these out before our next meeting. But could I say something?"

"Of course."

"I heard that you lost your brother in France. That's very sad and I want to say I'm sorry."

"Brendan, my brother." Thomas sighed. "Nothing stays secret for long." Thomas's eyes were glassy. He put his hand over hers for a moment but then pulled it back.

"Would you like to tell me about him?"

"Brendan was my hero, my big brother, my protector. When he left for France he was an even bigger hero to me ... to all of us. And I waited to welcome him back. The thought never entered my mind that he wouldn't come home. His death shattered my mother."

He looked into the distance. Neither of them spoke for a few moments. Then he broke the silence. "Let's keep at these math problems, shall we?"

Frances settled down to the work, pleased that she'd had the nerve to talk to him the way she did. But she wondered what he needed protection from.

"Well, Father Byrne, girls. Let's call it a day. We don't want to be late for our supper." Sister St. Maureen laughed as she clapped her hands in front of her chest. Frances felt a wave of affection for her, for her enthusiasm, her trust, her hominess.

Thomas and Frances stood and she gathered her things.

"Thank you for your help, Father." Frances bowed her head, made a small curtsy and went out to the corridor.

"Wait for me, Francie!" Mary caught up with her taking big strides – no running was allowed, ever.

⚜

Seeing Father Thomas for mathematics was the high point of Frances's dreary routine. One day in late May, after their afternoon tea, she and Mary walked to the senior classroom for their sixth and last session with Sister and Father Byrne.

"I don't know how you concentrate on mathematics with Father looking over your shoulder with those dreamy eyes of his," Mary said.

"Don't be so foolish, Mary.

Mary leaned close to her friend's ear and started singing a popular song they had all heard on the radio last summer. "Yes, I'm thinking tonight of my blue eyes ..."

They were at the door to the classroom. "Hush up, now, you're no Ma Carter," she said when she saw Sister and Father sitting together talking. They went in and took their usual seats.

Frances always made sure all her math problems were done ahead of time hoping that they would have time to talk. Over the course of their weekly classes together, Father Thomas had told her more about Brendan and how much he missed him. He also confided that his mother had died not long after Brendan did. Frances thought he was sad and lonely but she was reluctant say something so personal. She didn't dare.

They sat very close to each other, Frances holding her pencil over her copybook and keeping her head down. She kept her left arm tucked onto her lap, leaving room for Father Thomas to lean in toward her side as he watched her calculations. They had only ever touched hands twice, but once, his shoulder had pushed against her. He had raised his arm behind her and rested it behind her on the chair. Frances was giddy. The weather was getting warmer and she caught his scent – sweat and lemon soap.

Frances had never known anyone from away and Father Thomas gave her a sense of possibility. He expanded her world. "Tell me about Montreal, Father Thomas."

"Why? Are you thinking of taking a holiday, Miss Dalton?" he said in a teasing voice.

"No, no, of course not. The only way I'd get there would be to enter the convent!"

"There's so much to see, I don't know where to begin."

"What about where your family lives?"

"Griffintown doesn't have much to recommend it. I'll tell you about Sherbrooke Street. The seminary is there but there's so much more. It's very wide with majestic, old trees and gracious mansions. There's—"

Sister must have overheard them chatting because she was out of her seat and bearing down on them, her usual smile fading on her lips and a puzzled frown creasing her forehead.

"That doesn't sound like geometry to me, Father." Sister St. Maureen said.

"Well, Sister, no it ... I mean... I was saying—"

"Oh Sister, Father Byrne was telling me about Sherbrooke Street in Montreal. I asked him if he knows where our Mother House is."

"Our Mother House?" Sister paused, then started up with enthusiasm, "Of course, our Mother House. What a sight it is. The pale, yellow bricks glow and the gardens at the back of the convent are an oasis and the chapel ... the chapel is simply magnificent. I was very happy there." Sister fell silent and looked away, but only for a moment.

"But surely, Francie. What made you ask about the Mother House? You're not ... are you thinking ... well, I never. This is the first I've heard ... have you been called, my dear?" Called. The word they used for a religious vocation. As though it wasn't voluntary. If the call came you had to go.

Frances bowed her head. "Sister, please don't mention this to the other Sisters. I'm unsure." She couldn't look at Sister for fear of laughing.

The weight of such an important secret brought Sister to attention. She looked around. "Father, Mary, I think that's enough tutoring for today. Girls, you're dismissed."

As Mary and Sister gathered their things and straightened the chairs Thomas leaned toward her. "Frances, I had no idea you were thinking of a vocation."

"I'm not at all, Father Thomas. It was a little fib. I didn't want you to get into trouble with Sister. I hope you don't think less of me for it."

"On the contrary. I think you're very quick-witted and clever. Thank you, Frances."

Frances turned and left as fast as she could. She thought if she stayed one more second, she would give him a big kiss on the cheek.

⚜

Frances thought of Thomas day and night going over every word they had spoken to each other. It seemed to be a scant few lines to her. She longed to have a real conversation, to be able to speak openly, not to be on guard, not to whisper.

"Patsy, let's ask Sister St. Jerome if we can go to confession." She paused. "You ask her." Jerome was now in charge of the senior class.

"What are you talking about?"

"Well, the Graduation Mass and Tea is next week, right? I just thought we should go to confession. After all, it's our last special Mass at St. Bridget's."

"Frances Dalton, you're up to no good! What is it?" Patsy stared at her friend. "Aha! I get it. I get it. You hope you'll see your red-haired dreamboat. You're addled. Father Byrne is a priest. I know you're sweet on him but .... But ... it's not right, Francie, for you or for him."

"I know, I know. You're right. But he's the only person I know from away, from Montreal. I want him to tell me about ... about everything!"

Everything outside of her school and her tiny village. It was the pull of the unknown that drew Frances.

Patsy and Frances looked out at the waning evening light on the river. Frances would miss their special view when she was back in her tiny village of Armstrongs Brook.

"Soon school will be over, and I'll be home. It feels so final. The end. Talking to Father makes me feel hopeful. Please, Patsy? What harm can it do?"

⁂

Two days later, Frances sat with her wooden rosary beads twined loosely in her fingers. She was in the pew close to the two-door confessional. The priest's door had a carving of a dove with outspread wings and rays of light streaking from below it. The penitent's door had a sombre cross.

Patsy had been in and out of the confessional earlier. Frances was stalling for time. She wanted to be the last one to enter it. She recited the prayers automatically with no holy thoughts. Her thoughts were on Father Thomas.

She was out of line. Father Thomas as a math tutor was one thing but here, in the church, he was a priest. Confession is a Holy Sacrament. Patsy was right. Frances knew it was wrong. But what about him? He's a priest. He wouldn't do anything wrong, would he?

She lost her nerve and decided to leave but as she stood to go Avelda came out of the confessional and walked back to her pew to say her penance. Frances sat down again. It would look strange if she left now after waiting her turn. Five minutes passed.

Avelda glanced over her shoulder at her as if to say, "What're you waiting for?"

She was so confused. Father Thomas, Father Thomas, Father Thomas. She had never felt like this. Like what? What was it? Excited, alive, astonished, expectant.

Five more minutes.

A shuffle and creak came from inside the confessional.

He's going to leave!

She bolted up and rushed into the confessional. The light was very scant. She knelt and looked through the grill but could barely see him. She got a faint whiff of his lemony soap. She was tongue-tied.

Thomas leaned his head and shoulders sideways toward her, raised his right hand. *"In nomine Patris, et Filii, et Spiritus Sancti. Amen."* The words were familiar, but his voice was different. His priestly voice.

Frances was silent.

"Do you want to confess, my daughter?"

"No, Father Thomas, it's Francie. I want to talk to you. I didn't know how to see you, so I came here. I feel foolish now. I'm sorry."

The words rushed out of her in a stifled whisper and she started crying. She bit her knuckle and held her hankie over her nose to stop from snuffling.

"Frances ... this is ... unusual." Frances imagined she heard a smile in his voice, the voice she knew.

"I'm very sorry, Father Thomas. I wasn't thinking. I'll leave now." She stood to go.

"Take a moment to compose yourself. Wait for me in the front pew near the sacristy door. I'll be a few more minutes here." Thomas's voice was decisive. Frances was confused. Was he mad at her?

Frances blew her nose, made the sign of the cross out of habit, and left the confessional. She went over to the far side of the church and knelt in the front pew, pretending to pray. She swung her eyes around and saw she was alone. She sat down. The late afternoon sun was streaming through the west windows but the rays fell short of where she was sitting. The window to her right was open and she smelled the tang of fresh cut grass, the first of the summer. A soft breeze stroked her cheek.

Despite the quiet, peaceful setting, her mind raced. She stared out the window seeing nothing.

He was so abrupt. He must think she's a ninny. She knew she should go.

As she was about to stand she heard footsteps. Glancing to her left she saw Thomas genuflect in front of the altar.

Too late now. She bowed her head so low she thought the nape of her neck would snap.

"Frances ... Frances. Look at me ... please." His arms were spread wide and his hands were resting on the front of the pew. He leaned toward her.

Thomas smiled. "Frances, what is it you wanted to speak about?"

She was so relieved to see him smile the words gushed out. "Well, it's ... it's ... I'm going home soon, home for good. I won't be coming back to St. Bridget's and ... and ... we've never been able to talk freely. I want to know more about you ... to know about Montreal. I'm dreading going home, Father Thomas." The tears came again. She bowed her head and covered her face with her hands.

Quiet voices and the shuffle of feet came from the back of the church.

"Frances, the sacristy door is unlocked. Please go in there until you feel better. I need to speak with the Turgeons about their baby's baptism." He looked to the back of the church. "Leave by the side door when you're calmer. We'll find time to talk but it can't be now."

"But I still ..."

Thomas took her hand between his and led her out of the pew. "Go, Frances. We'll talk another time." As she turned toward the sacristy door he put his hand on the small of her back. His touch encouraged her and she looked at him. He met her eyes for a moment, removed his hand and then turned and strode down the aisle.

Frances waited until she heard the quiet but lively talk from the back of the church, then went up the three stairs and entered the sacristy. She remembered their first brief meeting here. Less than three months ago. How had he taken up so much space inside her in such a short time? She teared up again.

Dammit!

She paced from the table to the door.

Get a hold of yourself, Francie. Smarten up.

She walked to the back of the sacristy and was startled by her reflection in the mirror. Despite the dim light she could see what her foolishness led to – swollen eyes, red, mottled complexion, wisps of hair stuck across her damp forehead.

The old-fashioned, chaise on the back wall was inviting.

No, she had to get out of there.

There was a bit of water in the pitcher. She dampened her hankie, wiped her face and tidied her hair. She took a deep breath, straightened her shoulders, fixed her collar and tie, and left the sacristy and out the side door of the church. She bolted across the field and into the school.

Frances scurried into the dining room and onto her chair under the ferocious glare of Sister St. Jerome. Heads bowed, the boarders prayed, "Bless us O Lord and these thy gifts ...."

She was relieved to be there. Everything was the same and familiar – the girls, old Jerome glaring at her, even the stinky fishcakes.

Frances tried hard to concentrate in chapel that evening. All the girls were making a big effort. They were almost finished the provincial exams, summer was coming on, and they were ready for a change.

Patsy had grinned and nudged Frances a couple of times during the meal. Frances knew she wanted to hear about what happened in the church and why she was almost late for supper. The evening prayers gave Frances time to think up what she would say to her.

Sister St. Jerome came up to the dormitory to give them a pep talk for the next day. All the senior girls were sitting on their beds with their math books open. They were silent and attentive until her receding footsteps faded, then murmurs and giggles arose around the room. Patsy and Frances went to their bench in front of the window. The sun had set but the sky was still light. They watched the river in silence.

"Well?"

"Leave it alone, Patsy."

"Did you talk to him?"

"I can't talk about it."

Patsy took her hand and held it between them on the bench. They stared out the window.

"I knew it was wrong. You were right. I just went to confession and then sat in the church feeling sorry for myself." She turned and smiled at Patsy.

"I'm still glum about going home, being there with nothing to do, but I know that talking to Father Byrne about Montreal isn't going to change anything. What about you? You got a letter today?"

"From the Mother House. They accepted me."

"Of course they accepted you, Sister St. Patricia."

"Don't tease me, Francie." She covered her face with her hands and bowed her head.

"What? Aren't you happy to be going?"

"I'm not sure about being a nun. It's forever." Patsy rubbed her face, sat up straight and took both Francie's hands. "I'm being foolish. Don't worry about me. That's what being a postulant is all about

– getting your feet wet and deciding if it's for you. Let's go to bed. Math tomorrow."

They moved toward their beds. "I'm glad you came to your senses about Father B. He's a priest and that's definitely forever." Patsy rolled over and was soon asleep.

Frances lay there thinking about the lie she'd told her.

7

Feet of Clay

THAT EVENING THOMAS tidied the kitchen and then left the rectory for a walk while there was still some golden light. He headed east past the convent school and then through the apple orchard. The ground was littered with white blossoms gilded by the setting sun and he noticed the fresh green leaves filling out the branches above his head. He wondered if the rectory housekeeper, Mrs. Charlotte's baked apples were from last year's crop from this orchard. Everything here was connected.

The downward slope of the land led him toward the river's edge. The black flies were fierce. They batted and buzzed at his neck and ears. He swung his hands around in a futile effort to shoo them away and pushed on determined to untangle the mess in his head. He continued east. The gentle slosh of the brown river pulled him along with the current out toward the Northumberland Strait. As the river widened his mind opened and all the thoughts he was holding back were there in front of him.

Frances. He wanted her, to be close to her. And he knew she felt the same way. Her boldness in coming to the church today was her challenge to him, to his vow of celibacy. Even his thoughts were a breach of the vow.

He was striding now and the setting sun on his back made him hot. He reached one finger up to his neck to loosen his stiff clerical collar.

Thomas halted and stared into the distance. Was he hiding behind his cassock and collar? What was he doing here?

He pushed on. The ground softened underfoot. He was too close to the marshy shore. His shoes were filthy and the hem of his cassock was spattered with mud. He stood motionless. He didn't want to turn back to the rectory the way he'd come. If he went up the slope at a diagonal he thought he'd get back onto the track. The climb up was difficult. He was winded and stood there catching his breath then headed for home.

He let himself in and went straight to his room. He put his shoes on a sheet of newspaper by the door. He collapsed in his soft, old arm-chair and threw back his head. His legs ached from the long walk.

All afternoon he had meted out small prayer penances to the St. Bridget's girls who confessed their insignificant, made-up sins.

And him? What penance did he deserve? Is the priesthood his penance? Atonement for Brendan?

These thoughts were not new. Thomas had spent many hours, alone and with his fellow seminarians, contemplating and clarifying his reasons for wanting to be a priest. At the time of his ordination he was as sure as he could be – devotion to God, spiritual service to others and celibacy – that was his calling. But what could an inexperienced seventeen-year-old boy know of celibacy?

His muddy shoes mocked him.

Yes. You have feet of clay. Flawed. Weak.

He fell into a dreamless sleep. The sky was lightening when he awoke and, as usual, Frances was on his mind. He fell to his knees and prayed.

Lord, please, hear my prayer. Take this temptation and desire from me. I cannot do this without your help. My flesh is weak. Give me the strength and wisdom to walk away from temptation.

He resolved that he would avoid Frances.

※

After saying the six o'clock morning Mass, Thomas left the sacristy and went back to the rectory lured by the aroma of frying bacon and toast. Mrs. Charlotte was busy preparing breakfast for him and Father Donnelly.

"How many eggs, Father Byrne?"

"Two, please. And do call me Father Thomas. I think I'm here to stay."

When they finished eating the priests left the kitchen and headed off to their own chores. Thomas picked up his muddy shoes and headed for the back shed where the shoe kit was.

Mrs. Charlotte peered at his shoes as he passed. "Mercy, what happened there, Father Thomas?"

"Nothing serious. I went for a walk last evening. I wasn't paying attention and wandered off the track. Nothing a little spit and polish won't fix."

Mrs. Charlotte got out her baking pans. Thomas asked, "What marvel are you making today?"

"Squares for the senior girls. The Last Examination Tea we could call it. We even did it back in my day." Mrs. Charlotte stuck out her chest and raised her chin.

"You're a St. Bridget's graduate, Mrs. Charlotte?"

"Indeed. I was a student there, when her nibs, Sister Superior St. Benedict, CND, was a student." She punched out the words with a tense mouth and a wagging head.

"Before she got so high and mighty as a Provincial Superior of the Congregation of Notre Dame. She was plain old Beatrice Dalton then."

Mrs. Charlotte lowered her head and wiped the dish in the hot soapy water at a furious rate. "Pardon me, Father Thomas, that was unkind."

Dalton? "I haven't had the pleasure of meeting Sister Superior, but I take it you're not fond of her." Thomas was holding his breath as he waded into the pool of gossip.

"You know, that girl never lived at home again – after St. Bridget's, I mean. In the August of the year we finished, 1882, didn't she up and enter the convent? Off to Montreal she was, and we never saw hide nor hair of her until she turned up here as the Provincial Sister Superior."

"I understand she's had a notable vocation."

"Notable, my arse!" Mrs. Charlotte clapped her hand over her mouth. "Oh Father, forgive me." Her back was to Thomas. Her shoulders shook.

"What is it?" Thomas was surprised by the sudden sadness.

She lifted the hem of her gingham apron to her eyes. She turned toward Thomas and threw herself at him laying her head on his chest, her apron bunched up on her face.

Thomas hesitated then put an arm around her shoulder. "There, there, Mrs. Charlotte. Don't upset yourself so. What is it?"

"She left us all. No goodbye, no how do you do. I thought I'd see her again. She was my good friend, you see. I missed her for years. I kept it to myself, of course, but I missed her. Then, with one thing and another, I stopped thinking of her." The anger ebbed and a bitter sadness took its place. Mrs. Charlotte let out a big sigh and remained on Thomas's chest.

Thomas tried to comfort her. "To lose a friend, someone you counted on always being there, and with no goodbye, it's a hard thing. It leaves a hole."

Years later Thomas would think of this conversation. How like her aunt Frances was.

"You said Sister Superior's name was Dalton. There's a Dalton girl graduating soon."

"Oh yes, they've all been here, Josephine, Bernadette and now Francie. Their aunt saw to that, I'm sure. She'll snag one of them for the nunnery."

8

THE RED BROCADE CHAISE

WHEN THE EXAMINATIONS were over, the senior boarders started the usual June cleaning and packing. Many of the Sisters were away on a religious retreat and the other boarders had gone home for the summer. The senior class had to stay a few days until the graduation. Sister St. Joan was in charge. She was young and approachable and no one minded working with her.

Patsy, Mary and Francie went to the art room with Sister. They spent the morning in silence sorting through supplies, cleaning brushes and easels, and scrubbing the tabletops. They broke silence only to ask Sister for direction or help.

The practice of silence was a well-ingrained habit. It was also a protection. Frances was guilty for lying to Patsy and ashamed of her thoughts and feelings about Thomas. Enforced silence helped her keep her secrets to herself.

✤

They went to Mass together on Sunday morning. Frances was giddy when Thomas came onto the altar. She hadn't seen him since the day she had gone to the confessional, only a week ago but an eternity to her. She remembered the warmth of his hand resting on the small of her back. Her heart fluttered and she flushed all over.

She watched Thomas and listened to every word he said, Latin and English. When he got to the gospel reading, he went on about His Body, His Blood, His Flesh, saying that last word at least six times.

Frances knew it was the feast of Corpus Christi, the Most Holy Body and Blood of Christ, but she couldn't stop herself from thinking of Thomas's beautiful hands, his lush red curls and his lemon-scented skin. She kept her face neutral. Inside she was on fire.

Father Donnelly shuffled to the pulpit to deliver the sermon. If Thomas had set Frances aflame, Father Donnelly quickly doused it. He spoke for ten minutes about St. Thomas More.

He ended his sermon by admonishing the girls to follow their conscience and to recognize false or worn out allegiances, as St. Thomas More had done. Frances had to admit he was a good speaker. She loved words and he got her attention with "false allegiance". She rolled it over on her tongue.

Frances had gone to church with her family from the time she was born, and the catechism was drilled into her by rote in primary school. Religion classes were done every day at St. Bridget's. She accepted everything as true. Well, maybe not. She simply had never questioned anything – the sacraments, the rituals, the prayers, the mysteries of the holy rosary, the power and authority of the priests and nuns. She hadn't questioned anything but, she admitted to herself, she wasn't much of a believer. Her Catholicism was as much a choice as the colour of her eyes. It just was. Or maybe it was, as Father Donnelly would say, a false allegiance.

No one at home, her family or neighbours, was very devout as far as she knew. It was more of a social thing. They went to the Catholic Church on Sundays and Holy Days, to the picnic in the summer, to the Harvest Dinner in the autumn, and the odd lobster supper in the church hall in lobster season.

Frances was deep in thought when they filed out of the church. Father Donnelly and Thomas were standing on the small porch, waiting to shake everyone's hand. Father Donnelly almost crushed Frances's and when she winced he passed her hand to Thomas saying, "Don't be too rough with Miss Dalton, Father Thomas. I think I overdid it." Everyone in earshot smiled. Thomas took her hand between his, looked into her eyes and gave it a gentle squeeze. He let go immediately and turned to the next girl.

The boarders were sitting in the parlour after Mass doing the only things they were allowed to do on Sunday, reading or needlework.

"Girls, I have a surprise. We're having a picnic today." Sister St. Joan grinned from ear to ear. "Come to the kitchen and help carry things outside."

The groundskeeper, Mr. Leary and his helper Terry had carried a table out to the orchard. Sister Henriette and Mary laid out the food. There were chicken sandwiches, devilled eggs, pickles, coleslaw, and oatmeal cookies. The girls put down a few blankets and sat down with their legs folded under them.

Mary flicked the back of her hand at Frances. "Oh Francie, don't look now. Your blue-eyed math tutor is coming our way."

"Mary, your imagination is —"

Mary raised her voice to get Sister's attention on the furthest blanket. "Sister, do we have enough food to offer Father Byrne a picnic?"

"That's very thoughtful of you, Mary. Why not?"

Sister waved Thomas over. Frances resisted twisting around to watch him approach.

"Good afternoon, Sister, girls. What a fine day for a picnic. I imagine you're relieved to have the examinations finished."

They had all gotten up and now stood awkwardly, their abandoned sandwiches and cookies littered on the blankets at their feet.

"Please, please don't let me disturb you. Please sit."

"Father, we'd be pleased if you would have some lunch with us. I made the cookies right after Mass this morning." Mary held out the tin box to Thomas.

"Very kind, thank you." He took one and sat down closest to Sister.

Once he was seated everyone took their places on the blankets again. Thomas and Frances were facing each other, separated by plates of food and three other girls.

Frances's mouth had gone dry. The oatmeal cookie was stuck in her throat. She took a few sips of lemonade and tried to focus on what Mary was telling her, a long story about her sister's upcoming wedding and the preparations for it. As she spoke Frances turned her ear to where Thomas was sitting, wanting to scoop up every word he said.

"Mrs. Charlotte told me some of the Sisters would be coming over to do the spring cleaning in the sacristy in the near future. We are very grateful to all of you for your help."

At his mention of the sacristy Frances raised her eyes to him. He was looking at her. The colour rose in his face.

He turned to Sister. "I must be going now. Thank you for the refreshments, Sister. And congratulations to you girls on your graduation. It's a big step on your journey." He looked around to each of the girls but avoided Frances.

Frances let out a long breath and relaxed her shoulders.

✤

More cleaning followed the day of rest. There was a mountain of bedding to be mended and laundered and every window in the school and convent had to be washed. The twelve girls looked at each other and grimaced. Frances was assigned to the window-washing brigade with five others. They set off with rags, old newspapers, buckets of water, and two big bottles of vinegar, starting on the top floor.

It took them all morning to do the windows and they were happy to hear the lunch bell. They lingered over the meal, savouring every morsel. As they were drinking their tea, Mr. Leary came into the dining room.

"Pardon the interruption, Sister."

"What is it, Mr. Leary?"

"Could you spare one or two of the girls to help me with the windows over at the church this afternoon? Terry cut his hand the other day and he's no good for the job at all."

"Would one o'clock suit you Mr. Leary? I know you haven't had your meal yet. The girls will meet you at the kitchen door."

"That's dandy, Sister. I think I'll go see if Sister Henriette has one more of them sandwiches." He headed for the kitchen.

"Girls, let's take a twenty-minute rest. You may sit in the parlour or go lie down. We have more work this afternoon. Avelda and Frances, you will meet Mr. Leary at one o'clock."

Mr. Leary and the girls started on the west side of the church. It was hard work removing the storm windows but Mr. Leary was patient. Beads of sweat dotted his brow and his fringe of black hair clung to his head with dampness by the time they finished the six windows.

"Whew! That's one side done. Good work, girls. Let's go around the other side and tackle a few more."

Alveda grimaced and put her fingers on her temples. "I'm afraid I'm getting one of my migraine headaches, Mr. Leary. It's all the up and down in the heat. I must go and lie down."

Frances jumped in. "I'll stay. I've got the hang of it now and we can manage without poor Avelda."

Mr. Leary was looking at Frances. "You sure Miss Frances? I wouldn't want you to be poorly too."

"It's lovely being outdoors in the fresh air. And besides, it will be cooler on the east side of the church."

It was almost three o'clock when Mrs. Charlotte came around the corner carrying a small tray with cups of milky tea and fat doughnuts sprinkled with sugar for the three of them. She motioned with her chin to the old bench under the birch trees. They sat in the shade and sipped the tea.

Frances remembered what Thomas said about the Sisters cleaning the sacristy. She envied them being there, in his place. "Mrs. Charlotte, do you think it would be all right if I went into the sacristy to wash the windows? They're very dirty. Father Donnelly isn't in there, is he? He wouldn't mind?"

She didn't ask about Thomas. She thought if she said his name she would blush or stammer.

"He took the train up to Bathurst this morning, so no, he won't mind a bit. Father Byrne is doing parish visits. Sister Claire and Sister Henriette would be very grateful. The two of them are run off their feet with the graduation tea this week."

The church was empty when Frances went in the side door and slipped into the sacristy. The air was stuffy and the light and dim. She didn't bother turning on the light, starting on the grimy windows right away. Gradually, the pungent vinegar eclipsed the musky scent of frankincense and beeswax.

It was hot work. She rolled up her sleeves, loosened her tie, and undid her top button. She finished the last window.

"It's you."

A whisper of air on her neck, his lemon scent. His voice, so close, so soft. She didn't move.

Again, "It's you."

She lowered her arm, placed her rag on the windowsill and turned. She had to tilt her head back to look in his eyes.

She shifted her eyes away. "I ... I didn't hear the door."

Thomas said, "I came through the curtain from the altar. I was expecting Sister Claire ... the vinegar smell ... but it's you. A pleasant surprise."

Her mind raced with impure thoughts, thoughts she'd been told she shouldn't have. She dropped her eyes so he couldn't read them. She patted down her hair that was streeling out of its pins and began pulling down her rolled up sleeves as though she could contain her desire.

Thomas reached out and put his hands on her forearms. "Don't, please. You're over heated ... with all this." He glanced toward the bottle of vinegar.

They looked at his hands on her bare arms. Then looked in each other's eyes. He drew her arms around him and pulled her to him. Her hands rested motionless on the fine wool of his cassock, tingling, afraid at first to move, then she cupped them over his shoulder blades and held on. And in that instant of holding on she knew this was what she wanted.

His breath and murmurs in her hair thrilled her. He tilted her head back and they kissed. His mouth was soft yet urgent. The hard whiskers on his upper lip electrified her. He leaned into her and the damp rag on the windowsill settled at the small of her back. Their faces were slick and flushed and their mouths moved over each other from brow to jaw to ear to neck, hot and craving.

Frances pushed against him and turned her cheek onto his. "We're in the window. Someone will see."

He took a step back and turned, still holding her close until her back was against the hard edge of the oak table. She let out a soft puff of air as he pushed her into the table.

Suddenly he dropped his arms and moved away from her. "Frances. I'm sorry ... this is —"

"Shh ..." She reached out and put her hand on his lips, stepped closer and then covered them with her mouth.

He turned her again and again in an awkward dance away from the table, her legs catching in the swirl of his black robe. In the dim, stippled mirror, she saw the back of his head and her hands holding him.

Their knees hit the mahogany frame at the same moment. They stumbled, held on to each other.

He whispered, "Father Donnelly's chaise. Should we dare?" His face was flushed and solemn but then he swivelled his eyes around like a vaudeville clown. They were overcome with a fit of laughter.

"Might as well be hanged for a sheep as a lamb, Papa would say."

He drew her down onto the red brocade chaise.

❧

Frances left the bucket and rags outside the kitchen door and went in. "Sister Henriette, there's still some vinegar left. I'll leave it on the shelf in the pantry."

"My word, Francie. You've had quite a day of it. Mr. Leary told us about everything you did. You're a big help."

Frances kept her head down unable to meet her gaze. "No trouble at all, Sister. It was my pleasure."

"The others just sat down to eat. You go in. But first tidy yourself a bit. You look like something the cat dragged in."

She looked up, her eyes wide.

"I'm just teasing you, Francie. Go on, pin back your hair and button your sleeves. Everyone knows you had your hands full, what with Avelda's migraine." Sister gave her a conspiratorial smile and scooped mashed potatoes into the serving bowls.

She was grateful for the mealtime silence as she entered the dining room. She nodded at Sister and took her seat. Everyone peered up at her. It was rare that any of them went anywhere unaccompanied. It was as though she was returning with news from a foreign land. And she was. She had crossed a boundary and entered a new realm.

After saying grace, the clatter of cutlery and slurps of soup faded as her head filled with disjointed thoughts and memories. Time stretched and she relived the sensation of moving in his arms, the rag damp against her back, his body hard against her belly. Every sensation thrilled her, even the sharp pain, their inept fumbling, the sweating and panting, his final groan and collapse.

She remembered saying, "What is it?" He didn't answer. "Thomas, are you hurt?"

He had smiled against her damp cheek. "Oh God, no."

She'd waited. Then she'd squirmed out from under him and as she turned on her side, a warm, slippery wetness slid between her thighs. Her first thought was that her monthly visitor had come but she knew it wasn't her time. Then she realized what it was. She pulled her pleated skirt down over her, her modesty lying side-by-side with her exhilaration.

"I'm not hurt. That was exquisite," he said.

She thought her face would split from her grinning. "I have to go. I can't be late for supper."

Frances gathered her window cleaning things and went to the door. She turned back. Thomas stood beside the chaise, smoothing down his cassock.

They'd looked at each other. She'd put her finger to her lips, turned and left.

⚜

"Avelda left you high and dry with Mr. Leary today. It's a wonder the two of you didn't shatter a few of those windows," Patsy said as they got ready for bed.

"It was okay once we got the hang of it. He's patient and kind. I didn't mind doing it without her and it was a nice change from studying and writing exams. But I'm worn out. I'm going to bed."

Frances hoped Patsy would take the hint and stop talking. She couldn't look her in the eye and she wanted to be alone with her thoughts. Part of her couldn't take in what had happened, what she had done, what they had done. But she remembered how she'd looked at him at the communion rail four months ago and realized that had been the beginning.

"Of course, you're worn out. And you're a million miles away. Are you mad I didn't come to help you when Avelda came waltzing back here?"

"Oh no. That never even crossed my mind."

She paused a few moments. "I'm just sad about going home and leaving you. I don't have any good friends at home."

Patsy reached out and hugged her. Francie's eyes welled with tears.

Patsy hugged her harder. Her soft weeping turned to sobbing. They sat down on the edge of the bed and Patsy held her until she didn't have a tear left.

Patsy pulled the covers down and tucked her into bed. "You get a good night's sleep, Francie. You'll feel better for it. We'll spend tomorrow together, our last day here. Goodnight, my dear."

"Goodnight, Patsy."

Patsy was better than a sister, her closest friend. But entering the convent put her, too, in a new realm, a different world altogether. Patsy would never understand what she had done or what it meant to her. Might even blame her. Frances could never tell her, or anyone.

✤

June twenty-fifth, graduation day, went off without a hitch. It wasn't extravagant, just Mass at the church and then a tea in the school.

Thomas was saying the Mass with Father Donnelly. Frances had prepared herself. She was aware of every bit of her body, her eyes, her lips, her hands, her knees. She willed herself not to fidget or to give away her secret, their secret. When he rose to the pulpit she looked at him with no more, but no less, interest that anyone else. She didn't hear what he said. She watched his lips move and his hands gesture, the way his eyes scanned over the congregation.

Having a secret was hard. It was thrilling and wicked at the same time and she was torn between excitement and shame. The sisters had taught her to seek forgiveness and absolution for her sins but she knew there was no forgiveness for her. She was the only one who would feel thrilled by what she had done, who she was becoming.

Frances avoided Thomas as best she could during the tea. She was afraid she would give herself away if she came face to face with him. But as she looked around at her friends and their families she realized no one was paying any attention to her.

Mamma was visiting with old friends and the Sisters she had

known for years. Standing beside her, Frances was happy to see her so gay and light-hearted.

Frances felt a tap on the shoulder. She turned and saw Sister St. Maureen and Thomas. "Frances, dear, I've brought Father Byrne over to meet your mother," Sister said in a soft voice.

Frances glanced at him for a second and then away. She felt the heat rise in her neck. Was she blotchy?

"Oh ... yes, of course." She waited for a pause in her mother's conversation and then tugged at her arm.

"What is it, pet?"

Frances took a deep breath, as if it would settle her queasiness.

"Mamma, I'd like you to meet Father Byrne. Father has been at St. Bridget's since January. Father, this is my mother."

Mamma extended her hand. "It's a pleasure to meet you, Father. Frances has written about you and your mathematics tutoring. It's very kind of you to take an interest in the girls' schooling."

Frances lowered her head but peered up at Thomas as he spoke. His cheeks were flushed. "It's nothing really. My pleasure."

Sister's and Thomas's cups were empty. "May I pour you some tea?" Frances took their cups and retreated to the tea service.

When she returned Thomas took his teacup from her. "Thank you, Miss Dalton. Very kind."

"And what about you, Father Byrne? What brought you from the big city to this small parish?" Mamma asked.

He looked around, maybe for a way out, but then said, "I grew up in Montreal, Mrs. Dalton, and frankly, I'd had enough of it. Well, that's not quite true. I ... dear me. You don't want to hear about me, surely."

"Nonsense. Of course, I do."

"A lot of things changed after the war. It seemed a different place. Not as welcoming. When I saw the advertisement in the Diocesan News for the opening here I thought I needed a change. I'd had enough of Montreal. That's the long and short of it."

"And your family? You must miss them." Mamma reached out and put her hand on Thomas's arm for a moment.

"You're very kind, Mrs. Dalton. I can see that Frances takes after you." He turned to Frances and nodded at her, his eyes wide, trapped looking. Frances looked into her teacup then glanced around, anywhere but at him.

He continued. "My family is one of the things that changed after the war. My brother was killed in France, my mother died not long after and then my other brothers and sister either got married or moved away from home for work."

Frances was startled to see Thomas's eyes tear up.

"Well, you'll make a new kind of family here. It's been nice getting to know a little bit about you, Father. I mustn't take any more of your time. And thank you again for helping Francie."

"Goodbye, Mrs. Dalton. It was a pleasure to meet you. I hope you have a safe journey home."

Mamma turned toward the seats by the windows where Father Donnelly and Mrs. Charlotte were sitting. Frances gave her mother her arm.

"Hello, Agatha," Father Donnelly said as they sat down. "I see you met our Father Byrne. He's getting well-known around town."

"Oh?"

"Oh yes. Not a day goes by that I'm not reminded of what a help he is. The altar boys, the tutoring, trout left at the kitchen door for us. Why, I even heard from your sister-in-law."

"Sister St. Benedict?"

"The very one. Herself. She wrote to ask if she could enlist his help in the school come September. Latin, mathematics, that sort of help. I don't mind saying I'm glad of it. It's getting too much for me."

"You've been at it a long time, Father."

"He certainly has, Agatha," Charlotte said. "I've been telling him to take it easy. Father Thomas is a blessing."

"All I can say is that if he's looking for a life's work, he'll find it here. Early days though, early days." With that, Father Donnelly drew a line under the conversation about Thomas.

Mamma turned to Frances. "We'd better get going."

"Alright, Mamma. The Sisters are lined up at the front door for the final goodbye."

"Go ahead, Francie. I'll meet you in front in a few minutes."

Frances got in a line and shook hands with all of the Sisters. This was the official St. Bridget's farewell – leaving by the front door. When they got out Patsy and Frances hugged and looked back at the school together.

Patsy glanced over at her parents. "I've got to go now. I'll write as soon as I hear from the Mother House."

"Enjoy your last free summer, my friend. I'll wait for your letter." They hugged and kissed goodbye. Then Patsy was gone.

Thomas and Mrs. Charlotte stood by the huge silver maple at the edge of the laneway, like an honour guard, waving to girls and their families as they drove away in wagons and a few in cars.

Frances was in the shadow of the overgrown lilac bush beside the front steps watching them. The boughs were drooping around her shoulders, laden with their frothy purple cargo. She breathed in their fresh spring scent. Thomas and Mrs. Charlotte had their backs to her. The bits of conversation she had overheard about Thomas at the tea came back to her then. She was confused. In fact, she was irked that others had opinions about him, that they even thought of him at all.

Mamma came around the corner of the building and walked over to Thomas and Mrs. Charlotte. After a few minutes of chatting Mamma looked around and waved Frances over.

"I'd better get in there to help clean up," Mrs. Charlotte said. "Francie dear, I hope you'll keep in touch and let us know what you're up to. Send a letter to me, not to the convent. The Sisters get so busy I'm not apt to hear for ages."

"Good idea, Mrs. Charlotte" Thomas said. "I've enjoyed getting to know you, Miss Dalton. It would be good to know how you get on."

That's it then? Just good-bye?

She recovered and put on her manners. "Thank you both for your interest. And you Father, for your help. We'll see what comes of it."

Thomas frowned.

"When we receive our marks, I mean," Frances said.

Frances climbed onto the wagon after Mamma. The driver clucked at the horse . When Frances turned to look back, Thomas and Mrs. Charlotte were going around the corner of the school, likely to the kitchen door. Mrs. Charlotte reached out and took his arm in a familiar way.

I'll never get to hold him like that, Frances thought

It was a long evening of visiting and family gossip with Mamma's people across the river in Chatham. Of course, everyone at St. Bridget's, school and church, got a good going-over too. Frances was relieved when it was time to turn in and she could be alone with her thoughts. She couldn't bear to hear one more time what a boon to St. Bridget's Thomas was proving to be.

Father Donnelly's comments about Father Thomas made her see him anew. Perhaps he *was* looking for a life's work, a place to belong. He wasn't looking for a sweetheart. She couldn't avoid seeing herself too. Did she want someone exciting but somehow safe? She remembered Patsy's warning, "It's not right, Francie, for you or for him". Wise Patsy, she saw things for what they were. If Patsy were right here she would tell her everything. But no, she knew she wouldn't. She would never tell a soul. She knew it was wrong but she refused to feel ashamed. Her peevishness evaporated and she recaptured in her mind's eye every moment in the sacristy on the red brocade chaise.

9

A ROUGH LAD

FRANCES HAD NO immediate option after graduation except to go home. The teachers college in Fredericton had burned down just as Bernadette finished there. She joked that she had set a torch to it on her last day out the door. It was being rebuilt but wouldn't be open for a while. The future was uncertain for Frances.

Leaving the boarding school had been bittersweet. There were a few girls Frances knew she would miss, Patsy the most. She didn't know when Patsy was going up to Montreal to enter the Mother House, but it would be soon. They had talked about her stopping her train journey in Armstrongs Brook for a few days, so they could have a visit.

Frances was lonely without Patsy. She was easy to talk to. She never tutted about all the strange notions Frances had about what she might or could do in the future.

A couple of the Sisters at St. Bridget's told her they were surprised she wasn't entering the Mother House too. They implied that Frances and her sisters owed their education to their aunt, after all. Mamma and Papa had never mentioned Sister's letter from a few summers ago and Frances hoped the whole idea had been dropped. The only things appealing about it were that Frances and Patsy would be together and they would be in Montreal.

As familiar as the nuns were to her after four years at St. Bridget's, they were still a mystery. She expected there was more to them than what she saw but she found them so uniform and dull, interchangeable even. And so restricted.

She knew she would never be able to fit into the mould.

But what mould do I fit into?

The comfort and hominess of summer days put thoughts of the future out of her mind though. She had loved the summers during her boarding school years. The freedom to be outside, to run as much as she wanted, and to yell and make noise – leaving the studying and silence and ladylike behaviour behind – was exhilarating.

Every summer, she and Jimmy had explored the woods and made up pretend stories and games. They'd made jam sandwiches and gone to the beach where they would spend the afternoons skipping rocks. He was always the one with the good ideas and she followed along. She didn't mind.

But Frances was almost eighteen now. There was lots of work to do tending the garden and doing the canning. In the afternoons she and Mamma would have tea on the front porch and Mamma would tell her all the news and gossip she had missed when she was at school. Once a week Cecile came to help with the bread baking and the housecleaning.

One day, sitting on the porch they could hear Jimmy yelling at the hired man over near the barn. Mamma said, "Jimmy's become a rough lad, Francie. And the temper on him! He flies off the handle at the least little thing. One day I told him not to tramp mud on the kitchen floor. He ran at me with his hand in the air! Then he turned cursing and ran out to the shed. He'd wanted to hit me. Gave me a shock, I can tell you."

"Does Papa know about this?"

"Oh no, and don't you say anything to him." Mamma blurted. She continued in a low, breathless voice, "Did you see how white Papa is? And he always has to sit down to catch his breath? The doctor said he's sick, something about his blood being weak. I don't want him to worry. No, don't say a thing. Just be careful around Jimmy. Don't spark that temper."

They sat looking at each other and then at the hayfields at the side of the house. Frances wanted her to ask more about what was worrying her, but she didn't know how to ask. They went in to start cooking supper.

Frances hadn't told anyone, but she'd seen Jimmy throw a rock at their old dog, Prince, a few days before. She yelled at him, "Jimmy, stop that. Poor Prince didn't do anything to you."

"Oh, fuck off, you sissy. That's just the point. That old dog doesn't do anything for anyone. Especially me. He just lies around and sleeps while I hafta do all the chores."

Frances had been stunned. Jimmy had always been a tease, and sometimes a mean one, but she'd never seen him hurt anyone.

She thought of Jimmy as she stood at the sink peeling potatoes. They'd had so much fun in the few weeks she had been home in the summers. But he had also had a nasty streak of bullying when he was younger. He had never liked it when he thought his sisters had the upper hand or got more than he did. She had wondered back then if her sickness had something to do with his jealousy. She was definitely the centre of attention, and he'd made her pay for it.

Years ago when she had been sick and languishing on the kitchen cot, Frances had puzzled over how sure of himself six-year-old Jimmy was. She had always struggled to keep up with her sisters and especially since she had had typhoid. She kept quiet and took her cues from them. But not Jimmy, a year younger than Frances. It never seemed to enter his head that he couldn't do whatever he wanted or that everything he did or said wasn't of interest to all.

"Francie, Francie with poo in her panties," he had chanted, laughing and jumping around the kitchen after she had made a mess that Mamma and Cecile had to clean up. She knew it was because she was getting extra attention. She had been too weak to smack him like she wanted so she had turned on the cot and faced the wall.

✠

On the very next Sunday after she and Mamma had talked about Jimmy, Frances heard a shout from upstairs. It was him.

"Mamma!" Jimmy hollered. Frances was sitting in the front room trying to stay cool and not muss up her Sunday dress. Her stomach whined with hunger, but they could only eat after taking communion at Mass. She got up to see what the fuss was.

Jimmy's voice again, more urgent now. "Where's my shirt collar? Mamma!"

He was at the top of the stairs cupping his hands around his mouth to yell again when Mamma looked up, those two straight lines between her eyebrows in a frown.

"Jimmy! Quit your hollering. What are you in such a state about?"

"I need a collar. I'm getting ready to go to church."

"Miracles never cease," Mamma said under her breath. "What's gotten into you, Jimmy? You've made such a fuss about not going to Mass since Easter and now you're in a goll darn rush to get there!"

"Mamma! Just find me a collar ... please. I don't want to be late."

Frances and Mamma exchanged a look of exasperation. Mamma went upstairs and helped Jimmy find his church-going clothes.

At last they were all ready and left for church. They sauntered so that Papa didn't get winded. But Jimmy rushed ahead waiting for them outside where folks were mingling and the men were having a last smoke.

Once in their pew Frances noticed that Jimmy was on edge. Every few minutes he swivelled his head around. He cracked his knuckles, shuffled his feet.

Frances gave him a poke with her elbow. "Quit fidgeting, Jimmy. Got ants in your pants? Are you looking for somebody?"

"Shut up, Francie."

Father Gagnon came out with two altar boys and started the Mass. Jimmy stood, sat and knelt when everybody else did. Father Gagnon mumbled the prayers.

The priest read the gospel "...but some seed fell on rich soil and produced fruit ..."

"Wake up, Jimmy!" Papa poked him hard in the ribs. "Pay attention."

Frances was watching him. The only time he paid attention was during the communion procession.

Who is he looking for?

The Mass droned to its end. Folks filed out to the scrubby plot in front of the church to exchange bits of news and gossip. Jimmy stayed behind on his knees pretending to pray. Frances and her parents looked at each other with quizzical frowns. They waited for him, Papa talking to Mr. Borden about his account at Borden's store. Jimmy came barreling out the church door as if the devil was after him. He nodded at Mamma and ran off.

⚜

Later that night Mamma and Frances were washing the supper dishes in the hot kitchen. Mamma had her head bent down, scrubbing the living daylights out of the roasting pan. Frances waited, staring out the window, the red striped dishtowel over her arm, lost in memories of Thomas. The hayfield was gilded and shimmering in the evening glow.

Mr. McNaughton, their neighbour crashed into her daydream. He drove his old chestnut mare and wagon past the house, past the chicken coop, and back to the barn. He was going at a fast clip.

"Mamma, look!"

"What's going on?" Mamma raised her head, beads of sweat dotting her brow, and followed Frances's gaze out the window.

Mr. McNaughton pulled the reins back hard and to the left. The horse veered away, jerked her head and came to a noisy halt, her legs still stomping the dusty barnyard. The old wagon swayed and settled.

"What's he doing here? And at this time of day?"

They watched as Mr. McNaughton jumped from his wagon, drew himself up and marched toward the barn door, his head leading the way. Papa sauntered out of the barn and stood with his hands in his overall pockets. He extended his hand as Mr. McNaughton neared him. Papa's gesture was like the hard rein on the horse. It brought Mr. McNaughton up short, swinging his head from side to side. He paced a few steps and ignored Papa's hand.

They couldn't hear what he was saying but Frances could see Mr. McNaughton going at Papa for all he was worth – arms swinging, finger jabbing, pacing back and forth. He removed his dusty brown hat and threw it on the ground beside him.

"Oh dear, Francie. Where's your brother?"

"Why?"

A small shaft of light opened in her mind and she remembered Jimmy fidgeting in church, looking around. "Are you looking for someone?" she had asked. Now she knew. He'd been looking for Rita McNaughton. Jimmy was sweet on her.

"Where is he?" Mamma asked, impatient for an answer.

Frances said, "Maybe he's gone back to the creek." Mamma wrung her hands.

"What's wrong Mamma?"

Mamma hesitated. She pulled Frances away from the open window and spoke in a low tone. "Papa thinks Jimmy's been drinking with his friends. He smelled it on him a couple of times when Jimmy came home late. Maybe Mr. McNaughton saw them or heard about them. He's such a strait-laced busybody."

She glanced out the window. "Now you go out there and take a glass of water with you. He looks like he needs to cool down."

As Frances went through the back shed she wondered not about Jimmy drinking but about Jimmy and Rita. Were they sweethearts? What a fuss their parents were making. Why?

The air was sweet and the evening breeze cool after the hot kitchen. By the time she got to the barn Mr. McNaughton was back on his wagon and turning it around.

"I'm telling you, Edward. Keep that son of a — " Mr. McNaughton looked over his shoulder and saw Frances standing at the side of the lane. "Keep that son of yours away – away from my Rita." He flicked his whip over the horses' haunches and the wagon creaked and shuddered past.

Frances was right. Jimmy and Rita. It wasn't about drinking.

"Francie, dear. What are you doing here?" Papa was impatient, looking from her, back to the barn and then over to the house.

"He looked so angry, Papa! What was he saying to you?"

"That's not your concern, Frances. Now go in the house."

Papa glanced up toward the hayloft. One of the loft doors was ajar and they saw four dirty fingers around the edge pulling it closed.

"I'm going to have a word with Jimmy. We can't have McNaughton storming around like that. Go in Francie." Papa's shoulders were slouched and his mouth set in a hard, grim line as he turned toward the barn.

Uh oh. A word from Papa is usually delivered with a backhander.

Frances shuddered to think what she would get if they knew about Thomas.

Frances and Mamma stood by the kitchen window as though keeping vigil. Ten minutes passed and Papa came out the big door. He slumped onto a maple stump and sank his head into his hands. A few minutes later Jimmy burst out the side door holding his hand over his nose; he jerked his head to both sides then ran around the back of the barn out of sight.

10

GOSSIP

THAT NIGHT, FRANCES heard her parents talking in their bedroom in hushed, urgent voices. Mamma was pleading, and Frances thought she heard her name.

They didn't speak to Frances about what was going on. Mamma was distant and sharp. Frances began to feel like she'd done something wrong. She had. Though the ruckus was about Jimmy and Rita maybe they suspected her of being up to no good too. Had word gotten out somehow? A knot of worry and guilt formed in her stomach.

Jimmy came home in the late afternoon the next day.

He was sullen, saying, "I'm hungry. Gimme something." He threw himself into his usual chair at the table, head down, staring at nothing, knees jerking up and down.

Frances was shocked at the state of him. He had a blood-crusted, open gash across his nose and dark purple bruising under both eyes seeping into his cheeks. His upper lip was like a ripe damson plum. Bits of moss, twigs and grass were stuck on the back of his head and shirt. He stank.

"Jimmy, let me clean up that cut on your nose. There's dirt in it." Mamma went to the white, chipped medicine box on the wall in the pantry.

"Leave me alone, Mamma. Gimme something to eat right now. Before he comes in." Jimmy's fists were curled on the table, white-knuckled. Mamma gave Frances a curt nod and she went to the stove and piled up a plate of corned beef, cabbage and carrots. They watched as he shovelled the food into his mouth, snorting and gasping with the effort.

Jimmy pushed his empty plate away and stood. He glared from Frances to Mamma and back again. Frances thought he was about to speak but he grabbed the old blue and yellow quilt from the cot and rushed out through the shed.

"Go look, Francie. Where's he going?"

When she got to the shed door she caught sight of Jimmy going around the backside of the chicken coop where all the leftover, unwanted stuff was piled up. He was stepping over old burlap chicken feed bags, broken tool handles, a couple of oil drums, chicken wire, and some bald tractor tires. He lost his balance and flayed his arms, the blue and yellow quilt swinging around like a flag. Just as she thought he was going to fall he jerked himself at his waist, got his balance again and ran around the corner out of sight.

"I think he's going into the woodlot, Mamma," she said when she returned.

"He'll have another damp night out there." Mamma spoke more to herself than to Frances.

She knew better than to ask what was going on. The look of Jimmy's face said everything. Papa had had more than a word with him.

Frances didn't know what the story was but she knew enough to bide her time. Nothing stayed secret for long.

⁂

The next day Cecile came to help with the chores.

Mamma muttered to Frances as Cecile swung the back door open and put her basket on the low pine dresser. "Not a word to Cecile about the goings on here."

Cecile nodded at Mamma. They always got along fine but hardly spoke two words to each other. Cecile went to the pantry and started taking out the things she needed to make the bread.

Mamma was all business. "Francie, put the water on for the washing. Then clean up the kitchen and help Cecile. I'm going upstairs to strip the beds."

"How are you today, *ma petite?*" Cecile squinted at her as she carried the big bowls and blackened pans into the kitchen. Her intense black eyes pierced Frances's thoughts.

Frances looked away and busied herself at the sink. "I'm fine, *merci.*"

"And your brother? I 'eard some terrible ting about him."

"Oh, Cecile!" Frances looked up at the ceiling and shook her head. "I can't." She whispered, torn between her mother and her friend.

"I know, *petite. Quel dommage.* A pity. After, we talk." She jerked her head toward the back of the house. Frances knew she meant when they were hanging out the washing.

Whump! A pile of laundry landed in the hallway followed by Mamma's heavy footsteps coming down the wooden stairs.

"Let's get busy with this load. It's going to be a hot one today."

When they finished with the washing Mamma put the kibosh to Cecile and Frances having a quiet gab. Mamma came out to the clothesline with them, handing them the pegs and setting the prop high so the sheets were off the ground.

"Cecile, why don't you call it a day? Francie and I can finish up here. Have a drink of water before you go. And say *bonjour* to your sister and her family."

"*Bien oui*, Madame Dalton. Until next week. Bye-bye *ma petite Francoise.*"

Frances smiled. *Francoise.* Only Cecile ever called her that. Mamma sucked her teeth.

"What did she say about Jimmy? Tell me."

"Nothing."

"Francie." Mamma gave her a long stare.

"She heard something about him, Mamma, but she didn't say what … and I didn't ask."

They turned to go back to the house.

"Oh mercy! Look who's back early." Mamma was looking down the lane where Josephine and Bernadette were strolling arm in arm toward them.

Josephine and Bernadette both had teaching jobs down near Bathurst for the fall. They'd been down there for a week at Mamma's sister's making arrangements. They weren't supposed to be back for two days.

"Francie, put the kettle on. Bernadette, help your sister. There are some molasses cookies in the pantry. We have to say everything there is to say about this before your father comes in. He won't abide any gossip."

Frances thought about gossip. It was a contagious disease, like typhoid. You never knew where it came from, where it started, where it was going or what form it would take. One day you were ordinary, a part of the everyday landscape, unremarkable. Then all that changed. You had the disease. You stood out. People judged you.

Jimmy stood out now. A dust cloud of gossip and speculation rose and swirled around his head.

Josephine and Mamma spoke in hushed tones out on the front porch. Bernadette was more interested in the molasses cookies. Frances knew Bernadette would tell her what was going on so she sat in the kitchen with her.

"Papa sure gave Jimmy a walloping the other night, Bernadette. You should have seen his face."

"Well, maybe he had it coming to him. He's gotten away with lots of hell-raising ever since I can remember."

"He must have done something awfully bad. Papa always turns a blind eye to Jimmy and his high jinx. Mamma's worried. And what's it got to do with Rita McNaughton? Meek Mr. McNaughton was raging and stomping out there like Dan Cormier's bull!"

"Francie! What do you think? What do boys want with girls?" Bernadette reached for another cookie. "Oh, never mind. You don't know anything."

It didn't seem possible to Frances that a girl, even Rita Mc-Naughton, could think of Jimmy that way with his sulky, moony face and stinky feet.

And besides that, Bernadette's comment made her so mad, she could have spit. Her sisters treated her as though she was a baby just because, as far as they knew, she'd never had a beau and was only seventeen. But she was almost eighteen, and she knew lots.

She knew what boys wanted with girls. Her ears rang and a numb pounding hit her temples.

⁂

A few days later, Josephine was up to her ears in chopped tomatoes and onions. Frances was helping her make tomato chow but she wanted a break from the sharp vinegar in the air. "I'm walking over to Beaton's to see if we have any mail. I'll clean up here as soon as I get back."

Mrs. Beaton was rocking on her porch, fanning herself with the back pages of an old Eaton's catalogue.

"Good morning, Mrs. Beaton."

"Oh, Francie. I was wondering when one of you would show up. There's four letters for you Daltons." She wriggled herself forward on her rocker and heaved her bulky frame up with a groan. She went into the room that served as the post office.

Mrs. Beaton held the letters in her hand but didn't pass them through the wicket. She leaned forward on the counter and said in a confidential voice, "I saw young Jimmy and Rita walking by here half an hour ago. They were headed back to the creek." She looked at Frances with raised eyebrows.

Frances knew better than to say anything. She reached for the letters and Mrs. Beaton relinquished them with a sigh. One was from Patsy. Frances put it in her apron pocket.

"Thank you, Mrs. Beaton. I'd best be going. We're making tomato chow this morning."

She thought about Jimmy on the walk home. Jimmy's wounds had healed but the damage to his pride festered. He was humiliated and angry at all of them. He was working with the hired men – Papa was weaker and worked less and less these days – but Jimmy was moody and quiet, especially at mealtime when everyone was there. He always ate in a hurry and then stomped out to the yard to have a smoke. Often he didn't come home until everyone was in bed. Never said where he went.

Mrs. Beaton's comment, more like an insinuation, was worrying.

One walloping wasn't enough for Jimmy. Mamma will be fit to be tied when she finds out.

She was thinking about how to tell Mamma about what Mrs. Beaton had said but was no sooner in the kitchen door than Josephine started in on her.

"Francie! You went out wearing your apron? What would Sister St. Jerome say?"

"It's a good thing I have you to remind me, Josephine!" A gentle rebuttal.

Jo's nagging, the heat in the kitchen, and the tomato chow mess she had to clean up put Jimmy out of her mind. She laid the other letters on the pine dresser near the back door without looking at them. Then she cleaned up the mess and set the jars out to cool on the front porch.

Frances had been expecting Patsy's letter. Now that she had it in her hands an unexpected ache filled her.

Patsy is taking the train to Montreal.

She sat staring out at the dry hay field and said it over and over to herself. She didn't know if her longing was for her friend or for Montreal.

And as smoothly as a train pulling into a station, thoughts of Thomas filled her mind. They had said goodbye and she wouldn't see him again. He was the new boon to St. Bridget's and that's where he would stay. But now, the mention of Montreal brought up memories of their conversations. She imagined them walking arm in arm in the shade of the tall leafy trees on Sherbrooke Street; it was a wide, smooth road that stretched to the horizon he had said. They could do whatever they wanted there with no fear of being known, being seen, being talked about. Such a dream.

"Here you are. Josephine said you had a letter." Mamma came out to the porch holding the letters Frances had put by the back door. "What are you daydreaming about?"

She stared at Mamma, startled for a moment. "Nothing, Mamma. The letter is from Patsy. She's going to the Mother House on August eleventh and asked if she could come here for a visit on her way." She handed her mother the letter.

"Well, well, she's made up her mind. Her mother will be pleased about that, a priest and now a nun." Frances thought her mother didn't sound particularly impressed about Patsy becoming a nun. In fact, her voice had a note of doubt in it. Frances wasn't surprised. Mamma had never thought Papa's sister being a nun was anything special, except for being better educated. For some families, a daughter entering a convent meant one less mouth to feed, but that wasn't the case for either Patsy's or Francie's families.

Mamma looked at Patsy's letter again. "What's this she says about being worried? What in heaven's name could she be worried about? It won't be a lot different from St. Bridget's."

How can you say that Mamma? she wanted to ask. Patsy won't have any friends there. And it's not like going to teachers' college. It's forever.

But Frances just shrugged.

Mamma said, "Drop her a line and get it over to Beaton's this afternoon. Tell Patricia we'll be pleased to have her stay."

Mamma sat down and opened one of her letters. Frances closed her eyes and let her mind drift back to Sherbrooke Street.

11

THAT SURE STRONG VOICE

UNCLE FRANK AND Auntie Dorcas visited on Saturday night in early August to play cards with Mamma and Papa. What a racket they made, laughing and hollering about counting points and who was the biggest cheat.

Frances was on the porch with Josephine and Bernadette reading the Campbellton Tribune about the collapse of the fishery and closure of the lumber mills. Things had been getting desperate. They didn't understand what the stock market crash was but knew it was bad. But her sisters were excited about moving down to Bathurst and living with Aunt Maisie. Everything was changing for all of them. They were lucky to have any opportunities at all.

Everything was changing, except for Jimmy.

"I hope Jimmy straightens out after we're gone," Josephine said. "Poor Mamma. She's got to put up with him storming around, cursing and yelling,"

Bernadette added her bit of gossip. "Louise Hickey told me those fellas he chums around with are a bad lot. They've been going to a place back in the woods where someone is making liquor."

"Yuck. Maybe Jimmy will calm down when we're not here to remind him of how stupid he was to quit school."

"Maybe, maybe not," said Bernadette.

By now, Frances was resigned to her future plans; she was entering the convent in Montreal, accepting her aunt's "invitation". She didn't join in her sisters' predictions about Jimmy's future but he was on her mind. She remembered Mamma's warning about how edgy he was. Now he was like a powder keg. The humiliating beating from Papa, rumours about his romance with Rita, and now Frances going to Montreal had made things worse. When Mamma had told everyone about the opportunity Frances had his anger and resentment had been fierce.

"I'm going to bed. Are you two coming?" Frances asked. She and her sisters shared the big room above the kitchen. It had always been their room, even when they were at St. Bridget's. Now that they were all home and grown up it was cramped. Frances shared the double bed with Bernadette next to the window that overlooked the shed roof and Josephine slept on a narrow bed under the sloping ceiling. They made the best of it. By the end of the month they'd all be gone.

"It's still too hot to sleep," said Josephine.

"Well, I'm going to try. Good night," Frances said. She went into the kitchen to say goodnight to the card players.

⚜

Her bedroom window was wide open to catch the breeze. A light scraping sounds on the shed roof and the windowsill behind her got her attention. As she turned over in bed to look, Jimmy lurched through the window and fell forward landing half on her and half still on the floor. He stank of the cloying smell of liquor and sweat. He heaved himself up so he was lying on her.

"Jimmy, get off me. What are you doing? I'm going to —" Jimmy clamped his hand over her mouth and heaved himself on top of her, knocking her breathless.

"What are you going to do, Miss Snot, Miss Convent Girl Snot?" he said in a nauseating whisper, slurring his words.

He pushed down hard on her mouth and nose. Her teeth gnashed against the inside of her lips. She tasted blood. Her hair was caught under his elbow and her scalp burned. She tried to punch at his back and sides but it was futile. He was like stone.

"You're not gonna do nothin', Miss Snot. I'll do it all."

He yanked the thin sheet off her and pulled her nightgown up around her hips. His thick calloused fingers dug into her inner thighs and wrenched them apart. She strained to buck him off and at the same time grabbed at the hem of her nightgown to cover herself. When he moved his hands to undo his trousers she twisted her torso away from him and tried to close her legs but his weight on her shins was too much. He pushed her onto her back again.

In a moment he had pinned her shoulders and upper arms down and pushed himself inside her, grunting, snorting and slamming, grating her insides with a savage rage. She kicked her legs and tried to shrink away from him.

"Yeah, yeah, you squirm, you snot."

The top of her head crunched against the headboard. He guffawed and jerked her down the bed a few inches.

Defeated and helpless, she turned her head away from his foul mouth and went limp. A burst of laughter came from the kitchen below. Chairs scraped across the floor. Mamma was getting up to put on the kettle and Papa and her aunt and uncle were going out to the porch. The sounds that reached her were familiar and homey, but far from where Frances was now.

He rocked faster, his face contorted and blazing. In another moment he grunted and rolled off her and onto the floor.

She pulled the sheet over her and lay still. Tears rolled down and began rinsing her blood and Jimmy's spit and snot from her lips and cheeks. His wetness seeped between her legs. Her tongue quivered and her mouth watered. Her stomach heaved.

As he jerked and staggered to his feet, stumbling over his trousers, he spat at her, slurring, "Go to Montreal, you stupid quiff. See how holy they think you are now. I don't give a fuck about you."

He stood swaying with his arms held out to his sides and looked around as if he was lost. He belted his trousers. He turned to the window, took three steps and climbed out the way he'd come, over the shed roof.

She rolled onto her side and put her legs over the side of the bed and onto the floor. She used the chamber pot letting Jimmy's filth slide out of her. Her stomach heaved again. She pulled the pot around and vomited, drained and limp.

She was at the basin rinsing her face when Bernadette and Josephine came in. She was grateful for the dim light from the hallway.

"What a stink, Francie. Were you sick?" Bernadette wrinkled her nose.

"Yes. Just now."

"Pass me the pot," said Josephine. "I'll take it out and clean it. Bernadette, check if she has a fever. I'll get Mamma."

"No." The urgency of her voice startled them all. They looked at her.

"I don't want to ruin her evening. Let her have her tea in peace. I feel fine now. Please?"

Bernadette had her hands on her cheeks. "No fever but look at the mess of your hair. Let me brush it for you. I'll put it in a nice braid."

Josephine left with the pot and they sat on the edge of the bed, Bernadette brushing her hair, Frances sinking into her sister's tenderness.

"I had a nightmare. Maybe that's why my hair is such a mess."

"Well, it's neat as a pin now. You get under the covers and I'll join you in a minute."

Josephine came back and handed her a glass. "Here Francie, some water and a bit of baking soda to settle your tummy."

"Thanks." Frances couldn't look either of them in the eye.

"Go to sleep now and we'll see how you are in the morning," Josephine said.

Bernadette climbed in behind her and put her arm around her.

"There, there, Francie. Stop that shaking. You'll warm up in a minute. You'll be right as rain tomorrow."

But Frances knew Bernadette was wrong.

She would never be right again.

❧

Everything was the same in the morning. No one gave her a second glance or mentioned her swollen lips, her memento of Jimmy's rough paw. They got ready for Mass and left together.

"Where's Jimmy?" asked Bernadette.

"He's in no shape to be going to Mass. I saw him when he brought in the milk," Papa said. They knew enough not to ask more.

In the church Frances went through the Sunday morning rituals – greeting friends, making small talk, kneeling, standing, sitting – but part of her was gone, replaced with something that was never there before: shame. It filled her up and coloured everything. She hesitated before going to communion. She was full of sin now. But she was more afraid to draw attention to herself by staying in their pew.

She didn't care what God thought.

After Mass everyone milled around in front of the church. They avoided the McNaughtons as best they could, but Frances looked Rita up and down, taking in her loud good nature, her laugh, her ease.

You should have been the one, not me.

Why it had been her? Was it simply because she was there? Would he have done it to Bernadette or Jo if he'd come upon them instead?

But no, he wouldn't. Never.

He thinks I'm weak, Frances thought.

Two of Jimmy's pals were on the edge of the gathering looking worse for wear with flushed, pimply faces and red-rimmed eyes. They sized her up and made remarks to each other out of the sides of their mouths. Frances turned away.

Everywhere she looked things made her think Jimmy, Jimmy,

Jimmy. She remembered him saying that night at supper when Mamma had told them she was going up to Montreal, "What about me? I never do nothin'."

She stifled a scream.

You did everything, Jimmy. You took everything.

⚜

The next day Mamma watched her as she pushed her breakfast around her plate. "Francie, you've hardly eaten anything. All right?"

"I'm okay, just not hungry. Can I lie down for an hour?" Frances motioned to the kitchen cot.

Mamma reached over and put her hand on her forehead. "You don't have a fever. What is it dear? You've been listless since Sunday at church."

"I'm okay. I think my monthly is starting, that's all." "

"You must be worried about going to Montreal too. It's a big change. You go on up and lie down. I'll call you in an hour so we can go through your things and decide what you'll take with you."

Panic gripped her. Frances didn't want to be alone up there. "No, Mamma. I just want to lie down here in the kitchen."

How could she tell Mamma any of it – the thrilling gentleness of Thomas or the wretched violence of Jimmy? She couldn't, she mustn't.

She stretched out and turned her face to the wall wishing she could fall asleep forever. But unwanted thoughts pushed their way in. His face above her again, red and sweaty, his piggish grunts, him ravaging her. She tried to banish him with memories of Thomas, his gentleness. Despite their urgency and the overwhelming sensations, Thomas had been tender and thoughtful. Jimmy had been nothing but rage.

Why didn't she scream for Bernadette and Josephine, hit him harder, bitten him? Why did she let him do that?

She was in the barn on a moonless night walking with her arms outstretched toward the small, side door but it wasn't there anymore. She turned in circles, panicking, looking blindly for the way out, hearing the pigs' snuffling and the cows' tails swaying and swishing.

Mamma was shaking her shoulder. The aroma of cinnamon and nutmeg tickled her nose.

"I doubt you got much rest, Francie, the way you were carrying on. I'd swear the devil was after you."

"I was dreaming. I was trapped in the barn." She shook her head and rubbed her face.

"Help me get these pies out on the veranda to cool," Mamma said. "Your sisters have gone over to McNaughton's to have a word with Rita."

"Oh?"

"Here. Take the oven mitts. I'll hold the cookie sheet and you put a pie on it. Steady now. Don't spill the juice."

After they got the three pies out on the veranda, Frances asked, "Why are Bernadette and Jo seeing Rita McNaughton?"

"Short of killing Jimmy, I don't know what to do to keep him away from Rita. I think they've been carrying on all summer."

Frances busied herself sweeping the floor and avoided looking at Mamma. Part of her hated Rita and another part pitied her.

Mamma continued, "Josephine was Rita's teacher for a couple of years. Jo thought she'd be able to talk sense into her. You know ... the perils of getting too close to a boy. Oh mercy, if your Papa knew what was going on, if he knew the half of it, he'd throttle Jimmy."

Frances picked up the dustpan full of crumbs, flour, bits of raw dough, and dead flies and went outside to empty it. She slumped onto a wooden box by the back door, the dustpan discarded at her feet.

If Papa knew the half of it ... if he knew ... if they knew.

The thought went around in her head. Her heart withered when she thought of Mamma and Papa's faces if they knew. Their son, their daughter. She had to protect them. She couldn't bear their shame and disgust.

They don't have to know. It's up to you.

Her voice, but icy and sharp. She'd never heard it before. The idea became clearer in her head and a resolve settled on her, a sense of control.

No one will ever know.

She said it over and over to herself and as she did, she sealed over her shame, her rage, and part of her heart.

⚜

Mamma was helping Frances pack a small bag of personal things to take to Montreal. As usual, she'd be wearing a uniform there so packing wasn't a big chore.

"Sister St. Benedict went to university, you know," Mamma said.

"What? At the Mother House?" Frances had never heard that.

"Oh no. It was years after that, after she'd been a nun for more than twenty years. She went somewhere in the United States – Washington, I think. She's the only one of Papa's or my family who went to university."

That frigging letter, again, she thought.

Frances realised that according to Mamma being a nun was nothing to brag about, but being a university graduate, now that was something.

She took her nightgown out of the bag and refolded it.

Mamma took it from her to stop her fussing. "I know you're unsure, dear, but this is a special opportunity for you. Imagine, she went to university."

"I'm not smart enough for that. Besides you need to be holy to be a nun. I'm not holy, Mamma."

"Frances, you're every bit as smart as the next one. And, as for being holy, nobody expects you to be a saint. What about Patsy? She's no holier than you.

"No. But she's got something inside her that tells her to be a nun."

"Maybe so, but maybe it's just family duty."

Same as me, thought Frances. Payback.

"Maybe. She talked about her brother, Father Tim a lot when we were at school. Her parents are so proud of him."

"No matter what you do, Francie, I'll be proud of you. You give it a try and if it's not for you, at least you got some more education."

No matter what you do. No, she wouldn't be proud if she knew.

"And I can say I've been to Montreal." She smiled at Mamma.

"You'll see the inside of the convent at any rate." Mamma put her arm around her shoulder. "I haven't seen that smile all week."

⚜

It was haying time so Jimmy was out every day working but Frances couldn't avoid him at supper each evening sitting in her usual chair opposite him. She shrank into herself, pulling her feet under her chair and holding in her elbows. One night, Bernadette told a funny story about something Mr. Borden had said to her at his store. Jimmy's braying laughter and snorting grated on her. She felt filthy sitting across from him.

Her family's laughter and chatter faded away behind a tinny ringing. She looked at all of them at the table out of hot, feverish eyes. She was curled up, a frightened rabbit and him, the hungry fox across from her. And Mamma and Papa, her sisters, the same as always.

They don't know. No one will ever know.

That sure, strong voice. There were two of her now. The little sister, the third daughter, the follower, the one Jimmy thought was weak. And the strong, shrewd one who would keep her secret at all cost.

"Francie, quit daydreaming and pass the potatoes." Bernadette's voice echoed around the kitchen and drew Frances back to the table.

She and Jimmy reached for the potatoes at the same time. She flinched and jerked her hand back.

Jimmy laughed without humour. "She's gone, Bernadette. Gone to Montreal already and left us behind."

"Yes," Papa said. "Soon you girls will be gone just like when you were in school. It's good to know you're out in the world making something of yourselves."

Everyone avoided looking at Jimmy.

12

BREAKING FREE

FRANCES AND PATSY were on the front porch. They got some time alone between all the visits with neighbours who dropped by to wish them well. Patsy wasn't from the village, but she was still a New Brunswick girl and their going into the convent was both a loss and a source of pride. The neighbours wanted one last look at "their girls".

Patsy was thrilled about Frances going to the Mother House. "We'll have each other. That'll make it much easier."

Frances couldn't muster any enthusiasm. She wanted to forget what Jimmy had done, to look forward to her adventure with Patsy, but he was always on her mind.

"I feel like a phoney. I'm just doing it for my aunt," Frances said.

"I guess that's why the whole thing is done in stages – postulant first, then novice, then first vows, and then final vows. It takes years. No one could be sure right off the bat."

"Mamma thinks we'll get more education." Frances made a quizzical frown.

"Maybe more Latin, some Church history, religious studies sort of like philosophy. I don't know."

"Oh Lord, here's Mrs. Beaton the Postmistress." Frances stood to greet their newest visitor and introduce her to Patsy. This would be the last visit of the day.

⁂

On Sunday afternoon the whole family came to the station to see them off. Cecile was there too and stood close to Frances, holding her hand. It was a celebration but with a sombre, conflicting undertone. Everyone knew that girls who were successful in the convent rarely came home again, even for funerals. This was a final good-bye.

All the usual promises were extracted – write often, study hard, help each other, pray for us – and then they heard the screech of the train whistle and saw the towering, belching machine approach. They backed away from the track as if to give it more space. As soon as the train stopped, and the doors clanged open everyone went into motion, kissing, hugging, wiping tears, and getting the bags and the girls onto the train. In all the fuss Frances avoided Jimmy who was slouching against the station wall, looking at his feet.

She and Patsy claimed their seats and waved to the party on the platform. "Whew, off at last," said Frances.

"It seemed the whole town came out on Friday when I left for your place," Patsy said. "Sister St. Maureen was there. I told her that you were joining me in the convent. She was thrilled and wished us both well. She hadn't known. I guess your aunt kept it to herself."

"Maybe she's as unsure as I am."

"Father Byrne was there, too, with Sister. They've become great pals since the math tutoring days. He's as handsome as ever. No wonder you were sweet on him."

Frances struck a casual, funny tone. "I just liked the thought of him being from away. Now I'm going to Montreal and he's stuck back there."

"Well, don't forget, you are going to a convent." Patsy dragged out the last word in a spooky voice.

They had to change trains in Campbellton. They showed their tickets to the stationmaster. "You have a bit of a wait, young ladies. The Ocean Limited won't be leaving until seven forty-five." He looked over his shoulder at a handsome wall clock, its gleaming brass pendulum marking time behind a glass door. They had almost three hours to wait.

He pointed over their shoulders. "There's a waiting room behind that door in the corner."

The waiting room was at the east end of the station and had windows on three sides. The station roof had a deep overhang so the waiting room was cool and dim, despite the hot afternoon sun. Some people were sheltering in the shade outside, mostly young boys with flat caps, smoking. Hooligans Mamma would say.

The boys reminded Frances of Jimmy. She shook her head to rid herself of the image.

Stop it. Don't give him a minute of your time.

Frances and Patsy sat down to wait for the train that would take them away from New Brunswick.

⚜

The Restigouche River flowed under the train, the clocks rolled back an hour and she was on her way. The openness of the fields and the radiance of the wide bay gave way to the shadows of the steep mountains closing in on both sides. Despite the narrowing outside the train a spaciousness grew inside her, a newness.

⚜

Patsy gave her a poke. "I have an idea. Let's be Frances and Patricia from now on."

"Are you reading my mind? I was thinking about how new I feel, different, free."

"We are different now. We're going toward something special, something we've chosen." Patsy leaned over and took her friend's hand.

"Oh, don't scowl at me like that. I know you have your doubts about the convent. Maybe it's not for you, but you can find out."

"I suppose. I've been thinking of my aunt though. This was *her* idea. No one at home, my family, I mean, ever talked about vocations."

"Sister Superior is like a magician in your family. You and your sisters don't really know her, but she makes things happen."

"My father hardly knows her either. He was a child when she went into the convent." Frances paused a moment. "She's more like a puppeteer ... and she thinks I'm her puppet. If I choose the religious life it'll be because I want to, not because of her."

"I've been thinking about it for years and I'm still not even sure." Patsy craned her neck around. "There's the porter. I'm tired. Let's move so he can make up the berths. I want the top one."

"I won't argue with that." They moved to the end of the car while the porter assembled their berths and pulled the curtains down in front of them.

"Patricia, I like your idea about our names."

"Oh, good, Frances. Let's try to remember. It'll remind us that we're grown up ... even if we don't feel like it all the time."

They got into the berths. "Good night, Patricia."

"Good night, Frances."

⚜

Frances lay awake surrounded by blackness. Every now and then a distant light or two would flash by the window, illuminating nothing. Her mind wandered. She remembered the quilt Mamma was working on, probably right now, called Drunkard's Path – forward, backward, up and down. She rolled from side to side, finally settling on her back, staring into the dark.

Father Byrne. Thomas. She hadn't said his name once since leaving St. Bridget's, but he'd never been far from her mind. After Jimmy had hurt her, thoughts of Thomas had comforted her. The two encounters were worlds apart, one full of pain and shame, the other, exhilaration and mystery. Her experience with Thomas didn't match the little she knew about sex. It was supposed to be either dangerous and shameful – she thought of Isabelle being banished to Newfoundland

– or necessary and routine, a wife's duty. But sex with Thomas was something else.

Love. Maybe it was love.

She thought of him now, his long, gentle fingers, his lips and tongue and the softness of his skin. Their fumbling and stumbling over the old red sofa, laughing and holding on to each other. She reached under the covers and touched herself, remembering what came next that afternoon. The short, sharp pain and then her opening herself, the warmth, and his controlled urgency. She kept rhythm with the train's rocking, feeling her wetness and heat until she was outrunning the train, moving to her own rhythm. The spasm drove her hips into the mattress and she arched her back. She cupped her hand over herself, sliding two fingers inside. She lay there stunned, feeling her insides soften and relax. Her breathing eased. She lifted her damp hair off her neck and rolled toward the dark window, keeping her hand between her legs.

She flushed to remember what Thomas had said after they made love. She had asked, "Thomas, are you hurt?"

Now she knew what he had felt. It *is* exquisite. And she could feel the same thing without him..

13

A Long Way to Go

FRANCES WAS WALKING in the Mis courtyard as Sister Dolorosa had directed her – get some fresh air and exercise. Two full weeks had passed since she'd escaped from the CND convent. Sister Geneviève approached swinging her arms and looking up at the bright blue autumn sky.

"You have a visitor, Gemelle. It's your cousin. Come with me." Sister took Frances's hand and tucked it into the crook of her arm.

Sister didn't ask questions about the visitor. They walked in companionable silence. Frances liked Sister Geneviève. She reminded her of Bernadette, tall and thin and always telling jokes. She was in charge of the baking in the kitchen on Tuesday and Thursday. The rest of the time she helped Sister Thérèse, the *Secrétaire des Visites*.

"This is the first time anyone has come to see me," Frances said.

"I know. Visits are recorded in the visitors' register. Mrs. Egan was surprised by our procedures. Thank heavens she remembered her visitor card."

"What's that, Sister?"

"It's a card with both your names on it and your registration number. Sister Thérèse mailed it to her as soon as you were registered. She's the only person who can visit you and she must have the card with her every time. See, I've marked in today's date, September twenty-first."

Frances had heard the visitor rules her first day here but forgot them. They hadn't been relevant then. She had only wanted to hide herself away.

"I can't imagine anyone wanting to come here unless they had to." Frances realized her gaffe and hurried to explain. "I mean except for you Sisters."

Sister laughed. "Don't worry, Gemelle. I knew what you meant."

They were in the main floor corridor and stopped at the door where the old nun had left Frances the first day she was here. The door was closed.

"Here we are. You have thirty minutes. I'll be in the office across the hall." Sister knocked and opened the door. "Here she is Mrs. Egan. Enjoy your visit."

Frances was surprised at how young Mrs. Egan looked, probably in her early forties. She was a tall sturdy woman with dark wavy hair. Frances did a fast calculation and figured she must have been a teenager herself when she had Rosemary.

"All business, that one." Mrs. Egan took a step forward and raised both her hands toward Frances. "At long last, we meet. Distant cousins." She screwed up her face and made a careless sign of the cross to cover her small lie.

"Let me look at you, Frances" She held her new "cousin" by the shoulders and studied her face.

The sound of her own name pierced Frances's heart and brought her to tears. She fumbled for her handkerchief.

"There, there, none of that. We haven't time for it." She led Frances over to the sofa and sat down.

Frances started, "Mrs. Egan, I want to thank —"

"You must call me Ellen, since we're pretending to be cousins. I'm happy I could help. You've little enough to be thankful for right now. I hope this place is a help?" She peered around and tilted her head.

"Oh yes, Mrs. – Ellen. I can't say I like it but being in the convent or at home now would be a thousand times worse. We're all strangers here and we get by, day to day."

Until she said it, she didn't realize she had chosen to be here rather than at home. And she knew it was more than shame. It was pride, too.

"Speaking of home, I had a letter from your mother. And she sent this one for you. I showed it to that one." She jerked her head toward the door indicating Sister Geneviève. "She read it but didn't say anything." She handed the white envelope to Frances.

"And here's another from Rosemary. I think my job is going to be the postmistress." She gave a hearty laugh and patted Frances on the knee.

"Now tell me, if you don't mind, how far along are you?"

She couldn't look Ellen in the eye. "Ten or twelve weeks, they said on the day of my examination. That was a week ago or more."

"God bless you, girl. You have a long way to go."

"One of the girls said that too, that I'd be here a long time. I didn't understand but was too shy to ask what she meant."

"Sister Ignace didn't pull any punches in her letter. By the time your wee one comes you will be here about seven months, give or take. Then you'll have to work a few months more to pay that off."

Frances hung her head. "It's no worse than I deserve."

"You've certainly got yourself in trouble, but there's enough folks willing to say what you deserve or don't deserve. Let's not join that chorus."

Ellen took Frances's hands and was still. Her calmness was soothing. "I'd better be going. I'll stay the full thirty minutes next time. Rosemary asked me to see you first and then come to her. She misses you and wants to know how you're managing."

"Please tell her I'm alright. In some ways it's not as hard here as it was in the convent. We don't have to ask forgiveness for small failures and lapses every day. All of us here have one big mistake to think about. We don't burden everyone else with it."

Frances took a deep breath. "I'm sorry, Ellen. I shouldn't talk about convent life like that. I just wasn't suited to it. I was a pretender."

"That's all right, dear. I'm not sure it's for Rosemary either, but she wanted to find out." She stood and put her handbag over her arm. "I'll come next Sunday if the weather is fine."

"I'll get Sister to show you out." Frances turned toward the door but stopped. She spoke with her back to Ellen. "I was ashamed to meet you, Ellen, but I feel relieved now. You're very kind."

"It's a shame this happened to you, but it doesn't mean you are shameful. Just unlucky."

Frances opened the door and left.

September 19, 1930
Dear Frances,

I hope you are well. Your letter was a great shock to me, as you can imagine. I would like to know more about the circumstances but will not press you. I have decided that no one else, no one but us, needs to know for now. I don't know if we can keep it a secret, but we'll try.

I am grateful to your cousin for being such a help. I hope she continues to visit you. Please give her my regards.

I would like to see you dear, but I can't manage it. Your father is holding his own, no better than when you left, but no worse either. I hope to hear from you soon.

I am thinking of you every day, dear daughter.
Love,
Mamma

It didn't sound like Mamma at all. No news of Bernadette and Josephine or even Jimmy. No funny stories about Cecile and her family. Nothing about the garden. It was the kind of letter Frances had learned in school, a business letter, short and to the point. Frances understood that Mamma was thinking about other people reading her words and was being cautious. Talking freely belonged to the past now.

She thought about what Ellen said – having a long way to go, at least seven months. She would keep her head down and not draw attention. But confused, jumbled thoughts hammered at her. Since Sister Dolorosa had said, "not less than ten weeks", Frances had counted backwards over and over and tried to remember when she had had her monthly visitor but she couldn't.

Ten weeks brought her back to the hot night, the card game in the kitchen, and Jimmy, drunk and reeling, spewing his hateful words. She'd heard vague stories, mostly related to farm animals, about the dangers of inbreeding – monstrous deformities. Unlike animals though, women had the added burden of shame, sin and rejection. She covered her ears as if she could stop remembering.

But twelve weeks, would make it Thomas. They did it together, completely blind and unthinking, driven forward by months of secret touches, innuendos, and looks, a longing kindled in the silent oppression of the boarding school. She thought about him now, living his life, saying Mass, visiting people, laughing with Mrs. Charlotte. Did he ever think of her? What would he think if he knew?

Frances looked down. She was holding her belly. Some girls here did that, encircled their bellies or rubbed them. And they talked about their babies, even talked to them. They all knew there was little chance they could keep them, but for a short time they were connected. Frances had never joined in, until now. She held onto her baby and thought of Thomas.

14

THE ASSIGNMENT

FRANCES WAS SITTING at the Director's sturdy desk, her head bowed in deference to the nun. She didn't know why she'd been summoned but she was wary. Her gut told her she was wise to be wary of Sister Philomène.

"*Bien, Gemelle.* You have been here for several weeks. Sister Dolorosa tells me you are healthy but a little underweight. I hope you are eating well." It was a command.

"*Oui*, Sister Philomène. I eat very well. Sister Geneviève is a good cook ... and a good teacher. I am learning a lot."

"Yes. I have had a report from her also." She made a dismissive gesture as if to say I know everything about you.

She continued, " Sister Geneviève was surprised you are so capable in the kitchen. Sister has had very little experience working with you English." Sister Philomène said no more about Sister Geneviève's viewpoint, but Frances could read between the lines. The Sister thought all the English had servants and never did their own housework.

"So, you are able to get along in a French-speaking community?"

"Sister, I am grateful to be here. Many of the Sisters and the other girls —"

"Penitents."

Frances winced at the harsh words.

"*Oui*, Sister, penitents. They help me when I don't understand what is needed in the kitchen."

"But the rest of the time, Gemelle? You are not lonely, wanting to talk with the others?"

It was a test. None of the girls ever mentioned being called into the director's office.

"I am used to silence, Sister. And the rule of privacy is important to all of us. Sometimes we talk about things in the newspaper if Monsieur Leber leaves it in the kitchen. There is a lot about *la Grande Dépression.*"

Sister squinted at her. "Do you read French, Gemelle?"

"*Pas beaucoup*, Sister."

"Sister Dolorosa has asked me to consider assigning you to the antenatal clinic to help with filing papers."

Frances thought of her humiliation on the examining table and wanted no part of it. But getting out of the kitchen and the laundry was considered a step up at the Mis. Working in any of the nursing areas was a good way to reduce her debt but she was wary of appearing overly enthusiastic.

"It would be an honour to help Sister Dolorosa. She is very busy. Would I be able to do what she has in mind, Sister?"

"Yes. And your lack of French is an asset. Everything in the clinic is confidential. The less you can read and understand, the better." She paused to look at a file on her desk.

"You will finish in the kitchen on Sunday and start with Sister Dolorosa on Monday."

"Yes, Sister. Thank you for your confidence."

"We will see. Good afternoon, Gemelle."

"Good afternoon, Sister."

Frances returned to the kitchen as the afternoon tea break was ending. She poured a cup and gulped it down.

Rogata motioned to Frances to take the other handle of the potato basket and they scooted over to the peeling bench. "Where've you been? I came back from the cold pantry and you were gone."

Frances took a paring knife from the table. She kept her head bent toward the basket.

"Philomène's office. I have a new job." She winked at Rogata.

They had become very close, what the nuns called *particular friends.* Sometimes at night they lay side-by-side in Frances's cot and talked. They'd even told each other their real names. Rogata's was Mercedes. One night, she leaned over Frances, whispered *"Tu es belle, ma Francoise."* and kissed her, a long, soft kiss on her mouth. She pulled back and looked at Frances. *"D'accord ma belle?"* Okay, my beauty?

Frances had answered by drawing Mercedes close to her and covering her face with kisses. After, when Mercedes went to her own cot Frances thought about what they had done to each other. She liked it. She ached to feel close and special to someone in this harsh, impersonal place. Every day she buckled under, swallowed the hard stone of shame that was the Mis. Mercedes would be her resistance.

Frances and Rogata – Mercedes – would have many nights of lovemaking. And they weren't the only ones. The lonely and forlorn found comfort where they could.

⚜

Frances took the stairs two-by-two immediately after chapel and breakfast on Monday morning. She was due at seven-thirty, but she wanted to get there early and wait for Sister Dolorosa.

"I'm going to miss you in the kitchen, Anglaise." Rogata had said the night before. "But it's a lucky break for you."

Frances was eager to learn something new. She remembered how the two men had touched and questioned her. Sister called it an antenatal examination. That meant there were right answers and wrong answers. She wanted to know the answers and what they meant for pregnant girls. It would certainly be more exciting than learning Latin cases and declensions or how to calculate the area of a nine-inch pie.

Sister Dolorosa came down the hallway carrying a stack of thin brown folders. She was trying to balance them in one arm while getting her key out of her pocket.

"Please, Sister, may I take those from you?" Frances asked, remembering what she'd learned in the convent about the Vow of Obedience. An obedient nun does not assume to know, only asks for direction.

"Oh, Gemelle. I forgot about you." Sister heaved the bundle to Frances and shook out her arm. "Yes, that's better."

Once inside Frances stood aside while Sister settled at her desk. Frances glanced around the room remembering it from when Sister had given her the results of her ante natal examination. The violets still bloomed. Sister picked a file from the stacks on her desk and told Frances to put the rest on top of the wooden cabinet in the corner.

"Pull over that chair. I'm going to show you what to do with all these reports." She pointed to a pile of loose papers on the desk. There was a meditation book atop the pile to prevent it from sliding to the floor.

"Each penitent has a hospital record and all the information about her is filed in the record in an orderly way." She made a face. "It's supposed to be, anyway. This section is for information from *le laboratoire*, mostly just urine tests and blood tests. This section is for *les signes vitaux. Comment on dit ca, Gemelle?*"

"I think it is vital signs, Sister."

"*Oui, c'est ca.* Another section is for the doctors' notes. Your job is to put the papers in the right section of the right file and then put the files in those drawers, *par ordre alphabétique.* If you find something that doesn't go in those three parts just stick it in this section here. Each paper and each file have the penitent's name and number on it."

"I understand, Sister."

"The only thing you need to read is the name and number." She stared at Frances.

"Yes, Sister."

"I will be seeing penitents in the examining room. You will work here. Do not disturb me or leave the room. Someone will bring coffee at ten o'clock. Knock on my door then."

Frances got to work sorting the papers into alphabetical order but soon realized it would go faster if she made more than one pile. She cleared everything from Sister's desk, putting the stuff on the desk chair. She also cleared the narrow table with African violets, putting the small plants on the other chair. She designated the small table for the A to F papers in three piles and the desk for the rest of the alphabet in five piles. Frances spun from table to desk and back again, papers flying from her hands. When the box on the desk was empty she looked at the piles and smiled.

Frances put the files into the cabinet drawers first, despite Sister's instructions, so that both the files and the papers would be in alphabetical order and she could match them up systematically.

Using the names, numbers and dates of confinement Frances had everything filed away by nine-thirty. Her curiosity won out and she looked at a file marked Gemelle. It wasn't hers. She pulled another file at random and tried to read it.

The information from the laboratory meant nothing to her, just letters and numbers. She never imagined there could be so much to say about urine and blood. The vital signs pages weren't much better but she did recognize weight. The girls were weighed every time they came to the clinic. Sister Dolorosa said she was underweight. Compared to what?

The doctor's notes would have been indecipherable, even if they had been in English. There was lots of different handwriting and Frances remembered the troop of young men looking at her private area. Did they all have to write something about what they saw?

She was wondering how else she could be useful to Sister Dolorosa when the clink of crockery and a soft knock at the door brought her attention back to the office. She jumped up and knocked on the door to the examining room.

Sister swept past Frances and opened the door to the hallway. *"Merci ma Sœur, une bonne tasse du café,"* thanking the Sister for the coffee. She took the tray from the kitchen Sister, closed the door and turned toward her desk.

"Gemelle! Where are all the files? What have you done?"

"I finished the job, Sister. Everything is filed."

"Ma bonne fille. Tu es très vite. Very fast. I will check after we have coffee. Sit there."

"Sister, may I pour your coffee for you?"

"Oui, s'il te plait."

They sat blowing and sipping in silence. Sister gazed out the window and then looked at the table beneath it. "Did you move my violets? The purple one was on the left."

"Yes, Sister, to make more room for sorting the reports. I should have asked. I didn't want to interrupt you."

Sister flicked her wrist. "The violets don't mind. They can get the light whether they are on the right or the left."

She smiled. "It's silly but I love those little violets. My brother gave them to me a few years ago. Sister Philomène allows me to keep them here."

Frances remembered what she'd learned about the Vow of Poverty. Sister had had to get permission to have the little plants and yet still, she didn't "own" them.

She never thought of the Sisters having a life and family outside of the hospital and convent. Maybe because she herself felt so bereft and isolated here. She didn't know whether to bow her head in the usual posture of respect or to meet Sister's gaze. She opted for the latter trying to encourage Sister and extend the moment.

"They looked well cared for, Sister."

"They ask for nothing. They are here to cheer me. It's the least I can do." Sister put her cup on the tray. "Now let's take a look at a few files, shall we? Hand me four that you worked on."

Frances pulled out the files at random and handed them to Sister. She stood and waited for Sister's verdict.

"These are perfect, Gemelle. I hope the rest are as well done. Did you have any difficulty?"

"There were some penitents with the same name, but I soon saw their numbers and dates were different." There are only so many ridiculous names to go around, she thought.

"It's a relief to have this done. Now I can move to the next step."

"I would be happy to help, Sister."

"Sister Rosario in the records department wants all the records from the clinic prior to 1930 for a big reorganization, by decade. What a job! There's only the 1920's left to do. Get some boxes in the big closet next door. When they are ready Monsieur Leber will take them to Sister. I'll be busy in the clinic." She got up and returned to the clinic.

By the time Frances finished she had eight large boxes of files from 1920 to 1929 on the floor. Her hands were filthy, but she was elated. Sorting and filing and organizing gave her a feeling of orderliness and control she hadn't had for a long time.

Francs jumped up when Sister swung open the door. Sister glanced at the boxes and opened the top drawer of the filing cabinet. "What a difference. Room for a new decade. Time for chapel, Gemelle. Come back at one o'clock." She was smiling as she gestured toward the outer door.

After the noon meal Frances helped Sister empty the glass cabinets in the clinic. She didn't dare ask how they got into such a mess, but she plucked up her courage to ask what had been on her mind for a while.

"Sister, I am interested to learn about the information in the files. I didn't know there was so much to know about pregnancy."

Sister was sorting through a heap of linen. "I cannot talk about your record, Gemelle. That is against the rules. You are fine, everything is as it should be."

"Oh, I didn't mean mine, Sister. I meant the antenatal clinic in general. Why you weigh us, what is in our blood and urine that's important, all the things you do. What does it mean?"

"It is information for the doctors and nurses, not a penitent like you."

They focused on their tasks on opposite sides of the small clinic and spoke in low voices as if telling confidences. The separation emboldened Frances to continue.

"I won't always be a penitent, Sister. I need to think about the future and I've been thinking about nursing. Perhaps you could help me to learn something about it?" She didn't know she'd been thinking about nursing but once she said it she knew it was right.

When Sister hesitated, Frances realized that the nun couldn't make a decision herself to help Frances. It was against the Vow of Obedience. Frances had only been at the Mother House about a month, but she knew that, for a nun, initiative, acting on your own idea, was not only frowned on, but forbidden. Sister had to ask the Director's permission.

"I will think about it. Come tomorrow, Gemelle."

Frances went to bed that night feeling more hopeful than she had for a long time. Maybe she could find a way to support herself and her baby. Could she? Must she leave her baby behind? Mamma's sister was a nurse and after her wartime experience she worked in Boston. But how did her aunt become one? How could Frances?

15

A Way Out

FRANCES AWAKENED DESPERATE to pee. It happened every night now as her belly got rounder and bigger. She tiptoed to the bathroom and as she finished she heard a garbled moan. She left the stall and looked around. Nothing. She started back to the dormitory but then heard it again, clearer this time. Maybe one of the girls had gone into labour. She looked in each of the stalls and headed for the section with the bathtubs. She turned the corner and was brought up short at the sight of bright red blood.

"Holy Mother of God," Frances held her hand over her mouth to stifle a scream..

It was the new girl. Frances ran to the bath. The girl was the colour of the porcelain tub, her eyes half closed, staring blindly. And so much blood. It was congealing on the girl's nightdress and splattered on the sides of the tub. Her arms were resting next to her belly, gashed from her wrists to her elbows. A knife was cradled in the crease below her belly.

Frances sprinted to the dormitory.

"Mercedes, wake up. Come." She pulled her girlfriend's shoulders and whispered, "Come, come, *maintenant, vite, vite.*" She ran out.

Mercedes was behind her a few steps and entered the tub room just as Frances knelt down by the bleeding girl. Mercedes stared. "*Calice.*"

Frances was surprised to hear Mercedes swear but ignored it. "What should we do?" she asked.

"You stay with her. I'll get Sister." Mercedes bolted away.

Frances didn't want to stay but was frozen. A moment passed. There was a towel in a heap on the floor. She laid it across the girl's belly and arms and pressed down on her arms to staunch the flow of blood. The sticky warm blood seeped onto her palms and fingers. It was futile. Frances reached out and touched the girl's clammy cheek. She stroked the hair from her forehead. The girl moaned. Startled, Frances pulled her hand away. The girl's fingers twitched and she mumbled. Frances leaned her ear toward the girl's mouth.

"*Désolée.*" The girl's head fell to the side and the dim light in her eyes faded.

The instant between life and death was unmistakable but still Frances shook the girl's shoulder and rubbed her arms begging her to wake up.

When three Sisters ran in, Mercedes trailing after them, Frances was sitting with her back against the tub staring ahead, tears running down her cheeks. She wiped at them with her bloody hands.

Sister Leonie took charge. "Sister Paulin, take the penitents to our lounge. We'll take care of this." She raised her chin toward the tub.

Sister Paulin brought Frances a basin of warm water and a towel and instructed her to clean the blood from her hands and face. Afterward, Frances and Mercedes sat side-by-side holding the hot tea Sister gave them. They didn't speak. Sister wrapped a blanket around their shoulders then she paced and fretted.

Time dragged. There were many footsteps and low murmurings outside the lounge and then the squeaky wheels of a stretcher. Sister Superior Philomène swept into the lounge. Sister Paulin sprang up and the girls followed suit, their empty teacups and saucers crashing to the floor. Sister Paulin squatted and tried to brush away the shards with her hand.

"*Laisse faire, laisse faire,*" said Sister Philomène waving the nervous young nun away from the broken crockery.

"*Rogata, Gemelle, venez avec moi.*" Come with me. She walked to a table in the corner of the spacious lounge.

The director took a mere moment to sympathize for their gruesome discovery but then blamed the penitent, Magdalene, for her mortal sins of suicide and murder. "She 'as condemned 'erself to everlasting 'ell and 'er child to limbo," she said with contempt.

Frances noticed the lapse in Sister's usually perfect English. She's not as in control as she likes to appear, she thought.

"*Et puis,* what about you two? You have seen a terrible ting, *c'est vrai* but it is *impératif* dat you forget what you saw and do not say one word to anyone else. To speak of such *une horreur* is a sin." She fixed them with a stern stare and waited.

Mercedes poked Frances. "*Oui, ma Soeur,*" they said together.

"*Et bien, au lit. Oubliez tout ca. Pas un mot!*" She whipped her index finger across her fleshy lips and dismissed them with a flick of her wrist.

They got into bed and clung to each other. "Why'd you leave me with her? What took you so long? She spoke to me – she said *deux soleils,* I think – then she died." Frances was crying.

"Maybe *désolée.* It means I'm sorry. I'm sorry too that I took so long. I went to her bed. I thought she might have left a note so I went to look. It was on her pillow. I put it under my mattress and then fetched the Sisters. They took a long time to answer the door."

She kissed Frances on the cheek and stroked her hair. "Let's sleep now. We'll read what she wrote when there's light."

The next morning they got up well before six o'clock Mass. The bathroom had been cleaned, showing no evidence of the mayhem of the night before. Only in their memories. Philomène's command to be silent and forget what they saw was futile.

They crowded into a toilet stall. "It starts, 'Papa'", Mercedes continued reading. "Oh, *Jésus.*" She dropped the hand that clutched the letter and blessed herself.

Frances took the letter from her friend. The printing was childish and uneven, some words running off the edge, others crammed in. "I don't understand this."

Mercedes took back the letter. "*C'est dificile.* I'll translate. 'Father, You did this to me and now ... you hide me here because of shame. It is your shame... I will not stay here and I will never go back to your house where I am your ... slave. Mama was smart to leave you. Now I am leaving too. I have no choice... Going to hell will be better than returning to you. Jacqueline.'"

Frances whispered the girl's name. "Jacqueline."

⚜

Ellen came to visit that Sunday. Frances was in knots, constrained by her obligation of silence, but when Ellen took her hand and said, "You're very quiet today. Has something happened?" Frances couldn't hold back her tears.

Sobbing she said, "I can't tell you. Sister will kick me out. And it's a sin if I tell."

"Sister will never know what you tell me, I promise. Only God can judge if it's a sin."

Frances cried and blew her nose but said nothing.

"Maybe it will do you some good to get whatever it is off your chest. Did something happen to you?'

"Not me. Another girl ... in our dormitory."

Ellen was silent. It had the intended effect.

Frances blurted, "She killed herself, Ellen, and I found her. There was blood everywhere; she cut her arms. She was still alive."

A fresh spring of tears. "She said sorry then she died. I couldn't help her. I couldn't do anything."

Ellen looked stunned at the talk of suicide and murder, mortal sins in the Catholic Church, crimes too. She didn't move for a few moments but then she nudged closer and hugged Frances.

"Of course you couldn't. It wasn't your fault she died. The sin is hers, not yours. Sister is trying to frighten you into silence. Was the girl your friend?"

"No. She came here a few days before. No one knew her. She didn't talk to anyone even in the kitchen where there's usually some chatter."

"That's a terrible secret to keep. I won't tell anyone, not even Rosemary." She gave Frances a fresh hankie. "Were you alone, the only girl who knows?"

"My friend Mercedes was there. She found the girl's – Jacqueline's – note and read it to me. It was in French, with lots of mistakes Mercedes said. Not much education."

"And?"

"Jacqueline's father was to blame. And she would suffer more of the same if she went home. She was trapped and hopeless."

They sat in silence. Then Frances jumped up and paced. "It broke my heart but my will got stronger. I am going to have a baby, Ellen. My baby deserves a chance. It deserves to have its own name and a life. Jaqueline didn't have a chance and neither did her baby."

Frances covered her face with her hands and sobbed. Ellen pulled her down next to her.

"A tragedy. Would you like to say a prayer together for the poor girl?"

"No, prayers are useless. The Sisters didn't even have a special Mass for her. Hypocrites. It's as if Jacqueline and her baby never existed. They erased her."

Frances stood again and rubbed her face. She whisked her hands down her sleeves and over the front of her dress as if brushing the tragedy off her. "I can't talk about it anymore."

Ellen gestured to the seat beside her.

"I have a new job now." Frances sat down. "I told Sister Dolorosa I was interested in learning about what nurses do. It took her a while to clear it with the director but now I'm working in the antenatal clinic."

The shock of Jacqueline's suicide hung between them. Frances struggled to go on. "Often the Sisters aren't kind to us. They never let us forget how shameful we are. But they do their best for the babies."

"Rosemary will be happy to know you're settled here."

"Settled? No, I'm not ... I'm just useful. I don't want to be settled." She emphasized the last word in disgust and threw up her arms.

"I meant you've landed on your feet. You're safe here. That's what Rosemary was worried about."

"Even though it's like a prison it's given me time to think about the future."

"The future? What do you see ahead of you?"

Frances bowed her head, but Ellen reached over and lifted her chin, so they were looking at each other. Frances's eyes brimmed with tears. "My baby," barely above a whisper, caressing her belly.

Ellen was silent giving Frances time. After a few moments Frances said, "I see my baby and wonder how I can manage for the two of us. I won't be helpless like Jacqueline."

16

ROSE

FROM THE MOMENT Frances saw her Rose, she was filled with desperation to keep her daughter safe and close. She didn't give one thought to either Thomas or Jimmy. Rose was her daughter. A sharp determination arose in her and she knew she would do anything to keep her baby.

Rose was born on Good Friday, the most solemn day in the Catholic world but only another day of birthing at the Miséricorde. The Sisters were, as usual, quiet and competent. They smiled when she was safely delivered but offered no congratulations.

Rose's arrival was straightforward. She was robust and healthy. Frances knew the Sisters were going through the motions, as attentively and efficiently as they did everything, but their souls and hearts were on another plain with the passion of their Christ. She didn't mind. When they put Rose on her chest and went about their delivery room duties, Frances clung to her and asked for nothing except to marvel at her perfection.

⚜

"Can I call you Mother?" Frances heard the soft whisper and opened her eyes. Ellen was standing beside her bed, smiling. She put a bunch of daffodils in a jar on the table.

Frances had finished nursing Rose an hour before and then had sunk down into her bed to doze. But now, she focused on Ellen with uncommon intensity.

"She's the most beautiful little thing I've ever seen." She beamed and clasped Ellen's hand. "Please help me, Ellen, I can't let her go."

Ellen seemed taken aback. She said nothing.

"I was feeding her, and she held my finger. Her nails are perfect, like the shiny shell fragments I used to find on the beach at home. She looked right at me. She knew me."

Ellen finally spoke. "Yes, of course. The wee ones are perfect. And what about you?"

"Sore but fine otherwise. I was in labour through Holy Thursday evening. The Sisters called Sister Dolorosa and she came and stayed with me all through Friday morning. And then before I knew it, Rose came." Frances pushed herself up in the bed.

"Help me. Please think of something. The adoption paperwork will start soon", Frances said, pleading. "I can't do it. I won't."

They looked down the row of beds. A Sister was making her rounds. She was two beds away. Ellen's time was up.

Ellen extricated her hand from Frances's desperate grip. The Sister was at the next bed. "Stall. Don't sign anything. They're not above the law." She tilted her head toward the approaching nun. "I don't know how I can help but I'll think on it. I'll come next week. Rest up now and God bless you and the little one." She turned to go.

"Rose, her name is Rose," Frances said.

&

Frances smiled when Sister Geneviève came to get her a few Sundays later during visiting hours but her happiness turned to caution when Sister said, "Mrs. Egan is really stretching the rules. She brought a priest with her. She knows she is the only one allowed. I didn't know what to do."

To convince Frances to relinquish Rose? Give her away to a Catholic family, one with a mother and a father?

"A priest?" Frances asked.

"Yes. I had to ask Sister Thérèse what to do. She said we couldn't turn away a priest. They are waiting for you."

They walked to the visiting room in a dark silence. Frances was preparing to fight for her Rose.

The tall, broad priest gave the room a cramped feel by virtue of both his physical stature and his authority. Ellen took the lead. "Father, this is Frances, the girl I told you about. Frances, please say hello to Father Monahan. Father is the parish priest in Griffintown. He may be able to help you."

"How do you do, Father?"

The old priest didn't reply and didn't waste any time. "I'd like to talk to Frances in private, Ellen." He gestured with one arm to the door and with the other to the sofa. The two women took their cues.

The priest began. "We have thirty minutes so let's get right to the point. Ellen has told me a little of your story. Very sad but not unusual. The unusual part, according to her, is that you think you can manage, or rather you want to manage alone, with no husband to provide for you."

Her insides were like jelly, but she sat up straight and looked him in the eye. "Yes Father, that is what I want. Rose is my daughter."

He looked at her, leaning forward. His soft eyes were very kind. "Go on."

A surprise. He wasn't telling her what to do. She thought of the parish priests at home cajoling and sometimes bullying folks into doing what they, the priests, thought best. Could she trust him?

She continued. "I would like to become a nurse and raise Rose myself."

"A nurse? What gave you that idea?"

"I work with one of the nurses here. I have to continue until August to pay off my debt and Sister Philomène said I can do so in the clinic. I like the work, Father. My family always thought of me as weak when I was young, but I'm not. I like working hard and I like being busy. Sister Dolorosa says I'm the most organized person she ever met in her life."

She paused, "She herself, bless her, couldn't organize a breadbox, so she's easily impressed."

Father chuckled. "Yes, I can see you've got something of a nurse about you. But what about your child?"

"There are some children here who are not up for adoption. Their mothers visit them and support them. They pay the Mis a dollar a day for the baby's room and board. When they get back on their feet, they are going to take them home. Maybe a word from you might influence Sister Philomène to consider it."

"I'm sure I could persuade her, but you must know I can't offer any financial support. I'm only a priest." They both smiled

"When Ellen told me about your idea, I thought about St. Mary's Hospital. No time for all the details." He waved his hand from side to side.

"Suffice it to say they are building a new hospital and I'm doing some of the fundraising. Imagine, a new English Catholic hospital ... about time, too. I know the Sisters there, the Grey Nuns, are going to need to train more nurses to staff it. Perhaps there would be a spot for you in their program that starts after the summer."

"Father that would be wonderful." Frances couldn't believe how simple it sounded.

"But that doesn't address your need for financial support. Nursing school is three years long."

"If they let me into the nursing school, I will ask my family for support. It won't be easy, of course. They know almost nothing of ... of recent events. Only my mother knows a little. And we aren't wealthy. But there's always food on the farm and both my sisters are teaching now."

A dollar a day for three years during these wretched times.

"But what about going home, returning to your family?"

"Armstrongs Brook is a poor village in a poor province. There is no work. Rose and I would be dependent on my family's charity, forever." She hesitated before going on. "Besides, people in small communities are not kind to unwed mothers." She did not say the words whore and bastard.

"How will you, shall I say, break the news to them?"

"I would ask my mother to come here to meet her first granddaughter. I'll ask her for help then. Perhaps Ellen could find a place for Mamma to stay."

"I can see what Sister Dolorosa means. You think of everything. What if help is not forthcoming?"

Frances didn't look away when her eyes filled with tears. "I will stay here working for the Mis until I can think of something else. I won't relinquish Rose."

Some of the girls, after delivering their babies, entered the Madelon, an order of Oblates, lay people who spent their lives in service to the Church. Frances couldn't bear the thought of serving the Sisters of the Miséricorde for the rest of her life but she would for a short time if she had to.

They sat in silence for a few moments. "I will consider your situation. Let's call Ellen in here and say a short prayer."

After the prayer Frances motioned Father aside. "Thank you for not enquiring as to Rose's father. It seems to be the first thing people ask."

"You are a smart young woman. I expect you have every good reason not to want to prevail upon him for help."

"I do, Father." Later she wondered about what he'd said and thought of all the stories he must have heard as a parish priest. And that thought led to Thomas.

She wondered if Father Monahan would be so helpful if he knew the whole story.

Frances thought about all the nuns involved in her life and began to see that each order had carved out its niche in 1930's Montreal – the CND for teaching, the Grey Nuns for nursing, and the Sisters of the Miséricorde for a very specialized, even secret, kind of nursing.

By August all the pieces of the puzzle of Frances's life had fallen into place and she had a clear picture of her immediate future.

⚜

Mamma's visit had been a victory. She had come up to meet Rose in the spring. Things had changed at home since Frances left. Papa had died. His never meeting Rose or even knowing about her left Frances with an odd mixture of sadness and relief.

They were in the visitors' room with the picture of the Madonna and Child. Mamma removed her white gloves and put them on the side table. She held out her arms. "Give her to me Frances."

Mamma held Rose close to her and when she began to whimper Mamma paced back and forth, cooing and rocking her. She examined her face, stroking her brow, her small nose and her lips. She released her hands from the blanket and turned them front and back as if looking for clues.

Frances knew the identity of Rose's father was on Mamma's mind. She interrupted Mamma's scrutiny, "The only ones you need to know are Rose and me. There is no one else. I'm struggling to make sure I am enough for her and I'm asking you to help me to keep Rose here while I do my training. Please, Mamma." She struggled to keep her voice even.

Frances herself sometimes peered at Rose looking for clues. Did she see Thomas? Jimmy? But as Rose grew and her unique personality asserted itself Frances saw only her daughter. Thomas and Jimmy were the past. Her life was going forward. She put the past where it belonged.

"I told the girls about Rose," Mamma said.

Frances knew she meant her sisters.

"All of us, including Jimmy, will help support you and Rose until you finish nursing school. Jo and Bernadette don't have much. Sometimes they don't even get paid. They're thinking of looking for work down in Moncton or Saint John. But we'll manage to make sure Rose is taken care of."

Frances felt her body loosen, a sag of sorts, a relief, as though she had been guarding herself against her family's rejection.

Mamma continued to pace and rock until Rose fell into a deep sleep. She laid her down in the maroon armchair and sat beside Frances on the sofa. "I've been worried about you for months, on your own in this place with strangers. It's changed you. You've become strong-minded and confident. "

"Mamma, I —"

"Let me finish, Frances. You need to be strong-minded and confident to raise your daughter, but you don't have to be alone. You're my daughter and Rose is my granddaughter. We're a family and you're welcome at home."

Frances had flung herself at her mother, put her arms around her and sobbed. She gulped at the air and moaned through her tight aching throat, "I'm not strong, Mamma. I'm not strong. I'm just pretending."

"There, there, Francie. I know it's been hard. I can't say I'm happy about what happened to you, but you've done the very best you could. And Rose is beautiful and a lucky girl to have you for her mother."

She had held Frances for a moment or two then pulled herself away. "Don't wake the baby with your caterwauling." They both smiled remembering how Papa used to go on about the cows caterwauling in the barn.

Mamma reached out and smoothed Frances's hair and offered her a hankie. They both looked at Rose, peaceful and unaware of the seismic shift that had just occurred. Frances was forgiven. She could go home ... if she wanted to.

❖

Once Frances had received the letter of acceptance from St. Mary's she requested an appointment with Sister Philomène. She explained what she wanted to do and showed her the letter.

Sister tossed the letter back across her desk. "I know all about your little plan. I know more about it than you."

Frances struggled to maintain her composure.

Sister pulled a piece of paper from the side of her desk and stared at Frances who said nothing.

"Sister Dorothy, the nursing director of St. Mary's, has requested my assurance that I will continue to care for your child."

She wants to see me beg, Frances thought

" I would be very grateful, Sister."

Sister nodded. "But I cannot agree to this ..." She folded the letter.

Frances almost spoke out but Sister continued. "... without some assurance regarding payment of our fees."

"Yes, Sister, of course. I will write to my family immediately. I understand. I appreciate your help." Frances cringed inside at her placatory words.

Sister couldn't resist a pessimistic jab at Frances at the end of the meeting.

"You will never succeed. Now go."

❖

Frances spent her last month working off the debt for her confinement, labour and delivery. She recalled what Ellen had said. "You have a long way to go."

She'd been captive at the Mis for eleven months.

She wished Mercedes was still there to join in her quiet celebration. Mercedes's family had welcomed her back home. Her infant son was the latest in a large tribe of cousins. She was her first real friend outside of her New Brunswick circle of family and school. She missed her every day.

But Frances's excitement was tinged with sadness and worry. She would have to leave Rose at the Mis for three years and she had to think up a story to live by when she moved to St. Mary's nurses' residence.

17

THE PARADE

FRANCES FLOURISHED AT St. Mary's. The nursing students lived on site. She learned something new every day and worked hard. She sometimes had backward glimpses of her time at St. Bridget's.

Her memories of Patsy never dimmed. She thought about sitting at the dormitory window talking about their futures. Now she was in that future and it wasn't a speck like anything they had imagined. It had been so vague then, like the muzzy horizon they saw when they looked down the river. Now it was piercingly sharp. Her future was Rose. Remembering Patsy's talk about having a place of her own made her smile. Although she had a long way to go Frances felt herself moving inch by inch into her own place in the world.

She imagined telling Patsy about the time her new friend Ena had tried to make their supper when they were on night duty.

"Frances, Frances, come look at the soup they left for us. Something is wrong with it." Ena Hewson clomped down the basement stairs ahead of Frances. She was a tall, solid girl who moved decisively but without grace.

Frances looked into the pot Ena was heating for them and the on-call intern. She tried to stir it, but the wooden spoon stood up straight in the pasty congealed mess.

Frances groaned. "This isn't soup, Ena. It's pancake batter! It's ruined now."

Ena had roared with laughter. "I thought it was cream of corn soup. I wondered why they left syrup to go with it."

They'd all gone without a meal that night. Frances could hear Patsy's deep-throated laugh.

Frances missed Patsy and wondered if they would ever be able to share all their thoughts again after her abrupt departure from the Mother House and long silence. Both Patsy and Rosemary had taken their first vows shortly after Rose was born and they were now teaching, Rosemary in Montreal and Patsy in Kingston. Frances only knew this through Ellen. She still kept a safe distance between herself and the Mother House.

⚜

Frances had one day off each week and spent it at the Mis visiting Rose. Sister Philomène kept tabs on Frances. About once a month she called her into her office to ask her about St. Mary's.

"I read in the newspaper that the new hospital near *l'université* is almost finished."

"Yes, Sister. The hospital is too small. It must have been a very grand house in its day, but it doesn't do for a hospital. There are no elevators and the staircases are narrow and steep for carrying stretchers up and down. It's agony for the surgical patients."

Frances kept some of the stories about the old mansion to herself, stories about the cockroaches and rats that infested the place. Sister was smug enough about the tight ship she ran at the Mis without help from Frances. She continued, "They expect the new hospital to be open in three years."

"I guess you English are not suffering like the French during these hard times. Where is the money for a new hospital coming from?" Sister sniffed, not expecting an answer.

Frances knew Sister's reference to "you English" was an ignorant generalization. Indeed St. Mary's was an English Catholic hospital but the word English only referred to the language. The majority of the patients she took care of were of Irish descent, many of whom lived in Griffintown. And many of them were poor and destitute. Yes, they suffered.

Sister never asked about Rose although Frances was sure she got reports about the baby and saw the mounting bill she owed. Sister had given up calling her Gemelle, but she wouldn't acknowledge Frances as a young mother. Frances thought Sister had locked that information in a place in her brain with a sign: Do not open. Frances was resigned to it. She couldn't waste her time or energy on what Sister thought of her.

Rose was her delight once a week. Her heart ached every time the nurses told her about another thing Rose had done that she had missed but she accepted it with grace as best she could and kept her focus on the future when she and Rose would be together. They had come this far. But doubts crept in. Sometimes after a particularly tiring stretch of work, she wondered if she could keep it up, wondered if Rose deserved more than she had to offer. The doubts knocked her back and she struggled to regain her determination.

⚜

She didn't see Father Monahan after the day they had met at the Mis but somehow he had influenced the St. Mary's bigwigs to accept her. One Sunday morning in her last year of training she was pouring tea at a Communion Breakfast fundraiser. She was in a freshly starched bib and apron with her name pinned high on her chest. An elegantly dressed man with steel grey hair combed back from his prominent forehead was sitting beside a priest.

The man looked at her name and then looked at her. "Miss Dalton. So you've gotten this far." He looked away and sucked his teeth.

"How do you do, sir? Milk and sugar?" Frances was flummoxed.

He waved his hand at her, a gesture of dismissal.

When Frances got a chance, she pointed out the man to Ena. "Do you know who that man is, the one beside the priest?"

"MacDougall, MacDonald, something like that. I was off duty last St. Pat's and saw him in a big, black car in the parade waving to us as we shivered on the sidewalk."

She continued. "He's the chairman of the board of directors of the hospital. The priest is on the board too."

Frances recalled how Sister Philomène at the Mis and Sister Dorothy at St. Mary's had negotiated about Rose's care. The two Sisters were forces unto themselves in their own spheres, but they didn't question directives that came from priests or chairmen of boards.

Later that evening after the fundraiser, Ena asked Frances why she asked about the man.

"He seemed to know me, but he was rude." Frances said.

"Of course he knows you. You're the only one of us, the only girl in the hospital who is married —" She stopped. "I'm sorry, *was* married, and has a baby."

Frances said nothing. Ena reached across and took her hand. "We know you must have had some help, some kind of pull. Even if that bigwig didn't like breaking the rules for you he had to go along. The board knows it couldn't run this place without us. None of us girls begrudges how you got in, Frances."

Frances doubted that but said nothing. Indeed the nursing students were valuable providing free service in the hospital, but she also knew she had been favoured. She ached to confide in Ena, to be real friends but she was isolated by her own reticence. Her story was that she was from a small village in New Brunswick, a widow with a child. The reason her daughter was at the Miséricorde was that Frances's mother was ill, and her sisters were single and working, unable to care for Rose. And that Frances wanted to be close to her daughter.

Ena said, "You don't have to tell me more. I don't care who went to bat for you. You're the best night-duty partner anyone could have."

⚜

Frances adapted well to the routines at St. Mary's. Regimented communal living was familiar and comforting to her. The nursing students' quarters were on the top floor of the mansion, in what were probably servant rooms in Lord Shaughnessy's day. They worked day and night shifts six days a week with one day off duty. Someone was always trying to get some sleep, so they spoke in whispers or not at all on the top floor.

Frances loved wearing her nurse's uniform. The crisp bib and apron suited her tall slender figure. Her friend Henny, on the other hand, had a generous bosom that buckled the bib out in front of her like the prow of a ship. To avoid creasing their bibs and aprons they hung them from lines up near the ceiling above their beds. Late at night they wafted in the air, like ghosts haunting the place.

One day when they were working on the women's ward Henny grabbed her by the arm. "Come on, Dalton. Time for lunch."

All the girls were called by their last names, sometimes turned into a nickname, like Henny for Hennessy. Frances was happy she wasn't nicknamed Dolly.

"Give me ten minutes. I have to go see Mrs. Giovanni. I've put it off. I promise, ten minutes," Frances said. Henny rolled her hand in the hurry-up motion and turned on her heel.

The women's open ward never had fewer than fifteen patients – women birthing, women dying and everything in-between. A curtained alcove at the end of the ward was reserved for special cases – sometimes it had well-to-do patients – bankers' or politicians' wives. Mrs. Giovanni was its current occupant.

But "Mrs." Giovanni wasn't anyone's wife. She was a seventeen-year old who had delivered a healthy, eight-pound baby two days earlier. But she would not be feeding her baby at two o'clock. This afternoon Mrs. Giovanni would sign the first adoption papers relinquishing her son to a family she would never know.

The alcove was dim. Mrs. Giovanni was lying on her side facing away from the curtain with the bedcover pulled over her head. The air was stale with the meaty, milky smell of a postpartum woman.

Frances called her name in a soft voice and touched her on the shoulder.

"Go away."

"I'm here to see that you are all right, Mrs. Giovanni."

"Don't call me that." Her dull, sad voice was muffled by the covers she huddled under.

"What do you want me to call you?"

"My name is Valentina. Everyone calls me Tina. What's your name, Nurse?"

"Frances Dalton but just call me Nurse when anyone else is around. Especially the nuns." The girl uncovered her face and they both smiled.

"I have to check a few things. How are your breasts feeling?" Frances reached for the ties around Tina's neck, undid them and pulled her gown and the blankets down.

"I'm leaking some sticky stuff and they're getting sore."

"I'll get you a basin of warm water. And a breast binder. Your breasts will get full for a few days before your milk stops. It may get uncomfortable."

"It's no worse than I deserve."

Frances remembered saying the same words.

Always the same. Unwed mothers, feeling unworthy and undeserving.

"It's not a punishment, Tina. It's just what your body needs to do. Don't be hard on yourself. There are enough people willing to take that on."

She made sure she caught the girl's eye. "I have to go and get my lunch before the kitchen closes. I'll be back with the binder in about forty-five minutes."

Frances was happy eating alone. Whenever there was a girl like

Tina on the ward it piqued everyone's curiosity about Frances. Her nursing school friends knew she had a daughter, and no husband despite the thin gold band she wore, but that's all they knew. She was sure they talked, sure there were rumours, but her resolve was hard and fixed. Her past was private. She sometimes thought she would like to confide, to let down her guard but her habit of silence and secrecy was well honed.

Back at the Mis, when the babies were brought in for their feedings, their cries had always sparked something in their mothers. Sadness and anguish at the thought of relinquishing their babies, relief to get on with their lives, or resentment and anger toward the couple who would raise the child legitimately. Perhaps Tina would feel all those at once, a confusing sea of emotional ebbs and floods. Frances had seen it all at the Mis.

⁂

One day in the spring of 1934, her third year at St. Mary's, she went to the Mis to visit Rose and she couldn't find her. She moved quickly from room to room in the nursery section of the hospital. Sister Jeanne was in the large dormitory folding diapers.

"Est-ce que Rose est dans le jardin avec Sœur Evangeline?" Frances asked. Is she in the garden?

Sister's eyes darted from side to side. She twisted around and knocked a pile of diapers on the floor. Bending to retrieve them she looked at Frances, panic-struck.

Decorum and her well-seasoned deference to the Sisters who cared for Rose vanished. "Tell me. Where is she?"

Silence.

Frances's voice, loud and demanding, boomed in the sparse, high-ceilinged room. "Where is my daughter?" Two Sisters dashed into the dormitory. One got a small chair for Frances and the other reached for her shoulder. *"Asseyez-vous,* please." Sit.

Frances shrugged off the Sister's arm. She wouldn't sit. She took a breath, trying to calm herself. "I'm sorry for yelling, Sister. Please tell me where Rose is."

"She is in the adoption parade."

Frances spun around, knocked over the flimsy chair and ran toward the stairs leading to the first floor. She flew downstairs. Several couples were walking toward the door to the parlour that was used for what they called the parades, the viewing of prospective children for adoption. She cut off a well-dressed couple just as they got to the door. The man jumped back holding onto his wife. *"Mon Dieu,"* he said. Frances dashed in ahead of them.

There were ten children on display, some new-borns and some older. Rose was on a blanket on the floor playing with a doll. Frances overheard the two Sisters hosting the parade talk to a couple about Rose. Frances lifted Rose and hurried to the door. She didn't know where she was going. She had no time to think. She had to get Rose out of there.

Sister Philomène, doubtless having been warned by the Sisters upstairs, cut off her escape. *"Mademoiselle* Dalton, stop."

"Sister, what are you doing? Rose shouldn't be here. She's not an orphan."

Sister glanced at the couples that were watching them. "We will go to my office to talk. Give Rose to Sister Clarisse."

"No."

Sister eyed her for a cool moment but capitulated. *"Comme tu veux."* As you wish.

Frances wouldn't put Rose down in the nun's office even though Sister put a small blanket on the floor and waved her hand at it. Frances pulled some keys from her purse and gave them to Rose to distract her. She waited for the nun to speak.

"We have a couple coming today who are interested in an older child. Sister Clarisse wanted to see their reaction to Rose."

"Rose is my daughter. She is not up for adoption. We have an arrangement."

"You and your arrangement." Sister gave a hollow laugh. "It is falling apart. Your payments are two months behind."

"I have no money. My family is strapped for cash because of my sister's upcoming wedding. You know that I am graduating in two months. And I have a job at St. Mary's." She cringed inwardly at the desperate plea in her voice but kept her shoulders and back erect.

"These are very difficult times and they will not improve soon. A nurse doesn't earn enough money. You can't manage, an unmarried woman with a child. A disgrace. Rose needs two parents. And you would be better off too if you relinquished Rose. We would erase your debt for Rose's care." Her voice had a baiting tone.

Rose was priceless to Frances but she realized that the adoption fees the Mis would receive for her would far outweigh what Frances owed. Erasing her debt was nothing more than a shrewd business strategy.

Frances noted Sister's contradictory message, shaming her and showing concern for her welfare at the same time. But she did not argue. She let the shaming and false concern roll off her.

She knew she had advantages that the majority of the girls at the Mis didn't have. Her education was one. Most of the girls were poorly educated rural French-Canadians. Many of them were servants or farm workers.

Because Frances was an anglophone perhaps Sister mistook her as somehow privileged.

And finally, Father Monahan, the priest who had interceded on her behalf, and her aunt at the Congregation of Notre Dame were authority figures in her background that Sister might consider. Frances gambled that those factors gave her the upper hand.

Frances played her trump card. "I have not signed any legal documents that entitle you to offer Rose for adoption. And I will not."

Sister fidgeted with the papers on her desk.

"If you want me to remove Rose now, say so. But do not put her in the adoption parade again. Is that clear enough for you?"

Sister snorted. "You *anglaises,* even a sinful, sexually incontinent one like you, you think you can live however you want."

Frances rose. "I am taking my daughter upstairs to Sister Evangeline. Good afternoon, Sister."

She was shaking when she got out onto Dorchester Street. She had never raised her voice to a nun. But it was Sister's snide criticism about what Rose needed that undid her. It echoed her own doubts about whether she was good enough.

Her only comfort was knowing that, without the official papers relinquishing Rose, the Miséricorde could do nothing. She gave an inward nod of thanks to Ellen for her wise counsel.

She scrambled for ideas for what to do if Sister called her bluff about removing Rose. Her only possibilities were Ellen or Mamma. Frances pictured Rose, three years old, in the kitchen at home running circles around Mamma and Cecile. If she had to move Rose from the Mis, it would only be for six months. Still, her heart was bruised.

As it turned out, Sister Philomene had been bluffing, taking advantage of her vulnerability and fear, for what reason Frances never knew. She had never warmed to the Director and now thought of her as a pathetic bully. Once Frances graduated, she signed a lease on an apartment, and moved in with Rose and her nurse friend, Ena, as fast as she could.

PART 2

18

RECONNECTING

FRANCES AND ENA had the same day off and were busy in their kitchen making supper. There was no counter-space, so they did most of the work at the rickety table set up beside the narrow pantry. Frances had baked some apples and they were swimming in golden syrup on the back of the stove.

Rosemary was coming for supper. She and Frances hadn't seen each other for almost five years. Rosemary had recently left the Congregation of Notre Dame.

"What do you think was the straw that broke her back, Frances? Five years is a long time to stick with something and then just up and leave."

"Yeah. Maybe she'll tell us tonight," Frances said, reluctant to talk about others. "I think we need a couple more potatoes. The meat was a frightful price so we'll have to make a little go a long way."

"What was it like, being in the convent?"

Frances stopped browning the onions and stared at the wall, which was still grimy even after all their scrubbing. During the three years of their training she and Ena had become close friends, and Frances had broken her promise to herself never to reveal her past. She had told Ena about her poorly thought out move to the Mother House, her pregnancy – nothing more – and the escape to the Mis. Frances swore Ena to secrecy and begged her to ask no questions.

Ena's question was out-of-bounds but Frances continued. "I was there less than a month and I was frightened and worried the whole time. I don't remember much of it." She stared off again. "We were silent almost twenty-four hours a day. I think some girls found that very hard. I didn't. My mind was either racing with horrible thoughts or just numb and blank."

She left the kitchen and poked her head into the front room to check on Rose, who was carrying on a lively conversation in English and French with her dolls.

Back in the kitchen, Frances said, "I only went because nothing else was open to me. The Congregation of Notre Dame is a teaching order and my aunt was a bigwig CND teacher so I thought I would at least be furthering my education, maybe learn something about teaching. But all I learned was how to be a nun – poor, chaste, and obedient."

"Well, Rosemary sure learned it and now she has to unlearn it. But at least she got around to becoming a teacher," Ena said.

Rosemary had left the order at the end of the school year and then was hired by the Sisters of Charity as a lay teacher in one of their schools.

Frances and Ena's apartment was near the hospital. The landlord, a beefy man ironically called Mr. Lord, had looked askance at two women with a child. There were other women sharing apartments but none with children. But Frances and Ena's letters of reference, one from the director of the board of St. Mary's, and the other from the director of nursing, had allayed his fears.

They finished their training, took jobs on the maternity ward and decided to share an apartment. They had an easy way of being with each other. Neither of them had any family in Montreal; in fact, Ena hardly had any at all. Her parents had died within months of each other when Ena was in training. She had no brothers or sisters. She was born after her parents had been married for twenty years.

"They thought it would never happen and then when it did, they were stunned. I remember coming home from school sometimes – I had to knock on the door to be let in – and my mother would look surprised to see me, as if she'd forgotten all about me in the six hours I'd been at school." She looked at Frances for a long moment. "It's as though we were never meant to be a family. I feel more at home with you and Rose than I ever did with my parents."

Frances was grateful for Ena. She accepted Rose and never pried about who her father was. She was a buffer between Frances and their nursing friends. Ena was confident and outgoing and Frances was happy to be in her shadow.

When the stew was simmering Frances took off her apron and went to lie down for five minutes. Ena's question about the convent – what was it like? – irked her. How could she know? She wasn't herself then. She was as an escapee going from one new place to the next, never sure if it was right or safe, having no choice. The hardest part had been leaving Rose at the Mis. But Rose was her choice and come hell or high water she would make sure they were safe, even more than safe.

Raucous laughter from the front room. Rosemary had arrived. Frances jumped up, straightened her skirt, slicked on a smear of lipstick, and strode out to greet her friend. She found her luring Rose out from behind Ena's knees with a soft, knitted doll.

"This is Miss Monique and she's come to meet a little girl called Rose."

Rose peeked out and said in her strongest voice, "I'm Rose." Then she ducked back to safety.

"Well then, Rose, this doll is for you. Please come out and say hello to her. You can hold her."

Frances said, "Would you like to see the doll, Rose?" She gave her daughter an encouraging nod.

Rose darted forward, took the doll from Rosemary and held it toward Frances. "*Regarde, Maman, une poupée.* The lady gave me a dolly."

"What's the polite word, Rose?" Frances asked in a gentle voice.

"*Merci* and thank you, Madame." The three women watched Rose as she took her new treasure to the blanket on the floor and introduced her to her other dolls, forgetting about Maman and her friends.

"What a sight for sore eyes you are, Frances Dalton." In one step Rosemary had her arms wrapped around Frances and almost pulled her off her feet. They hugged for a moment and then held each other at arm's length with broad smiles splitting their faces.

"I don't think I ever saw you smile, Frances. It suits you."

"Let's sit down. Supper won't be long. I guess you and Ena introduced yourselves while I dozed."

"Yeah. She's been asking me how I like life on the outside, as she said."

"Ena, you could have waited at least until dessert." Frances wagged her finger at Ena and shrugged. "Convent life seems so mysterious to those who haven't been there."

Rosemary threw up her arms. "It's more mysterious to those who have." She let out a whoop of laughter. "I'll tell you what I told Ena. Life on the outside is noisy, busy, distracting, and wonderful. I'm having a ball."

"You two have a lot of catching up to do," Ena said. "I'm going to the corner store to get some cream for the apples."

Awkwardness nudged in between the friends. They looked at Rose prattling away to Miss Monique and the other dolls. Rosemary broke the silence. "She's lovely."

"I think so too. Some days I can't believe we're together. I brought her here from the Miséricorde nursery the day Ena and I moved. She was thin and had nothing but the stained hand-me-downs on her back. It was heart breaking." She paused then looked at Rosemary. "It was exactly four years to the day you and I made our pilgrimage to Notre Dame de Bon Secours – September eighth. I'll never be able to thank you enough for what you did for me that day."

Frances slid over on the couch and took Rosemary's hand. "I didn't know if I'd ever see you again. But here you are. I'd love to know about your decision to leave, but I won't press."

"How about another time, Frances? I promise I will, but frankly, I'm getting tired of talking about it. I went over the story with Father Monahan today. Do you remember him?"

"Of course. I owe him a lot too. I don't know what he did, but St. ·Mary's accepted me."

The front door open and Ena called out, "It smells great in here. Let's eat."

*

Frances and Rosemary met often over the summer. They told their stories recalling details and anecdotes that barely registered with them at the time.

"My friend at the Mis was Mercedes," Frances said one day at the Egan's. "She and her baby went to live with her sister's family in the Eastern Townships. We were the lucky ones."

"Lucky?"

"Life at the Mis is a secret that few know about. Most of the girls left their babies there to be adopted. A lot wanted to, mind you, but some didn't. Their families were nasty, and the girls had no chances." Frances shook her head. "It was sad watching them leave in the baggy clothes they came in with."

"And I suppose you left in your habit." Rosemary grinned at Frances.

"I never saw it again. I put those months I stayed to good use. Sister Dolorosa found some old dresses that had been left behind and asked the Sisters in the laundry to help me make them over. When I wasn't working in the clinic or the kitchen I was learning how to sew. The Sister who ran the workshop had us recite the rosary as we worked, the Hail Mary's running together with the sound of the treadles and knitting needles."

"It sounds like more fun than where I was. I thought if I heard one more thing about poverty, chastity and obedience I would scream. I've been poor all my life and I've certainly been chaste, except for the odd impure thought ..." They burst out laughing. "But obedience; it was too much. Blind, unthinking obedience."

Frances was part of Rosemary's family now, little Rose calling her parents Nanny and Grandpa. They often took Rose out for a walk in the neighbourhood so Frances and Rosemary could have some time alone.

"What about Patsy ... Patricia, my friend from home?" Frances asked on one of her visits to the Egans'. "I know she's in Ontario now but back then when you were postulants ..." Frances looked down at her empty teacup.

"Did she ever ask about what happened that day?"

Four years after Frances had disappeared from her best friend's life she still thought of her daily.

What would Patsy think of her if she knew?

"Oh, did she ever. Eventually, I begged a girl who was working with her on sacristy duty to give Patricia a note. I wrote, "She will contact you when she can. She loves you. Be charitable." That last bit was some nun flourish!" A sheepish smile. "I guess I forgot to tell you."

They both knew passing notes from postulant to postulant was against the rules. The lack of names was a sort of protection.

"Should I write to her?"

"I'll give you her address. It's up to you."

"But I .... Oh, here's my little angel." Rose climbed onto her mother's lap.

Rosemary's mother said, "Sorry we're a wee bit late, Frances. We ran into Mary Kelley and she talked our ear off about a tea party at the church for Father Monahan next month – fifty years since his ordination. Please come with us. I know it's an age since you clapped eyes on him, but he'd be delighted to meet our little Rose." She cupped

Rose's cheek in the palm of her hand.

"Thank you, Ellen. We'll come if we're off duty. Let me know the date when you know it." She stood and pulled out her chair. "You and Kevin sit down, and I'll put on a fresh pot for you. Then we've got to run."

Keeping pace with four-year-old Rose, Frances had lots of time to think as they walked to the streetcar on Guy Street. She looked around at the rundown buildings, the broken pavement, and the potholed roads. Griffintown. It was Thomas's old neighbourhood, an insular Irish Catholic pocket of Montreal. It was little wonder to her that he had wanted out. And things were even worse now than they were when he entered the seminary. Since the Depression had put a stranglehold on the neighbourhood, the poverty and hardscrabble existence had only intensified. Frances was grateful to the Egans for everything they had done and continued to do for her and Rose. But she was also grateful she didn't live in the Griff.

19

Particular Friendship

Frances slid her key in the lock, opened the door and tiptoed down the hall. Mrs. Stern, their next-door neighbour who was minding Rose that morning was dozing in the armchair but opened her eyes when Frances appeared.

"There you are. Busy night?"

"No, it was quiet." Frances sat down opposite Mrs. Stern. "Fingers crossed it will stay that way for the rest of my nights. All quiet here?"

"Still sound asleep." She ran both hands around her bulging belly. "I hope this little one sleeps as well."

"The first few months won't be as easy but you'll do fine."

Mrs. Stern was on the roster of people who took care of Rose. Frances and Ena usually worked opposite shifts, twelve hour days or nights, so Goldie, as she asked them to call her, would come in for an hour or so when one of them left for work and the other hadn't arrived home yet. Her husband, Jake, did shift work too, and Goldie accommodated herself to the erratic schedules. She was expecting her first baby and was thrilled to have two nurses next door. The first time Frances opened her purse to pay her she'd jumped back.

"Not on your life. When our baby comes I'll collect from you likewise. I don't have my mother or sisters here and I know I'll need some help in the beginning. Please, Frances."

Frances had a burden of human debt on her shoulders and added Goldie to the accounts. Ellen, Rosemary and her sister Colleen, Ena, and Goldie – they cobbled a schedule together. Sometimes, Rose stayed overnight at the Egans'. Rose had taken it in stride going from being one among twenty or thirty children at the Mis nursery to being the sole focus of everyone's attention. In the first year she called everyone *ma Sœur,* but eventually they all became Auntie, except Nanny Ellen and Grandpa of course.

After Goldie left, Frances put on her nightdress and sat in the kitchen nursing a cup of tea. Now that she had Patsy's address the only way to get some peace of mind was to write her. Rosemary had told Patsy, "She will contact you when she can".

Well? What about now? She had time now. What was stopping her?

Pride. Shame. Fear. Secrecy. Patsy knew her, knew her from that time, especially those last six months at St. Bridget's when Frances had been infatuated with Thomas. Would Patsy guess her secret?

Rose stirred in bed and called out. Frances opened their bedroom door. "Good morning, my angel."

Rose sat up in bed, rubbing her eyes and pushing her chestnut curls away from her face. "I want to wear my pink dress, Mama."

"Let's have breakfast and then I'll help you get dressed. Nanny Ellen is coming to get you this morning so no dilly dallying."

As soon as Rose and Ellen left, Frances penned her letter then collapsed into bed.

June 5, 1935
Dear Sister St. Zita,

I hope you are well, my dear friend. You may not think of me as a friend now, but if you do, please write and let me know. I'd like to explain my actions when we were postulants. None of the CND Sisters knows what happened to me, least of all, my aunt. It's hard for me to ask this but my story has to remain between the two of us.

I've thought of you more often than you can imagine in the

*last four plus years. I'd like to know about what you are doing
now, your school, the students, your community.*

    Your old friend,

    Frances

She wouldn't blame Patsy if she didn't want to be friends, after
Frances shunned her at the Mother House and disappeared. She probably thought that her old friend's confiding in Rosemary, a complete
stranger, was a slap in the face after all the years they'd spent together
in school.

✤

About a month later, Frances came home and saw an envelope on the
kitchen table addressed with Patsy's familiar scrawl. Ena had placed it
on top of the week's pile of mail. By now, Ena knew about the girls'
history. Frances tore open the envelope.

July 3, 1935

Feast of St. Anthony

Dear Frances,

    *Your letter was the answer to my prayers. I've thought of you
and prayed for you every day since you left. Isn't it rich that I am
writing to you on the feast of St. Anthony, patron for finding lost
things? You are not a thing but you know what I mean.*

    *Of course you are my friend, but please, no explanations.
The religious life is not for everyone and I know it was thrust on
you. The way you left, though, leads me to believe there was more
to it than a lack of vocation.*

    *My Vow of Obedience binds me. Sister Superior St. Benedict
was at the Mother House shortly after your disappearance. She
was ill and came to the infirmary. She summoned me asking
what I knew. I was relieved to be able to say I knew nothing. It*

is more than enough that I now know where you live. Your aunt
is the Provincial Superior for our American missions now. I
doubt if I will see her again, but I need time to meditate more on
how much I can know about you.

I heard through the CND grapevine that Sister St. Brenda
(Egan) left our order. I'm guessing that she is the reason we
are writing to each other. I never cared for her as a postulant
(I must confess to my jealousy!) – but please thank her and
give her my best wishes.

Your sister in Christ,
Sister St. Zita

Ena was putting away their meagre groceries while Frances read
the letter to her. Ena said, "Vow of obedience, eh? Never thought of
that."

"Me neither. I had these memories of us in school together and
thought it could be the same. I really didn't think. Patsy is a nun now."

"Who is the Superior she mentioned?"

"Oh, lord. That's part of the story I never told you. Come on. Let's
go out on the stoop and have a cigarette."

After Frances finished, Ena turned to her. "Do you think the old
bat really cares where you are now?"

"Probably not. Mamma doesn't seem to care what she thinks.
Here's the letter I got from her yesterday."

July 10, 1935
Dear Frances,

The weather is very fine here. Rita, Cecile, and I got the
garden in, these past three days. Rita is as big as a house.
Rose will have a little cousin before July is over.

I had a letter from Charlotte last week saying they all like the
new Provincial Superior. A breath of fresh air compared to your

aunt. You know, we didn't hear a word about you from that one
except the nasty letter she wrote shortly after you went to the Mis.
I don't think she really cared about you, just her blessed pack of
nuns. She sent a sympathy note after Papa died, and that's the
last I heard from her.

 All my love to you and Rose and Ena,
 Mamma

"Remind me. Rita's your sister-in-law, right?"

"Yeah, she's married to my brother, Jimmy."

Frances folded her letters. Her thoughts turned to Jimmy and Rita. Despite Mamma's worrying the summer before Frances left for good – the summer he raped her – they had managed to avoid what Mamma feared most and were now married, expecting their first.

Rape. It had taken Frances a while to call it what it was and to admit that it was criminal and she, a victim. But she had kept her vow – no one would ever know, no one would call her a victim.

Ena was still holding the letters. She nudged Frances. "Well, these say a lot. I think you're yesterday's news to your aunt."

"Maybe." Frances stared off and lit another cigarette. "I hope Patsy comes to that conclusion. I want her to know I'm not a big failure. I've been working so hard to make up for ..." Frances began crying, and she crumpled into Ena's arms.

"Come on, Dalton. Let's not cause a scene out here. Time you were in bed. You have to work tomorrow."

⚜

Frances held her past deep inside like a dark, hard chestnut. She almost believed the lies she told in nursing school: An unnamed make-believe husband, a phoney wedding ring, a pathetic widow. But she had cracked open the nutshell by asking Rosemary about Patsy.

In time, Frances and Patsy would write often. Patsy would ask

Frances not to write about the time they shared in the Mother House. Frances would write about Rose, but never mentioned a husband. Patsy never enquired.

But the current talk about Patsy brought Frances's mind back to St. Bridget's and, of course, to Thomas. Frances was coming apart. She was tired of being on guard, keeping her stories together. She craved the lightness of truth and absolution.

Frances awoke and looked over her shoulder. Ena was lying beside her, curled against her. It felt good. It awakened something in Frances. "Ena?"

"Shh. It's okay, Frances. You were crying, having a bad dream maybe. I stayed with you. I didn't want you to wake Rose."

Frances rolled over and propped herself up on her elbow. "I don't remember having a dream."

"Probably just as well." She moved to get up.

"Don't go ... please. You're so good to us. I'd be lost without you."

Frances leaned down and kissed her on the cheek. She pulled back, surprised at herself. She looked at Ena as if her eyes were a key that would unlock everything inside her friend. She realized in that instant that she was more than grateful to Ena. She loved her toughness, her sense of humour, her confidence, her disregard for petty opinions. Most of all she loved her because Ena loved Rose.

Frances kissed her on the lips, startled by their warmth, softness, and openness "Stay with me."

Ena touched her own lips and moved her other hand to Frances' mouth. A long pause, then, "I wouldn't be anywhere else." She reached up and pulled Frances to her. "Let's try that again."

Rose's presence, five feet away from them on her cot, lent an urgency to their passion. With long, deep kisses, like blind explorers they searched out every surface and crevice with their fingers and their tongues. The oppressive night air was cool on their steaming skin as they pulled their damp, cotton night dresses over their heads.

Ena took Frances's nipple in her mouth. Frances grasped the pillow over her face and sounded a groan from deep in her chest. Ena moved the pillow away and found Frances's eyes. She held them as she moved her mouth from one breast to the other sending a sharp, electric current down over her lover's belly, between her legs and deep into her. As if she sensed it, Ena followed the current with her hand. Frances could only moan as her long-held passion burst open.

Ena leaned over her, her heavy breasts resting against Frances. She stroked the damp hair away from her lover's forehead and neck and smiled. Frances gave her a weak smile in return and looked over at Rose. She looked back at Ena, took her face in her hands and then kicked up her legs and let out a whoop of laughter.

Rose rolled over and resettled herself.

"You're a dark horse, Miss Frances." They were overcome with quiet laughter.

✤

Frances sprinkled Yardley talcum powder around her starched waistband and uniform collar to absorb sweat on the hot summer day. A glimmer of sunrise framed the sides of the window blind. She leaned over Rose; she fussed with Rose's sheet; she tidied the top of her dresser. All to avoid looking at Ena who was just waking up.

"Good morning. Sleep well?" Ena asked.

Frances spoke into the middle of the room. "I'm off now. There's sausages in the icebox for tonight."

Ena sat up and took her hand. "We'll be all right. I promise."

"Yes. You and Rose are taking the streetcar up to Mount Royal today, aren't you? You'll have fun."

"You know that's not what I mean, Frances."

"I can't talk about it now. It's too ... too ... I'm going now. Miss Sullivan will be as mad as a wet hen if I'm late."

✤

Frances arrived at the maternity ward ahead of time. She hung up her cape and adjusted her cap, pinning every stray hair in place. As she ran her hands over her bib and smoothed down her apron a mere shiver whispered down her thighs reminding her. She caught herself smiling, but she put on a serious face and went to the back room to listen to the night nurse's report.

She tried to empty her mind. How many times did she tell herself, "Don't think of it ... of her. Think of Rosie. Think of anything but that." But it was no use. Ena's eyes watching her as she ran her tongue around and around her dark nipple. "Stop it, it didn't happen, it was a dream." But she knew it wasn't, and as she remembered, her insides flipped over, and she felt a warmth and a pressure below.

"Morning, Dalton. Nice to see you early for a change."

Frances came out of her reverie and looked at her Head Nurse. Miss Sullivan had the unfortunate combination of close-set eyes, a hooked nose, and a receding chin, giving her a wedge of a face. The severe cut of her thick, black hair did her no favours either.

"Good morning, Miss Sullivan. It's a lovely morning."

She listened carefully to the night report about the newly delivered mothers, but her concentration was shattered by her memories of the previous night's ecstasy.

Was that her? Whatever made her kiss Ena?

Ena had been a part of Frances's life for four years, three during nursing school and one sharing the apartment. Early on Frances focused her attention on the Mis where she had left Rose but now the three of them were a family. She trusted Ena. She loved her.

In between breast checks, fundus massages and perineal cleanses she couldn't help herself: she thought of nothing but sex. She relived the kiss, a single, ashy grey coal that ignited a bonfire.

As the day wore on, Frances became less shocked. She remembered her furtive lovemaking with Mercedes at the Mis. They had had moments of ecstasy, but after Jacqueline's suicide, their lovemaking had been more a comforting and a soothing.

And with Thomas? Urgent, blind, unthinking – the culmination of months of secretive flirting and tamped down passion. But last night was different. Urgent, yes, but controlled, restrained. She and Ena had watched each other, paid attention to each other, thrilled each other.

The walk home was just the right distance, long enough to shed thoughts of the mothers and their new-borns, Miss Sullivan's ever-watchful eyes, and Doctor Hurley, the over-eager obstetrical resident. She passed people going about their early evening business. No one paid any attention to her in her scarlet-lined cape. The new hospital had been open less than a year and already the nurses were an accepted part of the urban landscape. Frances was reminded again of what she loved about living in Montreal. Anonymity. She was just a face in the crowd. Her uniform gave her respect and belonging without having to be known.

She liked it that way, belonging but not being known. As much as she loved Rosemary and her family she wouldn't want to live in Griffintown. It wasn't a nice place to begin with, in fact, a recent article in the Gazette referred to it as a slum. But being so close, knowing all her neighbours and them knowing her, wouldn't suit her. There was no anonymity in the Griff.

She thought of the Mis. She had liked the anonymity there. All of the girls belonged there by virtue of their "sin", but the nuns made sure no one knew you at all.

Shame crept in as she turned off Côte-des-Neiges Road and entered the leafy street of three-story apartment buildings. She knew no one would ever suspect, but still, if what she and Ena had done were known, the respect and belonging would evaporate like the curl of steam from a fresh cup of coffee. The acceptance would grow cold.

She was no stranger to shame. She had been draped in it day and night when she was at the Mis, the heavy folds falling from her shoulders. It seemed that aside from bearing a child the penitents had been there to learn how to be meek and shameful.

With dogged determination during her nurse training, she had muted the shame and gained respect for her discretion, loyalty, and competence. She had friends now and the speculation and gossip had abated. Still, she was vigilant. She knew what they had done the night before would outrage many, if not all, and that the outrage would extend to Rose. She couldn't let that happen. But as she approached their building her resolve to set things straight with Ena melted.

Over the following weeks she and Ena didn't talk about what they were doing or what it would mean to others. They went about their usual routines, working, taking care of Rose, visiting the Egans. Frances kept her shame apart, pushed down. But every minute that was theirs alone, they spent in bed revelling in the pleasure of each other.

Eventually, they moved Rose into Ena's room. "It's better for you to have your own room, Rosie," Ena explained. "We're coming and going on different shifts, disturbing you when you're trying to sleep, especially on school nights."

Rose was excited about starting kindergarten soon so the mention of school nights clinched the deal.

They put up some bright wallpaper that Rose chose and Frances was relieved to see Rose claim the room as her own. She could hardly stifle a laugh when Rose told them they would need to knock before entering her new territory.

"That's a good idea," Ena said. "And you can knock on ours."

Frances and Ena exchanged looks.

20

An Unexpected Guest

THE TEA FOR Father Monahan was on Sunday afternoon in the church basement. Frances and Ena took the streetcar down to Dorchester Street and then walked to the Egans'.

Rose was sitting on the front steps waiting for them. She had been at the Egans' for two nights. Frances ran to the steps and swooped her up in her arms, covering her face in kisses.

"You look like an angel, Rosie. You'll be the belle of the ball."

"The ball?"

"It means you'll be the prettiest girl at the party." They both looked up from the sidewalk and saw Ellen standing on the porch in her Sunday best. "With the exception of Nanny, of course."

Frances held Rose's hand and listened to her prattling about her visit with Nanny and Grandpa. There were twelve of them strolling in twos and threes to the church.

St. Anne's was the centre of community life in Griffintown. Rosemary's brother, Peter, belonged to the church's Boys Club and Ellen often attended the Sodality of Mary activities. Frances had sometimes thought about Thomas's life in the Griff, wondering if, despite the poverty and overcrowding, he had felt embraced by his community. She never mentioned his name to any of the Egans for fear it would breach her well-guarded secret.

Peter, now sixteen, swung a stick at the leafy branches above them. "Fifty years a priest. I bet he could tell some good stories."

Ellen's sharp ears caught his comment even though she was fifteen paces ahead. "You hush up, Peter Egan. Father Monahan keeps himself to himself and tells no stories. That's why he's lasted so long here. Imagine you talking like that and saying just last week you were thinking of the priesthood."

Peter yowled. "Mama!"

Rosemary sidled up to Frances and leaned in close. "Mama's right about Father Monahan No gossip. You can be sure."

When they got to the church Peter took Rose's hand and, in a flash, had her up on his shoulders. He turned to Frances and said, "She'll be able to see everything this way. I'll take good care of her." He made his way through the crowd shaking hands and clapping friends on the back.

The church basement was a dingy, low-ceilinged room. It was divided, similar to the church upstairs, with an open central space and two side areas set apart by thick pillars every twenty feet or so. Water pipes snaked along the upper walls staining the wall here and there with rust streaks.

The church ladies had tried to cheer up the place with streamers and balloons. There was a banner – 1885 to 1935 – Father's years as a priest, and a raised platform for speeches.

Frances leaned over to Rosemary and Colleen. "Ena and I will get tea and some sweets for your parents." She left with Ena close behind her. The parish hall was heaving with people. They squeezed their way to the sweets table.

"This is just like home," Ena said. "It's a lot smaller there but the atmosphere is the same. Everyone belongs, everyone knows everyone."

"Do we belong, Ena? I wonder."

Ena took her hand and gave it a quick squeeze.

Ena held a plate out to Ellen and Kevin. "The ladies of the parish have been baking all week." Kevin took the plate, his eyes sparkling.

Ellen glanced over at the raised platform at the front of the hall. Several men shuffled into position and then faced the crowd. "Just in the nick of time. It looks like the bigwigs are going to start talking."

And talk they did. First the Archbishop, then a couple of Montreal politicians, someone from the board of St. Mary's and two younger priests who had worked in the parish under Father Monahan's tutelage but left for richer parishes.

Father Monahan ended the formalities in his usual style. "My thanks to everyone here. I would also like to remember those parishioners unable to be here, most especially those who lost their lives in the Great War. It has been a privilege to serve you all these years. I know times have been tough recently. But this Depression has brought us closer. I have seen more faith, hope and charity demonstrated here in Griffintown in the past few years than ever before. Now, let's have our tea and celebrate. And if I catch any of you young fellas having anything stronger than tea, watch out."

Father stepped off the platform to great applause and cheers. He walked among the crowd, having a word here and there.

"Let's find Rosemary and Colleen," Ena said.

The Egan sisters were standing near the raised platform, talking to some friends. Among the crowd was a tall, burly man with black hair. Rosemary introduced him as Danny. When Frances saw the scar at the corner of his mouth she knew it was Danny Boyle, the man Rosemary was sweet on.

Frances enjoyed listening to everyone. She paid close attention to Rosemary and Danny and noticed them touching hands from time to time. Rosemary was flushed and for the first time since Frances had known her, she would have said she was giddy. The thought of sensible, reliable Rosemary being giddy made her smile. She was lost in thought when Ellen tapped her on the arm.

"Frances, Father Monahan would like to say hello."

Frances turned. "Congratulations, Father. This is a ..." The words caught in her throat. Standing beside Father was Thomas.

A high-pitched whine echoed around in her skull. Her eyes scalded on the inside. The corners of her mouth twitched in what might have been a smile. The bitter smell of over-steeped tea clung to everything. The only thought in her head: Where is Rose?

Father Monahan said, "Congratulations are due to you, my dear. I hear you are an asset to St. Mary's."

"I ... uh, it's ..." The whining was getting louder and chaotic.

Father saved her from her senselessness. "May I introduce Father Byrne? Father this is Frances Dalton, one of our nurses at St. Mary's."

Thomas was looking at her. He hesitated and clutched his hands together until she heard his knuckles crack. He looked like he felt as trapped and under scrutiny as she was. He turned to Father Monahan. The old priest was his usual genial self, waiting for a response.

"I ... uh ... I. Forgive me Father. It's just that I'm surprised. Hello Miss Dalton." He extended his hand to her. She took it for an instant and then pulled her hand away and gave him a curt nod.

"Father, Miss Dalton and I are acquainted. She was a student at the boarding school during my first year in Newcastle." He turned back to her. "It's a pleasure to see you Miss Dalton. May I also congratulate you on your accomplishments."

Still stunned, she said thank you with a croak in her throat. She did not meet his eyes but instead looked past his shoulder.

Father Monahan spoke. "Oh, yes. I didn't make the New Brunswick connection. She's one of ours now." He gave an avuncular laugh.

"Father Byrne was an altar boy here years ago, Frances. His family is gone from the Griff, but not forgotten."

Brendan, of course, gone now. One of the war dead Father Monahan remembered.

A loud shout caught their attention. "Father Tommy. Long time, no see." It was Danny. He grabbed Thomas by the upper arm and pumped his hand. Soon the whole group of them surrounded Thomas and fired questions at him. Frances melted out of the circle and away from his line of sight against one of the pillars.

When Ena came over to her Frances gripped her hand and whispered, "Let's go, Ena. Let's find Rose and go."

"You look terr —"

"I'm sick. Get me out of here."

When they got outside Frances put her backside against the church wall, leaned over with her hands on her knees and gasped for air. She had a spongy, off-kilter feeling. Ena ran back downstairs and got a glass of water. She dampened her hankie and put it on the back of Frances's neck. She gave her a sip of water.

"Mama, are you sick?"

Rose was standing in front of Frances when she opened her eyes. "No pet, I'm just hot. And I think I had too much cake."

"Me too. But I'm not sick." Rose had a chocolate ring around her mouth and a smear across her cheek. Frances smiled.

"You're the lucky one. Let's walk to the streetcar."

Ena handed the glass to Peter who was too nonplussed to say anything. He'd never seen Frances anything but one hundred percent competent and in control. He'd adored her from afar since he was twelve and this new picture of her was confusing.

"Thanks, Peter. Say bye to everyone for me. Tell Rosemary I'll call her as soon as I feel better."

"Sure thing, Frances," he said.

21

KNOCK KNOCK JOKE

THOMAS WAS WRUNG out. Seeing Frances, holding her hand, even for a moment, and then the effort to cover his shock, especially when he saw the cool, guarded look on her face, had been an ordeal. And her disappearance. Panic had risen in him, a demand to do something, anything. But he was stuck here in the rectory keeping the old priest company. He pulled his thoughts away from Frances and back to the dull meal.

Father Monahan put his knife and fork on his plate and smiled ruefully. "My parish is dwindling Thomas. Families have been leaving here as fast as they can. It's only the Depression that's slowing them down now."

Neither of them spoke for a moment.

"It's changed a lot since you were here," Father Monahan continued. "I saw your old crowd laughing and carrying on with you."

"It was all Danny could do not to call me Firecracker. He slipped once and then went back to Father Tommy."

"Firecracker?"

"It was a nickname – red hair, Byrne – only teasing. I'd forgotten about it. It seems more like a century than a decade since our school days."

"Tell me about St. Bridget's."

"All the usual parish duties. Father Donnelly is pretty well retired now and I manage things." He went on, "The Miramichi is a lovely spot. It doesn't have all the amenities of Montreal, of course."

"I imagine the nuns at the convent school are a big help. I know I couldn't do without them here."

"Well, time for me to call it a day. Goodnight, Tommy."

"Good night, Father. I'm going out for a walk. I'll lock up when I get in."

⚜

Thomas was distraught and marched down the street as if a brisk stride could lift him out of his misery. The narrow dismal streets closed in on him. Many of the buildings were in disrepair; some were squalid. The hot summer evening thickened the air and the stench of sewage and outhouses settled on random corners and alleys. Trains clanked by on the elevated railway that was being erected around the time he left. And the number of taverns was out of proportion to the dwindling population.

He passed Murphy's, Izzy Moore's, and Paddy Carroll's and knew there were more a few blocks away. He marvelled at how unwelcoming they were with their windowless, dirty fronts and bolted doors, especially knowing that, to their regular patrons, they were oases of comfort and, for some, oblivion.

Thomas thought of his drunken father with bitterness and hatred. He prayed for forgiveness and wondered if he could ever forgive his father.

He passed a cluster of boys on a street corner, smoking and playing cards in the waning evening light. One of them scooped up the cards and shoved them in his pocket as he approached. "Evening, Father."

"Good evening, boys. Mind if I join you for a few minutes?" He pulled a crumpled cigarette packet from his cassock pocket. One of the boys struck a match. "Thanks."

"Are you Father Tommy?"

"Yes, I'm staying at the rectory a few days. I haven't been back here for years. I thought it would be nice to celebrate with Father Monahan.

What's your name?"

"Peter Egan, Father. You met two of my sisters this afternoon, Rosemary and Colleen."

"Yes, I remember. They were with Danny. We had quite a time reminiscing. Rosemary seems keen about her new teaching job," he said. He threw his cigarette on the sidewalk and stepped on it. "I'd best be getting on. Nice chatting."

Thomas was more than a block away when he heard footsteps. He turned and saw Peter.

"Father, will you be at the rectory on Tuesday afternoon, about four?"

"I could be. Why do you ask?"

Peter fumbled with his cap and looked everywhere but at Thomas. "I want to talk about something, Father."

Thomas waited.

"The priesthood, Father. I've been thinking about it and seeing as you're here I thought I might as well."

"Have you spoken with Father Monahan?"

"Well, no, I haven't. But I'd like to talk to you. Father is ... well, he's ...., I'm afraid he might not know .... I just think you'd understand me better."

"I think we both have something to offer you. I'll see you on the condition that you see Father Monahan also, within the month."

"Okay, Father, it's a deal. I'll see you at four on Tuesday."

After Thomas bolted the rectory door and tiptoed to the small guest room he let out a long breath as though he had been guarding himself all day. He shrugged off his heavy cassock, kicked off his shoes and sat on the edge of the bed in his undershirt, trousers, and socks.

Memories filled his mind. All he could see was Frances, her grey eyes and soft hair, her playful, discrete smile, her quiet sureness. Their intimate secret.

Frances had never been far from his thoughts but until today he'd had no idea where she was. And her child, where was her child, their child? Adopted? Or back in New Brunswick with her family?

Her cool demeanour and her vanishing act today sent an unmistakeable message. Stay away. But maybe not. Maybe she was as shocked as he and needed time. They could meet in a quiet place, a private place. No, not private, a neutral place. On and on his thoughts went. How could he meet her? What would he say?

He paced back and forth, avoiding the squeaky floorboards, and finally knelt and looked up at the image of St. Joseph. It flickered in the light of the votive candle.

Thomas took his rosary from his pocket and ran the beads through his fingers over and over. He prayed to the icon on the wall, asking for guidance. Very soon his thoughts were back to Frances. He let the rosary fall to the floor and ran his hands through his hair. How he missed her. She had been such a brightness in his days. He was lonely without her.

What did she mean to him? He had tried not to think of it; had pushed the thoughts down, submerged them. But today they pushed back at him.

Thomas thought he understood passion and the desire for connection with another. He celebrated it all the time with his parishioners at marriages, baptisms, and funerals even though the unspoken, carnal aspect of human connection was cleaved from those sacred rites as if it didn't exist. But Frances made it alive. For a short time, Frances had brought him into a fuller sense of life, of living.

He looked at the image of St. Joseph, the role model of fathers.

There was no sense in praying. The saint couldn't help him None of it could.

❖

"Tommy, I'll leave you to yourself today. I have a meeting at St. Patrick's this morning and then some parish work in the afternoon."

"Of course. I ran into Peter Egan last evening. He wants to see me tomorrow afternoon. Thinking of the priesthood."

"Yes, his mother spoke to me," Father said. "Looking for a younger opinion, I imagine. He's in good hands with you."

When Father left, Thomas asked the housekeeper the way to St. Mary's Hospital.

"I hope you don't have family ill, Father Byrne?"

"No, no, nothing like that. I've heard a lot about the new place and just thought I'd take a look at it."

"It's a long way off but it's grand, everything that opens and shuts, you know. Get the streetcar on Guy Street. It goes around the mountain to Côte-des-Neiges. Anyone can tell you where to get off."

✤

Thomas sat in the empty hospital chapel for two hours. Around eleven, a few nurses came in and knelt for a short time then got up and left. He approached one as she was leaving.

"Excuse me, Nurse. Perhaps you could help me."

"What do you need, Father?"

"Do you know Frances Dalton?"

"Of course, I do, Father. Everyone knows everyone here."

"She's an old friend from home. I don't want to bother her at work, but I don't know how else to reach her. Perhaps you could give this to her?" He held out a sealed envelope.

"I don't know if she's on duty today but I'll leave it on the maternity ward."

"That's very helpful. Thank you." As soon as she had gone he sank onto the hard pew. His hands were shaking.

✤

Miss Sullivan was bearing down on Frances at a clip. "Dalton, someone left a card for you at the nurses' desk. My ward isn't a post office so don't make a habit of it. I don't care if it was a priest. I won't have it on my ward." She barely drew a breath. "Doctor Bailey will be here soon to see his patients. Make sure they are all presentable for him." She turned and marched away.

Frances was too stunned to react to Sullivan's overbearing commands. She walked to the desk, grabbed the envelope, stuck it into her waistband behind her bib and then got on with her work.

Dear Frances,

I was sorry to hear that you were taken ill so suddenly yesterday. I hope that you are feeling better now. Seeing you was a pleasant surprise and I was looking forward to talking with you. I was caught up in reminiscing with my old school friends and when I tried to find you I learned you had gone home.

I am staying at the rectory until Friday evening. I would be very grateful if you would telephone me. The number here is WE3-2617.

Sincerely,

Fr. Thomas

Their apartment was as quiet as a church. Rose was asleep after three fairy tales and a lot of questions about Cinderella. Ena was on night duty. Frances read the letter several times trying to find some special meaning or message. She chastised herself. There was nothing to find, nothing between them. She looked at the door to Rose's room.

⚜

She woke up when she heard Ena's key in the door. She stayed where she was and a few minutes later Ena flopped onto the bed beside her, still wrapped in her cape. "What a night we had, Frances. Twins and a breech. I'm beat."

"Everything turn out okay?"

"Doctor Hurley is pretty good. Cool as a cucumber. I was glad old Sully wasn't there though."

"Get out of your uniform and have a wash. I'll make you some tea. Do you want an egg?"

"Yes, please. I'm starved."

After they finished their tea and scrambled eggs, Frances said, "Remember the priest we met at Father Monahan's do?"

"The tall redhead?"

"Yeah. He left a note for me on the ward yesterday – asked me to telephone him."

"Lucille Payette told me you got a letter at work. I thought it was strange. Sully must have had fits about that. He's from New Brunswick, right?"

She was glad she'd told Ena about the letter. Lucille was the cleaning lady on their ward. If she knew about the letter, everybody did.

"He's from Montreal but he was, still is, one of the priests at St. Bridget's, the parish where I went to school. He tutored us in mathematics before our provincial exams. I guess he just wants to have a chat."

Ena tilted her head toward Rose's door. "Does he know?"

Frances struggled to be cool. "No. And he won't. I don't really want to talk to him but I don't think I can ignore him."

"No, I guess you can't." Ena said. "I'm going to bed. I can hardly keep my eyes open." She leaned over and kissed Frances. "Oh, delicious you."

Frances laughed. "Have a good sleep, darling."

After getting Rose her breakfast and setting her up with her dolls Frances went out to the shared telephone in the stairwell. She dialled the rectory. A woman answered.

"May I speak to Father Byrne, please?"

"It's a little early for telephone calls, don't you think? Just hang on. He's eating his breakfast." The telephone clattered down, then she heard loud footsteps and a door being opened.

Frances laughed to herself. She could picture the housekeeper, put out, feathers ruffled.

"Father Byrne speaking."

The squeeze of her heart was unexpected. Her voice was a gasp, "It's Fran ..." She cleared her throat, "It's Frances, Father Byrne."

Thomas was speechless. A moment passed.

Frances was embarrassed. She stammered. "Father, I shouldn't have called. I won't disturb you again."

"Frances, Frances, don't hang up, for God's sake, don't."

She was startled by his urgency.

"I'm so happy you called. I didn't know how else to reach you. I hope it wasn't a nuisance at your work. It's wonderful to hear your voice."

"A nuisance? I only have to explain myself to every Tom, Dick and Harry in the place. Who is the mystery priest?" Despite herself, she was laughing.

"I guess it's safe to say you are not at work right now?"

"No. It's my day off."

"It would be lovely to have a visit. Can you come to the rectory today?"

"No, Father."

"Oh. Well, I could take the streetcar up to Côte-des-Neiges."

"No, Father." Her heart was hammering. She couldn't think of what to say. Not there, not here, too exposed.

Silence again.

She took control. "Do you know where Ogilvy's is, on the corner of St. Catherine and Mountain Street? They have a coffee shop on the fifth floor. I can meet you there at eleven o'clock. Will that do?"

"Yes, yes, it will be perfect."

"Alright then. See you later."

"Goodbye, Frances."

❖

She knocked on Goldie Stern's door. Her baby was two months old and Frances could hear her singing to the infant.

"Hello there. You're up and about early for your day off. I hope the baby's crying isn't bothering you?"

"No, no. We never hear a thing. I have a big favour to ask, Goldie."

"Shoot. What do you need?

"I have an appointment I can't change, and Ena is sleeping. Can you take care of Rose from ten to one?"

"This is your lucky day. Jake is home so the two of us can manage. Rose is no trouble."

Frances stared past the rows of tombstones as the streetcar trundled past the cemetery on Mount Royal. She thought about their telephone conversation, recalled everything he'd said. She told herself to smarten up and stop behaving like the schoolgirl she had been but she couldn't stop the fluttery feeling inside. It was just like back then; she felt special, she felt seen, she felt connected. After five years of silence, sealing over her emotions and acting a role, her reserve loosened and a lightness came over her.

She entered the elevator and told the operator, in her kilt and white gloves, that she was going to the fifth floor. The operator closed the gleaming grill. "Certainly, Miss."

He was in a booth near the front and rose when he saw her. He looked very modern in a black suit and shirt, the cassock gone, but the gleaming white collar reminded her of what he was.

"Frances, I'm so glad you came. Please sit down."

"Thank you, Father."

When the waitress came, Thomas asked Frances what she would like. She spoke to the waitress, "I'd like coffee with cream and a slice of your banana loaf, please."

"I'll have the same, please."

An uncomfortable silence set in. He turned his coffee cup around and around in its saucer. Frances had her head down, but she lifted her eyes enough to watch his fingers on the rim of the cup.

She glanced at him and looked down again. "You're going to wear out that saucer, Father."

"I guess it shows, my nervousness I mean. I wanted to talk to you so much and now I'm tongue-tied. For a start, please call me Thomas."

"Why don't you tell me about St. Bridget's? How are my old teachers?"

"They are all very much the same. The same classes, the same people, the same little ceremonies and rituals."

They went on in this vein for a time until he erupted. "Enough, enough. I want to talk about you Frances."

She didn't hesitate. She assumed the guarded stance she had taken for the last five years when anyone got too close. "There is little to say. The years since I left St. Bridget's haven't been easy. I entered the CND after school. It wasn't for me. But I was lucky. I found my niche in nursing."

He looked around the coffee shop, up at the lights, down at the floor. He looked at her then looked away, then back again. He put his arms on the table and leaned toward her. "Did your mother ever tell you that she came to see me at St. Bridget's?"

"Mamma?"

"Yes. She came to ask for my help. I'm sure she was desperate to confide in me."

Frances turned to stone. She stared at him, holding her breath. "Confide?"

He looked away. His voice was low and broken. "She told me what happened to you, why you left the CND. She —"

"No! Don't say another word." She grabbed her handbag and started to stand up.

He reached over and held her arm. "Please, Frances. Don't go. I won't pry. Your mother was trying to help. She asked if I'd seen anything, anyone who might have ... She had no idea about me, that it was me she was after. I didn't say anything. She said you were being taken care of by French nuns on Dorchester Street. I knew it must have been the Miséricorde Hospital."

He paused, "I've thought about you every day since then, Frances."

He thinks he's the one, she thought.

She supposed that was better than him thinking he was one of many. But he wasn't the only one. She looked at his hand on her arm then looked at him. He pulled it away and sat with his hands clasped in front of him on the table as though praying.

She straightened her back and stiffened her shoulders. Her armour. "I had no idea you knew. It doesn't change anything though, and your thoughts, as kind as they may have been, didn't help me."

She had known back then that he, a priest, could be of no help. And he hadn't been, not even a letter. She scoffed at the idea of his prayers. They prayed all the time at the Mis. Prayers did her no good.

"I did what I could with the help of strangers. They are like family now."

"The Egans?"

She nodded. She still held her handbag but the impulse to run was fading. Whatever was between them was stronger. The spark, the passion, the comfort, all of it was right here. He knew the secret she had kept from everyone. She looked at him. She sat back in her seat, her shoulders dropped and she smiled.

"I have a daughter. Her name is Rose."

He leaned forward and tilted his head. "You have ... you kept ... Rose?"

She nodded.

He teared up. "Rose," under his breath.

She called the waitress and asked for more coffee. She was a French-Canadian girl in whom reverence for the clergy was drilled from birth. She approached with her coffee pot as though going to the

communion rail and then tiptoed away. The distraction gave him time
to collect himself.

"Tell me about Rose," His voice was constricted and weak.

"She's lovely, Thomas." It was the first time she said his name.
Their eyes met.

"She's four now. Her birthday is April second. She's tall for her age
and thin but everyone is thin these days."

He nodded. "Food isn't plentiful."

"But she's healthy. She has hazel eyes and curly chestnut hair. She
talks non-stop and loves stories."

He started to speak two or three times but couldn't say anything
except "Please, go on."

"I hope you're not shocked. Or even worse, ashamed of me."

"No, of course not. Most of all I admire your strength, your guts."

"I had a lot of time for recollection and meditation at the Mis. The
nuns expected penance also – in fact, we were called penitents – but I
resisted it. I resisted. I wouldn't be a sinner no matter how much they
told me I was. I never begged for forgiveness."

"I'm the one to beg forgiveness from you and God."

"I have nothing to forgive you for. Rose is my treasure. As for God
..." she shrugged. "Even as a schoolgirl I chafed at all the rules of chaste
behaviour and the threats of punishment, from God and others. When
I look at Rose I don't care a fiddle what God thinks of me."

Thomas didn't speak. After a moment they began to laugh in quiet
tones. She said, "Maybe that's why things turned out the way they did."

They sipped their coffee in silence, looking at each other from time
to time. "I heard stories from the girls at the Mis about how they got
in trouble, the fathers of their babies, their families. Some of them
were stories of misery and violence but some were just unlucky circumstances. That's how I came to think of my situation. Unlucky,
that's all. Not shameful, not sinful."

He looked at her for a long moment. "Do you think ... is it possible

... our circumstances ... can they change?"

"Thomas, you're a priest. That won't change ... ever."

"But Rose is ... my daughter."

A cold caution startled her. *His* daughter? The vast authority of the Roman Catholic Church pitted against the lowly station of an unwed mother flashed a warning. Canon law and civil law. Could he take Rose from her? Might he think he knew what was best for her?

"You may be Rose's father, but she is not your daughter. She is my daughter." She grabbed her purse and stood. "Goodbye, Father."

Frances had a hard time controlling herself on the streetcar home. She stifled her tears and got off a few stops before hers, so she could cool off. She had loved Thomas. Maybe that hadn't changed in the five years since she'd last seen him. But that love was encased and put away. Rose was everything. And Ena. The three of them were her family now.

✤

Thomas watched her leave the coffee shop like a drowning man watching his ship sail toward the horizon. He sat there another half hour, hopeless and lost in thought.

He recalled his conversation with Mrs. Dalton in the autumn after Frances had left St. Bridget's. She had approached him in the church where he had been hearing confessions. He was attentive and asked questions to learn more about Frances but was guarded. Only later did he see his cautiousness for what it was – cowardice.

After Mrs. Dalton had left the church that day, he sat in the last pew at the back staring into the darkening space. Images of Frances crossed in front of him like a picture-house newsreel. Doing math problems with a stub of a pencil, her necktie askew and a faint ring of grime inside the collar around her slim neck. In her white graduation dress the last time he saw her, poised and gracious, attending to her mother. Standing to attention with a load of linen in her arms. At the sacristy window, vinegar wafting on the air.

Four months had passed since they'd made love on the brocade chaise, but time hadn't dimmed his shame at his weakness or his longing for her. He had continued with his parish duties knowing he'd besmirched the sanctity of the Holy Sacraments while still thinking of the urgency and intensity of their passion.

Frances, her wry sense of humour, her curiosity, her openness.

He had snapped out of his reverie and jumped up from the pew.

God help us, God help us, God help me. What have I done? She is paying for my sins.

Thomas had walked down the dark centre aisle, drawn to the glowing red sanctuary lamp, a reminder of the ever-present Lord and Saviour. He knelt.

Don't look at me God, don't look at me. Mea culpa, mea culpa, mea maxima culpa. Were you watching over us then?

He had been chilled to the bone and went into the sacristy. He'd wrapped himself in an old sweater and collapsed on the red brocade chaise. Waves of helplessness and remorse had lapped around him until, covered in shame, he had fallen into a troubled asleep.

⚜

After Frances left the coffee shop, he walked east along St. Catherine Street and then down Peel to Dorchester. He went into St. James Cathedral and walked around in a vague, abstracted way. When he did pay attention, the opulence, the gold leaf and the grandeur dismayed him. He felt nothing, no, even worse, a sense of meaninglessness. The place he had loved as a boy and a seminarian, this replica of St. Peter's Basilica, the seat of his faith, now meaningless.

He trudged back to the rectory and waited for Peter Egan to arrive for his precious discussion. The priesthood? What could he say about it? It was a lonely, solitary life, seeking solace in long-dead people, arcane philosophy and well-worn rituals and regalia. He compared what Frances had endured since she left St. Bridget's to his own experience.

He didn't know half of it but he knew she'd emerged from her trial sure of herself and of what she valued.

Imposter. The word came back to him and he remembered thinking it of himself when he first was intoxicated by Frances.

Imposter. He hid within this revered role.

Reverence. It was absurd. He tried to remember the last time he had prayed with reverence and faith, the last time he had said Mass as a true embodiment of Christ. He went through the motions, that was all.

Seeing Frances again and learning about Rose challenged his shaky faith even more. Every day in his parish he saw hungry desperate people clinging to the Church, searching for answers to the misery of the times they were in. He had no answers for them. The shrivelling economy referred to as a great depression was great indeed. It was tearing families apart, wasting villages, even killing people. And faith was no comfort, for them or for him. Many evenings he longed for someone to talk to, someone to share the burden. He scoffed at the idea that celibacy would make him more devoted to duty, more available for his congregation. It bred contempt.

⚜

Peter knocked. "Hello, Peter. You're very punctual." They settled in the shabby front room. "Why don't you begin?"

Peter was sincere but Thomas recognized his motives. He was immature, naïve and, in his innocent way, wanted to bolster his rank at home and in his social group. Thomas saw himself in Peter and an image of his own mother, swamped in grief, played across his mind.

After some discussion Thomas said, "You've got a good head on your shoulders and the luxury of time. I think you could use both, to get a clear picture of the work priests do. We've talked about my small-town parish. Father Monahan has a wealth of experience in this working-class part of town. But there are lots of others. Learn as much as you can."

Peter was downcast. Thomas suspected he wanted more encouragement and admiration. But his strategy was to confuse and perhaps overwhelm the boy. "We haven't had time to talk about the orders: the Benedictines, the Oblates, the Dominicans and so on. Some do foreign missionary work, which is another area to look into. You're smart and young. I know you'll leave no stone unturned."

Remembering how he had longed to leave Griffintown, how unaware he had been that entering the seminary had been an escape for him, Thomas said, "Things are very tough right now. I imagine your family needs you to go to work for them more than to pray for them."

Peter was startled and frowned at Thomas. He took a deep breath and blew it out over his protruding lower lip. "I didn't think of all that, Father. It's complicated." He paused and looked around and then jerked his head back toward Thomas. "I almost forgot. Mama asked me to ask you for tea this week, any afternoon you have time. She said her youngest brother, Hugh, knew your brother."

"That's very kind of her. How about tomorrow afternoon, three o'clock?"

"I gotta warn you, Father, as many of us who can be home will be there. You might be from the Griff but you're a celebrity now, being from away."

"Who would guess it? A celebrity from small-town New Brunswick."

⁂

Thomas waited while Kevin Egan lifted the girl off his knees and rose with his hand extended. "It's a pleasure to meet you, Father Byrne."

"The pleasure is all mine, Mr. Egan."

They were both distracted by the girl. "Grandpa, Nanny has cookies in the kitchen. Can I have one?"

"Please say hello to Father Byrne first. Father, this is my granddaughter, Rose."

"Rose ... Rose ... a lovely name. How do you do?" He reached for her hand and held it between both of his as he squatted down to look at her.

Frances had said, "They are like family now." The Egans.

"I'm going to get a cookie. Do you want to come?" she said.

"Hold your horses, Rose. Go help Nanny. Father, sit down in this comfy chair. Ellen will be right in with tea."

Soon the small room was full-to-bursting with raucous Egans, talking at the same time and asking him questions. The only one who showed no interest in him was Rose. His eyes kept sliding over to wherever she was, absorbing every bit of her: her tinkling laugh, her mischievous eyes, her expressive hands.

"Grandpa, do you want to hear my joke? It's Uncle Peter's joke but he said I could tell it."

"Tell it to Father Byrne."

She turned to him and put on a serious face. Her small hand rapped twice on his knee. "Knock, knock."

"Who's there, Rose?"

"No, no. You just say, "Who's there?" We have to start again. Knock, knock."

"Who's there?"

"That's better. Rufus." She leaned in, her hair brushing his cheek. She whispered to him, "Now you say, "Rufus who?""

Thomas's heart was melting. "Rufus who?"

"Rufus the most important part of your house." Rose exploded with laughter and looked around to make sure everyone was laughing.

Peter said, "It's never so funny when I tell it."

Thomas was enchanted. "Tell me another one, Rose."

"I can't. I'm going to the park with Uncle Peter. I hafta go." She took Peter by the hand and pulled him toward the door.

The light went out of the room. They carried on with mundane conversation but there were no more knock-knock jokes. No one spoke about Rose at all. From his parish work he knew that grandparents often talked about their grandchildren; some talked of nothing else. He wondered if the Egans's silence was intentional, a protective strategy for everyone involved or simply an unspoken habit.

He lingered as long as good manners allowed, but Rose and Peter didn't return.

⁕

Two days after their encounter at Ogilvy's, Frances telephoned the rectory. The same bossy housekeeper answered. "Ah, it's you again, is it? Hang on, I'll see if he wants to speak to you."

Despite her nerves, Frances couldn't help but smile. She thought of Mrs. Charlotte.

Priests' housekeepers. Guard dogs.

"Father Byrne here. Can I help you?"

"It's Frances."

A pause, then, "I didn't think I'd hear from you again."

"I'm sorry I ran off. I was frightened ... for Rose."

Thomas was confused, couldn't think of what to say. "Frightened?"

"Some people are very unkind to women like me. They don't think we deserve to have our children—"

"But I—"

"I was frightened, Thomas. I've had to fight for Rose, to prove my-self. When you called her your daughter, I panicked. I won't let anyone get between Rose and me."

"I would never do that. I'm in no position, you know that. I was so flabbergasted that Rose is ... is a person ... your daughter ..."

There was a long silence. Thomas broke it. "Did Rose tell you she met me yesterday at the Egans? No, of course not, she's only four. And I was just another grown-up in the room."

He met Rose? Her heart leapt to her throat. But she forced it down – what harm could come of it?

"No, Rose didn't say anything except that Peter took her to the park. She has her priorities, you know," she teased.

He cleared his throat. "She's enchanting, Frances."

She sighed. "Isn't she?"

"I'm returning to Newcastle tomorrow. May I write you?"

Frances hesitated. "No one knows about you."

"I'll be discreet. Just news from the hinterland."

✤

When he started writing, Frances shared the letters with Ena and Rose, explaining that Father Thomas was an old friend from down home. His tone was friendly but not curious or intimate.

"You remember him, Ena? He was at that party for Father Monahan."

"No, I didn't meet him. I just remember Sully's tempest in a teapot about you receiving personal mail on her ward." Ena put on a fake voice of disapproval. "Most unprofessional.".

But after reading two or three of his letters, Ena and Rose had taken a pass on them. His descriptions of his parish duties and who said what to whom did not pique their interest or curiosity.

The Thirties dragged on. Frances and Ena worked; Rose went to school. They had what they needed but nothing more. Frances reflected once that it was like being in boarding school or the convent. Routine was everything.

When the war started, things didn't change immediately but life was marked by tension and vigilance.

22

THE SNAPSHOT

FRANCES AND ENA were in the kitchen talking in low voices, their tea abandoned, pushed away. Rose had gone to bed an hour before. Frances got up to check on her, to see if she was sound asleep.

She returned to the table and took Ena's hand. "You don't have to go."

"I know I don't. But as soon as I read that Gazette article, I knew I wanted to."

Frances was crying. She took a hankie from her apron pocket and blew her nose. It did little good. She was sobbing.

"Shhh ... you'll wake Rosie." Ena tried to console her, patting her on the shoulder.

Frances jumped up scraping her chair across the floor. "Oh, don't give me that horseshit. If you cared about Rose, you wouldn't be talking this foolishness."

She put on a nasty mocking voice, "It's a war. I can do some good."

"Don't be mean," Ena replied

Frances tried to squelch her rising voice. "Mean? What about Rose? You're the mean one leaving her."

"Rose isn't a baby, she's eleven. It's 1942. She knows there's a war on." Their silence was interrupted by Frances's blowing and sniffling.

"And it's not *if*, Frances, it's *when*. I've been accepted."

There was a long silence and muffled crying. Ena, exasperated, said, "We've been over this and over it. I'm going out for a walk."

Frances tried to calm herself by clearing the kitchen table. It was no use. She sat and stared at the wall. She and Ena had been living to-gether raising Rose – Mama and Auntie Ena – for eight years. They had been lovers for almost as long. Frances fell to pieces when she thought of losing Ena.

Ena insisted that she wasn't losing her. "You're just lending me to the war effort," she had said, trying to strike a jocular tone.

Frances wasn't consoled. She knew Ena was unhappy and bored with the routine of the maternity ward. Frances had turned that around, accusing Ena of being bored with her and Rose.

"Frances, there's a war on, the world is on fire," Ena had said.

"Stop being selfish. And stop doubting yourself. You and Rose will be together, you'll be fine without me. I love you Frances but I'm going. This war won't last forever, and I'll come back to you."

After ten minutes of anguished ruminating Frances turned off the kitchen light and went into their bedroom.

⚜

"Are you ready to go, Rosie Posie?" Ena asked.

Frances and Rose looked at Ena in her Bluebird uniform with the brass buttons. Rose saluted her. "Yes, Lieutenant."

The train station was mobbed with people – civilians and soldiers – coming and going but it didn't take them long to find the other army nurses in their bright white veils. They were taking the train to New Brunswick, and then a ship to England.

The nurses' friends and family came to see them off and Ena was no exception. Nurses from St. Mary's and all the Egans came to say good-bye. Peter Egan swung Rose up onto a cart with bags and boxes, so she could see over the heads.

There was a change in the crowd. People started shuffling their feet and standing up on tiptoes. They looked at the train and then back at the soldiers. Women – mothers, girlfriends, sisters – of the depart-ing soldiers, cried and blotted away tears.

Everyone backed away from Ena and watched as Frances hugged her. Then Kevin Egan nudged Rose toward them.

Ena let go of Frances and put her hand out to Rose. "I'll think about you every day I'm over there, Rosie Posie." Ena was the only one allowed to call Rose that anymore. Rose had a new rule – no more nicknames.

Ena hugged Rose so hard that Rose's hat tipped back and fell onto the platform. Ena was talking into the side of Rose's face and her tears and lipstick smeared across her cheek. "I want you and Mama to take care of each other. Practise your writing by sending me a letter every week."

Rose pushed back and wiped her cheek with her sleeve. Everyone laughed. "I promise."

Frances hugged Ena one last time. "It's the right thing you're doing but that doesn't mean I like it." She lowered her voice. "Let's not make a scene. Just take care of yourself and come home to us."

⚜

Ena wrote them individual letters most weeks but sometimes they got one letter for both of them. That was when Ena had extra-long hours. She said all she could do was work and sleep and "dash off a quick note".

Frances brought home three empty chocolate boxes from the hospital to keep Ena's letters in – Rose's, hers, and the ones to both of them.

"Why are the boxes empty? I'd like a full one." Rose smacked her lips.

"Me too." Frances laughed. "Fathers give the nurses chocolates after the mothers have their babies."

"All of them?"

"No. They can't all afford it. But the ones who can often do."

Rose hesitated. "Did my father?"

Frances stopped stirring the pot on the stove for an instant. She took a deep breath and went on stirring. "No, darling. Chocolates were too expensive for us. Dinner will be ready in a few minutes. Go wash your hands."

Lately, Rose had started asking about her father. Frances tried to change the topic and distract her. Rose's best friend, Doreen, was fatherless too, hers killed overseas. Doreen had shown Rose a picture of him in his military uniform, which was what had brought on Rose's new interest in knowing who hers was.

Rose had gone into her bedroom after washing up and now she emerged with something in her hand. "Is this my father?" she asked sounding defiant. She held a photograph of four children posing against the wall of a house. The one in front was a boy.

She had rummaged around in a box of old pictures Frances kept in her closet. Frances was hopping mad. She snatched the picture away from Rose. "You have no business looking through my things. It's a rude thing to do."

"I think it's rude that you won't show me a picture of him. He's my father. It's not fair." She was crying. She clenched her fists and stamped her foot.

Frances knew she couldn't brush her off. She was quiet for a few moments, staring at the picture.

"I don't have a picture. I wish I did. That's your Uncle Jimmy, tough little guy, glaring at the camera." Her heart lurched looking at her brother.

"And these are Bernadette and Josephine. Can you guess who this is?" She pointed to the skinny, pale girl on the edge.

Rose thought a minute. "Is it you? You look so small compared to Aunt Josephine. Look at her big, fat face."

"Aunt Josephine is three years older than I am. And I'd been sick for a long time then."

Rose took the picture from her mother. "Look how white and

squinty you are and how you're sort of disappearing."

"This was taken as I was getting stronger. I remember it was my first day outside."

Rose traced her finger over the pale image of the emaciated girl. "You look like a ghost."

"I do, don't I? I sometimes felt like a ghost that year, fading in and out."

"What made you sick?"

"I had typhoid fever. It's a contagious illness."

Rose didn't ask anything else about it. She squinted at the picture again. "I didn't know you were younger than Aunt Bernadette and Josephine."

"I was the third daughter – not a position of honour, if you want to know."

"What does that mean?" Rose asked.

"I think my father was hoping for lots of boys, strong boys to work on the farm. We all have boys' names – Joe, Bernie and Frank."

Rose laughed.

"Now let's eat, my number one and only."

Later that night, Frances studied the photo. Tough little Jimmy. He was tough all right. But then Frances saw him surrounded by his well-educated sisters, and he the only one there to do the farm work. Maybe he had felt trapped too. And angry. She remembered Rita's father coming to the house and the subsequent beating Jimmy got. He'd been angry and humiliated. She could never forgive him, but she understood more now.

Frances thought of Rose's questions. The time was coming when Rose would not be so easily distracted.

Who is your father, Rose?

23

Twenty Questions

One afternoon on her day-off, Frances lay down and picked her library book off the bedside table. She read a few pages and nodded off.

When she woke up she was on her side facing her bureau. The hem of her blue pyjama top was sticking out of the bottom drawer. She refolded it and tucked it away again, glancing at her letter boxes. Since Ena had started writing so many letters, Frances had had to re-organize her letters. She liked to keep them separated.

She had a box for Ena's letters to her, a box for Patsy's, a box for Mamma's and her sisters', and a box for Thomas's.

He was a good storyteller and often made her laugh at the antics of the people in St. Bridget's parish. He was never unkind but had a keen eye for peculiarities of speech and manners. One time he wrote about a strike at all the lumber mills along the Miramichi River. Frances was surprised at how involved he was in the local politics.

I spoke to a woman after Mass whose husband was on strike. She can't feed her children with the low wages he earns. It made me question what use I am, what use the Church is, to people who are hungry. They can't eat prayers.

After the war started his letters were darker. He regretted not en-listing and resented the Bishop's directive to stay in the parish and take over most of Father Donnelly's duties. Speaking to war widows, trying to help them find meaning in their loss, gutted him. Although no one said it, he couldn't help but think they thought he should be serving overseas. Frances could write little to comfort him. She didn't try. Instead she kept her replies light-hearted and, she hoped, amusing.

It's become very "patriotic" to eat lobster! Reminds me of the rare picnics we girls sometime had at St. B's. Lobster sandwiches – much nicer than the ghastly Canada War Cake that's served everywhere in Montreal nowadays. It's a dreadful time but I can't help thinking it's better than the Depression.

Frances knew Rose missed Ena. She spoke of her almost every day.
"I wonder if she eats fish and chips."
"Will she have an English accent when she comes home?"
"I didn't know Auntie Ena could ride a bicycle."
Rose memorized every word Ena wrote. Although she wrote almost the same things to both of them, Rose pored over her mother's letters as much as her own.
Frances didn't mind her reading her letters. She and Ena were used to discretion and subterfuge, living as they did, and it carried over into their letters. Frances could read Ena's affection between the lines.
Another letter came from Ena. Frances and Rose read it together.

March 17, 1943
Dear Frances and Rose,

I hope you are having a grand St. Pat's Day. Did you go to the parade?

I went out with two of the girls this evening to a pub in the village. Warm beer mixed with ginger ale – not so nice. The roads here are in a terrible state and we decided not to risk riding our bicycles in the dark coming home. One of us surely would have gone bottoms-up in a pothole. It was a long walk.

*I'm at a new place now and they're putting me to good use.
There's an obstetrical unit here for Canadian Forces wives and
military women. It's a nice break from the soldiers. The women
aren't coddled after they deliver. They have to be up on the third
day, make their own beds, and stand to attention when the doctor
does his rounds. All very military. I don't think it does them any
harm.*

*We do everything here, antepartum, labour and delivery,
and postpartum. They are using a spinal anaesthetic procedure
I haven't seen before for the deliveries. I had to deliver a baby
alone last week. It was her third, so she came along nicely, no
need for anaesthetic.*

*I'll wish you a happy birthday now, Rosie, in case I can't
manage it closer to the day.*

Love to both of you,
Ena

"I guess that's why she hasn't written for a while, moving to a new
hospital." Rose said.

"I think you're right. It must be hard to get settled, get to know the
routines and the people and then be packed up and moved along. It
wouldn't suit me."

Rose pointed to a word on the second page. "What does that
mean?"

"Anaesthetic? It's medicine that stops you from feeling pain. A lot
of operations wouldn't be possible without it."

"Did Mr. Stern have a nanasetic when he had his tummy oper-
ation?"

Frances corrected her. "It's an anaesthetic. Difficult word. Yes, Mr.
Stern had one."

"So it's not just for mothers having babies?"

"No. Not so many years ago, mothers didn't have any anaesthetic."

"Did you?"

"No."

"Was it very painful?"

"Well, yes it was. But I had some lovely women who helped me, and when it was over, I had you and I forgot all about the pain."

"Did Auntie Ena help you?"

"No. I didn't know her then."

They were quiet for a few moments. "I want to know all about when I was born."

"It was in a Catholic hospital in Montreal and—"

"Not St. Mary's?"

"No, dear. Let me finish." Frances took a deep breath. "The hospital was run by nuns and a very nice nun named Sister Dolorosa sat with me the whole time I was in labour."

Rose frowned when she heard the word labour, but Frances continued with her account.

"It was Good Friday. You know how solemn nuns get on Good Friday." She laughed a bit. "I think they were praying under their breath the whole time. It was quiet and peaceful. And you were a perfect, beautiful baby."

"Was my father there?"

"No, he wasn't. He was gone." Her voice was very low. "Rose, I know you are curious about your father. I'll tell you about him when you're older, I promise."

"Don't be so mean. He's my father. Tell me now."

"I won't, Rose. It was a difficult time for both of us and there are things that are hard to understand, even for me. I'm not making this promise lightly. When you are older I'll tell you what you want to know."

Frances swept her fingers in a cross over the front of her blouse. "I promise."

She got up and filled the kettle. "Tea?"

"Can I ask some questions about him?"

"I thought we were finished with that for now."

"Like the twenty questions game, I'll ask easy questions and you can answer yes or no."

"Okay, but only three questions."

"Was he a bad man?"

"Heavens, no."

"Did he go because of me?"

"No, no, no."

Frances banged the wooden spoon on the table in time with her words.

Rose mumbled. "That's good."

A moment passed. "Mama?"

"Only one more."

"Not about him. Can I call you Mum? A lot of girls at school call their mothers Mum. Mama sounds babyish. And I want to call Auntie Ena just Aunt Ena. What do you think she'll say?"

"I think she'll say, 'just don't call me late for dinner'." She reached out and grabbed Rose in a big hug. "You're getting very sophisticated, my almost-twelve Rose. I'm your Mum and I said so.

24

THE INHERITANCE

ROSEMARY WAS ON the stoop when Frances got home from work. A small pile of cigarette butts was beside her. Rosemary didn't give a hoot about social niceties and if she wanted a cigarette she had one, ladylike or not.

"You've been here awhile by the looks of it."

"Not too long. Are you going to ask me in or do I have to beg?"

"Come on, don't be so foolish. I've got to get out of this get-up. You can put on the kettle. Pick up those butts or the janitor will scold me."

When they settled down with their tea, Frances said, "You must have some big news that you couldn't just telephone me. Something about Danny Boyle, maybe?" Frances teased.

Rosemary turned beet red from her neck to her forehead. "Nothing on that front yet. No, it's about your aunt."

No need to name her. Frances knew Sister St. Benedict had retired from her mission in Rhode Island and was living at the Mother House. Rosemary kept up-to-date with a few of her former Sisters and passed on any news of Frances's aunt. But Frances never saw her.

"She died, Frances. I'm sorry to tell you."

"Ah, that's a shame. But there was no love lost between us."

"I came to ask you if you would go to her funeral at the Mother House with me. It will be a big deal, a Provincial Superior, you know. And she published that book."

Frances knew about the book too, a biography of Margeurite

Bourgeoys, the founder of the congregation but she'd never seen it.

"Go to the Mother House?"

Rosemary said, "I haven't been back in years. It'd do me good. Slough off the shame of not making it. I think it would do you good too."

"Do *me* good?"

"You've done really well – Head Nurse at the most modern hospital in the city. I've done well too. We have nothing to be ashamed of."

The last sentence hung heavy in the air between them. "I'm not sure about that. People have long memories," Frances said.

"Frances, I don't want to be mean, but I doubt anyone even remembers you. It was 1930, fifteen long years ago. You were there barely a month. The only Sister your presence had meaning for was your aunt and now she's gone."

Frances grew teary and Rosemary added, "Oh dear, I think that was too much. I'm sorry."

"You're absolutely right." Frances wiped her eyes. "It was the biggest moment of my life, the bravest, the scariest, the loneliest. But it was all mine, except for you. Why would any of them remember me?"

Rosemary seemed at a loss and said nothing.

After a time, Frances said, "I feel foolish. Me, me, me."

"So? Is that a yes? You'll come?"

"It's a scary thought but yes, I'll go. When is it?"

"Saturday, eleven in the morning."

"I'll be there to represent my family, as Sister's niece. That's all."

⚜

Frances mingled with some of the Sisters at the reception.

"Her niece? Lovely of you to come. I didn't know Sister well. We were never in the same mission but, of course, I know of her. Her book on our Venerable Mother is truly remarkable."

And another. "You must be very proud of her, so accomplished and yet so humble. A long, outstanding vocation – 1884 to 1945."

When she saw Sister Alfonse – the Great Snorer as she and Rosemary had dubbed her – Frances, emboldened, went and said hello. She had thought Sister was old years ago, but now she was truly aged.

"Hello Sister. My name is Frances. How do you do?"

"Well, Frances what?" Sister's impatience and bluntness hadn't waned.

"Frances Dalton, Sister St. Benedict's niece."

"Oh yes, it's good to see you again, Sister. Ooh, my feet are killing me."

Frances smiled to herself, being called Sister. "Please take my arm, Sister. You can sit over there." She pointed to a chair a few feet away. "May I get you a cup of tea, Sister?"

"*Merci. Tu es un ange.*" You're an angel. She blew on her tea, sipped it and blew some more. "What became of you?"

"I'm a registered nurse, Sister, at St. Mary's Hospital."

"Good for you. I always wonder about the ones who leave."

"I'm surprised you remember me, Sister," Frances said.

"Something about your eyes and then when you said your name I remembered. Dalton, of course. You disappeared into thin air. Caused quite a stir. But new things cropped up and you were mostly forgotten."

"That's good to hear, Sister, very good to hear."

The old nun laughed and paused for a few minutes.

"Yes, I suppose it is. Forget about mistakes and move on." Frances wondered whose mistake she meant.

After the reception, Rosemary and Frances walked to Guy Street. "I saw you talking to old Alfonse."

"She remembered me. Called me Sister! After so many years in the community I guess to her, every woman is her Sister. She said the same thing you did. I was one of hundreds who started and left. No cause for concern."

"Yeah, it's funny how we're each the main star in our own life but usually incidental to others. It's humbling," Rosemary said.

"Sure is. The one in charge of the service, Sister St. Rita, said my aunt's necrology would be available soon. I could come back to read it. Fat chance." Frances laughed.

"There's my streetcar." Frances ran across the street and yelled back "I'll see you next week at the Dominion Day party."

Giddiness bubbled up inside Frances. She put her head down to hide her grinning. It was as though she had just removed the tightest girdle in the world and could finally breathe.

⚜

Frances couldn't think straight, couldn't think of anything to ask Mr. Dupuis, the elegant, bookish man behind the desk. "I don't understand, sir. Would you please explain?"

"*Oui, c'est vraie que* ... Pardon me." He waved his hand off to the side as if shooing away the French words. "It's true. These things are sometimes a surprise, but it is simple. Your aunt, Sister St. Benedict, left you some money."

"With respect sir, my aunt and I have not spoken or seen each other since I was a child. Also, she was a nun living under a vow of poverty. There must be a mistake."

"Her Congregation contacted us after her death and gave us her will. We have followed the necessary procedures to determine that you are her sole beneficiary."

Her mind was blank. She looked around the spacious, book-lined room. The early summer sun poured through the tall windows and across the rich, red oriental carpet. When she returned her attention to the lawyer, he was sitting with his large hands folded in front of him, an onyx pinkie ring glinting at her. She nodded and he continued.

"It's a pleasure to settle a will like this. Your aunt had good counsel and it is clear that she intended her estate to be yours. There is a letter for you. Sister wrote it when she made her will." He shuffled some papers and checked a detail.

"Yes, that was five years ago. It may answer some of your questions" He opened the folder on his desk, removed an ivory-coloured envelope and handed it to her.

She took it, and as though in a trance, said, "Thank you, Mr. Dupuis, I'll be in touch." She came to her senses when the elevator door opened and she found herself amid smartly dressed businessmen coming and going in the lobby. She checked her handbag to see that the letter was there and took out some coins for the streetcar.

August 15, 1940
Feast of the Assumption
My dear Frances,

No doubt this will surprise you, so I will be direct. The money I am leaving you came to me from my father, your grandfather. As I was in the convent, the only thing I could do with it was put it in a trust many years ago.

I believe your strength, fortitude, and discretion are remarkable. I cannot tell you how I know of the struggles you have had. It is enough to say that I admire you.

When I left home for the convent, I had a true vocation, but I also knew it would be a place of safety and support unlike my parents' home. I flourished in my blessed congregation, but I was never blind to the ways of the world and what young women are up against.

I am confident you will use this money well for yourself and your daughter.

With love and blessings from your Sister in Christ,
S.S. Benedict

P.S. You owe nothing to the CND. I made a healthy donation.

Frances sipped her tea. Murray's restaurant was a better choice than the counter at Woolworth's. The lunch crowd was gone, and it was quiet. She had a small table, her aunt's letter in front of her.

"More hot water, hon?"

She stared into space and didn't answer.

The waitress bent down and got her attention. "You're off in another world, aren't you? I hope it's not bad news. They say the war is over but you never know."

"No, not bad news." She put her letter away. "Good news, actually. I'd like a fresh pot of tea, please."

"You relax. I'll be right back with it."

She had lots of questions for Mr. Dupuis. Who knows about the inheritance? How much money is it? When will she receive it? What would Mamma say? Mr. Dupuis couldn't answer that last question but it was the most pressing one. And her sisters, what about them? Would they see it as her being rewarded for being the black sheep, the one who left? She stopped short of thinking: *the bad one.*

Frances pictured pious Sister in her chaste habit and was stunned that she and her aunt had had such a horrific secret in common: that sometimes girls weren't safe in their own homes. The secret Frances had learned the summer before she went to Montreal.

She and Rose had started going down home in the summers when Rose was seven. Jimmy and Rita had two children by then and Rose loved playing with her cousins. It was an unspoken rule that no one mentioned the absence of Rose's father. Mamma loved all her grand-children and would brook no criticism or sly questions about Rose.

Frances developed a careful stance around her brother. Fatherhood seemed to have extinguished Jimmy's anger and resentment. He was hardworking and quiet. She and Jimmy never spoke about their shared secret; in fact, they were never alone together. She always stayed at a distance, keeping Mamma, Rita, and the children between them.

25

Moving On

"If you thought convents and hospitals were militaristic, you ain't seen nothin' yet. The Canadian Army is the real thing," Ena said.

"When will you be "demobbed" as you say?"

"I'm trying to explain. It's not up to me. It's the army. The war might have ended months ago but there are still sick and wounded soldiers who need nursing right here in Montreal."

Ena had been home for a month. She was still in the army and working at the veterans' hospital on Queen Mary Road. The military procedure for getting out of the service was a mystery to Frances.

Ena held out her glass to Frances. "Be a love and get me another drink. Ple-e-e-ase."

" Yes, sir." Frances stomped off to the kitchen.

"Oh, don't be so pissy, love."

When she returned she almost threw the scotch and soda at Ena. "Stop calling me love. And that's your last drink tonight."

"Why end the fun?'

"I'm not having fun and Rose will be home soon."

Ena grabbed her by the wrist, pulled her down on the sofa and wrapped her arms around her. "Relax, Frances. It's just a few drinks."

She leaned in to kiss Frances on the mouth. Her balance was off though and her lips slid across her face.

Frances jumped up, wiping her face. "Stop it, Ena, that's enough. I'm going to bed. I'm working in the morning."

"Suit yourself, love." Ena swung her feet up onto the chesterfield and soon dozed off.

Frances was wide-awake listening for Rose. Babysitting upstairs worked out well. Rose earned a little pocket money and felt independent and grown up but she was as close to home as could be. Frances didn't worry but she couldn't drift off until Rose came in.

But Ena was the real reason she was still staring at the ceiling. The happy homecoming had been short-lived. Ena had changed during the war, and Frances wanted to think she had too. She hadn't really though. Her life was going to work, taking care of Rose, doing housework and having the odd bridge night with the same old friends. And she liked it like that. Everything in order and no surprises. The change in her was that she was more secure and less at the mercy of things she couldn't control.

But the change in Ena was the opposite. She thrived on change. She was bored already at the veterans' hospital and was casting about for something new. She had little interest in the old gang from St. Mary's.

Frances had hosted two tables of bridge one evening and Ena had drifted in and out, getting the girls drinks and emptying the ashtrays. She joined them for their midnight lunch.

The next morning Ena had said, "I don't know how you can stand listening to all their chatter."

"They're my friends. I'm interested in their news. They might not tell exciting war stories but I'm still interested in them."

"Marriage, children, buying houses, shopping for curtains. You're right, dull as dishwater. Never my thing."

Frances bit her tongue and said nothing about thinking of buying a house herself. Except for the marriage part, all the talk of domestic life was right up her alley. Ena didn't know about her inheritance yet. At first Frances felt bad for withholding a secret but when Ena started talking about taking advantage of the war veteran's benefit to go to university, Frances knew she didn't owe Ena anything. She needed to make her own plans. She had thought of the four-year separation as a hiatus, merely an interruption but now she recognized it as truly liminal. Everything was in transition.

✤

Frances had enough money to make a substantial down payment on a house and still keep some money aside for things that would crop up. She had never thought about such a thing. People like her were tenants, not owners. The banker and real estate lawyer, that Mr. Dupuis had recommended, both said it would take some extra paperwork, her being an unmarried woman. Women had gotten the vote in Quebec only a few years earlier. A single woman owning property was another battle. But they were confident they could make it happen.

The lawyer told her to take her time and to call him when she was getting serious. He would give her the names of some agents and they would take it one step at a time. She marvelled at how simple he made it seem.

She could make the phases of labour and delivery sound simple too.

Frances's world was small so she made it her business to learn about areas of the city other than Snowdon, where St. Mary's Hospital was, and Griffintown.

"Rose, I'm going to Notre-Dame-de-Grâce today. Want to come with me?"

"NDG? Sure. Will we be back by two o'clock? Doreen and I are going to the library to study."

"I suppose Frank and Tommy Carson will be studying there too?"

Rose put on a casual tone and smiled at her mother. "I suppose they might be."

"Come on my boy-crazy gal. I'll be ready in ten minutes."

Frances was happy for Rose, having friends, leading a carefree life. But that could change. Two months ago Frances had run into Peggy

Miller, one of Rose's teachers, at the grocery store. She was the same age as Frances and had a sister who was also a nurse. After a few niceties Peggy had said, "I don't want to worry you but I overheard a couple of the nuns just before assembly last week. Nothing specific, just ... well ..."

"C'mon, Peggy. Tell me."

"Sister St. Jude, who will likely be Rose's teacher next year, was talking about *you*. She gestured toward Rose and said, "The mother, I never see her at Church for the novenas and the like. I wonder who she thinks she is, flaunting it like that." Sister can be pretty spiteful. Thought you'd want to know."

Frances had been furious. She had no idea what Sister St. Jude knew or thought she knew. Flaunting? Rose was sixteen now. Surely her father's identity wasn't still of interest? War widows weren't uncommon. Or was it about Ena? But Frances had been warned. She would always have to be on guard for self-righteous meddling into her single parenthood and her choice of housemate. Most people were naïve about women living together; it was seen as an economic necessity. But the nuns, with their fear of 'particular friendships', might have a different view.

As it turned out Sister St. Jude had become ill and was no longer at the school when Rose had moved to the next class. Rumour was that Sister had cancer. Frances bit her tongue not to say aloud, "Serves the old bitch right."

It was a long bus ride to NDG. Frances talked about Frank and Tommy and their mother, who worked at St. Mary's too. She wanted to give Rose the impression she had eyes in the back of her head and knew everything she was up to.

They got off the bus at Décarie Street and walked arm in arm along Sherbrooke looking in the small shop windows. They went into the park at Girouard and sat on a bench. Plump grey squirrels scurried about.

After a while Frances said, "Let's keep going. I want to get off Sherbrooke Street and take a look at the side streets." They resumed their stroll.

"What are you looking for, Mum?"

"I've been thinking of moving."

Rose stopped and grabbed her mother's arm. "What?"

"Our apartment is too small. And the landlord isn't keeping it up. It seemed like a palace to me when we moved in, but now the building is getting very shabby."

"It's too far from school. I'd have to take the bus. I couldn't stay for after-school clubs." Panic was rising in Rose's voice. "Why didn't you ask me what I thought? I don't want to move." She stood on the sidewalk with her arms clamped against her chest, glaring at her mother.

"Calm down, dear. This isn't going to happen overnight, if it happens at all. I'm just trying to get an idea of other parts of the city."

Rose stopped sulking after they'd walked a few blocks. She was looking at the red brick two story houses and their neat patches of lawn. "There are no apartments here, Mum."

"The girls at bridge last week said there are lots of duplexes in NDG. Let's cross over to the other side of Sherbrooke."

⁂

Frances and Ena were getting along better than they had when she first came home from England. It was clear though, that things between them were different.

One evening they were in the kitchen listening to the news before they started the dishes. Ena said, "Rose is so grown up now. Sixteen – it's hard to believe. She stayed a little girl in my mind the whole time I was away. Seems ridiculous now. And she's babysitting, when that's what you and I used to worry about – who's taking care of Rose? Juggling schedules, taking her to Ellen and Rosemary, begging Goldie and

Jake for a few hours – what a time we had. She hardly needs us now." She looked down at her hands and then up at Frances. "And you hardly need me."

"It's not ..." Tears burned Frances's eyes. "We've both ..." She loved Ena but knew they'd come to a crossroads.

"Don't try to explain, Frances. You don't need to." She scooted her chair closer to Frances and took both her hands.

"I was away four years, you raised Rose, and now we both have chances we never thought possible. Imagine! You can buy a house and I can go to university." She wiped a tear from her lover's cheek.

Ena knew about the inheritance now. Frances had asked Ena to go with her to look at the duplex on Grey Avenue that she was thinking of buying. Despite Ena's lack of domesticity, she had a good eye for detail. She'd been only mildly surprised about the inheritance. Ena's war experience seemed to have made her very open to change.

Ena had said, "What great news! Have you been able to figure out how your aunt knew about you all these years?"

"No and I'm not investigating too closely. I suspect Father Monahan. He would only have to mention the name Dalton in the presence of one of the CND nuns in his parish and it would wend its way to someone in the Mother House and then to my aunt. They never had last names to us, just Sister St. So-and-So, but among themselves they always kept track. Many of the nuns were sisters, aunts and nieces, or sisters of priests. As thick as thieves they are."

Now, they stood at the sink, Frances washing and Ena drying. She had to pile the dishes on the table before putting them away because Frances was in the way. "I hope you find a place with a big roomy kitchen and lots of cupboards. This kitchen is like a closet."

"Careful there, you're verging on the domestic." Frances laughed and swatted her with the dishcloth. "What have you decided about university?"

"I think it will be Toronto."

"Oh. Not McGill?" Frances curbed her disappointment. She'd assumed Ena would be close by.

"No. I want a change of scene. I don't want to be running into the same old crowd, present company excluded."

"Do you mean that, Ena? You wouldn't mind running into me?"

"Of course not. I'll be here to see you and Rose as often as I can. There's an express train every day of the week."

"It's a long way to come."

"We've been pals, and more, for a long time." She moved behind Frances and wrapped her arms around her waist. "And Rose is like a daughter to me. It'll be different but it's not the end. You're my family, the best kind."

26

COURTING

March 12, 1950

Dear Francis,

Thanks for your Christmas card and letter. I'm happy you are well settled in your new place. I laughed when you described yourself as a foreigner at your new hospital. I'm sure being close to home is a great advantage but leaving the security of St. Mary's must have taken some courage. But you know I have always thought of you as courageous.

There was a great turnout for Father Donnelly's funeral. Many graduates from the convent school attended. I saw your mother in the crowd but didn't speak with her. She was laughing with her friends and looked well.

There was sadness of course, but a sense that things were as they should be. After all the misery of the war and the news from Europe about concentration camps, reflections on Father Donnelly's long life of service gave us a sense of comfort and peace.

It's hard to believe that twenty years have passed since I came here. Some of my first altar boys are fathers now.

This brings me to my personal news. I am leaving St. Bridget's. I've taken a teaching position at Loyola College in Montreal. It's a great opportunity for me as well as a great surprise, not being a Jesuit. I guess they thought they could trust me to teach basic mathematics.

I'll be leaving early in the summer. Getting settled won't be difficult, as they have offered me a small apartment in the priests' residence on campus.

I hope that we can have a visit when I arrive. Please write again soon.

Sincerely,

Fr. Thomas

Frances didn't write anything to Thomas about his move. She couldn't sort out her stew of emotions. It had been almost a year since she and Rose had moved to NDG and she had left St. Mary's. It was an exhilarating time that Frances thought of as her liberation. Even though she was successful at St. Mary's and had a lot of friends, she could never quite forget the circumstances of her introduction there and the favour that had been granted her. She'd been accepted for a job at the Homeopathic Hospital based on her work record and good references. It was clean and unmuddied.

Now Thomas brought the past into the present again. She was curious and excited to see him after fifteen years but also on guard, the familiar, constraining feeling that wore on her. Her thoughts and feelings were contrary, not to be trusted. The one thing she was sure of was that she had to be careful. Twenty years ago – when Thomas was the brightest light in her dull life, when thoughts of him made her giddy, made her warm and silky, made her crave his touch – she didn't give a hoot about consequences. She knew about consequences now. In June she sent a short letter and ended on a casual note giving him her telephone number and vague encouragement to call her.

❧

Ena was in Montreal for the Dominion Day weekend. "Here's to Canada and here's to friends." Ena raised her ginger ale and clinked glasses with Rosemary.

Frances and Rose came out from the kitchen. "We'll drink to that," Frances said as she clinked with them and sat down, grabbing a magazine to fan herself.

"I hope it cools off a bit for the fireworks tonight. Rose and her friends are going to watch them over at Westmount Park."

"How's work going, Rose?" Rosemary asked.

"To be honest, it's pretty boring. Answering the phone, filing, taking dictation, all very routine."

"Tell them what you told me last night," Frances said.

"Mum and I talked about me going to university." Rose had her head down. She paused a moment then looked up to see their reactions.

"The best thing I ever did," Ena said.

Rosemary reached out and took Rose's hand "I wouldn't pass up the chance if I got it. If you and Frances can manage, jump in with both feet."

"You don't think I'm too old? I've been out of high school for two years."

"Absolutely not. Don't go looking for excuses, Granny."

Rose went to the kitchen.

Ena said, "She's got a good head on her shoulders, Frances. Don't let her talk herself out of this."

"I think it was you going to Toronto for university that got her thinking."

"What's she interested in studying?" Rosemary asked.

"Social work, whatever that entails. All I know is that they arrange adoptions but there must be more to it than that."

Rose called them to the table. As soon as she finished eating she jumped up. "I've got to get ready. They'll be here in fifteen minutes."

"Get cracking. Rosemary and I will do the dishes."

"Thanks, Aunt Ena. I'll see you when I get back if you're still up." In ten minutes she was sitting on the front steps waiting for her friends.

"Well, it's after five. I guess we can have a decent drink now. Three rye-and-ginger-ales coming up."

Frances passed the amber drinks around and they continued their usual conversation. Everything about their work – their students, patients, bosses, co-workers – was of interest to them. They were working women who liked to talk about it. Frances sometimes joked about the "playpen crowd", women she worked with who had young children.

"If I have to go through one more lunch break listening to them talk about formula and diaper rash I'll go mad."

Family and friends were also grist for the mill. "Danny has the patience of a saint," Rosemary said. "He knows I can't leave Mama and Pop yet. We have the longest engagement on record."

Ellen had had a stroke and still wasn't able to manage the shopping and cooking. Rosemary and Danny were as good as married – he had an apartment in Verdun – but no one mentioned their "arrangements".

"Why can't one of your sisters live with your parents? It's not fair that everything falls to you," Ena said. Frances shot her a withering look. "Okay, okay, none of my business. Previous question struck from the record."

"That's okay. I know you mean well."

The telephone rang in the kitchen and Frances went to answer it. When she came back, Rosemary was standing at the door. "We're going to early Mass in the morning, so we'll have time to get to the picnic. I'd better make tracks."

Ena was peering at Frances, who was acutely aware of the blotches that had surely risen on her neck. "Are you all right? You look sick."

"It's stuffy in here, that's all. Let's walk Rosemary to the bus stop."

⚜

Thomas called the next afternoon at three o'clock. She was sitting at the kitchen table looking at the telephone but she let it ring four times before picking up the heavy black receiver.

"Hello?"

"Frances, how are you?" Thomas didn't bother to say his name. "Are you able to talk now?"

"Yes."

"I'm sorry I bothered you while you had guests. I should have realized you would be busy on a Saturday night and it being Dominion Day too."

"It was only Rosemary and Ena." She had written him about them over the years.

"They wouldn't mind. It's just that ... you took me by surprise."

"How are they? I feel as though I know them."

"They're both fine. Ena just left for the train station. I don't think she'll ever come back to live in Montreal. She thinks the public health nursing department in Toronto would fall apart without her." They both laughed.

"Sorry to be catty. I don't mean to be. Things probably would fall apart. Those ex-military nurses are a force unto themselves."

"And Rosemary? Any progress on the courtship of Danny?"

"All status quo there." She knew the next question would be about her, so she finessed the conversation.

"How are things at Loyola? When did you arrive? Have you started teaching yet?"

"I'd like to tell you all about it. Why don't we have tea soon? Could we meet somewhere?"

She'd expected this but she hesitated a moment. "I'm off duty on Thursday. We could meet at Murray's. It's on Sherbrooke near Claremont Avenue."

"How is Thursday at two?"

"I'll see you then."

"Bye Frances." She could hear a big smile in his goodbye. She put the receiver back on the hook. She stared at it for a few moments before a broad grin split her face.

❦

Frances stood across the street from the restaurant in the doorway of a hardware store. The steep red and white awning provided deep, cool shade. She was looking at the selection of tools and canning supplies in the window. She kept her head down but swung her eyes sideways to the street when she heard the squeal of the bus. Thomas got off and passed in front of the hardware store. His head was turned away from her, looking toward Murray's. He crossed the street and went in.

She knew him immediately. He looked the same as she remembered, tall and slim, but something was different. He was more loose-limbed and confident with a spring to his step that was unfamiliar. She thought back to their tutoring sessions and how held-in and controlled his movements had been. She smiled thinking that the Sisters' admonition to exercise "custody of the senses" extended to all who entered their realm.

He was sitting in a booth near the window and had taken off his lightweight fedora. His hair was muted now with a touch of grey. He rose the instant he saw her.

He reached out and held her at arm's length. "It's wonderful to see you again."

Frances was frozen on the spot, her arm flexed holding her straw purse, his hands burning into her upper arms. Despite all the internal rehearsals she had gone through, she was speechless.

"Let's sit," he said lowering his arms and gesturing toward the booth.

"Yes, of course." She slid into the booth, laid her purse on the seat and took off her gloves. She arranged the folds of her skirt over her lap. "It's good to see you too, Father. I lost my voice for a minute. It's been so long."

"Too long. I was —"

The waitress arrived at the table.

"I always have the toasted fruit loaf. It's slathered in butter," Frances said.

"That settles it then. Tea for two and toasted fruit loaf." He beamed at the waitress, then turned back to Frances.

"Tell me, how are you and Rose doing?"

"She's working at the hospital, as you know, Father, but she—"

"Please call me Thomas."

She carried on as if he hadn't spoken. "She wants something more challenging, so she's looking into social work at McGill. Her high school grades were excellent and she's been saving every penny."

"University? It's hard to believe. I still remember her telling me that knock-knock jokes A big change in fifteen years."

"The whole world has changed, Fa—" She stopped herself from saying Father but couldn't go as far as Thomas. The waitress came with their order. They busied themselves with the tea and toast and the unspoken remained unspoken.

Frances went on. "McGill seems very foreign to me. I asked her to look into Marianopolis College too."

"What does she think about that?"

She raised her hands, palms out, and shook her head. "She's not saying much at all. I just have to stand back, not meddle. She seems to think I've never had to make a decision in my life."

They looked at each other for what seemed a long time. Frances fought not to be the first to look away.

He reached out for her hand. "We know better, though."

After a minute she pulled back her hand and pressed it to her blotchy neck. "This is difficult, Thomas. Let's talk about something else."

His eyes widened and he smiled when she said his name. "Of course."

He told her about his last few months in Newcastle. He talked a lot and Frances was comfortable listening. She encouraged him by asking questions.

"Tell me ... how are Mrs. Charlotte and Sister St. Maureen?"

He filled her in on all the small-town anecdotes making her laugh and capturing her and interest. When the waitress refilled their teapot Frances looked at her wristwatch.

"Heavens! It's four o'clock. I'd better get going, Thomas."

"I've taken up all our time talking about other people. I wanted to hear all about your new job."

"And yours too, Father Professor."

"I'm a mere associate for the time being. May I telephone you? Perhaps we can get together again?"

She hesitated, looking down at her lap for a moment then she looked at him with her head cocked to the right. "Yes. Why not? I've enjoyed this. You're a refreshing change from gossip about hospital politics."

"That's faint praise but I'll take it, Miss Dalton."

⚜

In the following months Frances and Thomas spent many afternoons together, usually walking in the steep, green park just off Sherbrooke Street. Their conversations became less nostalgic, less centred around their past in New Brunswick, and more focused on the present in Montreal.

She was surprised when he spoke at length about the Asbestos strike of nineteen forty-nine. When it was going on a year ago she had read a few accounts and soon forgot about it. Striking miners in a small Quebec town meant nothing to her.

Thomas spread his arms and shrugged. "I know, what's a union strike got to do with someone like me? It was the actions of some clergy that got me interested."

She frowned. He'd lost her.

"The Church and the Quebec government are like this." He held up his crossed fingers. "Duplessis thought the Church would push the union to back down. After all, it is a Catholic union. He thought it would be business as usual in a day."

Frances had no love for Premier Maurice Duplessis. She remembered the extra steps, the paperwork she'd had to go through to get a mortgage. Duplessis was keeping Quebec in the dark and using the Catholic Church to do it.

Thomas faced her and gripped her by the arms, speaking with rapid-fire excitement. "But the Bishops sided with the union – Charbonneau in Montreal, Roy in Quebec City, Desranleau in Sherbrooke – they stood up for the workers. They gave speeches criticizing the bosses. They raised money for the strikers' families."

"I didn't pay a lot of attention," Frances said.

"With the mountains of editorials and reports about the strike it would be easy to miss but many priests paid particular attention. They saw the miners pitted against the companies. A David and Goliath message for the clergy or remembering the Beatitudes that inspired them. Whatever it was, they spoke out."

"What was the outcome?"

"Only small gains for the workers after four months and then Monsignor Charbonneau *resigned* less than a year later even though he was young, popular and healthy. Resigned? I don't buy it. Duplessis made sure he was punished. People won't forget."

He talked about what he hoped could be a new role for the clergy, less tradition-bound and more modern.

"Is that why you left New Brunswick?"

"I think Quebec is on the cusp of change and I want to be part of it."

"Teaching at a Jesuit college?"

He gave a hollow laugh. "It's not ideal but at least I'm closer to things than I was in Newcastle."

✤

Frances and Rose took turns handing out apples and molasses candy kisses to the ghosts, princesses, cowboys, and scarecrows who came to the door. They wore thick woolen cardigans to fend off the chill.

"They'll catch their death out there."

"The thought of the Halloween candy and all that running around keeps them warm enough, Mum. I was never cold when I was trick or treating."

Rose started to speak a few times but kept being interrupted by the doorbell. At eight o'clock she said, "Let's call it a night. We only have a few apples left. I want to tell you my plans."

"Oh?"

"Give me a few minutes." Rose turned off the porch light and the hall light and took the apples to the kitchen. When she came back she said, "Let's sit in the kitchen. They'll get the message."

A fan of pamphlets and papers had been spread across the table. "What's all this?"

Rose cleared her throat and said in a clear voice, "Mum, I've been accepted to the University of Toronto."

"Toronto? You're going to Toronto?" She put her hand on her chest, took a deep breath and stared at the array on the table. "Toronto?"

Rose's tone was sheepish but, at the same time, defensive, the tone she took when she was determined to do something Frances didn't like.

"It's the oldest and the best social work training in Canada. It's all here. You can read about it," Rose said.

"But how will you manage? Who will take care of you?" She bit her tongue. She knew Rose would chafe at that.

"Aunt Ena said she would help me to get settled. I can live with her if I want or I can live in the student residence."

"Aunt Ena? Ena is in on this? You two planned all this behind my back?"

"Mama, please don't be mad. I thought you wanted me to make up my own mind. You've haven't been interested in the pamphlets I've given you."

"You didn't want my opinion!"

"Of course I did! But you've been in your own world. I thought maybe you were regretting leaving St. Mary's. I didn't want to give you another thing to worry about."

"Well, now you have. Of course, I'll worry about you."

She patted her pocket and looked around. "Get my cigarettes for me. They're beside my chair. Please."

Frances glanced at the brochures and looked away. Then she reached for one and started reading. Rose came back and handed her a lit cigarette. Frances continued reading. When she finished, she reached for another and read it cover to cover.

"What do social workers do? Where will you work?"

"I don't know but it will be interesting and more important than what I'm doing now."

"Important? How?"

"There are lots of war widows with children. The government is setting up programs to help them and I think social workers will have a role in that. And also for injured veterans. And all the people coming to Canada, the ones who were displaced by the war."

"I thought the charities and do-good ladies took care of all that?"

"I don't know, but I'm going to find out. I'm going in January."

"In two months?" She reached out and hugged Rose. "What am I going to do without my Rosie?" A few tears came to her eyes, but she brushed them away.

"You'll be the best darned social worker in the world. Now tell me about all the secret plans that you and Ena have hatched. You know she's not much of a cook but I'd rather you were with her than in a residence with strangers."

✤

When she finally went to bed, Frances couldn't sleep. She went from one thought to another and on to another and back to the first, over and over, nothing settled or clear in her mind. Rose's news about Toronto upset the apple cart. They had gotten into a smooth routine since moving to NDG and now everything was changing again.

She knew now that she wanted Thomas in her life. Though they had only a few hours every week, they were the best hours, the time she felt most herself. She knew all the lies and stories she had told herself over the years had been just that, stories.

It was a schoolgirl crush.

He took advantage of me.

We meant nothing to each other.

But what did he mean to her now? How could he fit in her life? Was she satisfied with walks? What else could there even be? He was still a priest. Did she want to continue keeping a secret? Around and around these questions went with no answers.

Then Patsy's voice from their high school days came back to her. The priesthood is forever. It's wrong for you and him. It didn't feel exactly right but surely it couldn't be wrong.

She had been thinking of telling Rose about Thomas, not everything but that he was in Montreal and that they sometimes met for tea. Rose knew of him, from his letters, the ones she had said were boring. But she and Rose had always been a duet, with Ena as their accompanist early on. Frances had never seen men socially. Her world was Rose and the bridge club. What would Rose think of Frances having "dates" with a priest?

She wondered what Thomas would want. He always enquired about Rose but never raised the question of meeting her. Even though he believed he was her father.

27

A Kiss to Build a Dream On

Frances was glad for the dark winter weather. She looked at the Christmas tree, dry, unlit, waiting to be undecorated and tossed in the back lane. She and Rose had had what Frances thought of as their last Christmas together, just the two of them. She was sad and lost but also free and unencumbered. In an instant, guilt was nipping at the heels of that feeling of freedom. She looked at the tree again.

She'd get to it when she felt like it. And she didn't feel like it tonight.

Rose had left a week ago and Frances felt her absence strongest at home. She almost regretted having this weekend off, two whole days by herself. All her daily routines and habits, the special occasions and outings, the decorating and sewing projects – everything was planned and done with Rose in mind. There was so much looseness around her now. She could do anything she wanted. She could have popcorn for supper and pork chops for breakfast if she wanted. She didn't have to set a good example. She didn't have to have an ear out for Rose's key in the door.

Faint strains of music came from the radio in the kitchen. She picked up and read, for the fourth time, Rose's first letter from university. She relayed all the excitement of new beginnings. Everything was special and perfect, with one exception.

You were so right about Aunt Ena's cooking. Last night
she made sausages and eggs. The sausages were underdone and

transparent and the eggs were fried to a crisp. Quite a feat to
underdo (is that a word?) one and overdo the other. When
the time is right, sooner rather than later I hope, I'll offer to do
the cooking.

She's a great help, though, with figuring out whom I need to
speak to about my courses and financial aid. Starting in January
is unusual as I'm out of step with my class – neither fish nor fowl.
I'm taking three electives now and will start the first-year
program in September.

I miss you every day. I'll be home for Easter, just two
months away.

Frances dozed on the sofa. The doorbell startled her. She looked
at her watch, nine o'clock. Probably her neighbour asking her to take
in her milk bottles in the morning so the milk didn't freeze. She
switched on the porch light and opened the door.

"Thomas! What on earth —"

"Good evening, Frances. I was —"

"Is everything all right? What's happened?"

"May I come in? It's freezing out here. I'll explain."

"Of course." She swung the door open, stepped aside, then closed
and bolted it.

Thomas stomped his feet to get the snow off his boots. "Nothing
is wrong, Frances. No need to worry. Danny and I went to a hockey
game at the Forum. I was on the bus on my way home and decided I'd
drop in to see you. I hope you don't mind."

She reached up and patted her hair and straightened her skirt. "No,
of course not. I'm surprised that's all. Dropping by is a down-home
habit. People don't do it here. But I'm not working this weekend so no
need for an early night."

"Give me your hat and coat and sit in here." She gestured to the
living room. "I'll put on the kettle. You look frozen."

"I went past your street, as far as Girouard, and then walked back. I wasn't sure I'd be welcome."

He came into the kitchen and stood behind her. "Your home is very comfortable. I've imagined it many times."

"Except for the dead Christmas tree. I really have to get to that. Pass me the teapot on the shelf behind you."

He passed her the pot and took her free hand in his. "I have a confession. It wasn't a spur of the moment decision, to drop by, I mean."

She put the teapot on the counter and took his other hand. "I didn't think so. I'm glad you're here. I wanted to invite you but didn't know how. Silly to feel awkward."

He put his arms around her and she held him around the waist resting her cheek on his chest. They stood still a few moments.

"The kettle," she said, pulling away.

He reached around her and turned off the gas. "It can wait, Frances." He turned up the radio. "May I have this dance? I think this song is for us."

They glided around the kitchen while Louis Armstrong serenaded them with *A Kiss to Build a Dream On*. Thomas sang along in her ear.

"You're very up-to-date on your music, Father Byrne." Frances laughed.

"Oh yes, Miss. We priests have a lot of long and lonely nights to listen to the radio."

As the song was fading she looked at him and took his face between her hands. "You're not alone tonight."

⁂

The morning light was pouring through the window so Frances knew it was well past her usual waking time. She raised her head a few inches and looked around. The curtains were open, there was a tray of cold tea and half-eaten toast on her dresser, her bed looked like a tornado had gone through it and Thomas was beside her, sleeping soundly. Nothing about this morning was usual.

She propped up her head and leaned over to watch him sleep. His eyes moved rapidly back and forth under his blue-veined lids. A copper shadow spread across his jaw and upper lip. She thought of kissing him and felt an immediate, intense clench between her legs. She reached out with one finger and touched the curve of that lip.

He opened his eyes. "Good morning."

He reached around her and pulled her on top of him. "A perfect morning." He kissed her as he slipped inside. They rocked together in smooth arcs.

They repeated last night's lovemaking but this time without words, only small moans and short, ecstatic gasps. Afterward, the sheen of sweat on her breasts and belly cooled in the morning air. She shivered. Thomas pulled the covers over them and held her close, as they dozed off.

A snowstorm started in the afternoon. The wind howled pulling up vortexes of snow and spinning them around the house.

Frances stood at the living room window watching a car inching its way down the street. "He's mad to try to drive in this storm."

"Must be something pretty important he has to get to."

"I guess we never know what another person has on their plate."

"I'm so happy I dropped by," he said with a laugh. "I can't think of a better place I'd want to be snowbound. Come sit with me." He patted the sofa.

She stretched out and put her head in his lap and looked up at him. "I like you without the collar. It suits you." She reached up and caressed his bare neck.

"Literally and figuratively."

"Go on."

"Well, the first is obvious. I'm more comfortable without it. I'm struggling with the second part though, the meaning. You're the biggest part of that."

He paused for what seemed a long time then he moved Frances out of her lounging position. When she was seated beside him, facing him, he took his hands in hers. "I love you, Frances. I have for a long time. I want to be in your life. I want you in mine."

They sat looking at each other. Her heart pulsed in her ears and she felt the usual blotches on her neck. She was steaming. She had to unknot the kerchief from her neck and undo her top button.

"Whew! Hearing that out loud is ... well, I don't know." She drew him closer and put her arms around his neck. "I love you too, Thomas."

They stayed like that for a few moments then drew apart.

Thomas said, "Being a priest and loving you, wanting you, aren't compatible. That part is easy. It's the rule, the way it is. But even if that weren't the case, if I could be a married priest, I don't know that I'd want that, to still be a priest, I mean."

"Priests have always been in my life. I've never really thought about what it means to be one."

"Well, it's a full-time service job, sort of like nursing but there's no time off, no private life. It's tending the flock, managing the congregation, helping people feel the love of God and not break any of the rules. It's repetitive and often boring."

He took a deep breath and blew it out through pursed lips. "I've never said this aloud."

Frances was surprised. It was like a confession. She touched his knee, "And ..."

"For the believers, I provide a space and the rituals and regalia for them to celebrate their faith. For the shaky ones I'm like a salesman trying to convince them of the quality of the goods, the value of believing. I find it tiresome sometimes and often meaningless. People need more than prayers and rituals. Less fatalism, more opportunities."

"What did you think it would be when you started?" she asked.

He said nothing.

Frances poked him. "Well?"

He looked at her, "I'm embarrassed to say."

"I might be embarrassed to hear it. But we've hidden a lot for a long time."

"I wanted to get away from my family – my father, to be honest – and out of Griffintown. I wanted to wear clean clothes and have indoor plumbing. I wanted to make my mother happy. I wanted to atone for Brendan's death. I was only seventeen, for God's sake. I didn't know what I was committing to. I didn't know what celibacy was." He was almost shouting now.

"So many rules, so much ritual, so much tradition. We spend all our energy repeating the same things over and over to keep people in line but not seeing how we can take action to help people in need."

She got up and motioned for him to stretch out on the sofa. She tried to snuggle behind him, fitting her shape to his, but the sofa was too small. She went in the kitchen and lit a cigarette. The truth-telling had begun.

⚜

The weekend passed in an ecstatic blur. They made love at all hours, ate snacks when they were hungry and talked about their past and their future without constraint. They talked about Rose. Early Sunday evening Frances prepared a meagre meal from what was available. They sat at the table looking at each other.

"This has been the most wonderful weekend of my life," he said. "I don't want to go."

She reached over and kissed him. "Me neither."

"Can I drop by again?"

"You'd better or I'll come to Loyola and make a scene."

"Do you remember dancing to Louis Armstrong on Friday night?"

"Of course. Do you think I'd forget?"

He laughed and shook his head. "This weekend is like the song, a kiss to build a dream on. Only we've had a whole weekend."

He paused, took her hands and pulled her close. "But I want to have a future with you, not just a dream, a real future."

"I can't picture a whole future, Thomas. I just want us to be able to love each other." She stopped short and looked away.

"What is it?" he asked.

"I ... I need to tell you something."

"Sounds serious. Let's go sit in the front room." She started to clear the table. "Leave it Frances. We'll do them later."

She'd gone over it to herself many times but when she started she stalled.

Finally, she spoke.

"It's about Rose. No, no, it's about me. I mean ... In the summer after I left St. Bridget's something happened. Someone hurt me. I mean he ..."

She held her breath and then blurted out, "I don't know if you're Rose's father." She turned away from him and bent over holding her head.

A moment or two passed. "Hurt you?"

She got up and went to the window; she couldn't face him. She spoke in a low voice, "He forced himself on me. I look at Rose and I see you, I want her to be yours, but I'm not sure."

"Forced himself? You mean ...?" It was a question, but it was said almost like he was saying it to himself.

"Don't ask me anymore," she said.

They sat disconnected, in their own thoughts, for a few moments. He moved closer to her and put his arms around her. Neither of them could put their thoughts into words.

"It's late, work tomorrow. I'm sorry I ruined our beautiful weekend but I had to tell you."

"You didn't ruin it. You couldn't. It's not simple but it doesn't change the fact that I love you."

Frances lay awake for hours after Thomas left. This weekend they had crossed a line into unknown, forbidden territory. All the things that Frances had never voiced even to herself rose to the surface.

Thomas was pursuing her and she was not resisting. Why should she? The vow of celibacy was his, not hers. She wasn't doing anything wrong. But why did it feel wrong? It was the question that had lain under the surface from the beginning.

28

DREAMS AND NIGHTMARES

THOMAS WOULD HAVE liked to talk to Father Monahan, his old mentor, but he had died a few years ago. He hadn't kept in close contact with any of the men he had been with in the seminary. And his fellow teachers at Loyola were definitely out. They were congenial with each other but nothing more.

The person he was obliged to speak to was Father McCallum, the rector of the college, his superior and his employer. He knew not to expect a warm show of support and understanding.

"This is very serious Father Thomas."

"Yes, Father, it is."

"How long has this been going on, this ... this "loss of faith"?" He said the last words as though he'd sucked a lemon.

"During the last few years ..."

"Last few years? Dear God. Go on."

"Yes. I questioned my purpose in parish work. The congregation was happy with me but I was not happy. More importantly, I felt like an imposter."

"You're well-named, Father Thomas."

He said nothing about his namesake: Saint Thomas, the doubter.

"So you thought teaching might ... what? Inspire you? That's ridiculous. Teaching mathematics is no way to restore your faith and improve your vocation." He drummed his thick fingers on his blotter.

Thomas sat with his head bowed and was silent.

"I'm very disappointed." Father McCallum stared out the window at the leafless trees and the few patches of brown grass showing through the melting snow.

He turned back to Thomas. "But better now than later. Your responsibilities at the college will cease in June."

Thomas snapped up his head and looked at Father McCallum.

"You're surprised? There's no question of you staying on. Impossible. You are in daily contact with our youngest, most impressionable students."

"Yes, of course, Father. I understand."

"I'll inform the Bishop's office. I'll send for you when I hear from them. I expect they will send you on a retreat, offer counselling, and then reassign you."

He leaned forward. "Is it safe to assume you have spoken to no one else about this?"

"Yes, Father. You are the only one."

"Keep it that way. You're not the first and you won't be the last but we must preserve the sanctity of our Holy Orders and the integrity of Mother Church. At all costs. Do I make myself clear?"

"Yes, Father. I will be discreet."

"You must have lessons to prepare." Father McCallum turned to the window.

⚜

"And that was it. I haven't heard another word from him or the Bishop's office."

"He didn't ask you anything more?" Frances said.

"No, just what I told you." Thomas paced the kitchen floor.

"He sounds awful, to me. Not a bit of concern or support."

"Oh, he's concerned, but not about me. He's running a parish and a college. I'm a major problem now and he's passing it up the line. The sooner he sees the back of me the better."

"Do you regret it?"

He came back to the table and pulled his chair close to hers. He took both her hands. "Not at all. Have you ever seen a piece of amber?"

"I don't think so. Why?"

"It's hardened tree resin. Sometimes when it is still soft an insect, say a fly, will get trapped in the sticky resin. It hardens and then the fly is preserved, trapped forever.".

"And ...?"

"I'm trapped, Frances. I'm the fly." He stood, pacing again but then looked at his wristwatch. "I'd better get back. I don't have more classes today but ... I'm under scrutiny now. Probably my imagination, but still."

⚜

The exterior of the Miséricorde Hospital hadn't changed, not since it was built in the mid-nineteenth century. More effort was evident on the interior. An exuberant young nun showed Frances in and asked her to wait in the same small room she was shown into twenty-one years earlier. The dark Madonna was gone, a painting of tulips and daffodils in its place. The room had a fresh coat of paint and sheer white curtains. Frances didn't think the new décor, however, would alleviate the misery of a young woman seeking the hospital's particular help.

The door opened. "What a pleasure to see you Frances." Sister Dolorosa looked around. "*Mais*, you have not brought *petite* Rose to see me." She turned down the corners of her mouth in an exaggerated frown and then laughed.

"Rose is still in Toronto, Sister. Thank you for seeing me. It means a lot to me." She handed her a brilliant purple African violet. "For your windowsill."

"Thank you. It's a beauty. I realized you must have something important on your mind, more than you could say in a Christmas card. Come, come, let's sit."

They had kept in regular touch over the years and had moved beyond their penitent and mentor roles. Sister had been very happy when Frances became a maternity nurse and liked to take small credit for her success.

"What is it, my dear? Even though you are no longer a penitent here, you can rely on my discretion."

"I want to tell Rose about her father, Sister. It is time."

"I don't see how I can help."

"I would like you to look at my record, about the particulars of Rose's birth. I didn't pay enough attention then, and I knew nothing of obstetrics."

"And we did not, even now we don't, encourage penitents to learn much. We ask for blind faith and ignorance. But what are you getting at?"

"I need to know if Rose was a full-term baby, if there's enough information in my record that you could say so with confidence."

Frances looked away and let out her breath. A few moments passed. Sister was silent.

Frances couldn't look at her. "Shame has followed me my whole life, Sister. Every time I think I've moved past it something will happen that brings it to the surface again."

"What is your shame?"

"I think Rose's father is the man I love, a good man. But there was another, a man who forced himself on me."

Sister didn't miss a beat. "One worthy, the other unworthy."

"Yes."

"These ... incidents? They were so close together you can't know for sure?"

Frances bowed her head. "Nineteen days."

After a long pause, Sister shrugged. "I can look. But some records are scanty. If I find anything I'll let you know."

"Thank you, Sister.

"Be patient. I'll need to think up a good reason to be looking into the past. Sister Rosario guards those records like they were the Vatican bank."

"I've waited a long time. I can wait some more."

Three weeks later they were back in the small room. Frances was dismayed to see Sister had no files with her. But before she sat, she reached into her capacious pocket and pulled out some folded sheets of paper.

"I'll show you what I learned and you can make up your own mind."

They pored over the papers.

"*Et bien?* What do you think?" Sister asked.

"I don't understand all the French. Please translate for me."

"The facts, weight and length, are here." She pointed to some numbers.

"Rose was big, wasn't she?"

"Eight pounds, not so big, but this may be more important." She indicated some handwriting that was impossible for Frances. "Sister Violette describes how lively and alert your little one was. She's almost poetic: *une belle chevelure roux châtain, les yeux brillants.*"

"Her hair and eyes?"

"Yes, a lot of beautiful red hair. No, not exactly red. I don't know the right word in English." She continued. "And bright eyes. And she also says the baby would need her nails trimmed soon."

Frances couldn't contain her smile. Her whole face lit up remembering. "She was full term wasn't she Sister?"

"Look at my notes from the clinic."

The page listed Frances's weight gain and girth. "I was carrying her low before she was born."

"Yes. But it's impossible to say with complete confidence. You know that, Francoise. *Tu t'accroches désespérément à un semblant d'espoir.*" Grasping at straws.

Frances walked aimlessly through downtown, not noticing any of the shop windows that usually caught her eye. Sister was right. It could be either of them.

⚜

It was their winter of love. Thomas got away from the college as often as possible and they spent the time enthralled with each other. Though they knew of each other's disappointing efforts – to leave the priesthood and to determine Rose's paternity – they ignored them and clung to some shred of hope that they could have a future.

One day in early April, they sat on a park bench on Mount Royal. A sloping carpet of daffodils spread in front of them and beyond it, lay the city skyline. Spring was unfolding. As the cycle of new life accelerated around them, it emphasized the inertia of their own situation. Thomas had heard nothing from the office of the Bishop.

"I remind myself of one of the horses my father used to have," said Frances.

"How come?"

"Papa would get the mare ready and then think of something he'd forgotten, hitch her to the fence and go back into the barn. She'd start going forward a few steps, feel the rein, go back and settle for a moment then start going forward a few steps again. She'd paw at the ground, shake her head then settle. Ready to move but held back."

"Can you picture us going forward?"

She hesitated, pulling her collar tight around her neck "No, not really."

Thomas deflated. "I have to confess, I can't either." He paused, "I love you, Frances, with all my heart. But I am tied to the Church and can't be untied easily just because it's what I want."

"And I'm tied to Rose."

His face was wet with tears. "My daughter. I should be tied to her too, but I don't even know her." Frances almost reminded him about the uncertainty of Rose's paternity but thought better of it. She took him in her arms and held him until his sobs wore him out.

She said nothing more until after they got back to her place. They had a small meal of beans on toast and then sat in the living room with their tea.

"Rose will be home in ten days," Frances said.

They knew Rose's being home for the spring and summer meant the end of their secret trysts.

"This is a nightmare I've created. I never should have left Newcastle. I was a fool to think I could ignore twenty years of my vocation and vows."

"That's a lot of I's. What about me? What about us?"

"It's a dream, can't you see? You don't want to risk your family on a dream with me. I have nothing to offer you; no home, no job, no future. Nothing."

He jumped up, almost knocking over the coffee table, strode across the room to the window, and then paced in front of the window, clearly agitated.

She stared into the distance for a few moments, stunned by his vehemence. Then, "Come, help me with the dishes." She picked up their cups and went to the kitchen.

He didn't follow so she washed, dried and put away the dishes by herself; she was grateful for the short reprieve. She went back to talk to him but the front door was ajar. He was gone.

29

NOTHING BUT THE TRUTH

FRANCES MULLED OVER Thomas's words all the time. He had said their relationship was a dream. No, a nightmare. Risky. No future. No way forward.

They had spoken on the phone often since he left her home so abruptly. He was contrite, apologetic but adamant that they had embarked on a fool's journey.

"We can't undo the last twenty years without you getting hurt. I could give up my priestly responsibilities and nobody need be any the wiser. That's the way the Church operates, no big announcements. But you ... you have Rose, your sisters, the Egans, your nurse friends. So many people will judge you. And for me? I won't let you do it."

He was like a phonograph needle stuck in a groove. She couldn't convince him of her love or of the freedom and ease she felt being with him.

But it was so muddled. What did she want? Why was she so confused? She was tidying her knitting basket one evening undoing knots of yarn and as she pulled strands apart it came to her. Her motherhood might be entangled with Thomas – although she now accepted Sister Dolorosa's verdict that she would never know for sure – but she could separate the two. She thought of Sister's words, a desperate hope. She was tired of it.

As much as she loved Thomas, she didn't owe him anything, least of all her daughter. Frances thought of what she had told Father Monahan years ago, that she wanted to raise Rose on her own. And she had. She was sure now what she would do.

✤

Rose came home on a Saturday afternoon. The station was mobbed but even with all the jostling Frances picked out her daughter the instant she came through the wide doors. Her hair was pinned up in a sleek French roll that seemed to add inches to her tall frame. Her green tweed suit flattered Rose's slim waist and long legs. She caught Rose's eye with a discrete wave. Rose approached smiling and gave her mother a bear hug. Frances picked up Rose's suitcase and they headed toward the exit.

"You're a real fashion plate with that hairdo."

Rose patted the side of her head. "Do you like it?"

"I do, very elegant. And you look much more rested than you did at Easter."

"C'mon Mum, those exams knocked the stuffing out of me. I was cramming every night past midnight."

"And?" Frances gave her a wide-eyed look prodding her to continue.

Rose beamed. "First class on all three courses."

Frances grabbed Rose's hand and gave it a quick squeeze. "Good for you. I'm very proud."

As they came in the front door, Frances looked at her watch. "Perfect timing. I put the chicken in the oven just before I left. Let's get the vegetables on and we'll have a homecoming celebration supper."

Rose put her suitcase in her room and went to the kitchen. "What a treat to have roast chicken. Is it stuffed?"

"Well of course it is. What's the point otherwise?" They both laughed. That was Ena's catch-phrase when she stated her expert opinion on any given topic. "Look in the pantry, dear."

Frances had made a layer cake piling it with stiff peaks of Seven-Minute Boiled Frosting that gleamed in the kitchen light as Rose pulled open the pantry door. Rose swiped a taste from the bottom edge of the cake and smacked her lips. "Chocolate?"

They intoned in unison, "What's the point otherwise?" and burst out laughing.

After supper Rose sat back and rubbed her belly. "It wasn't that long ago everything was rationed and now we have a whole roast chicken *and* chocolate cake. I'm stuffed."

Rose was full of stories about the university, her classmates, the professors, and Toronto in general. She wound down, yawning, just as they were finishing the dishes. Frances almost lost her nerve but she was determined to carry through with her plan.

She gave the table a final wipe and took off her apron. "Let's take our tea into the living room. I want to tell you something."

They sat side by side on the sofa. Frances turned toward Rose and held her hand.

"When you were younger you used to ask questions about when you were born."

Rose stared at Frances her brow furrowed, silent.

"I told you your father had died, that I was a widow. But ... well, that wasn't true. I ... I was never married, Rose."

"Never? ... What?"

Frances steeled herself and continued. "I left home when I was eighteen to enter the CND convent."

"What —"

Frances waved her hand. "That's a different story for another time. Soon after I got there I discovered I was pregnant. Aunt Rosemary and Nanny Ellen helped me get into a hospital called the Miséricorde. That's where I had you."

"That place on Dorchester Street?" Frances and Rose had been to the Mis a few times over the years to visit Sister Dolorosa.

"Yes. My friend Sister Dolorosa was there with me when you were born."

"So ... if my father didn't die, who is he, where is he?"

"I'll tell you as much as I know."

Rose looked baffled. "What does *that* mean?"

"In the summer after I finished school I had two ... experiences with men." She took a big breath. "One was with a nice young man. We were sweet on each other. One thing lead to another and ... well, you know."

"Mum, you were seventeen!"

"Almost eighteen. Do you want me to go on?"

"Of course. Who was he? What was his name?"

"Let me finish." She took another deep breath. "Two weeks later something horrible happened. A man ... hurt me. He raped me."

"Mum!"

"Let me finish. The long and short of it is I do not know who your father is." Frances turned away from her daughter and began to cry.

Rose was stunned, still as a stone.

After a few moments Frances turned back to her daughter and took her in her arms. "I'm sorry."

Rose let Frances hold her a few moments then she squirmed out of her mother's embrace. "It's a crime. Did you tell anyone? He's a criminal."

She sat bolt upright. "He might be my father?"

She got up and paced in front of Frances. "You know them. You know their names. Who are they, Mama?"

Frances shook her head, her face wet with tears.

Rose yelled. "Why did you tell me this? What good does it do me?"

"I don't know. I don't know. Was it a mistake?"

Rose ignored the question. She stood over Frances, her face flushed. "You won't tell me who they are. Will you tell me anything about them?"

Frances paused. "Yes. The man who raped me was young, angry, and drunk at the time. He's not like that now. He's just an ordinary man."

Frances looked at her daughter. Rose was holding her head and shaking it from side to side. She spoke in a flat tone. "And? The other?"

"The other man ... became a priest."

"My father might be a priest? This is too much!" Rose threw up her arms. "I can't do this now. But we're not finished with it." She spun on her heel and stormed to her room, slamming the door.

Frances sat unmoving as the daylight faded and the gloomy evening wore on.

Rose was standoffish after her mother's revelations. She went to her summer job and went out in the evenings with her friends. Frances didn't know how to talk to her. She was miserable and regretted saying anything.

⚜

It was mid-May, a warm evening. "Let's go for a walk," Frances said.

Frances was relieved when Rose picked up her purse and headed to the door. "Okay. I'm ready."

They were climbing the gentle slope in the park on Girouard Street in silence. "Rose, please talk to me. You can't stay mad forever."

Rose said, "There's something I don't understand. Why didn't you tell your mother? When you were raped, or at least when you found out you were pregnant. You just snuck off. Weren't you scared? Why didn't you ask Grandma for help? I would ask you."

How could Frances explain her family life without sounding petulant or whiney? "It's hard to compare our lives."

"What do you mean?"

"It was long ago. I don't like to think about all that."

"Now you're shutting me out. Please, Mum." Her tone said she wasn't buying it.

Rose sat on a bench and patted the spot beside her.

"You know I was sick for a few months when I was seven or eight.

Typhoid was contagious. There were no antibiotics then. I made a lot of work for everyone as well as, I suppose, a lot of worry."

"What kind of work?"

"I had to have my own bed, my own dishes. In the beginning I vomited a lot and soiled the bed linen so there was a lot of laundry, too, that had to be done separately with no running hot water or even a proper washing machine."

She stared into the past. "I missed school for months. Someone had to keep an eye on me all the time. I was the third daughter and sickly at that. Not much use to a farming family."

"That's horrible. Did someone say that to you?"

"No, but that's how I felt. So I think it was because of that time, being dependent on them and feeling so embarrassed, that I became determined to take care of myself, not to ask for help." She hesitated. "And I was ashamed to have let it happen. I couldn't bear to see my parents' faces. The disappointment."

"But you were raped."

Frances told her about Isabelle, the girl who was banished to Newfoundland. "You know that girls who get in trouble, regardless of how, are treated badly. When the chance came for me to hide myself away, I took it."

Frances had never forgotten Jacqueline, the girl who had killed herself at the Mis. In fact she sometimes dreamed of that horrific night. But Rose didn't need to know everything.

"What a horrible secret", Rose said.

Frances turned to face her daughter. "It was horrible for a while. But it's been the best for the last twenty years – because of you." She took Rose's hand and squeezed it.

Rose said, "Tell me more about when you were a girl."

Frances talked about her sisters going to boarding school and being left at home with Jimmy, living in the glare of his wild and reckless personality.

"Uncle Jimmy? Wild?"

"He was a different boy then. Rita and their brood have clipped his wings. A good thing, too." She paused, "It's getting dark. Let's go home."

Rose wanted to know more so they sat on the front porch. Frances's tales of boarding school were brighter. She told Rose about sitting at the dormitory window with Patsy after lights-out, going over their days and imagining their futures.

"I thought boarding school was for rich people like that place in Westmount," Rose said. "Miss So and So's."

"Wait here." Frances went to her bedroom and pulled out a dusty shoebox from under her bed. She rifled through it until she found what she was looking for. She handed some papers to Rose.

Rose looked at the sombre, black and white portrait on the funeral card, then, turned it over to read the back. She flipped through her great aunt's necrology that Sister St. Rita had mailed to Frances. "Dalton? Is she related to us?"

"She was my father's sister, your great aunt. She's the reason Josephine, Bernadette and I went to St. Bridget's. Don't waste too much time on the necrology. It's a florid bit of congregational aggrandizement."

"Mum, you're so unsentimental," Rose said, giving Frances a gentle poke in the ribs.

They talked late into the night. Frances had been reluctant, had thought the past would be of no interest to Rose. In truth, she hadn't been interested in it herself. She was surprised at the relief, the lightness it brought.

"Boarding school suited me. I liked the three R's – rules, regulations and routines. I tried never to draw attention to myself. My aunt was the Provincial Superior, after all, so the nuns' expectations were high. A loose shoelace was practically a mortal sin. Imagine being pregnant."

"She had a lot of sway."

"Patsy called her the ghost. I guess you could say she set the course of my life, and yours too. When I fled from the Mother House it was mainly because of her. I was in her house, by her good grace. I couldn't bear to face her wrath and that of all the Sisters who thought I was destined to be a nun."

Rose put her arm around her mother's shoulder and pulled her close. "You have more secrets than that gossip Hedda Hopper."

"But I'm better at keeping them." They laughed then fell into silence.

Frances pulled back and looked at her daughter. She realized that the nuns' Rule of Silence she had lived under years before had become a lifelong habit. She withheld things, left much unspoken. "I worry about how you're taking all this."

"I'm okay. Knowing you have such big secrets and that you kept them for so long makes you ... what's the word ... mysterious. More than being just a Mum and a nurse. But a priestly father, maybe, and a ghostly aunt are about my limit. Tell me that's it."

Frances noticed Rose had left out the possible criminal father but said nothing about it.

"Just one more bit. Then it's time for bed."

"Mum!"

She told Rose about the inheritance she'd received from Sister Superior St. Benedict. "I used most of it as a down payment for our house. So, we are living by her grace still, but I believe, with compassion and forgiveness."

30

FLIGHT

THOMAS SPENT HIS free time in the chapel or walking around the college grounds. He had been meditating about vocation and reciting the mysteries of the rosary but Frances was always in his thoughts. He ached for her.

The office of the Bishop had issued its orders. Thomas spoke to a functionary on the telephone who told him in a cold, distant tone to report to St. Christopher House near the seminary on Sherbrooke Street on June twenty-fifth. Thomas had heard of the place. It was a retreat centre for priests.

"With all due respect, Father, the school term here is not over until June twenty-ninth."

"Be assured, Father, your superior, Father McCallum, is aware that you must be at St. Christopher's on the twenty-fifth. I'd advise you to speak with him and make plans to wrap things up."

"And after my stay at St. Christopher's?" Thomas regretted asking the question. It revealed how directionless and at their mercy he felt.

"You are getting ahead of yourself, Father. Good day." He had hung up before Thomas could say another thing.

He had no appetite for what lay ahead – so-called Spiritual Direction – and no hope that it would do any good. Couching the problem as a lack of faith was a lie he could no longer tell. His faith wavered from time to time but he had not lost it.

The rule of celibacy was not about faith. But it was everything to the Church authorities. Admitting that he had fathered a child with a young woman, whose welfare had been entrusted to him, sickened him. That Frances didn't tell him she was pregnant and raised Rose alone; that she loved him; that they wanted to be together – none of it would mean anything to the Church.

His transgression was paramount. His priesthood, his sacrament of Holy Orders was a sham. Everything he had done as a priest after that blissful, sinful afternoon – the baptisms, the confessional absolutions, the marriages, the anointing of the sick, the celebration of the Eucharist – was null and void. If he admitted it he would certainly be banished from the priesthood. He wasn't worried about public embarrassment and shame. He knew the Church never admitted that priests were anything but perfect Vicars of Christ. The problem of Father Byrne would be dealt with discreetly.

⚜

He would leave Loyola College in a week. He met Frances at Murray's to say goodbye and they struggled to keep up a conversation.

"What do you think it will be like?" Frances asked.

Thomas was desultory. "Prayer, meditation, confession, counselling about the meaning of vocation, that sort of thing."

"It's odd to think of priests going to confession like the rest of the poor sinners." Frances laughed a little, trying to lighten the dreary conversation.

"Oh, you think we don't sin?"

She blushed but carried on. "You told me a few months ago that you didn't like parish work. Are there other things, other assignments you could do?"

"I don't know, I don't know." His voice was rising, "I have no idea what I want or how to be a better priest." He caught himself and lowered his voice. "I don't know."

Thomas promised to write if he was able to. "I think it will be restricted at first but I'll do my best."

He told Frances what he thought might happen if he owned up to his connection with her; she might be required to appear before the Church authorities to support his reason for seeking release him from the priesthood.

Frances said, "I can't imagine the Church powers-that-be would want to question me or be interested in my story. I don't think a woman could say anything to interest them or sway their opinion."

"Ouch."

"It's true." She gave him a hard stare with one eyebrow cocked.

He put up his hands. "No arguments from me. But ..." He stopped and looked into his teacup.

"But what?" She reached over, rattled his cup and took his hand. "You're wondering if I'd do it, go present myself to them? No, I wouldn't."

He looked at her, his eyes wide, waiting for more.

Frances said, "I made a decision. I've told Rose about what happened and that I don't know for certain who her father is. So I definitely won't tell a pack of Bishops that you —"

Thomas interrupted. "But I wanted —"

"It's too complicated, Thomas. You may or may not be Rose's father. We have to accept that."

Thomas had been speechless, not looking at her.

Frances had continued, "You said you weren't sure you would want to be a priest even if you could be a married one. Remember? You need to sort out your vocation without considering me or Rose."

⚜

Thomas hadn't told Frances his plan. He had written to his sister in Hamilton three weeks before his last day at Loyola College asking if he could visit her, nothing more. On the morning he was expected at the retreat centre, he left the college after the six o'clock Mass with no ceremony or fanfare, the same way he had left St. Bridget's almost a year before. He headed downtown to the train station. Before boarding he went into the washroom, removed his clerical collar and black shirt, put on a plain white shirt and striped necktie and put the black shirt and collar in the trash. He reached for the door handle and stopped. He went back and retrieved the collar, tucking it into his small bag.

After he boarded the train, leaving behind Loyola, his responsibilities, and Montreal, relief overcame him, like he had made a narrow escape. The train journey was long and his thoughts soon turned to Frances and Rose. His farewell with Frances had been painful. She had become so determined, so detached. "Sort out your vocation," she had said. And she had cut off his hopes of connecting with Rose. She did say she loved him but she had set him adrift. An escape yes, but no, not a relief.

Her reminder of what he had said about being a priest, struck home. Was it true he would want to leave the priesthood if Frances wasn't in his life? Despite his love for her, his faith was still alive. And despite his complaints about the monotony of the rituals, he knew he was a good priest. He had helped many of his parishioners live more faithful, hopeful, and charitable lives.

He got a taxi outside the Hamilton station. Despite the rain, he asked the driver to let him off at the corner of his sister's street. He needed some time to collect his thoughts. Going to his sister was an abstraction he had held at bay but now, panic rose in him and he felt like a fool. They were almost strangers.

The wind and rain picked up. He hunched his shoulders and walked until he found her address. A light was shining through the sheer white curtains of the front room. He straightened up and rang the bell.

The door opened immediately. Had she been waiting for him? Had she seen him standing in the rain? More the fool.

They stood still, smiling nervously, looking each other up and down. Thomas hadn't seen Nora since his ordination, twenty-three years ago. She had been thin and pasty, still in mourning for their mother. She had worn black and was solemn and reticent. The contrast to her present appearance couldn't have been more dramatic. She was stout with cropped pale ginger hair and outfitted as if for a Christmas play in a bright red pleated skirt and a shiny green blouse. Her alarming make-up consisted of dark brown arched eyebrows and traffic-stopping red lips.

Nora's eyes darted from his face to his neck and back to his face. She peered into his eyes, looking for something familiar, her mouth agape.

"Can I come in Nora? It's pouring out here."

She stood aside and motioned with her arm never lessening her scrutiny.

They were standing in the front hall. She was still staring and hadn't asked him in any further. He said, "Thank you for letting me come. I've left my last assignment. I have nowhere else to go."

"Jesus, Mary, and Joseph." She took him by the hand, dragged him into the living room, and pushed him into an overstuffed armchair in the corner. She strode out and returned a minute later with a bottle of scotch and two small glasses. She poured some and handed him a glass. "Tell me everything."

Thomas had decided to give her the loss of faith story. Nora took it in stride. "Can't say I blame you. I'm still a Catholic, but barely. You know, Christmas and Easter. I look at the nuns at my school and wonder how they stick with it."

"We can talk more about that later. Tell me about yourself and your life here."

She didn't need any more encouragement. He learned about her grade four students and their percussion band, her choir, and her boyfriend Stanley. Stelco Stanley he calls himself. Four more years and he'll retire."

Awkward silence. Nora continued. "Stelco is the big steel plant here. Just about everyone works there. But you'll learn more about it later." She patted his knee. "But I have a question. Did you ever go back to Griffintown after you left New Brunswick?"

"No. The last time I saw anyone I knew was in 1935 when I went home for Father Monahan's fiftieth anniversary celebration. Griffintown is a ghost town now. So many have moved away and the slummiest buildings have been demolished. You wouldn't recognize it."

Nora had lots of interests and no reluctance to talk about them. She also filled him in about their brothers. They avoided talking about him and his plans. He was grateful. In the evenings he pored over the classified ads in the newspaper. He knew Nora noticed, but neither of them mentioned the future.

⚜

Nora invited Stanley to dinner the second week Thomas was there. "He's dying to meet you. He's never met any of our family."

"What did you tell him about me? I mean, being a priest?"

"Stanley was raised Catholic, too, but he's like me, not practising. I told him you are a priest but you're taking a break. You can speak for yourself."

The nickname, Stelco Stanley, had given rise to many images in Thomas's mind – hard, cold, strong, dirty – and none of them matched the man who came to dinner. Stanley was the tallest and thinnest man Thomas had ever met. Unlike many tall people, he did not stoop, and had broad straight shoulders supporting a long slender neck. The back and sides of his head were shaved and he had a thick black brush cut.

"Stanley, this is my brother, Tommy; Tommy, my friend Stanley.

Stanley extended his hand. "Welcome. It's a pleasure to meet you. I imagine Tommy is a family moniker. Are you more accustomed to Thomas?"

"Yes." He was moved by Stanley's genuine warmth and welcome. When they sat down to eat Thomas bowed his head. Stanley noticed. "Thomas, Nora and I don't usually say grace but we'd be happy if you would, this once. Nora reunited with family is a special occasion."

Thomas started the usual grace. "Bless us, O Lord, and these, thy gifts ..." He stopped and looked at his sister and Stanley. "I think I can do better than that." They both nodded. "Let us give thanks for the companionship and generosity of family and friends, for this meal prepared by Nora and for the fruits of her garden. Amen."

"Amen. My garden never got a mention in a prayer before."

When dessert was finished, Nora struck a bargain. "I'll do the dishes —" Stanley started to object but she raised her hand. "— if you two will stake the tomatoes and water the garden. The stakes are under the back steps and the twine is in the red bucket."

"It sounds like she had this all planned, right, Thomas?"

They worked in silence, savouring the golden evening light.

"I think we've about finished our assignment. Let's go for a walk." Stanley turned off the water and coiled the hose. He rolled down his sleeves and put in his cufflinks. Thomas stored things under the steps.

"Nora tells me you've been scouring the classifieds. Can I assume the current hiatus in your priesthood is not temporary?"

Thomas frowned and looked at him.

"You're right. I need a job. But the classifieds all seem to want young men or veterans." He pulled out his cigarettes and offered one to Stanley. They paused to light them and continued around the corner.

"Stelco is the biggest employer here. Thousands and thousands of workers."

"I don't know anything about steel mills. A far cry from parish work."

"It is indeed. But it's not all about production, you know. There's accounting – that's what I'm in – and personnel, inventory, distribution, payroll. And on and on."

They stepped onto the street to bypass some girls skipping on the sidewalk. They were very earnest chanting the counting rhyme, their braids bouncing up with each skip.

"Even so." Thomas didn't know what more to say. As much as he felt a puzzling kinship with Stanley, he was accustomed to the distance, the aloofness of the priesthood. Though he had freed himself in one way, he felt constrained. He was still a priest after all.

"The belching smokestacks and rail yards – the Stelco Works – might give you the impression that it's all production but there is a lot of office work that keeps it all going." Stanley stopped and looked at his wristwatch. "I think Nora will have the kitchen all tidied up. Let's head back." He laughed and gave Thomas a gentle nudge with his bony elbow.

The three of them sat on the front steps for an hour and then Stanley said it was time to go. He and Nora made plans to meet at Gore Park for a concert later in the week.

"It was a pleasure to make your acquaintance, Thomas. I hope you'll think about what I told you about Stelco. It's not all hardhats and blow torches."

"Thanks. I will. I have a lot to think about. More than I knew." He extended his hand.

He and Nora watched Stanley stride down the street and around the corner. "You okay, Tommy?"

He let out a long breath. "Yeah. Stanley seems like a great guy. He took my renegade status all right. Not everyone will." They watched the night settle down on the street. "What do you think of Stelco?'

"It's what keeps this place going. More than half of my pupils are Stelco kids. If Stanley thinks there would be a spot for you, I'd bet on it. Did you notice his cufflinks?"

"I did. Pretty fancy."

"Thirty-Five Year Service Award. Thirty-five years, Tommy. Stanley knows a thing or two about Stelco. And just about everyone who works in the offices. You can trust him."

31

UNDER SUSPICIOUS CIRCUMSTANCES

THOMAS'S FIRST LETTER came the last week of June, less than two weeks since they'd said goodbye. But it was from Hamilton, Ontario. Instead of going to the retreat at St. Christopher House he had walked away ... but from what? The priesthood? No, she knew enough that he would have to go through some process to become laicized. Whether he wore a collar or performed the sacraments, he was still a priest.

But he didn't write anything about that. Just that he couldn't face the retreat and he'd write again. Was her challenge to him – to work out his commitment to the priesthood without considering her or Rose – the cause of his defection?

After that, he wrote often, sometimes three letters a week. He told her about his life in Hamilton. She answered every letter even if it was only a few lines. She thought of all the walks they had taken when he was at Loyola and marvelled at the fact they had had so much to say. How easy it was then and how difficult now. Sometimes when she was writing, struggling to strike the right tone, her mind said over and over, come back to me, come back to me.

Thomas had taken a temporary summer job at a company called Stelco, working in the payroll office and then in September he'd been hired as a math teacher at a high school. He wrote in great detail about the school and his students but no more about them or their future.

She missed him every moment, his smile, his touch, his optimism. But he was a priest and he belonged to the Church. Walking away didn't change that.

Christmas came and went. Winter dragged on. A new job came up at work in January, supervisor of the out-patient clinics, and Frances got it. She liked the regular hours, day shifts with no weekends. Then in February, Thomas sent a Valentine's Day card with a letter inside.

Dear Frances,

    Fond wishes on this day that celebrates love and romance. I love you very much and miss you. My time in Hamilton, almost eight months now, has given me the opportunity to think about many things, especially my vocation and us. By us I mean you and me, not Rose. She is very much a part of you but I accept that she can never be my daughter, even if she is. I love you. I have since our Newcastle days.

    I have applied to the office of the Bishop in Montreal for laicization. I do not know how long the process will take, but when it is finished and I am free I hope we can make plans to be together. Montreal? Hamilton? Anywhere so we can be together.

    All my love,

    Thomas

Frances was thrilled. 'Make plans to be together'. She wasn't sure what kind of proposal he was making but it was movement forward. He had raised her expectations again. But throughout that spring very little happened. He wrote that he had completed some forms.

Then the office of the Bishop requested an interview in Montreal. Her heart leapt thinking they would see each other, but he told her he couldn't take time off work to go to Montreal. He had asked the office of the Bishop if he could have an interview in Hamilton or if he could delay going to Montreal until after the end of June when his duties were over for the summer. She was dismayed.

What is he playing at?

✠

The tug of the locomotive pressed Frances into her seat as the train left Central Station and she relaxed. She was going down home. She didn't know the state of affairs with Thomas and his application and she was weary of always expecting something and being let down. She had a troublesome feeling – an instinct maybe – that she couldn't name.

It was her first time going home without Rose and she was lonely and light-hearted at the same time. When she stepped off the train she put down her suitcase and took a deep breath. Bernadette and her youngest daughter were waiting on the small platform. A surge of belonging flooded her.

Bernadette opened her arms. "Welcome home, Francie. How was your journey?"

"It was great. I treated myself to a berth and slept like a log." She let go of her and turned to her niece. "You're a foot taller than the last time I saw you, Clare. Come give me a hug."

Clare grabbed her around the waist. "Why didn't Rose come with you? We had so much fun the last time."

"She's working all summer."

"Poor her." Clare picked up the suitcase. "Let's go home." She marched off, the suitcase banging against her leg with every step.

Bernadette rolled her eyes and said in a low voice, "My Little Miss Take-charge."

Clare glanced back at them. "I heard that, Mama." She increased her speed.

The day was filled with chatter, gossip, many cups of tea, nieces and nephews. Even Jimmy dropped in. He stood at the kitchen door, cap in hand and head bowed, the light from the window glinting off his pristine bald head.

"Hello Francie," he said, glancing her way for an instant before looking away.

Rita was gone now. She had died in the spring leaving Jimmy

bereft, with a down-turned mouth and empty eyes. Bernadette told Frances this morning that he wasn't "coming around at all yet."

In the moment he said hello, the ember of contempt that had smouldered in Frances for so many years became weaker.

She went over to him and put a hand on his stooped shoulder. "Hello, Jimmy."

They had rarely spoken or touched since the night he raped her. He looked at her, puzzled and forlorn. She nodded. He muttered something and left. She hoped that was the last she'd see of him this visit.

"He'll be all right, Aunt Francie," said Heather, Jimmy's oldest. "It's hard for Dad being around a lot of people. It's not you. Come around after supper some evening and he'll talk your ear off."

When it was time for bed Clare reappeared from the porch where she had been playing solitaire. "Aunt Francie, you've got my bed. I cleaned my room for you and made up the bed fresh. I'll sleep on the porch with Pumpkin and Patch." The calico cats were never far from Clare.

Frances lay awake, staring out the window. It was a dark night with no moon. The summer air slid over her face like a silk scarf. It was down home air carrying scents from the fields, the forest, and the bay. She didn't miss it when she was home in Montreal but here, it was essential. It unlocked memories. Jimmy. She rarely thought of him. When Rita died Frances had sent the obligatory sympathy card but that was all. She raised her hand in front of her face. She couldn't see it but the sad slouch of his shoulder burned in it still.

⚜

One of the reasons Frances was home was that St. Bridget's was having a reunion. The CND Sisters had been running the school since 1869 and they celebrated their presence there every ten years or so, barring events like world wars. Frances wasn't that keen on it – it felt like the past was intruding – but Bernadette and Jo had asked her to come home for it.

"We won't know most of the Sisters, but we may as well put in an appearance," Bernadette said. "Josephine is over the moon, of course. She and Mamma are coming up from Moncton and staying at Louise's a couple of nights and then coming back home with us. We'll be at Margaret and Larry's."

Mamma had written to her over the years with all the news about her cousins, Louise and Margaret, but Frances had always felt distant. She was uncomfortable about staying with them but soon realized it was only her. Bernadette and Josephine were good friends with them. Frances was the outsider, the Montrealer. The one who left.

Bernadette's and Jimmy's lives, their families, their routines were constant and unchanged from that of their parents. Superficial things had changed; they had more comforts and conveniences, but the essentials were the same. They were part of a strong, long-standing community. Even Jo, unmarried, a school principal in Moncton, was still part of it. It could have been Frances's life too.

What drove Jimmy the night he raped her? It happened only days after he heard she was leaving. Was he trying to put her in her place? This place. Don't leave. You belong here.

No. I never did, she thought.

Clare had talked her into taking a walk and dropping in at Uncle Jimmy's. "Heather's a little bossy, especially since Aunt Rita died. Trying to take care of Rory and Al would make anyone bossy."

Frances had demurred but Clare kept at her until she gave in.

The evening was warm, so they sat on Jimmy's porch. In a few minutes Clare left to play cards with Jimmy's three youngest, Rory, Al, and Jane, leaving just Heather, Jimmy, and Frances having tea.

Jimmy gave a bashful laugh. "Nothing stronger to give you, Francie. That's Rita's doing, once the babies started coming."

Maybe he wanted to talk about Rita or the children but Frances cut it short. "It's perfect."

"It suits me, not having drink around." He stared into the distance. "Heather, pet, would you leave us for a while?"

Alone with Jimmy. Frances fought the urge to flee.

They sat in silence not looking at each other. Jimmy cleared his throat. "I got something to say to you Francie. It's hard but I gotta do it."

Frances slid her eyes away from his.

No, no, no. Don't go there.

"When Rita was dying – God Almighty she was in so much pain." His words caught in his throat and he clenched his jaw. He took a deep breath.

"When my Rita was dying, if she was having a good day, we talked a lot about the past. Some good memories we had." He paused, smiling. Then he shook his head.

"But not all good." He ducked his head down to catch her eye. "I'm sorry for what I did to you."

She turned her head away and stared into the distance. "I ... it's not ... it was a long time ago and —"

He put up his hand to stop her. "Don't matter how long ago it was. It was wrong and I'm sorry. You didn't deserve nothin' like that. Drink's no excuse."

She held onto the arm of her chair to control her dizziness. She felt her neck flush. "Did Rita know?"

"Yeah. She forgave me but said it didn't mean much if you didn't. I know you might not. I know you've hated me ever since. All's I can do is say's I'm sorry."

They sat with their heads down, lost in their own memories. Then Jimmy said, "I think I was jealous you were going away." He shrugged and the corners of his mouth turned up a bit.

"I knew I'd miss you. But jealousy, anger, drink – nothin' – don't make it right. Please forgive me."

She looked down to his outstretched palm then up at the fat tears quivering on his eyelids. She rested her palm on his. Absolution.

Frances nodded at him.

He said, "Thank you."

She choked, the words catching in her throat. "I can't talk about it anymore, Jimmy."

"I know." He dipped his head. "Let's go look at Rita's garden. Heather is taking care of it."

They walked in silence between the long rows of tilled, red soil.

"Heather just got the garden in last week. Nothing to see yet but it'll come along with the fine weather."

They lapsed into awkward silence. Jimmy turned at the end of the row. "Before we go back ... your Rose is a lovely girl. Rita asked me once if I thought ... Oh, Christ ... She wondered ..."

Frances cut in. "Is she your daughter? No. No, she's not. She's your niece, Jimmy."

She turned to face him. "Rose is your niece."

It didn't matter if she believed it, if it was true or not. She would not allow Rose to be the result of a crime.

She admitted to herself that she had been scrutinizing Rose's cousins for resemblances. She saw none. And even though she was half of Rose she saw little of herself either.

Jimmy's apology. It brought back memories of shame she could never erase. But he too was full of shame. He asked her to forgive him, to absolve him. All these years they both carried their black secret. She had only thought of him as he was in that horrific moment, a mindless brute committing a brutish crime, taking out his anger for his own shortcomings.

But she had never thought of him suffering too. She hadn't realized she had the power to forgive him.

✤

She hadn't seen anyone from St. Bridget's since the day she graduated more than two decades ago. Rose was not a secret in her family but there was a tacit understanding not to talk about her beginnings. She couldn't expect the same here. People would be curious; they might be cruel.

When they arrived at the school Mamma pulled her aside. "You two go ahead." She waved at Bernadette and Josephine.

She turned to Frances. "This is our first minute out of earshot of cousins and in-laws and what all. I just want you to know that your sisters and I are one hundred percent behind you."

Frances knew that wasn't exactly true. Josephine's acceptance of Rose had always been guarded, stinting. Frances had repaid her the money from the early days, but she knew Josephine's sense of propriety was greater than her feelings of sisterhood.

Frances hugged her. "Thanks, Mamma."

"Let's get some tea. I hope they have pecan squares." Mamma took her hand.

All the classrooms were open and there was tea service in the parlour and in the large class where Sister St. Maureen had held the mathematics tutoring so long ago. Both rooms were overflowing with lilacs and high-pitched chatter and laughter. Sister was sitting by the window, her hands buried in her sleeves, the sunlight bathing her shoulders. She was placid and, though she seemed to be listening to the laughter and stories the girls were telling, Frances had the sense she was off in a world of her own. She was surprised at how young Sister was. They all had seemed much older than the girls back then but now Frances saw Sister was probably only fifty or so.

She sat beside her. "Sister, do you remember me?"

"What kind of a question is that, Frances?" Sister reached for Frances and held her hand for a few moments.

"Of course, I remember you, one of my best mathematics pupils. You're a nurse now I hear."

No mention of her going to the CND and failing. "Yes. I'm not doing much nursing these days though. I'm the supervisor in the hospital out-patient department."

Sister smiled. "Good for you my dear. I bet you run a tight ship. Your aunt, bless her soul, was like that. She had high standards."

"I never thought I'd be compared to Sister Superior. She scared the daylights out of me when I was a girl."

"She scared me once or twice too. But I always believed she really knew me, had my best interests at heart. Despite all the missions and schools she supervised here and in America, she knew me and cared about me.

Frances smiled but said nothing about how well her aunt knew her too. "May I get you some tea, Sister?"

"No, thank you. You run along and find your old friends. Have you seen Sister St. Zita yet?" Sister lowered her voice, "Patricia O'Shaughnessy?"

"Patsy? Patsy is here?"

"Yes, and she's dressed just like me," Sister motioned to her habit. "So you need to keep a sharp eye out."

Frances went into the parlour and scanned the small clusters of nuns. One of them let out a very un-nun-like whoop and strode over to her with her arms wide open.

"Frances." Patricia wrapped her arms around her and held on. When she released Frances, it was only to grab her hands and scrutinize her from head to toe.

"I'm thrilled you're here. Let me get a good look at you, as beautiful as ever."

Patricia's hair, the small bit that showed under the peak of her habit, had some silver streaks in it and she was thin as a rail but her eyes still held the familiar mischievous sparkle. They had exchanged letters for several years and kept to their tacit agreement to avoid writing about the St. Bridget days. But since the end of the war, they had exchanged only Christmas and birthday cards. "What a surprise, Pats ... I mean Sister St. ..." They both laughed.

Patsy waved her hand in front of her face. "Let's sit in the orchard. I'll just tell my brother where I'll be."

Patsy gathered her long, black skirt under her and in one deft motion sat on the blanket of white blossoms. Frances had more trouble with her high heels, white gloves, and purse. Once she was settled, Patsy took her hand. "Tell me all about you and Rose."

"Wait, wait. What are you doing here? Are you teaching here now?"

"Oh, Francie, you don't know. Tim and I are home for Papa's funeral. It was yesterday."

"I'm sorry. What a sad time for you."

Patsy took out her handkerchief and wiped her eyes. "I'll have lots of time to think about him and pray for him later, but we only have a short time. How is your Rose?"

"She's loving university and they seem to like her, at least judging by her marks. Social work is a whole new world to me. She's quite the expert at comparing city and provincial government policies and programs, you know, funding, benefits and so on. I just listen."

They reminisced and gossiped about their old classmates. Patsy said her own life was very routine but that the students kept her on her toes. "It's exactly how I thought it would be, living with my Sisters and doing work I love. No regrets." Frances believed her.

They heard some laughter. A few people were leaving the school. Frances started to get up. "We'd better get back in there."

"Before you go ..." Patsy reached out and tugged on her arm. "Did you hear about Father Byrne?"

Frances's throat thickened. "Father Byrne?"

"Yes, our Father Byrne. You, of all people, would remember him. Remember how much you liked him?"

Frances hoped her blotchy neck wouldn't give her away. "Oh, of course. What about him?"

"He moved to Montreal, a very sudden departure. I was talking to Sister St. Jerome—" they both rolled their eyes— "and she said, 'good riddance', and zipped her fingers across her lips. Never the most charitable of my Sisters."

Good riddance?

Patsy continued. "I asked Tim if he knew why Father left. You know Tim is working in the Bishop's Palace in Montreal?"

"Father Tim is? What's he do there?"

Frances couldn't help but think of the Bishop's Palace and those who worked there as having all the power. Father Tim was one of the enforcers? She never talked about the coercive nature of the Catholic Church or her opinion that most people followed along blindly without questioning the worn-out traditions. She kept that to herself. She wouldn't draw attention or criticize others.

She lived in a glass house, better not throw stones.

Patsy replied, "I'm not sure. He just said I should know better than to ask ... about Father Byrne. Then he changed the subject. After Papa's funeral he apologized for snapping at me. Just said it's confidential. I'll bet there's a story there."

She sprang to her feet and held out her hand. "C'mon, you delicate one." Frances laughed, trying not to show how shaken she was.

⚜

Frances didn't have a minute to think about Patsy's revelation. In the evening there was a big family dinner with Mamma and her sisters, their cousins' families and a couple of people she didn't know at all.

Only when she got into the bed she was sharing with Bernadette did Patsy's words come back to her. A sudden departure? Zipped lips ... a secret? Confidential? No one anywhere knew what had happened between her and Thomas so long ago ... did they? Was it possible someone had gotten an inkling? And started a rumour that Thomas had lost his job. The thought made her sick.

The next morning, they were at St. Bridget's for the Communion Breakfast. During the Mass she got a brief respite from the non-stop chatter but soon afterward she found herself seated next to Avelda at the long table. Her golden hair was more silver now, but she still had the sharp, inquisitive look Frances remembered.

"Frances Dalton, what a pleasant surprise to see you here."

"Hello Avelda. I'm visiting Bernadette." She turned toward her sister. "You remember her?"

"Of course, I do." Avelda leaned forward and looked past Frances. "How are you keeping Bernadette?" She didn't wait for an answer.

"Remember our Sodality of Mary meetings? You weren't very devoted as I recall. You made us all laugh and Sister had the devil of a time getting us to say our prayers." She laughed. "I don't know now if the prayers were doing us any good anyway."

Avelda leaned toward Frances and whispered. "I don't suppose you've crossed paths with our Father Byrne up there in Montreal?"

Frances choked on her coffee and held her napkin to her mouth, breathing steadily through her nose until she could swallow it. "Pardon me, it's very hot. Father Byrne? The math tutor?"

"I used to tell Sally, my daughter, to show more respect for the clergy. She told me some of the girls called him all sorts of disrespectful names – Flirting Father Tom, Lonely Father Tom But when he left in such a hurry, and no farewell tea at all, I began to think it might be true."

"Excuse me, Avelda. I spilled some coffee. I need to wipe my dress." Frances fled to the washroom. The gossip wasn't about her or Rose. All the talk was about Thomas – Thomas and the young students. It wasn't a relief.

She wiped her dress and got her wits about her. When she returned, everyone was up from the tables and mingling. She looked for Avelda knowing it wouldn't be difficult to entice her to gossip.

"What did you mean when you said Father Byrne left in a hurry?"

"Well, you know. They usually announce parish changes from the pulpit and in the parish bulletin well in advance. Then there's a farewell do and everyone says nice things and ... well, you know."

She looked to her left, then to her right, and lowered her voice. "Not a peep. We came to Mass one Sunday two years ago and there was this new fellow from Bathurst on the altar. He just said Father Byrne had left St. Bridget's and we'd be getting a new priest in due course. There was something fishy, for sure."

Frances played along. "Shocking. And what about what Sally said? Is there a connection?"

"I don't know anything for certain and I'd hate to spread a false rumour but ..."

"Oh, go on. He's gone now." Frances kept pressing.

"Well, shortly after he left Lucille Gauthier's mother said something at the Women's Auxiliary about it serving him right after what he'd done to Lucille."

Her stomach lurched. "What he'd done to her?"

"Oh, she was right as rain as far as I could tell. I didn't want to ask more, you know."

"She didn't have to leave for a while?"

Avelda laughed. "You catch on quick. No."

"I'm a maternity nurse. I've seen it many a time." Frances picked up her purse. "I won't say a word to anyone. I've got to run, Avelda. Thanks for the news."

"Okay, Frances. Keep an eye out for that blackguard in Montreal!"

Frances found Bernadette leaning against the old silver maple tree. She reached for Bernadette's cigarette and took a puff. "That Avelda could talk both ears off a donkey."

"What was she saying?"

Frances lied. "Sally this and Sally that. Not a bit of interest in any of ours."

"Sounds like the same old Avelda. I think Mamma's had enough.

I'll have to drag Jo away from that new Sister Superior What's-her-name."

No mention of Father Byrne to Bernadette then. Really?

They went in and thanked the Sisters who were lined up at the door. Patsy wasn't among them as she wasn't a St. Bridget's Sister. Frances found her alone at the tea service putting the dirty teacups onto trays.

"I'm going now, Patsy. Seeing you made my whole trip worthwhile."

"I'm not far from Montreal, you know. Come visit me sometime."

Patsy hesitated, checking to see if they were alone. "We've never talked about our time at St. Bridget's and the Mother House but if you ever want to or need to ... I'll listen. I won't judge."

Frances hugged her old friend, her eyes welling with tears, then she left.

Patsy's invitation to confide undid Frances. Her mind swam with conflicting thoughts of Thomas and Jimmy, paragons of goodness and evil. She had kept them like that, intact and separate, for more than twenty years. Maybe things were not so black and white.

Her talk with Jimmy, short as it was, had opened her heart to him. Raping her could never be excused but her making an absolute judgement of him as evil, was also inexcusable. And now with these revelations from Patsy and Avelda she accepted that perhaps Thomas was not so good.

32

AMBUSH

FRANCES PUSHED HER food around her plate. She raised her fork to her mouth but gave up. She had no appetite; she shouldn't have bothered cooking. Several unopened letters from Thomas leaned against the sugar bowl, daring her. She didn't want to read one word from him, more reasons why things weren't moving forward. And what about the rumours? She scraped the food into the garbage, piled the dishes in the sink with the others, and went out to the front porch.

The evening was still warm, and the setting sun glowed yellow and pink through mackerel clouds. She was overcome with lassitude. She'd been back for several weeks and still she thought of nothing but the gossip from down home. Over and over it played out in her head. A scandal, rumours, but nobody really knew anything. What had happened at St. Bridget's? What had he done? And how could he have kept it from her?

Patsy and Avelda had asked her, did she know, had she heard, did she ever run into him? Patsy's promise not to judge her was like a wedge prying open the emotions churning inside Frances, scraping her raw.

She retraced every walk they had taken, to Murray Hill Park, around Mount Royal, along Saint Catherine Street. All their conversations came back to her. She had believed everything he had said, never questioned a thing, and never thought about what he might not be saying.

What a fool.

She had been a fool at seventeen but to have dropped her guard and allowed herself to be swept up now, that was the worst of it.

But no, that wasn't the worst. Her thoughts moved away from herself and she wondered about the St. Bridget's girls. Had there been another like her, frightened, alone, condemned to silence and shame? She couldn't bear it. His dishonesty and witholding crushed her.

Her anger and all her questions energized her in an instant. She stood up and started walking with no particular destination in mind.

She hated her helplessness, the not knowing. She rehearsed ways of confronting him – shouting matches, calm discussions, indirect questions. Her thoughts gave way to longing, swinging seamlessly into scenes of lovemaking – then back to confrontation. She composed letters in her head, crumpled them, started over.

"Hey! Look out, Miss!" Frances had bumped into a young woman, knocking her into a man.

She became aware of her surroundings. "I'm very sorry. I hope I didn't hurt you." She was embarrassed to look at them. She realized she was still wearing her apron. She started crying.

"We're okay. What about you? You don't look so good," the man said.

"I'm fine, I'm fine, on my way home. Goodbye." She turned and rushed away rubbing the tears from her face. When she got home the telephone was ringing. She looked at it but didn't answer.

She went to bed but lay awake for hours. When her alarm clock rang at six o'clock she was listless and bleary-eyed.

Being at work was a relief. The routine kept her going, although the same worries and thoughts about him and what he might or might not have done roiled around at the back of her mind.

There was a quick knock on her desk. She was startled to see Alice from the emergency department standing there. "How does a cup of coffee sound?"

Frances sighed and reached for her change purse. "Alright."

"Why so glum?" Alice asked. "Sorry to be back from vacation?"

"I've been back a month, Alice. It's just that ... I ... a headache, that's all. I didn't sleep very well last night."

"Drink up, my dear. We have a long day ahead of us." Alice turned to the woman beside her. Frances was grateful for her tact.

Frances never confided in anyone at work. She was friendly and interested in them but not close. When the break was over, she retreated to her desk, relieved to be alone. The nurses were busy with their various clinics and didn't bother her as she sat poring over staffing schedules and sterile supply inventory lists, the minutiae of her day.

The big wall clock ticked the hours away and soon it was quarter to five. She retrieved her purse and put on her coat. As she was walking up Marlowe Avenue, dreading the long evening and weekend ahead of her, Alice called her name.

"I thought it was you. What a great evening, so mild." Alice was breathless from running to catch up to her.

"We could do with some rain, though," Frances replied in a dull flat voice. She didn't look at Alice.

"Do you have any plans tonight?"

Frances frowned, "Plans? I don't know ... I never ... but ..." She stopped walking and looked at Alice. "What do you mean?"

"I just thought maybe we could have a meal together. I have some pork chops in the refrigerator. Nothing fancy but I'd really like some company. What do you say?"

"I don't want to be a bother."

"No bother. I live close by, on the other side of Sherbrooke."

" I don't know. I'm not really dressed for going out."

"C'mon, Frances. It's not as if I'm going to be dressed to the nines. It's Friday night!" She hooked arms with Frances and laughed. "If you don't like my cooking I'll never invite you again."

"Well, okay. It's very nice of you."

Alice lived in the bottom level of a duplex very similar to her own, long and narrow. Frances knew she was a widow – what people still called a war widow – but other than that she knew very little about her. Alice led her into the living room and offered her a drink.

"I have some sherry that my aunt gave me and I have rum and coke."

"Are you having one?"

"You bet."

"I'll join you then; rum and coke please."

They talked about the plans for the royal visit, the new medical director, and their sewing projects. They moved to the kitchen so Alice could cook their supper. She poured them another drink.

"I noticed the photo in the living room. Your husband?"

"Yes."

"When did he go overseas?"

"He did his RCAF training early in '44 and left in September, on our first anniversary, of all possible dates."

"Insult to injury."

Alice turned from the stove to Frances. "Yeah, when it comes around now I just think of it as the day I lost him, seldom of our wedding."

"Was it on a mission ... his death, I mean?"

Alice put their meal on the table and sat down. "I told you, nothing fancy," she said, passing the butter.

"It was a car accident in England. He was walking with some pals back to their base. Apparently, it was dark and rainy. A car went out of control and struck them. Len was killed on the spot and another fellow was badly injured."

Frances gasped. "That's horrible."

"Yes. It certainly wasn't how he imagined his wartime would go. I miss him sometimes but really, I've been without him much longer than we even knew each other. I'm thankful we didn't have any children. It would be awful to bring up a child without a father."

She covered her mouth. "God, I'm sorry, Frances. I didn't mean that."

"That's okay. It sort of answers a question I had. What do you know about me?"

Alice's tone was tentative and soft. "I've heard you have a daughter. How did your husband die?"

Frances stared at her for a moment. She took a long gulp from her drink. "Do you want to know the truth?" She said it like a challenge.

Alice waved her hands gently as if calming a child. "I'm sorry. I shouldn't pry. You don't need to tell me anything."

"I'd like to, I'd really like to." Frances pushed back her chair, leaned forward and gripped her knees. The words ran out of her, tripping over each other.

"I never had a husband, I raised Rose myself, and I thought my daughter's father was a good man, an honest man, and I thought we had a chance together, at last – you know that song, Our Love is Here to Stay – but I just learned that maybe he's not so good, not so honest, and I feel like a chump."

She stopped and stared at Alice. Then she dropped her head into her hands and blew out a long groan. "Oh God."

Alice spoke softly. "What did he do?"

"I heard rumours, just rumours." Frances waved her hand. "But I know from my own experience they might be true. I don't want to believe it but I can't help it."

She added, "And even if the rumours aren't true he didn't tell me the truth about why he left Newcastle."

Flummoxed, Alice stood and moved behind Frances patting her shoulders in smooth, slow strokes. Frances leaned into her. They were silent, staring ahead.

After a moment Alice said, "We need another drink."

Frances tidied her hair and wiped her face. She coughed, her voice cracked. "I'm sor ... sorry. I shouldn't have said all that. I lost my head."

"It's okay. Sounds like you needed to get that off your chest." She handed her a drink.

"I don't know if this will make you feel any better but ..." Alice hesitated. "I was pregnant when I got married. We didn't love each other, Len and I, but what else could we do? Then I lost the baby, then I lost Len." She snorted. "God really knows how to punish a girl,"

Frances raised her glass and clinked it with Alice's. "To us, unlucky in love."

⚜

She walked three blocks home at midnight feeling lightheaded and giddy, a combination of the drinks and Alice's company. She felt a warm connection to Alice, knowing she had a secret too. She couldn't remember ever feeling as free to be herself and say what she was thinking. Rose, Ena, Rosemary, Bernadette, Josephine – with all of them, there was always a role to play. "Anglaise, what about me"? Her old friend Mercedes piped up. Their friendship hadn't gone beyond the grey, stonewalls of the Miséricorde but it had been real. The anonymity of the Mis had liberated them to love each other for a short time.

And what about Patsy? She had offered her uncritical ear. Would Frances ever take her up on her promise and be able to say to Patsy what she'd said to Alice?

She was lost in thought as she turned up the path to her door. She didn't see him sitting on the porch.

"Frances."

Her heart clutched, stalled, and then sped away in her chest. "Thomas. What —?"

He took the stairs two at a time and swept her up. "I was so worried about you. I telephoned and telephoned. I left work early this afternoon and got the express train. How are you? Why haven't you answered my letters?"

She squirmed out of his embrace and away from his questions. "I have to go in. Right now." He came up the steps behind her.

She put her hand in front of his chest. "No, Thomas. Call me tomorrow. We can talk then." She closed the door on his protests. She went to her bedroom, shut the door, and sat in the blackness, shaking.

She awoke at five o'clock. She was still in her crumpled uniform. Her head was pounding, her eyes swollen. She sat on the edge of her bed for a few minutes.

She soon had a plan and moved without hesitation.

You won't ambush me again, she thought

Alice answered her door after some long minutes. Frances had gotten her out of bed by the looks of it. Alice eyed Frances up and down then looked at the bulging tapestry bag she was holding. "Come in. Tell me what's happened. No, before you do that I'll put on some coffee."

"Let me do that, Alice. You're hardly awake."

"Okay. The coffee is in the cupboard beside the refrigerator and the perc is at the back of the stove. I won't be long."

They lingered over their toast and coffee, and as much as they tried to talk about other things they always came back to Thomas. "He must have been shocked when you shut the door in his face."

"I think I was more shocked than he was. I don't know where I got the nerve."

"The rum." She put the back of her hand up to her forehead in a theatrical pose. "Dutch courage."

"Let's go to a movie this afternoon. There's always something good on at the Snowdon. It's my treat. We'll have lunch too."

"No, no, no. You don't have to do that."

"C'mon, Alice. You're a lifesaver letting me stay here tonight. I need to get my mind on something else."

Frances stayed at Alice's until Sunday evening about ten o'clock. When she opened her door a note was waiting for her.

Dear Frances,

I have to go back to Hamilton. I'm worried about you.

Why did you push me away? Please write. I love you.

Thomas

She was determined not to be ambushed again or under siege. She took the bold step of calling him later that week. Long-distance calls were reserved only for the worst news.

He was still living with Nora. Frances called at suppertime, when she thought they would both be home. The telephone rang twice.

"This is the operator. I have a station-to-station call from Montreal."

She felt a bitter satisfaction when Nora asked, "Who is it?"

"Go ahead, Ma'am," the operator clicked off.

"May I speak to Thomas?" she asked.

Nora's tone was hesitant. "May I tell him who's calling?"

"Frances."

"Oh mercy! Is everything all right?"

"Is Thomas there?"

"Oh yes, of course. I'll put him right on." She covered the receiver, but Frances could hear the muffled "It's her ... Frances. Something must be wrong. Here."

"Frances, thank God you called. What's happened?"

"I don't want you to write or telephone or visit me."

"What do you mean? What's happened? I've been beside myself."

"I heard disturbing things about you in Newcastle. I need time to think and sort out how I feel. Please respect my wishes."

She couldn't hear his breathing. Utter silence. Then, "Frances, I can explain—"

"Please, Thomas. I'll write." She hung up. Her hand was welded to the receiver, her other arm across her belly holding in a scream.

She wrote him many letters but sent none of them. They piled up on the corner of the kitchen table. She re-read them and then wrote more. But the writing and rewriting, the thinking and rethinking were helpful. What had she wanted from Thomas? What had she expected?

As autumn crept in, her thoughts and feelings were distilled, and she was able to write something that was unequivocal and did not invite discussion.

33

DEAR JOHN

THOMAS AND NORA avoided looking at each other when he picked the letter off the table and went into his room. They'd not spoken about Frances since the awkward telephone call at the end of the summer.

Thomas held the thin envelope in his hands. He put it down and picked it up again. Finally, he reached for his letter opener.

October 1, 1952

Thomas,

When I was at St. Bridget's in the summer two people spoke to me about you. You are the focus of gossip concerning your behaviour with St. Bridget's students. And a focus of gossip not only at St. Bridget's – apparently in the Bishop's office also. Based on my own student experience with you, I was alarmed.

When you returned to Montreal you did not explain any of the circumstances around your decision to leave St. Bridget's and I was happy to have you in Montreal so I didn't ask. But I remember you talking about being under scrutiny and people expecting perfection from a priest. Given what I heard I wonder if you were trying to tell me something.

Your vague explanations about your application for laicization – the delays and the lack of detail about the process – make me suspicious of you and your intentions.

I don't believe everything you told me. Put simply, I don't trust you – very shaky grounds for a friendship.

*When you returned to Montreal it was the happiest time of
my life but now it is spoiled. It is over. Please do not contact me
unless you are no longer a priest.*

Frances

He was stunned. He read it again. And again, hardly believing it was
from her. He ran his fingers over the blue ink, the familiar slant and
slope of her writing, looking for something more between the lines.
She had shut the door on him and he didn't know how to pry it open.
He had told her about the loneliness of those years, the isolation, the
tedium. Surely, she had understood?

"Tommy? Supper's ready." Nora waited outside the door.

He rubbed his face, shook his head. "I can't ...". His voice cracked.
He coughed. "Leave it for me, Nora. A bit of a headache, I'm lying
down."

He perched on the edge of his metal bed and looked around at his
shabby surroundings, the wire clothes hangers on the back of the door,
the chipped brown paint on the low dresser, the bare walls, the cracked
green blind curled at the edges. Nora had been kind to take him in. It
had been more than a year now. He knew she appreciated the extra
money but it was no better than a monk's cell. He thought of Frances,
her home, so warm and inviting. That was where he saw his future,
their future.

Damn Bishop Plessis. And that biddy of a mother. The girl was all
right, no harm done. Just gave herself a scare, that's all. Made a fool of
herself.

"I think you've been with us long enough, Father Byrne," the
Bishop had said his jet-black eyes piercing Thomas's chest. "Done
some excellent work in the parish. But I think I'll see if Montreal will
take you. A boys' school, perhaps."

He had planned to explain everything to Frances in due course,
how he'd been cornered, more or less trapped, by the girl. But the time

was never right.

He strode out of his room, past Nora in the living room, clutching the letter in his hand. "I need some air. I won't be long."

"What about your —"

He slammed the door.

Thomas walked for hours pushing himself to keep moving. The idea that had been lurking in a dark corner of his mind for a long time crept out and showed itself.

It appeared as his father's voice, himself a drunken failure and a bully, goading Thomas. "You have no backbone." "Make a decision." "Get on with your life." And now Thomas admitted to himself that his father had seen him clearly as he was, a follower. So the priesthood had been his choice; he had seen it as a safe path. Tradition, ritual, rules to follow.

And what about Frances? He was drawn to her because of her boldness, her courage, her strength. She intoxicated him. He thought he could be like her, wanted to be like her. But finally, the idea that he was not up to taking that risk, to taking an unconventional path with no rules to follow, shone its sombre light at him. Frances thrilled him but also threatened him.

34

A DENSE FOG LIFTS

TWO THINGS HAPPENED leading up to Christmas. The first was that Frances went to the hospital staff party at the Barclay Hotel. She usually went to the smaller socials held at the hospital itself but Alice talked her into it. She made a dress in emerald green taffeta with a flared skirt.

They sat at a circular table with some of the other single or widowed nurses, but in fact, they only sat to eat their dinner. The band played all the wartime favourites as well as some new tunes and the girls didn't hesitate to rush onto the dance floor together. Frances and Alice were swinging around in their own version of the Lindy and became the centre of attention. People formed a circle around them and cheered when the number was over.

Frances was hot and out of breath. Some of her junior staff nurses were laughing as they approached her. "Gee, Miss Dalton, you can really cut a rug. Where did you learn to dance like that?"

She laughed. "From my daughter. We used to dance in the kitchen when a good tune came on the radio. She'd love this."

She turned to Alice. "I'm going to sit this one out."

"Me too. Let's get a drink."

By midnight everyone was up dancing and laughing. A conga line started and Frances found herself between two men she didn't know. They shuffled and kicked around the room until everyone had joined up. The band wrapped it up with a wild crescendo and they all let out a cheer.

Frances and the two men talked about their Christmas plans. Frances was telling them about going to Toronto to see her daughter when Alice interrupted.

"C'mon Cinderella, time for us to get in our pumpkin coach."

Frances and Alice leaned back their heads in the taxi. "Thanks for talking me into going. I had a great time. I'm surprised how many people you know."

"I've been there since time began, it seems. The war years brought us together more than anything else. Everyone had a story to share and offered a shoulder to cry on in those days. Even though a lot of the cast has changed we still seem to follow the same script now."

The cab stopped in front of Alice's. "I'm going to have a great sleep-in tomorrow. I'll see you on Monday."

"Goodnight."

Frances couldn't sleep so she made a cup of weak tea and read Rose's latest letter. She wrote weekly and recently every letter had included a mention of her boyfriend, Hugh. Frances was going to meet him over the holidays. She was worried about Rose – she was only twenty-one, too young to tie herself to anyone – but she kept her thoughts to herself.

She sipped her tea and remembered the dance. The dinner hadn't been much to write home about but the dancing – oh the dancing. She was surprised how much fun she'd had. People had complimented her on her new dress. "Quite a change from the uniform," Jack, from the personnel department, had said when he walked her back to her table.

When was the last time she'd had such fun?

She searched her memory and realized the answer was never. Fun at St. Bridget's had been tepid and contrived, always with some odd overlay of Catholic guilt. Then the convent, the Mis, and nursing school. She remembered bright, magical moments with Rose and Ena, of course, but nothing like the carefree, let-loose kind of fun and laughter she had had tonight. Her long-time habits of frugality and vigilance had made no room for out-and-out fun.

Maybe that should be her resolution for 1953 – have fun.

⚜

The second thing began in front of Eaton's after doing some last-minute Christmas shopping. When Frances came out at four-thirty it was dark. Big, fluffy snowflakes were swirling around in all directions and the traffic on Saint Catherine's was snarled, horns blaring and tires spinning. She was staring into the big display window on the corner, mesmerized by Santa's train, laden with toy drums, and teddy bears.

"Mademoiselle Dalton?"

A tall man in a soft brown overcoat and a fedora covered with snow was looking at her, his head tipped to the side in a question. Frances couldn't place him. "Yes?"

He extended his hand. "Michel Dupuis. I handled your aunt's estate a few years ago."

She shook his hand. "Yes, of course. I didn't recognize you, Mr. Dupuis. How are you?"

He spread out his hand toward the street. "Fine, thanks, until I saw this mess."

"Yes. I won't be getting my bus anytime soon."

"No. It doesn't look good."

The silence between them was awkward. They looked left to right, right to left. When their eyes met they laughed.

"I might have a bite to eat, you know, wait it out. Please join me." He hurried on, "Unless you have another commitment?"

She laughed, "Where did you have in mind?"

"How about the Pam Pam on Stanley Street? It's not fancy but the food is delicious. It's Hungarian."

"Sounds good. I only had soup for lunch."

They walked to Stanley Street. He insisted on carrying her parcels and each time they stepped off a curb he put his hand lightly on her

319

elbow. By the time they got to the restaurant they had put aside the formality of last names.

The Pam Pam was five steps below street level. It had a low ceiling and about ten tables for two. The entire back wall was mirrored. There was a small bar in the corner festooned with multi-coloured lights.

"I've never even noticed this place. It's very cozy." She turned up her nose and sniffed, "And the aroma!"

They had a drink before their meal. "May I ask, did you ever buy a house?"

"Yes. It will be four years this spring. I bought a lower duplex on Grey Avenue. It's not grand but we like it very much."

"I'm happy for you. I remember saying I thought you were wise. I believe I was right." He raised his glass to clink it with hers.

"Wise, maybe. But careful? Definitely." She looked at him for a moment then looked down. "I believe you know a little of my story – a daughter and no husband – I had to use my aunt's money in the best way possible for Rose."

"Our children are our conscience."

He spoke a little bit about his two daughters. "They've been very attentive since Jeanne, my wife, died."

"Oh, I'm very sorry, Michel."

"Thank you. It was very sad for the three of us." He refilled their wine glasses. "But we go on."

The meal arrived. A comfortable silence settled between them with only the odd comment about the food. When the waiter took away their plates Frances looked at her watch.

It was eight o'clock when they climbed up the five steps. The storm had eased and the city was hushed. They walked to Burnside Street and hailed a taxi.

"Thank you for dinner, Michel. It was a lovely way to wait out the storm."

"My pleasure." He handed her the parcels he was carrying. "Are you sure I can't see you home?"

"Yes. This is no night for gallantry. Look at all the snow." She got in the back seat and rolled down the window. "Thank you again. I enjoyed getting to know you. Good night."

He stepped back from the curb and waved.

Frances remembered when she had first met Michel. She had thought he was very attractive. What had impressed her then was the same this evening. He was confident and attentive. What was different now was his genuine warmth and openness.

She smiled all the way home.

⚜

Rose had gone all out to make their first Christmas away from home special. Ena's Toronto apartment was decorated, the smell of spices and evergreen wafting in the air. Frances knew it was probably driving Ena up the wall, but she was taking it in stride.

Ena wrapped her arms around Frances and held on. "All this rigmarole is for you, you know."

Ena's friend Barbara gave Ena a friendly push out of the way and hugged Frances and kissed her on the cheek. "Don't mind her. You look wonderful, dear. How was the train journey?"

Frances and Rose liked Barbara and thought she and Ena were very well-suited. She had a way of softening Ena's rough edges that Ena seemed to accept.

Frances answered, "It was full to bursting but everyone was in good cheer and happy to be going home or wherever they were going."

They spent most of the first three days indoors because of a howling snowstorm but on the fourth day the city was sparkling. Frances went for a walk. The side streets had not been plowed and she trod gingerly.

Despite her firm conviction about not wanting to hear from Thomas, he was on her mind. He'd been gone now for a year and a half and that convinced her he questioned his passion and love for her. Her suspicions about him and the rumours took second place in her mind as time went on. She spent more time thinking about what she and Thomas meant to each other.

We don't belong together.

As she struggled through the snow she came to her own truth. As though a dense fog lifted, everything came into sharp relief. She had been infatuated, flattered that he hadn't forgotten her. He reminded her of the daring young girl she'd been and the secrets she'd kept. Letting go of some of them had felt like liberation.

But she wasn't liberated. For a year and a half, she'd been waiting for that one letter or triumphant telephone call from Thomas with news from the Bishop's Palace, news of a difference, a plan for the future. She wanted something to happen. She wanted to be in control of her life again.

She'd been waiting, but she was not waiting any longer.

Thomas had reappeared in her life at the perfect time, to fill the hole created by Rose leaving for Toronto. Frances had been afraid of being alone. She had lived with the comings and goings of women all her life: school, convents, nursing school, then Ena and Rose. But she had never been alone.

Hearing the rumours about Thomas had jolted Frances out of her dreams of a happy future. Over time she had given up wondering whether they were true or not and instead she'd been thinking about herself. What had she wanted from Thomas? Had she thought that by loving him, by reclaiming her love, she could somehow legitimize Rose and her own motherhood, get rid of the stigma? She had held her head high and shielded her small family from the arrows of disapproval for so long. It shocked her to realize how she, in some dark corner of herself, had internalized the labels of whore and bastard. And how she had hoped reconnecting with Thomas would somehow undo that.

The only way to really do that was to forgive herself. For being young. For wanting something more than the conventional choices on hand. For leaving home far behind. For failing to see Thomas as he was. For ignoring that troubling instinct that something was wrong. Infatuation had clouded her judgement. He had known about her pregnancy early on and had done nothing, and he was still doing nothing.

Rose accompanied Frances on her walk the next day. Frances told her about Alice and the hospital social committee. "We're already planning to go to the Robbie Burns dinner and dance next month. I'm making a red dress. I drew the line at tartan."

"What's wrong with tartan?"

"Too sturdy and functional. I want a skirt that twirls."

Rose reached over and rapped her knuckles on her mother's head. She put on a mysterious voice and said, "Hello in there. Where has my mother gone?"

"I'm only thirty-nine, Rose. It's time I lived a little. But I still have a job and pay the mortgage. You don't need to worry."

"Phew!"

"Speaking about the mortgage, I met an interesting man a couple of weeks ago."

"Huh? A man? Something I thought I would never hear you say."

"He was the lawyer who settled Sister St. Benedict's will that gave me the down payment for the house. That's the connection."

"Okay, okay. And?"

"We ran into each other downtown. I didn't expect to hear from him again, but he called to wish me a merry Christmas."

"And?"

Her mother's face lit up. "He asked me to go dancing on New Year's Eve!"

Rose grilled her about Michel until she got every scrap of information out of her – age, marital status, children, employment history, the works.

"I feel like I'm under a microscope. Do you interview your clients with such vigour?" Frances asked.

Rose laughed and waved off her mother's futile resistance. "I don't remember you ever going on a date, Mum. This is front page news."

"Yes, I suppose it is.

Rose put her arm around her shoulder and they went on.

"Did he say where you're going dancing?"

"No and I was too flustered to ask. He just asked for our address and said he would be there at eight o'clock."

"I hope he doesn't take you to a dive on the Main."

"He's much too elegant for that."

"Remember what you always told me when I went on a date. 'Pin a five-dollar bill inside your bra in case you need to make a quick getaway.'"

35

HER OWN LIFE

FRANCES, ROSE, AND Barbara hadn't been together since that Christmas more than a decade ago. It was now the sixties. They sat in the front pew as the priest spoke about the grace of God and everlasting peace. Their attention, though, was drawn to the casket and their own memories. Nothing he said would comfort them.

Ena was gone. In an instant. She was struck by a bus on Yonge Street. Barbara had telephoned Frances on Monday evening. Frances had called Rose and they'd agreed to take the train to Toronto the next day.

"I hate to think of Barbara being alone," Rose said. "I know Phyllis will come and stay with Hugh and the boys."

Phyllis, Rose's mother-in-law was ready, able, and willing to be the doting, grandmother. Frances knew she would arrive at Rose and Hugh's house with a tin of cookies or another treat.

Frances notified the hospital that she would be gone for the rest of the week. She telephoned her bridge partner and a few of the other friends from St. Mary's that she saw regularly. Word would get around fast. Some of that crowd thought Ena an "odd duck" but still, she was one of them and they would pay their respects.

The last thing she did before leaving for the train station was call Michel. They had planned to see a movie on Thursday.

"My condolences. So sudden, you must be heartbroken."

"I'm stunned." She couldn't think of anything else. "The taxi is here. I have to go."

"I'll wait to hear from you."

✣

As they left the church Frances noticed a tall, thin man standing at a distance. She stopped to get a better look. Thomas. She said to Rose, "I'll be just a moment. I need to say hello to someone." She moved away from Rose and Barbara.

"The car is waiting for us," Rose said, her voice urgent.

"Just wait. I'll only be a minute."

"Hello, Thomas. I'm surprised to see you here." She approached him tentatively.

Thomas started to reach out both hands but withdrew them. "I don't want to intrude. I saw Ena's death announcement in the paper and wanted to pay my respects."

Frances didn't know what to say. "I'm surprised to see you ... It's very kind of you ... I'd best get back to them."

"May I contact you, Frances?"

"It's been a long time." She hesitated then felt a pulse of confidence. "Yes. Why not? I'm at the same address."

She went back and got into the long, black car. She leaned forward and said to the driver, "I'm sorry I kept you. We can go now."

Frances took a break from going from group to group at the reception, offering sandwiches and thanking people for their condolences. She sat by a window and looked at Ena's friends. They were a noisy bunch but not all the talk was about Ena. The shock of her death was more than matched by the news of the American president's assassination. They had learned about it on the way to the reception. All the drivers had been huddled around a car radio when they came out of the church. It happened during Ena's funeral.

Rose sat down beside her. "How are you holding up?"

"Okay, you?"

"I miss the boys. I haven't had time yet to miss Auntie Ena. I can't believe she won't burst in here any minute and say, 'What's the point of all this falderal?'"

"She wasn't much for entertaining and ceremony, that's for sure."

Rose lowered her voice. "I know she was your special friend Mum." She reached over and held Frances's hand. "This is harder for you than any of us."

Frances was surprised for a second at Rose's perceptiveness, and then grateful. "You knew?"

Rose nodded. "After I moved in with Aunt Ena a lot of things became clear to me."

Frances blotted her tears. "You're right. This is very hard. I've never loved anyone like I loved Ena. I felt strong when I was with her. Not just strong but right, that fighting and working for you was right. When she went overseas in '42 I thought I would fall apart but I didn't. That's when I realized her gift. She gave me confidence and pride. Before Ena, I was faking it."

"I went to university because of her. I guess she gave me the same gift."

They were interrupted by friends who came to say good-bye. "Let's talk more later. I'm happy you told me," Frances said.

Rose took her hand and squeezed it. A look crossed Rose's face and lit up her hazel eyes. In that instant Frances saw Thomas. She peered at her daughter but then the resemblance was gone.

✤

The blessed relief of work and routine. Frances dove in and saved her ruminating for the evenings. Seeing Thomas at Ena's funeral had made her heart do a flip; she'd been sorry when he pulled back his hands.

There was something between them. Love or infatuation or nostalgia, it was something that pulled at her insides.

She had kept her long-ago resolution to stop waiting and to have fun. She and Michel had become lovers in the Spring after their snowy encounter. They saw movies together, went ballroom dancing, and every December they went to the Pam Pam for dinner. She spent a few weekends and sometimes a week or so with him at his summer place in Sainte Agathe. However, Frances was always more than happy to return to her own home on Grey Avenue.

Her feelings for Michel never pulled at her or confused her. They were companionable friends with common interests who came together to enjoy their time together. Rose seemed happy, even hopeful that something more permanent would develop. Frances didn't disabuse her about the nature of their relationship: casual and uncommitted.

Rose's revelation that she now understood Frances and Ena had been lovers made Frances wonder about herself. Her awareness and pursuit of love and sex had never been of prime importance to her. They had arisen out of her circumstances, unbidden, always answering a need. With Thomas, it had been for excitement and rebellion; with Mercedes, comfort in a bleak time; with Ena, support and strength. All three had been forbidden, had carried risk, but Frances had accepted the risk willingly. Now with Michel there was little risk and Frances was content with their understanding.

Her social circle since she had arrived in Montreal, and mostly before then, for that matter, was exclusively women. She and Ena knew other women who lived together. During the Depression and the war many women lived together. Frances didn't question why. Life was pinched and hard then and getting by was the thing.

When Frances and Rose took up their conversation about Ena, Rose had persisted in using the word lesbian. The world of social work had exposed Rose to things Frances had never thought of. The word seemed criminal or seedy to her. Frances couldn't relate it to Ena and her raising Rose as a family.

Frances had rekindled her friendship with Patsy and true to her word Patsy hadn't judged Frances. Frances knew Patsy was dismayed hearing about Thomas's behaviour.

"I know you were crazy about him and he was lonely but it was up to him to be the mature, sensible one."

They agreed not to dwell on Thomas's shortcomings. Frances said to her, "I remember when you said entering the convent meant you would have a place of your own. That stayed with me and I determined that I could have my own place too." She laughed. "It was a crazy dream when I was sixteen but now it's real. I won't let it go."

⚜

Frances still enjoyed the hospital parties and activities. There was always something on the go and she often joined in.

And she had Rose and her family. It wasn't easy with them living in Pointe Claire, but she went at least one Friday or Saturday for an overnight visit every month.

One Saturday morning when she was there for the weekend, she went into the kitchen. Rose had her nose in a book and the house was silent.

"Where are the boys?" No answer.

"Rose?"

Rose looked up. "Sorry, what did you say?"

"I asked you where the boys are. It's so quiet I actually slept in for once."

"Hugh took them to get new skates, then they're going to a movie. I have to give this back to my friend at work next week so I'm trying to finish it while I can." She held up the book.

"*The Feminine Mystique*. Is that the one that's been in all the magazines lately?"

"Yeah. I've never read anything like it. I bet you'd enjoy it."

"I stick to fiction. What makes you think I'd like it?"

"Maybe not all of it but there's a section where she describes women of the thirties and forties and compares them to younger women. She distinguishes between career women and homemakers. I guess in the past women had to be one or the other. Made me think of you. You don't fit the categories because you managed to be both."

She closed the book and changed the topic. "We have the day to ourselves, Mum. Let's go to Dorval. Morgan's is having a fabric sale."

"Now you're talking my language."

Rose's comments about the book, and more specifically about her, piqued Frances's curiosity and eventually she asked about it at her library. "No, we don't have it yet," the librarian said. "A controversial book like that takes a while to get through Acquisitions."

"I didn't realize it was so controversial."

"Oh, yes! It's stirring things up. About time too."

Now she was even more curious.

❖

It was early in the morning on Rose's birthday. Frances picked up the telephone on the first ring and belted out Happy Birthday. After the last note there was a pause.

"Frances, it's Thomas."

"Oh my God."

"No, it's just me."

She hesitated then laughed. "I'm surprised to hear your voice."

"You said I could contact you."

"Yes, I remember. I thought you'd write."

"Oh." Silence for a moment. "To be honest, I thought it would be nice to hear your voice again. It's been so long."

She sat. "It has been. Rose's graduation, her wedding, two babies, and Ena's funeral. Time doesn't stop."

"No. Ena's death was tragic."

"Thank you for the card you sent. I passed your condolences on to Barbara."

Their silence felt long. They jumped in together to break the tension.

"Frances ..."

"Thomas ..."

"Go on," Frances said.

"I've accepted a job in Saint Lambert. I'll be moving there in July."

"Congratulations. And good luck. Is it another teaching job?" Frances assumed he'd been teaching in Hamilton since the early fifties.

"No. They're setting up a new school board, a regional one. Initially, there will be —" He stopped. "Frances, my job isn't why I called." He rushed on. "I was wondering if there is any chance we could have a visit when I come to Montreal?"

She didn't say anything.

"Please think about it. It would mean the world to me."

"What would?"

"To see you again. To have you as a friend."

"I don't know... look, I'll think about it. I have to go now. I'm baking a birthday cake for Rose." She hung up.

❧

He was waiting in their old booth at Murray's. Frances tapped on the pane and waved. He jumped up and held the door open.

"I've already ordered the toasted fruit loaf," he said with a big grin, before they even sat down.

"Are you in a rush?"

His face collapsed.

"I'm just teasing," Frances said. "Come on, let's sit."

They looked around the restaurant. Frances thought about all the times they had sat here planning a future together. "Imagine. Our old stomping grounds."

He searched her face. "The years look good on you, Frances."

"Thank you. I've taken up ballroom dancing. And of course, I get a little help from Miss Clairol." She patted her hair. "Tell me how it's going in Saint Lambert."

He covered the basics in a few minutes. A small apartment near the school board office and an unusual interest in the Saint Lambert Lock. He had to explain that it was part of the Saint Lawrence Seaway.

She smiled. "That seems an odd thing to be interested in – for you, I mean."

"I know, it surprises me too. See what years of listening to Nora's friend, Stelco Stanley, can do?" He threw up his hands.

"Isn't he an accountant?"

"Yes." He waved his hand. "Maybe we can save that for another time."

He asked a lot of questions about Rose, her boys, and her family. It was clear to Frances that he hoped he might meet them someday.

There was a lull after they ordered more tea. Frances screwed up her courage and asked what she most wanted to know. "Did you ever —"

He put up his hand to stop her. She leaned forward and studied his face as he spoke. It was as if they both knew that this is what they came for.

"The priesthood?" He shook his head. "No, I didn't leave, officially. Time went on; I just let it slide. But I will never be a true priest again."

So much unspoken.

She couldn't think of anything to say for a few moments. Then, "Do you miss it?"

"The substance but not the form, is the best I can explain it. The powers-that-be," he looked away and shrugged, "would call me an apostate, but I don't like the term."

He gave a mirthless laugh. "Vatican II has energized the Church, but celibacy of the priesthood is still sacrosanct. Modernization can only go so far."

Frances noted his bitterness but knew there was nothing she could say that would help. She glanced at her watch. "I wish I didn't have to go. Just when we got to the important stuff. I'd like to hear more about it, the substance and form." They both laughed and, at the same moment, reached to each other and gave a warm squeeze.

"Let's not leave it so long," she said. "It seems our friendship is one of short intensity and long absence."

A warm lightness bloomed in his eyes. "Maybe we can strike a balance?"

"I'd like that. Will you call again?"

"You know I will."

⚜

Frances thought of this time as their third chapter. Their previous passion was gone or perhaps only tamped down, held in check. The intensity of their connection was inexplicable to her.

Early on, in their rekindled friendship, the rumours from the re-union, wove their way into their conversation. They were having a picnic at Beaver Lake and reminiscing about Newcastle.

He explained his side of the story. Apparently one of the senior girls in his Latin class – Lucille was her name – became overly familiar in a way that alarmed him. He distanced himself from her, which only emboldened her. He convinced Sister St. Jerome that Lucille would be better off in her class instead of his and they transferred her. The girl confronted him one day in his empty classroom. He was flummoxed and dashed from the room as she was still talking.

Soon, the rumours started. Within a year, he was before the Bishop and steps were taken.

"Even after almost twenty years in the parish, I was an outsider. The girl's family was well-known and very generous to St. Bridget's." He gave a shrug. "It wasn't a difficult decision for the Bishop and, honestly, I welcomed the change."

Frances didn't know what to think. Was it true? Was it partially true? Was it a lie he had convinced himself of? Or an outright lie? She decided she didn't care. If there were other girls who had suffered in some way because of Thomas, she could do nothing. Time had passed and she was very happy now, in her own life, and didn't want to belabour it. But she did want to speak.

"I felt betrayed when I heard the rumours."

"I know." He looked into the distance. "I knew it as soon as I read your letter. And combined with the meagreness of the life I had in Hamilton, it was enough to persuade me that the best thing for me to do was to stay out of your life. You deserved better than a failed priest, let alone one with rumours around him like the stink on a corpse."

She grimaced at the vile image, dismayed at how he thought of himself. "Didn't you think I deserved an explanation?"

"I took you literally when you wrote that you didn't want one, but truthfully that was just an easy out for me. The truth is, I was a coward. I was a coward thirty-odd years ago when your mother told me you were pregnant, and I was a coward about facing you and seeing what kind of life we might make together."

Frances had come to the same conclusion years ago. She felt a grim satisfaction.

"I had no expectations when I was expecting ..." She groaned. "You know what I mean, expectations of you. I didn't contact you or ask for anything. It was different later, though. I had hopes galore and —"

He started to speak but she put up her hand, a police officer's "Halt". He grabbed it from the air and held it in both of his. "Go on."

"My staff tease me when I stop them in their tracks like that. They even did it in a skit at a staff party last year."

"Sounds like they like you. But back to what you were saying."

"The first part is that I felt betrayed, I thought horrible things about you, I was humiliated and felt like a fool. I was keeping a wretched secret again and I hated it. I went on and on, it seemed, for months, to my friend Alice. No wonder she moved to Vancouver."

She glanced at him and smiled. "But the second part took me longer."

He wasn't interrupting now.

"I knew I loved you and I never, well almost never, doubted that you loved me. But it wasn't an everyday love, a practical love, one that could blend in and join the stream of my life. It was a love I wasn't proud of. I often asked myself why it, meaning us, felt wrong."

They sat in silence. She gave the thermos a shake to see if there was any coffee left and tipped the last few drops into the grass.

"Yes," said Thomas. "It was separate from our lives with too much going against it – mostly my vocation, I'd say."

"It was only after I gave up thinking *if only* and *what if* that I started to feel free. I always missed you, but I didn't miss loving you. I didn't miss holding out hope for the impossible. It was a relief, frankly."

What she didn't say – why she now believed it was wrong – was because he should have been a stronger man and not co-opted her in his cowardice, in his inability to make a difficult choice.

⚜

Frances and Thomas's pattern had been set in the tutoring classroom at St. Bridget's. They continued their friendship alone for the most part. They talked on the telephone regularly and saw each other every few months. It wasn't a secret, at least not from Rose or Michel, but it was private.

"He is something like a friend, but more and less than a friend," she told Michel. "I thought I had hardened my heart to him ... but I guess not. He just has a different place there now."

Frances still had all his letters and combed through them looking for clues about his self-imposed estrangement. She asked him about his excitement and empathy with workers during the Asbestos strike.

"What a dreamer I was. I didn't have a pulpit to preach solidarity from, like the Bishops in '49, nor any authority or prestige. I was just a high-school math teacher. I often used examples from industry – you know, wages, profits, benefits – to demonstrate math problems and calculations, hoping some curious student would ask more." He gave a rueful laugh. "A few did and we had some fiery out-of-class discussions about disparity, fairness, justice. But a far cry from how I had imagined the role I might have had."

⚜

Frances knew Thomas wanted to meet Rose and her family. He hadn't seen her since she was four. Rose was thirty-four now.

He had said, "Please Frances. I know there's only a fifty percent chance she is my daughter but she is one hundred percent your daughter. That counts for everything. I'm sure she is as delightful now as she was back then telling knock-knock jokes."

Frances asked Rose if she could bring Thomas to the next big clan gathering. Hugh had five brothers and sisters, all married with children. Frances marvelled at how Rose flourished in, and actually encouraged, the chaos and excitement of the family parties.

Frances said, "He's an old friend from down home who has recently moved to Montreal. He used to write to me. You and Ena read some of his letters but got bored."

"Sorry. I'm drawing a blank. But sure bring him along."

In time Thomas blended in, just an old friend of Nana's. He only visited a couple of times a year because of the distance from Saint Lambert to Pointe-Claire.

None of Hugh's family – his parents or siblings, the in-laws, nieces, nephews, aunts and uncles – showed the least bit of interest in Thomas's past. They talked about their jobs, the Montreal Canadians and, of course, because there were a couple of engineers, the Saint Lawrence Seaway. Frances felt a swell of affection for him when he was so engaged, so much a part of the hurly burly. But nothing more.

One day after one of Thomas's visits, Rose said, "Mom, I've remembered a couple of things you said."

"Only a couple?" Frances smiled.

"This is important, not a joke." Rose reached for her mother's hand. "What I remember is that you said one of the men who ..." She searched for the words. "...who might be my father became a priest. You also said Thomas used to write to you. What I remember is that the Thomas who used to write to you was a priest."

Frances fidgeted and looked away. She had known this day would come, known it was important to Rose. How could it not be?

"Be honest with me, Mum. Is Thomas one of the men ... could he be my father?"

That familiar look, the one Frances thought of as Rose's 'Thomas look' crossed Rose's face. It wasn't a certainty, wasn't enough, but it was what Frances had.

It gave her confidence to say, "I believe he is, yes."

"And? Come on, Mom. What else?"

"He knows he might be your father, but he also knows what happened to me and that he has to accept the uncertainty."

"Did he ask to come here, to know us, to observe our lives but to remain unknown?"

"He wanted to know you but I asked him not to impose, not to reveal himself. My concern wasn't for him but for you. I knew that you'd figure it out. You always look beyond the surface, you question everything. It was only a matter of time."

They sat with their private thoughts for a few minutes.

"Was he a priest then ... when ..." Rose's voice trailed off.

"Yes. He was my mathematics tutor when I was at boarding school in Newcastle. I didn't really need special tutoring, it was easy for me, but we all had extra tutoring. I always had the work done so we talked about other things."

"Like what?"

"Montreal, my family, the farm, the news, anything that came to our minds. He was my friend."

"And his family?"

"I don't know a lot about his family. He has a sister in Hamilton." Frances winced thinking how feeble this would sound to Rose.

Rose was silent, deep in thought. She blew out a long breath and said, "I don't know how I feel or what to do."

Frances knew Rose wasn't asking for help or advice and that she would do what was best for her and her family.

She said, "I haven't known what to do about Thomas for thirty-five years. For a long time my secret kept me distant from those I should have been closest to." She held onto Rose's hands. "You don't need to let that continue. It's not a secret now."

36

IT'S TIME

ROSE THOUGHT OF almost nothing else but Thomas for the next few weeks. She told Hugh about the revelation from her mother.

"I've known for years that my father might be a priest but it was ... just an idea ... not real to me. But since I put two and two together and asked Mum directly it's become more than real."

"What do you mean? Hugh asked.

"I feel obliged to do something now."

"Like what?"

"To know him, to know about his family. The boys may have cousins, aunts, uncles they should know about. They have a new grandfather!"

"Yeah. That's big news."

One of the reasons Rose loved Hugh was because he didn't tell her what to do, didn't try to solve problems for her. Once she made up her mind she didn't second-guess herself or procrastinate.

⚜

Thomas answered on the fourth ring. "Hello?"

"Hello Thomas. This is Rose."

"Rose? What a surprise. Is everything alright? Is Frances okay?"

"Yes, I didn't mean to alarm you." She took a deep breath to calm her nerves.

Thomas paused a moment then asked, "What is it, Rose?"

"It's time we talked ... as daughter and father. Don't you think it's time?"

"Yes I do."

✦

ACKNOWLEDGEMENTS

I AM GRATEFUL to the writing teachers who inspired me. Sharon Butala and Claire Robson made me realise it was not a memoir I was pitching but a novel and they gave me the confidence to write it. Peter Behrens taught me to pay attention to that ineffable, burning thing that wouldn't let go of me. He also talked about fear and courage in the writing process. June Hutton showed me that unremarkable everyday lives are worthy of stories. I am grateful for her enthusiastic response to the title. Robert Dugoni's respect for the craft of writing set a fine example. Cathleen With of the Vancouver Manuscript Intensive pointed me in the right direction when my story was going off the rails.

Writers need readers and I have had the best early readers. Patsy Morrison, Pat Hogan, Nancy Farran, Elaine Gibson, and Ann Svendsen were generous with their time and made astute observations. They challenged and supported me in equal measure.

Two publishing industry professionals who gave me helpful criticism and encouragement were Genevieve Gagne Hawes and Doug Richmond. My thanks to them.

Jess Shulman, my editor was creative, thorough, and responsive. She offered insightful comments every step of the way.

I am grateful to artist Linda Bell who took on the challenge of painting Frances. Her interpretation of Frances's restraint and determination is perfect.

Andrée Tardif helped me to find the right French words. Merci mon amie.

"It takes a village to ..." I am lucky to have fabulous people in my village, too many to name. To the voracious readers in my book clubs and writers groups, many thanks for your inspiration. To long-time friends and new-found allies I'm grateful for your support and confidence that this project would come to a happy end.

I owe a world of support to Ian Cameron. He knew when to get close and when to back off; when to suggest and when to be silent; when to make supper and when to offer wine. His timing was impeccable and I thank him with all my heart for that and for everything else.

The inspiration for *The Mother House*: My mother had two sisters and one brother. She and her sisters attended a Catholic boarding school in Newcastle, New Brunswick. That was it. Thanks to my mother's habit of reticence and her lack of nostalgia I was unencumbered by many facts of her early life. *The Mother House* is a work of fiction in which the main characters, actions, and events sprang from my imagination.

KATHERINE DOYLE WAS born and raised in Montreal, attending Catholic school for twelve years with nun teachers. In the 1960's she followed their expectations that girls should become nuns, teachers, nurses or secretaries, by studying at a hospital-based nursing school run by nuns.

She is delighted that those past limitations are gone and girls can pursue so many more ways to live their lives ... even as writers.

After a career teaching nursing, Katherine lives in Vancouver working on her next novel. When not travelling, she enjoys reading and writing, alone and with others in book clubs and writing groups.

CPSIA information can be obtained
at www.ICGtesting.com
Printed in the USA
LVHW020110030821
694218LV00008B/258